MICHELLE A. MARSH

HIDDEN
SCARS II

Extreme Overflow Publishing
Dacula, GA
USA

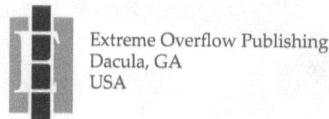

Extreme Overflow Publishing
Dacula, GA
USA

Extreme Overflow Publishing
A Brand of Extreme Overflow Enterprises, Inc
P.O. Box 1811
Dacula, GA 30019

www.extremeoverflow.com
Send feedback to info@extreme-overflow-enterprises.com
Author Photograph Credit Joshua Marsh

Printed in the United States of America

Library of Congress Control Number: 2019915898
Data is available for this title. ISBN: 978-1-7340638-1-3

HIDDEN SCARS II

MICHELLE A. MARSH

Growing up, I was a quiet child. Pencil and paper served as my voice but as I became an adult, my life experiences empowered me to discover and use my voice . . . no longer hidden.

Michelle A. Marsh, Author

This book is dedicated to everyone who's gone through a life-altering or traumatic event and suffered in silence.

Your voice matters.
YOU MATTER!

CHAPTER 41

Franklin paced back and forth in the hospital emergency room. The past few hours replayed in his mind like a bad dream. It was unimaginable all the things he'd found out.

His brain was spinning like a washing machine on the rinse cycle, as it competed with the sound of the rain beating down on the large skylight, from the thunderstorm.

He thought back to when Grace was a little girl, and how she would run into his room and cling to him for comfort at any sign of thunder or lightening. He was always there to protect her and regretted that he was not there to protect her from this pathetic rapist. He couldn't imagine the trauma she'd gone through.

He wished that he could be in the delivery room to support her but knew that he would not be able to hide his raw emotions. He was pissed at how she was robbed of her innocence. It made him sick to his stomach. Not to mention that he couldn't bear to watch his little sister grimace from those dreadful labor pains. He felt helpless. He knew that he had no experience in this department but felt relieved that she was in good hands with Macie, the labor and delivery nurse. All he could do now is support her and be there for her and his new niece or nephew.

He contemplated going to the police to let them know what this monster had done to Grace, but he wanted to wait until he knew that she and the baby were okay and after he filled Anna Mae in on what he and Grace discovered.

Franklin had mixed feelings about calling Anna Mae, even with Grace giving him the okay to share the news of her pregnancy. Against his better judgement, he knew that it was in the best interest of everyone to keep Anna Mae in the loop, although his gut was telling him that Anna Mae would only add more fuel to the already uncontrollable fire once she knew the truth.

He pulled his cell phone out of his pocket, contemplating if he should call Anna Mae. He dialed the number, then abruptly ended the call on the first ring. He paced back and forth. He pulled it out again, dialing Anna Mae in spite of his own reservations.

In classic Anna Mae style, she gave him the third degree for not telling her that his tour of duty had ended with the Army, and that he was home. Her confrontational attitude enraged him, making him change his mind about mentioning Grace's pregnancy. He informed her that there was a family emergency, and that she needed to come up to the hospital quick, fast, and in a hurry. That opened the flood gate of inquiries. She badgered him, asking a million and one questions, controlling the conversation, and threatening that if he didn't give her the reason why she needed to come up to the hospital, that she would stay home. He knew that wasn't true because she relished in others misfortune, especially if she knew it had to do with Grace.

Franklin tried his best to control his emotions over

the phone. He held back his anger toward Anna Mae for failing as a big sister. She had no excuse for not making frequent visits to check on Grace and David. In hindsight, he knew that he was just as guilty and wished that he'd done more too, knowing that Momma was no longer here to keep a watchful eye on them.

Franklin didn't fall for Anna Mae's empty threats, which continued for 15 minutes.

Finally, Anna Mae said, "I'll get there, when I get there!"

Franklin abruptly ended the call. He paced back and forth in the waiting room area, awaiting Anna Mae's arrival. He tried his best not to think about the con that he'd called a brother for the past 19 years. Just the thought infuriated him. He remembered the day that their family instantly grew, and how they welcomed the two-year-old little boy, who was left on their doorstep with a note attached to his lapel, into their home.

"Oh! When I see that bastard, I'm going to kill him," Franklin mumbled, loud enough to catch the attention of uneasy onlookers who stared him down.

"I cannot believe this! This is so unreal," he said, punching his fist into his open hand. At least 45 minutes had passed since he'd hung up with Anna Mae. He pulled his cell phone out looking for a missed call from her.

Nothing.

"Where is she at? What is taking her so long to get here?"

Inconsistent to his character, an unraveled Franklin knew he had to pull himself together and prepare for the firestorm that Anna Mae was about to unleash, if she showed up. He inhaled through his nose and exhaled out of his mouth, trying to calm his nerves. He stretched his arms high above his head as he cracked his knuckles.

But the rain continued to pound on the skylight.

The sliding glass door leading into the emergency room opened. A full-figured woman wearing a tightly fitted, floral print Juicy Couture jumpsuit, with a matching rain jacket and a jet-black front-laced wavy wig with a part in the middle, casually entered the hospital's waiting area. She shook her waterlogged, lime-green umbrella over the trash barrel, carefully placing it into its plastic sleeve before dropping it in her large pocketbook. Her slow movement was similar to her attitude, damp!

She snuck past the security guard, who was fast sleep. She stopped at the small table that held a box of face masks and hand sanitizer. She grabbed a mask and carefully placed it over her head, securing it over her nose and mouth. She began to douse her hands with sanitizer, as if she was a doctor preparing for surgery. She then proceeded to sashay past the secretary, whose face was immersed in a home furnishing magazine.

The secretary, whose platinum blonde hair was in

perfect tight spiral curls, quickly looked up.

"Excuse me ma'am, all visitors must sign in," she said, pointing up to the large sign that hung above her head.

The woman turned around, gawking at the secretary as she flared her arms in the air, speaking belligerently. She quickly wrote her name on the sign-in sheet, jarring the pen at the secretary, as if it were a weapon. Her voice muffled. She tossed the ball point pen on the desk and slid the face mask down, resting it on her chin.

Diamond, the secretary immediately recognized the woman. She looked down at the sign-in sheet, remembering a mean-spirited and evil Anna Mae, who found joy in torturing her anytime Ms. Leola wasn't looking. She recalled helping Ms. Leola in the soup kitchen, along with the other teenagers at their church, and how Anna Mae did everything in her power to break her spirit, every chance she got. She remembered the countless times that Franklin and the other kids would protect her from a devilish Anna Mae. Her mind went back to when she'd gotten married, and shortly thereafter, she heard that Anna Mae jumped up and got married too, more out of jealousy and spite.

Although Diamond's issues were solely with Anna Mae, she had so much respect for Ms. Leola and appreciated the guidance that she gave her. Like Anna Mae, Ms. Leola taught her how to burn in the kitchen, which didn't sit well with Anna Mae.

When Diamond announced her engagement, she

flaunted her three-karat diamond solitaire engagement ring, showing it off to their peers. She raved about how her fiancé, a successful business owner in the city, five years her senior, spoiled her rotten. She boasted about how he took her out to five-star restaurants and whisked her away on his business trips, the last one in Maui. One day she'd told Ms. Leola that she wanted to cook something extra special for him. She expressed his love for gulf shrimp. She remembered Ms. Leola staying late one night in the church's soup kitchen, showing her how to make southern style shrimp and grits, enlisting Anna Mae's help. Anna Mae seemed to have turned over a new leaf, helping out Momma and Diamond. Anna Mae neatly packed the food up, giving it to Diamond to take home with her that evening. The three of them prepared a meal fit for a king, so Diamond thought!

The next day, Diamond called Ms. Leola, hot as fire, saying how she and her fiancé became sickened after eating the meal and ended up in the very same emergency room with food poisoning. She blamed Anna Mae for it, although she wasn't able to prove it.

"Anna Mae Payne, you know that you have to sign in!" Diamond exclaimed.

"Do I know you?" Anna Mae asked, looking intently.

"I'm sure you tried your best to forget everything that you've done to me, but I remember," Diamond said, smirking.

Anna Mae quickly remembered Diamond and her high-pitched voice from when they both helped Momma work in the soup kitchen at the church.

"I see you're still just like your name, 'a diamond in the rough!' I almost didn't recognize you with that blonde mop on your head, looking like Wanda from 'In Living Color,' Anna Mae said, laughing, as she poked fun at Diamond.

"Do you need to see a doctor, because you sound like hell?" Diamond asked, smirking, hearing hoarseness in Anna Mae's voice.

"Does it look like I'm sick?" Anna Mae remarked, sounding pitchy. The volume of her voice changing with each word that she muttered.

"Well, you are wearing a mask, and it sounds like you have a razor blade stuck in your throat," Diamond responded.

"Bloop! Wrong!" Anna Mae said.

Diamond had waited a long time for this moment. She couldn't resist, as she clapped back, "That front lace wig on your head is all wrong!"

"Look here Goldilocks, I have a family emergency to attend to! Make yourself useful and tell me where I can find my brother before I report you to your supervisor!" Anna Mae exclaimed. "He called me in a frenzy, asking me to come up here. I've called him several times, but I cannot get him."

"If I had a sister like you, I wouldn't answer either," Diamond mumbled under her breath, neglecting to share with Anna Mae that she and Franklin spoke earlier and that he was just 50 feet behind her. "What was that?" Anna Mae said keenly.

Franklin leaned over the water bubbler, eavesdropping on the conversation between the loud woman with the raspy voice and Diamond, who seemed to be holding her own. He couldn't clearly make out what they were discussing but the woman seemed irritated. He shook his head in disgust as he mumbled, "You can take the rat out of the hood but you can't take the hood out of the rat!"

The more he listened, the more the woman's strained voice started sounding familiar. He looked keenly, watching the woman point her finger in Diamond's face. He didn't want to believe it, but it was Anna Mae, sporting a different look. His mind instantly went back to the countless heated interactions between the two girls in the church's soup kitchen, where he and others had to step in to separate them.

"Aw, hell, here we go!" He muttered.

Franklin had seen her from afar walk through the emergency room entrance, but the last time he saw Anna Mae on the day of Momma's funeral, her hair was four-inches long. Growing up in a house with three women, if there were things he learned to never, ever question, it was the length, color, and cut of a black women's hair. It can change in a matter of minutes, although he admired their versatility. Franklin walked to the center of the waiting area.

"ANNA MAE!" He called out. He waved his hand in the air, aborting the verbal beat down that she was about to unleash on Diamond.

Anna Mae turned around abruptly, looking toward Franklin's direction. She refaced Diamond, "You better be glad that I found my brother, WANDA!"

"Ms. Leola's not here to protect you, so you better watch your words!" Diamond said. "Karma is a…." Anna Mae cut Diamond off.

"Are you threatening me?" Anna Mae asked.

"You're a big bully! I got my eye on you! Get yourself some hot tea, put your mask back on, and say less! Have a good day, Mrs. Payne!" Diamond said, putting emphasis on Anna Mae's last name.

"You need sensitivity training!" Anna Mae said, as she walked toward Franklin.

"And you still need Xanax! Girl, bye," Diamond exclaimed. Franklin zoned in on Anna Mae, as she walked toward him looking like a steamed locomotive.

"Anna Mae. Just stop! You know better than that!" He said.

She wasted no time starting in with her theatrics. She threw her arms up in the air as she approached Franklin, not even greeting him, having last seen him five months ago.

"I've been calling you, but your voice mail is full!" she said.

"I checked my phone earlier. I didn't see any calls from you. I assumed the weather held you up." He said, taking out his phone. "What happened to you? You didn't sound like that earlier, when we spoke!"

"I lost my voice screaming at Rufus on the way over here! He made me so mad!"

"What did he do, that would cause you to strain your voice that much?" Franklin asked, as he began scrolling through his phone, noticing the recent missed calls from Anna Mae.

"He was driving all slow, taking every detour he could find to get here, and wasn't listening to me. We went all around Robin Hood's barn instead of just keeping straight! I don't know what was wrong with him. He said he was trying to protect his car's engine from the flooded streets. I called to tell you that I was on my way about 10 minutes ago! After trying a few times, I gave up! I'm here now!"

Franklin continued scrolling through his call log on his cell phone.

"My bad! I didn't realize that you'd called me so many

times. I didn't realize that my phone was on silent, so I didn't hear it ring. Dang!" He said, as he began to delete his old voice messages before slipping his phone back into the side pocket of his Army fatigues.

Anna Mae reached into her pocketbook for a lozenge, popping it into her mouth as she looked around the waiting area.

"The last time I was here was the day that Momma went into a coma. It feels kind of spooky being here. I feel something bad is about to happen.

"I didn't think about that. I remember that I was in the field and didn't find out until I returned to the base," he said.

"Since I couldn't reach you, I called the house phone, and it just rang off the hook. Rufus thought maybe you'd gotten sick and the military sent you home and that's why you were in the emergency room. He was watching a program on TV a few weeks ago about some agent orange chemical," Anna Mae said, talking a mile a minute while her voice was cracking.

"Anna Mae, that was back in the Vietnam War," Franklin said.

"Oh," Anna Mae remarked. "I told him, maybe David got into it with Grace like they did growing up, and he put her up in the hospital this time," she said, cackling. "I couldn't get her either!"

"That's not funny and no, that's not quite what happened," a serious Franklin said, stalling.

"Why are you wearing a mask? Are you sick? You sure sound like you are," he asked, commenting on the mask resting on Anna Mae's chin.

"No, fool! I'm trying not to get sick! Once I drink something hot my voice will go back to normal," she said. "Besides, this isn't about me."

The lights in the waiting area flickered. Franklin noticed Anna Mae looking up at the lights, as it began to thunder again.

"It's thundering pretty bad out there," he said.

"Yeah," she said, looking startled.

"Anna Mae. It's okay. Hospitals have a backup 48-hour generator. The lights have been flickering since I got here," he said.

"I was about to say, I'm getting up out of here," she said. Anna Mae quickly changed the subject to Diamond.

"That ghetto girl is so rude! You better be lucky that you saw me!" she said. "I was about to turn around and leave!"

"Oh, Diamond," he said.

"More like RuPaul!" she exclaimed.

"At first, I didn't remember her," she said.

"Anna Mae, you should remember her. She worked with us in the soup kitchen at church, and she was at Momma's funeral. She wasn't over there when I came in earlier, but then I heard someone calling my name, and that's when I went over to talk to her. We chatted for a while. She was telling me how she took Momma's death so hard, and how much she missed her, and the positive impact that Momma had on her life. I remember how close they'd gotten," he said. "She also mentioned that her husband is thankful that Momma taught her how to cook!" Franklin said, looking over at Anna Mae. "You used to give that girl holy hell! You were like a thorn in her side. Always picking on her. That girl used to be so afraid of you. You're lucky she didn't throat punch you!"

"I wish she would," she said, welcoming the confrontation. "Maybe that's why she was so salty toward me. She needs to get over it! Sorry, NOT sorry!"

"I guess she'd been looking for me on Facebook and Instagram. I told her that I don't do social media," Franklin added.

"Why is she trying to find you? Sounds like trouble in paradise." Franklin looked back at Diamond. "She looks great!" Franklin said, noticing the security.

"That outfit she has on does not! It looks like its gasping for a pocket or a buttonhole, or something. It can't breathe!" she said.

"I see that you still have that mean streak, but Anna

Mae, you can't talk about anybody," he said looking his sister up and down.

"I didn't come up here for you to insult me!" she said.

Franklin knew he had to appear calm before he divulged why he asked Anna Mae to come to the hospital. He continued.

"Diamond told me that her younger sister Dalia works for Misty at the hair salon. Isn't that where you and Grace go?" He asked.

"Yeah, but I don't pay those ratchet girls no mind," she said.

"She mentioned that Dalia plans to open up her own salon by the end of the year!" He said. "They're doing big things!"

"Good for them! About time!" she exclaimed.

"Oh yeah . . . now I remember her sister Dalia. She's the one with the jacked-up hair at the shop, who does Grace's hair. Rufus said the guys at the barbershop said that she has a crush on you!" she commented.

"Really?" He said, quickly changing the conversation back to Diamond.

"I didn't recognize her at first. Her hair is different than how it was at Momma's funeral," he said, looking in the area of where Diamond sat. "I like it!"

"Hmmmm! Looks like a bushel of hay that was left out in the sun way too long to me!" she said.

"Stop being mean Anna Mae!" He said.

"Did you know that Diamond still blames you for giving them food poisoning when they were engaged?" He questioned.

"I don't remember that," she said coldly.

"I do! She said, that you were trying to kill her because you were jealous that she had a man and you didn't. Right after your 18th birthday, you moved in with Rufus and ya'll eloped. That surprised all of us because you never mentioned that you were dating anyone. Now that I think about it, how did you meet that dude anyways? I know that he's not from here."

"No, he is not and don't worry about it," she said, sarcastically.

"Hmmmm!" He paused.

"Diamond said that's how she got the job here; from the time she came in here deathly sick with food poisoning. She'd told the nurse how she was working on her associate degree and was looking for a secretarial job. They pointed her to the website, she applied and got the job!" He exclaimed.

"Looks like she should be thanking me then," she said.

"Ya'll used to argue every time Momma put you two

together in the kitchen. It would get so bad, that we'd have to separate the both of you. I remember having to step in, like the day you hid her glasses in the flour container, knowing that she couldn't see. She told me that she wears contacts now. You were really mean to her!" He reminisced. "Do you remember the day that she prepared cups of soup to take home?" He questioned.

"Nope. I blocked all that out," she said.

"Well, let me remind you. Do you remember how Momma used to let all of the kids make cups of leftover soup to bring home, after we fed the homeless?" He asked. Anna Mae did not respond. "Well, Diamond placed her three cups of soup in a bag and put them in the fridge, with her name on it. You snuck into the refrigerator, went into her bag and poured the cups of soup back into the pot and replaced the emptied containers with raw potato peelings. You then had the audacity to place the bag back in the fridge. You don't remember Momma taking you over to their housed to apologize?" He asked.

"Nope. Maybe it was Grace," she said.

"No. It was you being petty," Franklin said.

"She was telling me that her cousin knows Grace. He's a popular grief and trauma counselor here," he said.

"Good for him! He needs to put his cousin on his couch, because she is truly disturbed! She needs to snap out of it and let all that go!" she remarked.

Franklin thought about Grace, as he listened to Anna Mae. He took a deep breath, mentally preparing himself to tell her why he called her up to the hospital.

"I know you didn't call me all the way up here to talk about Diamond! Miss me with all that! So, what's going on? What was so important that you couldn't tell me over the phone? How come you didn't tell me that you were coming home?" She badgered him with one question after the other.

"I did. I informed all of you after Momma's funeral that my tour was ending around April, but you were too mad at Auntie Mabeline to listen to what anyone had to say!" He barked back. "Besides, you would have known that I was home, had you been over the house helping Grace clean out Momma's closet, like you said you would!"

"Oh please!" she said, rolling her eyes. "I don't live there! Besides, she was acting like she was the only one helping Momma out anyways. When I told Rufus about all the stuff Momma had in her closet, he told me that I should just let Grace handle it. So, I did!"

"As much as you don't want to believe it, Anna Mae, Grace was there for Momma a lot more than we were, but we weren't there for Grace," he said, sounding somber. Their voices started to get louder.

"I see she's still manipulating you! Boy, bye! Speak for yourself!" she exclaimed, ignoring the latter part of what Franklin had said. "She wasn't the only one that was there for Momma. You don't even know what you're talking about!"

"Anna Mae, when was the last time that you were at the house?" He asked.

"That's not the point!" she exclaimed, her voice breaking.

"That's exactly my point. You have no idea of what's been going on!" He said, noticing Diamond talking to the security guard in the far distance.

The security guard began to walk in the direction of where he and Anna Mae stood before taking a sudden detour into the men's room.

"Well, you can blame Auntie Mabeline for that, because I took her advice. What Grace and David do is no longer my concern!" an insensitive Anna Mae responded.

"That's not what she was trying to say to you. She simply told you to stop treating them like they were your kids, always telling them what to do, when to do it, and how to do it! That's not what I called you up here for, but I'll wait until Rufus comes in. He should hear this, too."

"My husband doesn't have time to deal with this foolishness. He dropped me off. I told him to swing back and pick me up after he gets his hair cut and picks his clothes up from the cleaners, which should take him about an hour-and-a-half. So, instead of going back and forth with me, you need to tell me why you called me up here. I need to get home and get out of this nasty weather. I cannot afford to get sick," she said.

"Did you tell him that it was a family emergency?" He asked, looking puzzled.

"I most certainly did, and I told him that there's no reason for both of us to be stuck up here! It's probably nothing serious, or else you would have told me over the phone," she said. "Don't worry about Rufus. He's been very stressed lately with his own family issues. He got enough going on. Besides, you could have just saved me a trip and told me what you needed to say over the phone."

"WOW," he said, looking surprised.

"So, what happened to that little rotten egg, because I don't see her nowhere, and she didn't answer the phone when I called her?" a coldhearted Anna Mae said, referring to Grace, as she looked around. "And this better be good!"

"Chill with the name calling!" Franklin noticed the security guard coming out of the men's room and walking slowly in their direction before stopping for a drink at the water bubbler.

"If you can be quiet for a minute, I need to tell you something that's very important. Right about now, I am so angry that I can't even think straight," he said.

"Angry about what?" She asked. "You could have fooled me! You spent all this time talking about silliness! Well, spit it out!"

"Because I was waiting for your husband to come in!" He said.

"Just listen, Anna Mae. Stop talking and just listen," an aggravated Franklin said, as he placed his hands on his head.

"You're not saying anything!" she said.

"ANNA MAE, JUST STOP!" He shouted. His eyes fixated on the security guard who appeared to be listening to their conversation. The guard crouched over the bubbler, taking large gulps of water, looking closely in their direction.

Franklin took a hold of Anna Mae's arm, pulling her behind the frosted six-foot partition. They were out of sight of where the others sat and the security guard, was drinking from the water bubbler.

"Where are we going?" She asked, pulling away from Franklin. "I should be asking you if you're okay!" she exclaimed. "Are you suffering from that STD?"

"You mean, PTSD? No!" He said, shaking his head. "What I'm about to tell you is going to be difficult for you to hear."

"Stop playing with me and just tell me. I don't have time for this!" she said.

"It's very bad, and it's about David and Grace," he said.

"I knew it!" she said, sharply. "That little tattletale called you and falsely accused David about something he didn't do that landed her in the emergency room!" I told Rufus that's what it was!"

Franklin could see the security guards silhouette through the frosted glass.

"No! . . . Yes! . . . Well . . . that's partly true," he said. As he proceeded to talk, Anna Mae began to talk over him, sounding like a broken record.

"Since you were sounding as if you were stuck in your feelings earlier when we spoke on the phone, and I couldn't get a hold of that little rat, I called David's cell to see if he knew what was going on," she said. "I got his voice mail."

"YOU DID WHAT!" He exclaimed.

Franklin's knees buckled.

"Get up! What's wrong with you?" a careless Anna Mae said, smirking.

"Nobody got time to be playing charades with you. I left him a message and told him to call me back. He hasn't called me back yet, I told him that you were home, and that you called me from the emergency room acting like you're in the Secret Service, not telling me what was going on! I mentioned to him that I had a feeling it was about Miss goody two-shoe Grace, since I couldn't get her on the phone. She's probably looking for attention, since Momma and Auntie Mabeline aren't here to give it to her," she said, folding her arms.

"WHY ANNA MAE! WHY WOULD YOU DO THAT?" He yelled.

"Do what?" She asked.

"CALL DAVID, YOU FOOL! ANNA MAE, HOW COULD YOU? I TOLD YOU THAT I WOULD EXPLAIN EVERYTHING TO YOU ONCE YOU GOT HERE!" He yelled, as he paced back and forth, punching his closed fist into his open palm.

"I DIDN'T COME UP HERE FOR YOU TO INSULT MY HIGH IQ!" she said. "YOU ARE THE FOOL, BELIEVING EVERYTHING THIS GIRL SAYS! I DON'T REMEMBER YOU SAYING ALL THAT! YOU ASKED ME TO DROP WHAT I'M DOING AND COME UP QUICK, FAST AND IN A HURRY, AND THAT IT WAS A FAMILY EMERGENCY! SOMETHING LIKE THAT," she rambled on. "NEXT TIME DON'T BE SO SECRETIVE!"

"YOU'RE A PIECE OF WORK!" He yelled.

A stunned Anna Mae looked at Franklin.

"I SERIOUSLY DON'T SEE WHAT THE BIG DEAL IS?" She yelled. "WE ALL HAVE A RIGHT TO KNOW WHAT'S GOING ON!"

Franklin noticed the security guard moving closer, toward the frosted glass.

"You just got home. What do you know?" She said, sucking her teeth.

"Obviously more than you!" He exclaimed.

"Whatever!" she said, "Rufus went to the barbershop a few weeks ago. I know that David has been down on his luck after Momma died! He doesn't have no money, and we all know that he can't keep a job! He was in the barbershop, begging for a job and got turned down. He went over to Misty's, and she felt bad for him, since he was Momma's son, so she paid him under the table to take the towels to the laundry mat, to wash and dry them. This was up until the day that idiot went to hang out at the barbershop to kill time and forgot the towels were in the dryer. Once he remembered, the laundromat had closed. The next morning, Misty had to go to the store and buy more towels. Then she fired his behind!"

Franklin was speechless. His mind in overdrive.

"So, I know more than you think I know," she said.

Franklin looked inquisitively, "Since when did the barbershop start giving perms?"

"Huh?" She said, thinking about what Franklin said. "Oh . . . Rufus cut his jerry curl out. He told me it was too much for him to keep up with. I told him that it was out of style anyways, and I was tired of him ruining our pillowcases!"

"All I have to say is, if David shows up here, you have

your big mouth to blame for what's about to go down," a pissed off Franklin said.

Anna Mae started fishing through her pocketbook for her phone.

"Where's my phone" she said. "I don't have time for this. I'm calling my husband to come get me!"

"Yeah, you better call your Tyrone," he said facetiously.

Anna Mae looked up at Franklin.

"Since when did you become so afraid of David?" She asked.

"Anna Mae don't go there!" He exclaimed. "I'm not afraid of David! It's the other way around."

"So, who else did you call?" He asked angrily, clearly annoyed.

"Oh, I called Auntie Mabeline, even though I haven't spoken to her in months. I know Gracie got her on speed dial! I figured she may know what's going on," she said, mocking Auntie Mabeline. "That woman worked my nerves when she was here. She stayed up in my business. She needs some business of her own, and she needs to remember that I'm grown! I don't need her advice. She can't tell me nothing! People kill me, always trying to give relationship advice, and they don't have a man!"

"Did you get her?" He asked.

"I called her four times and gave up! She didn't answer, and she still hasn't set up her voicemail, so I couldn't leave her a message," she said. "She's a hot mess. She's probably screening her calls."

"You're the hot mess," he said, turning his back to Anna Mae. "One day your mouth is going to get you in a world of trouble!"

"How rude! I didn't come up here for this. Where's my phone!" she said.

Anna Mae continued fishing through her pocketbook, looking for her cell phone, just as the security guard peaked around the corner.

"What time is it?" She asked.

Franklin remained silent, noticing the guard.

"Excuse me. Is there a problem?" the security guard asked, as he came around the frosted partition. He looked to be in his mid-70s, but appeared to be light on his feet and physically fit.

Anna Mae turned around, noticing the security guard, as she continued to search her pocketbook.

Franklin refaced Anna Mae and the guard.

"We're good, sir," Franklin said.

"Did we report a problem, or did she send you over here?" She asked, referring to Diamond.

"You are in an unsecured area. You can't be back here, lady," the guard said.

"Thank you for letting us know! We are having a private conversation. We'll go back over there once we're finished," she said, sarcastically. "Sorry to wake you up from your nap. You can go back to sleep now!"

"My medication makes me doze off like that. The doctor changed my prescription and…"

Anna Mae began to talk over the guard.

"Why are you telling us this? We don't care!" a ruthless Anna Mae said.

"Anna Mae, stop! You need to be more respectful," Franklin said.

"You better hope you make it to my age. If you make it this long," the security guard said proudly.

"Well, maybe you should be working in a sleep lab! If you fall asleep, no one will know!" she said, sarcastically.

"I don't want anything to get out of hand, so I'm gonna ask you to keep your voices down and move back over to the waiting room area, or I'll have to ask you to leave the premises," the guard said.

"I will leave once my husband gets here," she said.

"I'm not standing out in the pouring rain! I'm already hoarse!"

The security guard paused.

"Ma'am, you are disturbing the peace, and I heard that you can be a loaded pistol!" He said, looking at Anna Mae keenly.

Anna Mae placed her hand in front of the stunned security guard's face.

"You don't know me, and she needs to keep my name out of her mouth!" she said, referring to Diamond. "Anyways, as I was saying to my brother, before this rent-a-cop rudely interrupted me..."

The security guard stood behind her, motionless, and in disbelief. Anna Mae turned back toward Franklin.

"You've wasted enough of my time with this drama, and you have nothing to tell me," she said. "Now, I have this little toad, in this polyester uniform, jumping up over here, harassing me."

"I'm done," Franklin said. "I knew calling you was a mistake. I'll just deal with this on my own."

"Ma'am, I will escort you out," the guard said. Against protocol, he placed his hand around Anna Mae's thick arm.

"GET YOUR HANDS-OFF ME!" she shouted.

"WE DON'T WANT ANY TROUBLE. SHE'S LEAVING!" Franklin yelled, as he positioned himself between Anna Mae and the security guard, breaking the hold on his sister's arm.

"That's it! You both need to leave! Come on! Get yourself on out of here lady! You aren't going to make me lose my job!" the guard said, pointing toward the entrance. "Come on here. Let's go! This a way!"

"Leave for what? For having a conversation with my sister? Man, please. Get out of here with that. I'm not going anywhere, and you heard her say that she was leaving," Franklin said, looking down at the grey-haired security guard.

Franklin began to walk away.

"Then where are you going?" Anna Mae asked, as she watched Franklin walk away.

"I didn't know that I needed your permission to use the men's room," Franklin said.

"I think you need to dig in that suitcase that you call a pocketbook, find your phone, call David and tell him that if he comes up here, there will be problems! I can't be held responsible for what's about to go down," Franklin said, disappearing into the men's room.

"Not on my shift! Come on lady. I don't want to have to call for backup," the guard said, attempting to get a stubborn Anna Mae to leave.

Anna Mae continued to exchange words with the security guard.

CHAPTER 42

The unkempt man rushed through the emergency room entrance. He had on an oversized, grey sweatshirt and baggy, dark blue denim jeans. He sported a tightly fitted baseball cap that hid his eyes. His clothes were drenched from the pouring rain. He appeared to know Diamond, as they hugged and chatted, as he signed the visitors log.

You could see him look toward the entrance, as if he was waiting for someone to come in.

About five minutes later, another man entered. He removed his black kangol hat and shook it outside the sliding glass door, before placing it in the inside pocket of his long black trench coat. The two men knew each other. The well-dressed man was about five feet, nine inches in height and wore all black. He sported a low, freshly cut afro, in total contract to his companion.

"You can look over there," Diamond said, directing the two men toward the waiting area, in response to the man's inquiry.

"Thanks," he said. "It's good to see you."

"Yeah, you too!" an unenthused Diamond said.

The two men scouted out the waiting area of the emergency room.

"There she is!" the unkempt guy said, picking up his

pace. The clean-cut man followed closely behind him.

Their attention drew toward the far end of the waiting room, where Anna Mae and the security guard had moved from behind the frosted partition and were in plain view, ragging on each other.

The guard grabbed a hold of Anna Mae's pocketbook, attempting to drag her out.

"Get your hands off my pocketbook!" she exclaimed.

"Wait! That dude's putting his hands on her!" the unkempt guy said.

He began to walk faster, looking irate. The other man trailed behind.

"Hey! Is there a problem?" He asked, towering over the security guard.

The guard quickly let go of Anna Mae's pocketbook, raising his hands in the air, to surrender.

Anna Mae looked up, relieved to see both David and Rufus.

"My husband and my brother are going to jack you up for putting your nasty hands on me!" she said to the security guard.

"What's going on?" Rufus asked.

"This rent-a-cop was trying to kick me out!" Anna Mae yelled. The security guard backed away from Anna Mae, noticing that he was outnumbered.

"I don't want no problems," he said. "She was being very belligerent and I was trying to get her to leave peacefully."

"What happened to just asking? You don't have to put your hands on her . . . I got her," Rufus said, in a calm voice, reaching out for his wife's hand.

"Baby, are you okay?" He asked, consoling his wife.

"I am now that you're here, sweets," Anna Mae said, as they embraced.

"Where's Franklin? I thought you said he was here?" He asked.

"He's in the bathroom," Anna Mae said.

"Oh," he said.

"Where's Grace?" Rufus asked. "Did something happen to her?"

"I don't know where she's at!" Anna Mae said, looking sharply at Rufus.

"Yeah, I called the house, and I didn't get her after I received your message," David said. "When I called you back, Rufus answered. He'd told me that he'd dropped you off up here. I was walking up here in the rain until Rufus pulled up beside me and picked me up. I see you've been yelling at Rufus again," David said, noticing Anna

Mae's raspy voice.

Anna Mae looked at Rufus intently, separating from his embrace.

Anna Mae started talking a mile a minute, trying to get as much out as she could, before Franklin returned from the bathroom.

"Listen, I don't know what's going on. Franklin started to tell me something but then this little leapfrog came over harassing me. So, I don't know what he'd planned to say," she said, looking at David. "Oh, he told me that you better not come up here, or else there will be problems! I don't know what you did David, but he's pretty pissed off at you!"

"For what?" He smirked. "What's Grace blaming me for now? I haven't even seen that girl in months," he said, looking irritated.

"Uh huh, I said the same thing! It's funny how she talks all this trash behind our backs but can't face us! She obviously said something, because Franklin knew that you hadn't been living at the house. I didn't dare tell him that we've allowed you to crash on our couch a few nights since he wants to withhold information from me," she said.

The two men stood fixated on Anna Mae, as she spoke. The security guard noticed Franklin walking slowly out of the bathroom toward them, with his head held down.

As he got closer, he charged like a bolt of lightning toward David, surprising all three. He tackled David to the ground. David's large body hit the floor like a pallet of concrete.

"I'M GOING TO KILL YOU!" He yelled.

As if they had a premonition, the people sitting in the waiting area began to scamper, heading straight out of the entrance.

The security guard and Rufus struggled as they attempted to pull Franklin off David.

"YOU GUYS NEED TO STOP!" Anna Mae said.

"Wow! Bro, that's the type of welcome I get after not seeing you for five months!" David said winded, attempting to get up off the ground. Franklin bum rushed him again, both of their bodies hitting the ground like a huge slab of lard as they began to scuffle again.

"Hey, hey, break it up," the security guard said. "I'm going to need all of you to leave right now! Don't make me have to use my stun gun! I'll zap you all like a mosquito!"

Franklin and David got up from the floor, panting, both fixing their clothes.

"What the hell?" David said. "What's your problem?"

Franklin grabbed a nearby chair in the waiting area and threw it in David's direction, as Rufus and the guard used David's body as a shield. The leg of the chair clipped David's leg before it slammed right into the glass coffee table, shattering it into pieces.

"OKAY! THAT'S IT!" the security guard yelled.

"OUCH!" David yelped.

"Can we all just get along?" Rufus asked.

"He's the one that you need to be escorting out!" David exclaimed.

The guard stepped behind the partition, quietly beckoning for help on his walkie talkie, peeking around the corner keeping a watchful eye on the four.

"DAMN! You mad or no bro?" David asked, looking at Franklin. "What was that for? What's wrong with you?"

"Stop acting like you don't know what you did!" Franklin exclaimed.

"Franklin, before you set it off again, you need to tell us what's going on!" Anna Mae blurted out. "You are the reason why we are here! What did he do, and what's up with Grace the gossiper!"

"Baby, I got this," Rufus said, stepping from behind David and getting in between Franklin and David.

"Hey, hey, cut it out guys! Stop this!" Rufus said, attempting to be diplomatic. "Ms. Leola is probably rolling over in her grave right now. She wouldn't want to see you all acting like this. We are family."

"We aren't family! Anna Mae, you better get this fake Sister Sledge wannabe backup singer out of my face, before I toss him!" Franklin said, angrily.

"That's it! Come with me," the security guard said to Franklin, trying to diffuse the situation. "Let me talk to you for a minute, young whipper snapper. You remind me of myself in my boxing days."

Franklin reluctantly walked away. The security guard was right on his heels. Both heading in the direction of where Diamond sat at the front desk. The guard abruptly stopped and whispered to Diamond, as he kept a watchful eye on Franklin, and stared out of the front entrance, his eyes fixated on the pouring rain. The security guard pointed in the direction of Anna Mae, Rufus, and David. Diamond stood up, keeping a close eye on the trio, huddled at the opposite end of the waiting area.

David moved closer to Anna Mae.

"What's he on? Because I've never seen him like this!" He whispered.

"I don't know. He's been acting weird since I got here," she said, looking in the distance to see Diamond peering in their direction.

"That bumble bee needs to leave me alone," she said, referring to Diamond. "She's so annoying!"

The three looked back to see Diamond slowly walking in their direction.

"Never mind her! I feel like you're setting me up, Anna Mae. You need to tell me what is going on!" David said.

Rufus stepped closer toward David and Anna Mae, listening in on the conversation.

"So, he didn't tell you why he's pissed?" He asked.

"I told you, I don't know what's going on with him," she said. "Since I've been here, he hasn't said anything. It has to be about Grace, since she's the only missing link."

"I'm sensing the same thing," he said.

Anna Mae looked at Rufus.

"I tried calling you but I couldn't find my phone," she said. "I was looking all over for it."

"You dropped it in the seat when you got out the car," Rufus said.

David began to look around.

"Where did she go?" Anna Mae asked.

David looked behind him again. "I don't care about her! I don't know. Maybe the bathroom," he said.

A loud thunderclap caught their attention, as they witnessed the lightning from the large window.

The hospital lights began to flicker off and on.

Anna Mae looked up at the lights.

"These lights have been flickering since I got here. I'm ready to get out of here, Rufus! Please take me home," she said.

"Oh no, ya'll are not going to get me to come up here and now bounce?" David said, slowly reaching into his pocket while continuing to look around.

Anna Mae saw another flash, as she looked up to see Franklin rush back toward them, outrunning Leroy. "Oh my God, he's coming back this way!"

Anna Mae got a glimpse of the gun. She dropped her pocketbook and screamed to the top of her lungs, "NO! STOP!"

"BANG, BANG, BANG!" Three shots rang out.

Anna Mae fell to the floor, along with the gun, the phone, and her pocketbook. Her laced front wig ricocheted in the air before falling in slow motion, landing by her side, looking more like a horse's shiny black mane.

"OH MY GOD! MY WIFE'S BEEN SHOT!" Rufus yelled.

David froze, standing there in total shock, just like he did he day that Momma had her bad fall.

"ANNA MAE!" Franklin yelled. Her lifeless body lay at the feet of Franklin, David and Rufus.

Anna Mae's whimpered, "Ahhhh! Help ... me ... I've . . . been ... shot!"

Rufus bent down beside his wife. "WE NEED TO GET HER SOME HELP!" He exclaimed. "Baby, don't die on me!"

Leroy hid behind the frosted wall. Out of duty, rather than sympathy, he grabbed his walkie talkie from his shoulder and frantically beckoned for help again; this time reporting the shooting.

"I NEED BACK UP NOW! THERE'S BEEN A SHOOTING IN THE EMERGENCY WAITING AREA! ONE IS DOWN!" He screamed.

"Copy that!" the male on the other end said.

"CODE BLUE! CODE BLUE!" blared over the loudspeaker.

The hospital was on lockdown, with an active shooting in progress. Security guards were called to stand guard in front of the operating rooms. Everyone in the operating area was on edge and in a state of shock.

The head nurse gave orders to the staff to shelter in place, limiting movement in and out of the area. For Macie, it meant that she would miss her dinner break. Macie had only seen these events play out on the news, but she never imagined something like this would happen at Lakewood Community Hospital.

Macie didn't have the complete details, but she couldn't help but think about Leroy, the security guard that greeted her when she would enter the hospital through the emergency room, and Grace's siblings, who she knew were also out there. The description of one of the guys involved in the shooting matched Grace's brother, who she'd met earlier when Grace was in labor.

Grace was awake and present for the birth of her son but after hearing all of the commotion, Dr. Freelance prescribed her a sedative. It knocked her out like a good right hook. She was sound asleep, but her face looked tense.

Macie recalled how Grace was overcome with emotions after hearing her siblings arguing in the waiting area before the gunshots rang out. She nearly delivered her baby right in the hallway.

She recalled how Grace violently shook the rails, as she screamed at the top of her lungs for her brother. Macie tried her best to calm down an unnerved Grace. Just the thought of seeing the fear on Grace's face plagued Macie. If there was one thing that was clear, she truly loved her brother.

Macie witnessed a doctor and two nurses hurry by, discussing the shooting. The doctor said one was down. Macie had no idea who was injured.

She didn't want to think that Grace's family was involved in the shooting; but if they were, she couldn't help but wonder what would spark such violence inside of a hospital. Macie wheeled Grace into the recovery room, positioning the bed just right before closing the curtain.

Macie looked at Grace with empathy as she stood at the foot of Grace's bed in a partially lit room.

"You poor girl. I don't know your story. We all have one, but my heart aches for you. You are stronger than an ox," she said. Macie walked alongside the bed, pulling the blanket up over Grace's shoulders, still shaken from the shooting earlier.

"Okay Miss Grace. Rest well. I'm going to check on your beautiful son," she said, as if Grace were awake to hear her.

CHAPTER 44

Diamond ran back near the front entrance and retreated under her desk. She frantically called the hospital's security office and let them know that Leroy was caught up in the shooting. The security officer calmed her worst fears. He told her that Leroy was fine and had just called them. He told Diamond to shelter in place and wait for the other guards to arrive on the scene.

Diamond let the security officer know that although she couldn't see who'd gotten shot, since she was under the desk, she didn't have a good feeling from the time that Anna Mae entered the emergency room. She ranted how bad things usually happen when Anna Mae is present because she's nothing but trouble and that's why she sent Leroy down there in the first place!

Although she couldn't hear what they were squabbling about, Diamond picked up on their body language that something was amiss. She let the security officer know that things went from bad to worse once their younger brother David showed up with an unknown gentleman. The security officer asked if Diamond could see Leroy from where she was. She responded "no" but said that she spoke to him earlier, before retreating under her desk, but that he was clearly outnumbered to take on the three men who were much younger than him.

The quick-thinking security officer quickly ended

Diamond's rant and contacted law enforcement to request back up.

"These fools are crazy!" Leroy said to himself, as he hid behind the frosted partition. He noticed that two of the three bullets penetrated the magazine rack and the other one hit Anna Mae, who was still laying on the floor moaning in a pool of blood, as her husband crouched over her stiff body. Franklin and David stood over them, arguing, placing the blame on each other.

Three minutes after hanging up with the security officer, Diamond heard footsteps as she crouched under her desk. She peeked over her desk and saw the police officers running through the entrance with their guns drawn.

The security officer called Diamond back and asked her to remain sheltered in place, until the police officer direct her to come out.

"Okay," Diamond said.

"FREEZE! NOBODY MOVE! PUT YOUR HANDS UP SO WE CAN SEE THEM!" the lead officer said.

Rufus slowly stood up. The three men slowly stretched their arms in the air.

"YOU! UP AGAINST THE WALL!" the one rambunctious officer said to Franklin, as he placed the cuffs on his wrists. He then cuffed him to the metal railing while two other officers grabbed Rufus and David, placing them in cuffs, as all three were read their Miranda rights.

One officer ran over to check Anna Mae's pulse, which was faint.

"WHERE'S THE FLIPPING SECRETARY AT? SECURITY SAID SHE WAS UNDER THE DESK!" He yelled.

Diamond's blonde head popped from under the desk.

"I'M OVER HERE!" she yelled.

"CALL FOR A DOCTOR!" He yelled.

"HELP IS ON THE WAY!" she yelled.

"LOOK WHAT YOU'VE DONE!" Franklin yelled, looking at David.

"NO! LOOK WHAT YOU'VE DONE!" David said.

"YOU BETTER HOPE SHE DON'T DIE!" Franklin yelled.

SHUT UP!" the rambunctious officer said to both men, as he surveyed the waiting area.

"WHY AM I BEING ARRESTED?" Rufus asked.

"All three of you are under arrest until we do our investigation and figure out who the gun-toting guy is! This woman has been shot! One of you were the trigger man! We need to know which one of you were stupid enough to bring a gun into a hospital!" the officer said.

"THAT'S MY WIFE! I NEED TO STAY HERE WITH HER!" Rufus said.

"That's not happening! You're all suspects!" the unsympathetic officer said.

One officer placed the 21 caliber gun, Anna Mae's cell phone, and pocketbook into separate plastic bags, as evidence.

"Those are my wife's belongings!" Rufus exclaimed.

"Well, it's all evidence now," the officer said.

"MY WIFE NEEDS ME!" Rufus exclaimed.

"SETTLE DOWN! HELP IS ON THE WAY!" the officer said.

Diamond ran over. "OH MY GOD!" she exclaimed, covering her mouth in complete shock seeing Anna Mae laying on the floor, looking like a beached whale.

"I heard the Code Blue earlier, but I called again," she said to the attending officer.

"Where's the security guard who made the initial call?" the officer asked.

"I don't see him," Diamond said. "His name is Leroy." Leroy popped out from behind the frosted partition.

"Are you Leroy?" the officer asked, noticing his security uniform.

"Who's asking?" Leroy said. "If it's any of my ex-wives, I'm only working part-time, and I've paid all that back-child support. They aren't getting another dime from me," he said.

"That's him," Diamond said, providing a positive identification.

"Where is the security room?" the officer asked.

"I can show you where it's at," Leroy said.

"Once I get an officer back here, we will need to review the video surveillance," the officer said to Leroy.

The officer removed his little pad of paper and pen from his pocket.

"I need your full names," he said.

"Mrs. Diamond Ponzitti!" she said.

"Yours?" the officer asked Leroy.

"Leroy Lamont Little, better known in my younger boxing days as the triple threat!" He said, smiling.

"Yeah, I remember watching you on television," the officer said, looking Leroy up and down. "You were a great fighter . . . back in the day."

"Yeah, but these cats tried to outnumber me today! Had it been one-on-one, you would have been coming in taking a body count," Leroy said to the officer, taking a boxing stance.

The officer seemed unamused.

"Okay, you two, just stand by. I'll need a witness statement."

"Yes, sir," Leroy said, looking over at Anna Mae.

"I didn't witness anything," Diamond said, noticing the large pool of blood that Anna Mae laid in. "Is she gonna make it?"

"I don't know. She's bleeding like a pig who's been poked!" Leroy said as he hopped over Anna Mae's body.

"HEY! THIS IS A CRIME SCENE! GO BACK OVER TO THE DESK!" the officer yelled at Leroy.

A voice came over Leroy's walkie talkie, asking him to confirm his name.

"It's Lima-Echo-Romeo-Oscar-Yankee," Leroy said. "Man, the cops are all up in here!"

The person on the other end exclaimed, "LEROY? OH DAMN! I hope you weren't asleep!"

"OH, shoot!" Leroy said, turning his walkie talkie off.

"Ya'll ought to be ashamed of yourselves!" Diamond said, looking keenly at Franklin, David, and Rufus. She smirked as she looked back over at Anna Mae, "Poor thing!"

She and Leroy headed back over to the front desk.

The officer ordered another cruiser to come to the hospital to ensure that all three men stay separated.

One officer escorted Franklin out first. The other two officers followed suit, escorting David and Rufus to their respective cruisers. All three men covered their faces for their walk of shame.

Suddenly the double doors flew open. The doctor and two nurses ran from behind the secured area, pushing a stretcher.

"She's over there!" Diamond yelled, pointing toward where Anna Mae lay.

"FINALLY!" The attending officer said impatiently. "OVER HERE! HURRY UP!" He said. "SHE'S LOST A LOT OF BLOOD!"

The doctor assessed Anna Mae's condition rather quickly.

"I'll check her vitals," the nurse said.

"I checked a few minutes ago. She has a weak pulse," the officer said.

"We are going to have to roll her over in order to get her on the stretcher," the doctor said.

The two nurses stood back. The officer assisted the doctor with carefully rolling Anna Mae over onto her back.

One of the nurses carefully cut the string to the face

mask, around Anna Mae's thick neck and her matching rain jacket, quickly placing an oxygen mask over her nose and mouth, as the other nurse started an IV.

"Ma'am can you hear me?" the doctor asked, as he checked Anna Mae's pulse. Anna Mae's eyes fluttered. "Stay with me."

"We have to get her into surgery stat," the doctor said, as they whisked Anna Mae behind the double doors, where Grace was.

"DON'T YA'LL FORGET HER HAIR," Leroy said, rushing over, scooping up Anna Mae's wig and tossing it on top of her stomach.

CHAPTER 45

The screams were bone chilling. Macie ran into the recovery room.

"It's okay Grace. You were having a nightmare," she said, gently rubbing Grace's arm. A groggy Grace woke up, looking frightened.

"Where am I?" She asked, looking around, as she gathered her bearings.

She felt her stomach.

"MY BABY! WHERE'S MY BABY!" She began to yell. "HE TOOK MY BABY!"

"It's okay," Macie said, consoling a confused looking Grace. "You're in the recovery room. You gave birth to a beautiful baby boy. Your baby is safe. He's in the nursery," the nurse said.

"Where's my brother!" She cried. "Is he dead?" Grace said reliving the sound of the gunshots.

"He's okay," Macie said, closely relying on the instructions that the head nurse gave her, to not inform Grace of what had transpired in the emergency room.

"Then where is he?" Grace asked.

Macie had to think quick. The head nurse didn't provide her with a script on how to respond to the questions, that she knew Grace would have.

"He had to leave," she said.

"LEAVE! TO GO WHERE? WHY WOULD HE LEAVE ME?" Grace asked, trying to sit up, "Aww!" she said, grimacing from the tenderness.

"Relax Grace," Macie said.

Grace leaned back, resting her head on the pillow, looking up at the white ceiling. Her mind in overdrive.

"My brother wouldn't leave me like that," she said, cutting her eyes at Macie. "There's something that you're not telling me."

"Do you want some water?" Macie asked, attempting to change the subject.

"No! I want my brother!" Grace exclaimed.

"Okay," Macie said. "Let me go see if I can find him," she said, not knowing what to do.

Macie returned 15 minutes later.

"Look who I found," she said.

Grace shot up from the bed.

"FRANKLIN!" she exclaimed.

Macie pushed the bassinet into the room, with baby Justice asleep inside.

"I haven't found him yet but here's your beautiful son," she said.

Grace looked disappointed, as she looked over in the bassinet at Justice.

"Is that my baby?" She asked.

Macie checked Grace's hospital band against Justice's.

"He is your son" she said.

"His feet and hands are pink!"

"Most babies are born pinkish-looking," Macie said. "It takes a few days for babies to get their color. This is all normal, Grace. Your son is perfect!"

Baby Justice began to fuss a little.

"Would you like to hold him?" Macie asked.

Grace looked at Justice.

"Grace, it's okay. You have to bond with your son," Macie said.

Justice started to whimper.

"Oh, he's getting fussy. He's probably ready to eat," she said. "Are you up to breastfeeding? I would encourage you to. If not, we'll have to start Justice on formula."

"O-kay," Grace said reluctantly. "I'll try it, although I don't know what I'm doing."

"That's why I'm here!" Macie exclaimed.

"Okay," Grace said.

"Before I went to the nursery to get Justice, I ordered you something to eat. You will definitely need to keep your strength up for both you and Justice," Macie said. "This is very important, Grace."

"Okay," Grace said.

"Are you ready to begin breastfeeding?" Macie asked.

"I guess," Grace said.

Macie carefully picked up a fussy Justice and gently placed him in Grace's arms.

"Okay, let's do this," Macie said, with a calming smile, as she pulled the curtain for privacy.

Chapter 46

On the count of three.... One ... two ... three," the doctor said, as he and the nurses struggled to help move Anna Mae from the stretcher to the operating room table. Anna Mae's body was limp.

"She's lost a lot of blood," the nurse said.

"WHERE'S THE ANESTHESIOLOGIST!" the doctor exclaimed.

"I'm here!" the anesthesiologist rushed in, working feverishly to hook up the intravenous needle in Anna Mae's arm before placing the breathing tube down Anna Mae's throat. "I'm done!" she exclaimed.

"Impressive," the doctor said. "We got it from here!"

"Good luck!" she said, as she quickly left the room. The heart monitor beeped, as the nurse kept a watchful eye on it.

"The anesthesia is kicking in," the other nurse said, watching Anna Mae's body become more relaxed, while the other nurse covered Anna Mae's neat cornrows with a plastic surgery cap.

"Did that x-ray come back yet?" the doctor asked. "I got to get this bleeding to stop, but I cannot go in until then."

"Yes," the nurse said to the doctor.

"What do we got?" He asked.

The nurse began to read the results as quickly as she could. "The bullet nicked her stomach, bypassing the kidneys, pancreas, and her liver. It remains lodged in her stomach."

"Did her blood tests results come back yet?" the doctor asked.

"Yes," the nurse said.

"What's her CBC looking like," he said.

"CBC looks good!" the nurse said.

"Her RBC is low," the nurse said.

"That's expected due to the blood loss," he said.

"Was any HCG found in her blood stream?" the doctor asked.

The room fell silent.

"WAS THERE?" He asked.

"Yes," the nurse said.

"Oh my God! Not what I want to hear!" the doctor exclaimed.

CHAPTER 47

The cruisers pulled up to the precinct, one behind the other.

Franklin sat in the backseat with his head resting against the back of the front passenger seat. He couldn't believe the chain of events. Although he was pulling for Anna Mae, he held resentment toward her for calling David.

He thought about Grace. Once again, Grace was left, all alone to deal with another traumatizing situation. He blamed himself for what happened. If only he hadn't involved Anna Mae.

The officer opened the passenger door.

"Okay, let's go! Watch your head," he said, pulling Franklin out of the car and escorting him into the police station.

Franklin was so embarrassed. He held his head down, as he walked into the police station. He shamefully looked around to see if he could see David or Rufus or anyone else that he may know.

It didn't surprise him that David would be carrying a gun. His behavior had been suspect for months. He felt so bad that Rufus got caught up in all this drama, but he was confident that they would both be cleared, once all of the facts come out.

"Who do we have here?" the booking officer said.

"Franklin Johnson," the officer said.

"Hey, was that the call that came in from the Lakewood emergency room?" the booking officer asked.

"Yeah," the officer said.

"I guess the victim was at the right place, at the wrong time," the booking officer said, poking fun at Anna Mae. "The weapon is being processed for fingerprints. The other two have been questioned, just waiting on this one."

"Sounds good," the officer said.

Two other officers were already in the room. They grilled Franklin like a toasted cheese sandwich. He remained calm, as he told the officers his account of what happened. Two hours later he was done and worn out.

The office who drove him to the station, helped him to his feet.

"It's light, camera, action time," he said to Franklin, attempting to make light of the situation. They walked to an adjacent room.

Franklin stood in front of the camera, feeling ashamed. He knew that Momma would be so disappointed in him. He was disappointed in himself.

"Face me," the officer said.

"Turn to the right ... and now the left." Franklin fought

back tears as he obeyed the officer's commands.

"Okay, let's get your fingerprints done," the officer said.

The officer escorted Franklin to another small dingy room.

"He's all yours. I'll stand here until he's done," the officer said, closing the door.

Franklin entered the room, where one officer sat at a computer and another officer walked him over to a machine and proceeded to take his fingerprints, saying very little.

Ten minutes later, the officer opened the door, as he escorted Franklin out.

"We're all set," he said to the awaiting officer.

The officer took Franklin into another area and began to pat him down.

"Do you have any sharp objects in your pockets?" He asked.

"Just my keys, my cell phone, papers, and a pack of gum," he said.

The officer patted Franklin down, double checking, before carefully emptying all of the content from Franklin's pockets. The officer handed Franklin a jumpsuit. He led him to an area to change before bringing him back to the booking officer.

"Hey, is he getting a screening!" the officer yelled to the booking officer.

"Yeah! Sarge ordered one for all three, for precautionary measures," he said.

"What does that mean?" Franklin asked.

"Health screening. Checking for diseases," the officer said.

"I'm clean!" Franklin exclaimed.

"I don't take orders from you," the officer said rudely, before escorting Franklin back to the booking area.

"He's all set," he said.

"Okay, let me see where he's going," the booking officer said, looking over Franklin's arrest file, as he began talking to himself done ... done ... done ... no DNA test requested ... done . . . done."

"YOU NEED TO DO A DNA ON DAVID JOHNSON!" Franklin blurted out.

"Buddy, remember your Miranda rights. Take it up with your attorney," the officer said.

Franklin felt helpless.

"Is he cleared for warrants?" the officer asked.

"He's clean, but one of his buddies got a little bit of a

record," the booking officer said.

"I TOLD YOU!" Franklin said. "WHEN CAN I MAKE MY PHONE CALL?"

Both officers ignored Franklin.

"Sarge has that one in protective custody," the booking officer said.

"Oh, wow!" the officer said.

"This one's going into holding cell 5," the booking officer said.

"The charge sheet set bail for $10,000.00!" the officer said.

"Yeah, two have a $10,000,00 bail but the other one, his bail is set for $100,000.00," the booking officer said, "but the victim is in surgery. If she doesn't make it, that may change. They will appear before the judge on Monday morning!"

Franklin's heart sank. He knew that he didn't have that type of money accessible to him. He wasn't sure if Rufus had $10,000 accessible to him, but he had the consolation in knowing that David wouldn't see the light of day for a long time.

Chapter 48

Grace laid on the nurse call button, as if she had a personal butler.

Macie came running in.

"Good morning sunshine," she said, sounding cheery.

Grace seemed surprised to see Macie.

"How are you feeling?" Macie asked.

"I feel okay, but my breasts are sore," Grace said, scrolling through the TV channels before tossing the remote on the bed.

Macie smiled.

"That's expected. Your breasts will feel firm and full because of the milk. Before you go home, we'll go over using the breast pump again. This will relieve some of the pressure."

"Okay," Grace said looking drained.

"… and Miss Grace, you will do just fine. It can be overwhelming at first, but you will be a pro at motherhood in no time," she said, grabbing the television remote and powering the TV off.

"Okay, come on. The shower is waiting," she said, helping Grace into the bathroom.

"Do you live here?" Grace asked facetiously.

Macie chuckled.

"I just cannot get enough of you," Macie said jokingly. "No, I picked up an early shift."

The truth was, some of the nurses had heard about the shooting on the news and refused to come to work; so Macie, along with some of the other nurses, was forced to stay to provide coverage.

"Did you find Franklin?" Grace asked. "I called his phone and he's not answering."

"I haven't seen him today," Macie said.

Macie had found out additional information from the head nurse. Franklin and the two other men had been arrested for the shooting in the emergency room. The woman who was shot was indeed Grace's older sister that she'd mentioned to Macie when she was in labor. She was instructed not to tell Grace.

"Something is not right," Grace said. "This is not like Franklin to come with me to the hospital and then vanish."

Grace looked puzzled.

"I left my cell phone at home, but I called the house and no one is answering that phone either," she said.

"I think he'll show up soon," Macie said.

Grace was in deep thought.

"Wait? Where's my sister?" Grace asked, reaching for the phone.

"Grace, you don't need to be stressed right now. Your family is fine, they probably just went out to dinner to celebrate the birth of their new nephew," Macie said, grabbing the phone and hanging it up.

"Not my family!" she said. "Definitely not my sister!"

"Grace, you are such a worrywart! I'm sure when they are able to, they will come in to see you," Macie said.

"Okay," Grace said. "I have no reason not to believe you."

Macie felt relieved that she was able to calm Grace down, if only temporarily.

"Here you go," she said, handing Grace the breakfast menu. "Why don't you look over the menu and tell me what you want, and I'll call the order into the kitchen," Macie said. "It shouldn't take that long."

"Okay," Grace said. "I hope they have French toast and bacon," she said, smiling.

"I'm sure they do!" Macie said.

"Yes!" Grace said with excitement, pointing it out on the menu.

Macie picked up the phone and ordered the food.

"Okay. Your breakfast should be here once you're

done. Let's get you in the shower."

"Okay. Is Justice up?" Grace asked.

"I checked on him earlier, and he was still asleep," Macie said.

"Good! He should be full!" Grace said. "The night nurse woke me up three times!" she said, sounding annoyed.

"Yes, remember I said that Justice needs to eat every two hours for right now," Macie explained.

"What if I forget to wake up once I'm home?" Grace asked.

"Well, you can set your alarm clock, and I'm sure you will have help once you get home," Macie said, before Grace had a chance to bring up Franklin again.

Twenty-five minutes later, the shower was complete. The food service worker had come in and delivered Grace's food, just as Macie was helping Grace get back into the bed.

"Great timing; your breakfast is here," Macie said.

"Thank you!" Grace said.

The young man nodded and walked out.

"I checked your chart earlier, Dr. Freelance will be coming by later this morning to check on you. You can ask him any questions that you may have," Macie said.

"Okay," Grace said.

"When am I going home?" Grace asked.

"Dr. Freelance will assess you, and he will let us know when you can be discharged. If all is well, you may be discharged as early as tomorrow," Macie said.

"Who's going to take me home?" Grace asked. "I don't have a car seat or clothes for Justice to go home in," she said with fear in her voice.

Macie realized that she may have set herself up.

"Don't worry about that! It will all work out," she said bluntly. "I just need you to take one day at a time and focus on bonding with Justice. Speaking of Justice, it's time for his feeding. I'll go get him ready and give you some time to eat."

"Macie," Grace said. Macie stopped at the doorway.

"Can you come home with me?" She asked.

"You'll be just fine Miss Grace. I have to admit you're starting to grow on me. How about if I give you my number and if you have any questions, you can call me," Macie said.

"Okay," Grace said. "One more thing. Do you have any headphones that I can borrow?"

"Yes," Macie said. "I'll bring them back when I return."

"Okay, thanks," Grace said. "I'm going to ask Franklin

to bring my phone up."

Macie smiled, as she looked at Grace. "Okay … now eat up! I'll be back!" she said, leaving the room to go get baby Justice.

Chapter 49

Were you able to get in contact with her next of kin?" the doctor asked.

"Unfortunately, that's not going to be possible," the nurse said.

"Why is that?" the doctor asked.

"Her husband was one of the men arrested on yesterday. He's being held in the city jail until his appearance in court on Monday," the nurse said.

"What in the world happened here? My God!"

CHAPTER 50

"Knock, knock, knock."

Grace pulled the curtain back to see who was at the door.

"Yes," she said, peaking behind the curtain.

"We have a flower delivery for Grace Johnson. Is that you?" the nurse asked.

"Yes," Grace said hesitantly, placing her fork down on the tray.

The nurse, wearing hot pink scrubs, walked into the room, carrying a huge blue and white beautiful bouquet in a baby blue alphabet block ceramic vase, with a 12-inch teddy bear attached.

"Where would you like this beautiful arrangement?' she asked.

"Are you sure they are for me?" Grace asked, looking puzzled.

If you're Grace Johnson, they are."

"I am," Grace responded.

"Now, where do you want this?"

"You can sit them on my side table over here," Grace said, pointing to the small table near the window.

"I guess it's safe to say that you had a boy."

"Yes, I did," Grace said.

"Congratulations on the birth of your baby," the nurse said.

"Thank you! Who are they from?"

"I don't know. The hospital security bought the delivery up to the nurse's station. But it looks like there's a card attached," the nurse said.

"Can you pass it to me?" Grace asked.

"Sure," the nurse said, pulling the card off the plastic card holder and handing it to Grace.

"Thank you," Grace said, holding onto the unopened envelope as she picked up the remote to turn the television on.

"Don't mention it," the nurse said.

Grace couldn't help but notice that she had seen the nurse before, but she couldn't place her. She wondered if it was one of the nurses that she saw when Momma was hospitalized? Her mind didn't feel as sharp as before. The lack of sleep, and the aftereffects of the anesthesia were affecting her memory.

"Have a great day Grace!" she said.

"You too," Grace said hesitantly, as she watched the nurse vanish.

Less than three minutes after the nurse had exited Grace's room, Macie entered pushing the bassinet that held Justice.

"We're b-aack," she sang, as she handed the headphones to Grace. Macie picked up the remote and powered the TV off.

"Thanks Macie. Now I can listen to one of my favorite songs that I used to listen to when I was pregnant with Justice."

"What song is that?" Macie asked.

"Well, I am huge Whitney Houston fan, but my second favorite artist is Andra Day," Grace said. "Do you know her?"

"Do I know her? Of course, I do! You have to be living under a rock to not know who she is. I love her!" Macie said.

They both started singing "Rise Up," laughing like school-aged girls.

"You got good taste in music, Miss Grace," Macie said.

"That song makes me feel better," Grace said. "It makes me feel like I'm a phoenix, rising up from the ashes ... you know, like I've been reborn. I've renewed my mind, redirecting my energy and my thoughts. Only positive vibes. Real positive vibes!" she snickered.

"Wow! Yeah, I can see that Grace. The song fits you

perfectly. You have a new beginning with your beautiful son. Just know that no one or nothing can stop you. I don't know all that you've been through, but I can tell that you've gone through some stuff, and you are a survivor."

"Yes, I am," Grace said, sounding confident. "You don't even know the half of it."

"I can tell that you're a fighter," she said.

"Yeah," Grace said.

"Ooooh, beautiful!" Macie looked up, noticing the flowers.

"Thanks," Grace said.

"Who are they from?" Macie asked.

"I don't know," Grace said, knowing that Franklin and Misty were the only two people that knew she was having a baby.

"What does it say?" Macie asked, as she took Justice out of the bassinet.

"I don't know," Grace said.

"Well, open up the envelope and read the card, silly," Macie said. "Inquiring minds want to know." Grace began to read the card.

"Read it out loud .... I mean, if you don't mind," Macie requested.

"What, you hiding from me? Glad I found you! Something messed up happened, as to why I haven't been around, but hope to see you soon. I hope you like the flowers and congrats on baby boy! Stay up."

Grace's entire demeanor changed. She became enraged.

"WHY IS HE DOING THIS TO ME? HE JUST CANNOT LEAVE ME ALONE!" Grace yelled.

"Who?" Macie asked, looking shocked at how quickly Grace transformed from a mythical bird into an angry bird.

"DAVID!" Grace yelled.

"And … who's David?" Macie asked.

Grace grabbed the vase and slid it off the side table. The glass vase hit the floor and shattered into small pieces. The blue and white flowers scattering all over the floor.

"OH MY GOD!" Macie exclaimed, shielding Justice from the flying glass.

"GRACE, WHY DID YOU DO THAT?" She asked, in total shock.

"DAVID IS THE ONE WHO ASSAULTED ME!" Grace yelled, as she started to get up out of the bed.

"OH MY GOD!" Macie exclaimed. "Don't move! I need to call the custodian to come clean this up. The last thing I need is for you to step on broken glass!"

Macie thought back to when Grace was in labor and she'd asked about the baby's father, if he was around. Grace had mentioned that he was around more than she knew. Macie realized that David was Justice's absent father.

Grace proceeded to share every detail with Macie, about that dreadful night, not sparing any detail.

Macie applauded Grace for her bravery and totally underestimated her strength, but as a health professional, she knew that she couldn't send Justice home with an unstable, angry mother, even if she began to grow fond of her. She was perplexed. She had to do something!

At that moment, nothing Macie said was able to calm Grace down.

Grace looked hotter than fire! She looked beyond angry.

"GET OUT!" Grace yelled.

Macie's priority was to protect baby Justice.

"Grace, I'm so sorry. I had no idea, but I think that it's best if I have the nursery feed Justice, and I will come back to talk to you!"

Shaken to her core, Macie placed Justice back in his bassinet and dashed out of the room. She instructed the neonatal nurse to feed Justice, so that she could look into getting Grace help.

Macie paged Dr. Freelance and explained what she had learned about Grace. She asked if he could prescribe Grace a sedative to calm her down.

Dr. Freelance refused to order meds since Grace was breastfeeding. He instructed Macie to call the grief and trauma office and ask if they could send someone to meet with Grace before she's discharged to help her cope with the sexual trauma that she'd experience.

As directed by Dr. Freelance, Macie placed David on the "privacy patient" list, so that he would be turned away if he came to see Grace.

Macie reluctantly returned to Grace's room. Before entering, she took a deep breath. She slowly entered the room, to find Grace sound asleep.

Macie closed the door and let her sleep in peace.

CHAPTER 51

Is she asleep?" He asked, leaning over Grace.

"Don't she look asleep, fool," she said.

"Look like she dreaming . . . about me," he said, laughing, with his red shopping bag over his shoulder.

"If that's the case . . . wait for it . . . wait for it," she said.

"Wait for what?" He asked.

"Her nightmare!" she said.

"Now, get out of the girl's face and go over there and sit your butt down! You gone wake her up with all that Brut you wearing. You got enough on to choke a horse!" she said coughing.

Grace peeked her eyes open, hearing the chatter.

"See that! Your ole' mean self, waking her up from her beauty sleep," he said, limping with his cane over to the empty chair.

"If you don't hush up!" she muttered.

"Look at her yawning.... catch them flies gal," he said, with a chuckle, as he sat down in the chair.

"Mabel, this gal's stomach is as big as yours! I thought that nurse told us that she had the baby already!" He exclaimed.

Auntie Mabeline playfully hit Old Man Joe on his chest as she walked around the foot of the bed and over to the window.

"It's depressingly dark in here!" she said, pulling the noisy blinds back.

"Well, if that didn't wake her up, your heavy walking sure enough will!" He said facetiously.

Grace's eyes started to flutter as the bright sunlight kissed her face.

Old Man Joe and Auntie Mabeline watched her every move.

Grace slowly woke up to see both of them staring at her.

"WHAT ARE YOU DOING HERE!" she exclaimed.

"I should be asking you that, Miss Gracie," Auntie Mabeline said, "Keeping secrets huh?"

"I bought you something," Old Man Joe said cackling.

"You did," Grace responded.

"I picked these up downstairs," he said, reaching into his red shopping bag, pulling out some pamphlets on sexual dysfunction.

"Joe, you are out of your mind!" Auntie Mabeline said, grabbing the pamphlets and tossing them in the trash.

"Never mind that right now. How are you feeling Gracie?" Auntie Mabeline asked.

"Besides being sleepy and sore, I'm feeling okay," Grace said.

"How was your delivery? It must've been painful?" Auntie Mabeline asked.

"Yes, the contractions were painful, but Macie, my nurse, was very supportive. She stayed by my side the whole time," Grace said.

"How'd you know that I was here? Did Franklin call you? He came home yesterday!" Grace asked. "I want him to bring my cell phone that I left on Momma's dresser. I called the house but no one answered."

"Franklin? No, I haven't heard or seen Franklin. I forgot his tour was ending this month."

"I knew it was this month, but he never told me the actual date. He surprised me! I spoke to him early yesterday morning, while I was cleaning out Momma's closet. I thought he was still on the base. He told me that he had to get off the phone, but he was actually right outside. He'd tricked me," Grace said.

"Well that's a nice surprise, but you know I'm going to get on his case for not reminding me. He knows my memory ain't good," Auntie Mabeline said.

"So, how'd you know that I was in the hospital?" Grace

asked again.

"You can thank me!" Old Man Joe said proudly.

"Yeah, he partly right. Now, you know, I don't answer my phone if I don't know whose number it is. I pay my bills on time, so ain't no bill collectors chasing me. But you had me so worried, Gracie! You know that I look forward to our daily chats. When I didn't hear from you yesterday, I figured you were asleep. I know how ya'll sleep like logs in the forest. So, I went out with the seniors at church to a matinee. When I got home in the evening, I had a few missed calls on my caller ID. You know I still don't have my voice mail set up on that answering machine. So, I just went on about my business. If someone wanted to reach me bad enough, they'll call back," Auntie Mabeline kept rambling on. "Then Joe rang my phone after eleven o'clock at night breathing all heavy on the phone. I thought he'd lost his ever-loving mind, calling me that late."

"You never complained about my breathing before," Old Man Joe said, tapping Auntie Mabeline on the butt with his walking stick.

Auntie Mabeline gave him the side eye.

"Joe told me that he had a splitting headache and was finally able to fall asleep in his chair, when he was woken up by a lot of racket going on above his head," she said.

"Yup, I told this woman here, I had stretched out in my bed, then I heard all this racket above my head. My head felt like it was about to explode. I just got myself up and walked into the living room to try to take my nap!"

Grace remembered that she and Franklin had been in Momma's closet. The noise that Old Man Joe was referring to was likely Franklin dragging the safe.

"As soon as I'd fallen asleep, I woke up again to all kinds of commotion in the hallway. I cracked my door and seen them people in uniform taking you out in a strait jacket. Uh huh, I told your auntie, they had you strapped in the bed tighter than these pants she got on here," he said, looking at Auntie Mabeline's polyester brown pants. "I told Mabel that every last one of ya'll are crazy!"

"Hush up Joe, before I commit you!" Auntie Mabeline said.

"You go first," he said. "Maybe we can get two for one!"

"You two are funny," Grace said.

"Don't pay him no mind baby," Auntie Mabeline said, looking over at Old Man Joe. "You know they had to strap her tight, so she wouldn't fall off the stretcher!"

"Hmmmm," Old Man Joe grunted, continuing. "I was gonna come out there, but I saw your big muscular boyfriend in them army pants. I said, he probably carrying a switch blade or something."

"Oh, that was Franklin," Grace said.

"Who? Do I know him?" He questioned, looking up at Auntie Mabeline.

"Earth to Joe? Is anything up in that head of yours? Yes, Joe, you know him. Franklin was the one who helped you out all those years with your errands, before he went off into the service."

"Oh, that was him? He grew into a nice-looking young man. That boy's head used to be so big, it needed its own zip code," he said, laughing.

"Once Joe described him to me, I put two and two together," Auntie Mabeline said. "I said that got to be Franklin." Auntie Mabeline changed the subject back to Grace. "Boy, was I shocked when the lady downstairs looked up your name and told me that you were in the maternity ward. I told that nurse she was dead wrong. I told her they must have your name spelled wrong. She ended up being right. Now, that threw me for a loop!"

Grace ignored Auntie Mabeline's comment and focused on Franklin.

"I've been asking Macie about Franklin, but she can't seem to locate him," Grace said. "He came with me to the hospital. He met Macie, so she knows what he looks like, and now she's not telling me nothing!" she said.

Against policy and out of frustration, Macie had filled Auntie Mabeline in on what had transpired in the hospital. Auntie Mabeline was not ready to share it with Grace, after learning about the fit that she had over the flowers. She wanted to proceed with caution.

"Shut your mouth!" Auntie Mabeline said.

"Yes, Franklin was out there. I told him that it was okay to call Anna Mae and tell her that I was pregnant. We both know that she would want to come up here to see for herself," Grace said.

"Well, don't worry yourself about that now. Put your energy into you and your son. We'll figure all this out together. They'll turn up!" she said.

Auntie Mabeline grunted. Grace continued her rant.

"I was in so much pain, it felt like time was flying by fast. One minute I was pregnant, then next thing you know, I was holding my baby. Who knows, Franklin could have been right by my side, and I wouldn't have even known it," she said. "My mind is still scattered from that medicine that put me to asleep."

"What did I just say?" Auntie Mabeline said. "You're being hardheaded," she said, quickly changing the subject.

"What did you name the baby?" Auntie Mabeline asked calmly.

"Justice," Grace said. "I wanted Franklin to help me think of a name, but when he didn't come back, I went with my first choice."

"You should have named him "Mo Money," for all

them times your Momma sent you downstairs, begging me for my money after all I've done for her!" Old Man Joe said. "Now don't you go training this kid to be knocking on my door. I'll have to take my cane here and rat-tat-a-tat his behind."

Grace ignored Old Man Joe.

"Have you met Macie?" Grace asked Aunt Mabeline.

"Oh baby, I don't know. There are so many nurses out there. I could have."

"She usually comes in before she leaves, to say bye," Grace said.

"Guess what Gracie?" Auntie Mabeline asked, trying to cheer Grace up.

"What, Auntie?"

"I broke down and bought me a cellular phone!" she said.

"WHAT? THAT'S GOOD! ABOUT TIME AUNTIE," Grace exclaimed.

"Oh yes. Joe's the only one who has the number to my cellular phone, since I couldn't reach you. The hell with them other kids," she said, showing off her canary yellow phone case.

"Nice!" Grace said.

"Yeah. I'm just trying to stay up with the changing

times. Irma tried to explain to me how to use my new cellular phone. Then, she started jumping all over the place, confusing me, telling me that I had to put in my contacts. I told Irma that she knows I don't wear no contacts."

Grace laughed, knowing that Auntie Mabeline totally misunderstood what "contacts" meant.

Auntie Mabeline continued, "Hell, she sat on my glasses before the movie started and bent my frame. Luckily, Bessie carries an extra pair of them glasses she got out there at the dollar store, so she let me borrow some.

Where was I at, before I get off track?"

"Off track? That train done jumped the tracks and headed in the opposite direction," Old Man Joe said.

"Joe, hush up now," she said.

Grace looked at them, as if she was watching a comedy show. Auntie Mabeline cut her eyes at Old Man Joe.

"You need to keep that gingko for yourself! Never mind trying to give them to me! I have enough energy," he said.

"Fool, it's for memory. You ole' absent minded ant!" she said.

"Auntie, you'd mentioned your contacts," Grace said, attempting to get her back on track. "Your contacts are the people that you want to add in your phone and save their number. When they call you, their name will show up on your phone. This way, you'll know who's calling you."

"Oh, is that what she meant?" Auntie Mabeline said.

"Yes," Grace said.

That's too much! I'll stick to using my landline," she said looking frustrated. "Ain't nobody got time for that foolishness!"

"It's not hard. I can show you," Grace said.

"Thank you, baby," Auntie Mabeline said. "Where was I at ... oh yeah ... so, my caller ID at the house showed that there were two numbers that had called me repeatedly, while I was out with the ladies. I figured it was probably not a bill collector. I ended up being right this time!"

"When I called the last number back, I got your sister's crazy husband. He answered her phone."

"What?" Grace said. "Why would he have Anna Mae's phone, I wonder?"

"I don't know. It was strange to me too! Well, they both strange!" she said.

"Enough about that. So, you had a baby, and no one knew that you were pregnant. How in the world did this happen?" Auntie Mabeline asked, with her flight of ideas.

Grace was interrupted by a familiar voice walking into the room.

"Hey, I see you have some company!" Macie said,

pretending as if it was her first-time seeing Auntie Mabeline and Old Man Joe.

"Chile' you know we already met in the hallway," she said. "This is Grace's neighbor. He was in the bathroom earlier when we spoke."

"That prune juice was working overtime!" Old Man Joe said.

"Joe . . . TMI! Anyways, he was the one who told me that Grace was taken away in the ambulance. I called around to all the hospitals and found her," Auntie Mabeline, said sounding proud, yet scripted.

"I am so glad to see that Grace has support," Macie said, looking relieved.

Grace studied Auntie Mabeline and Macie's behavior.

"Auntie, I didn't know you've both met?" She said. "I asked you earlier." For once, Auntie Mabeline was speechless.

"Yeah, briefly," Macie interrupted Grace over the lie that she told.

"EVERYONE IS LYING TO ME! I DON'T KNOW WHY YOU ALL ARE LYING TO ME! I SHOULDN'T HAVE TOLD YOU ANYTHING!" she yelled, looking at Macie.

"Watch your mouth!" Auntie Mabeline said. "Now don't you come calling me no liar! Gracie, I don't know what's gotten into you!"

"Gal, don't you go copping no attitude with me neither!" Old Man Joe exclaimed. "You want some licks with this cane I got here?" He said, raising his old beat up cane in the air.

"MACIE, DID YOU TELL HER?" Grace asked, referring to the sexual assault.

"OH NO, GRACE! I WOULD NEVER BETRAY YOUR TRUST!" she said.

"Tell me what?" Auntie Mabeline asked.

"How do I know that?" She asked, ignoring Auntie Mabeline's question.

"Because I'm telling you the truth," she said. "Grace, you have to trust me."

"What is she talking about?" Auntie Mabeline asked Macie.

"I'm sorry, but I cannot divulge that information. Patient confidentiality," she said.

"Why are you not being honest with me! I want to see my brother," Grace wailed…. "I just want to see my brother."

Auntie Mabeline walked over to Grace and began to cradle her. She knew that she owed Grace the truth, and Grace was smart enough to figure out that they all knew more than they had let on.

Macie and Old Man Joe looked on as Grace wept in Auntie Mabeline's arm.

"I can give you a minute," Macie said. "How about I go get Justice and come back. I'm sure your Auntie and her friend would love to meet your bundle of joy."

"Joy? She looks like she in pain!" Old Man Joe exclaimed.

"Joe!" Auntie Mabeline exclaimed, before looking back at Macie. "Yeah! Bring that little rascal on out," she said, giving Macie the side eye, realizing that she hadn't been forthcoming.

Macie hurried out of the room.

"Calm down little girl … now, just calm down," Auntie Mabeline said, as she took a deep breath.

Auntie Mabeline sat on the side of Grace's bed, facing Grace as she held her hands.

"Gracie, I didn't want to tell you this, but I see that you just gonna work my nerves until I tell you what happened yesterday. I'll tell you what I know."

Grace listened intently drying her eyes.

"Is Franklin dead?" She asked.

"No … no … thank God, your brother is very much alive, but Gracie, he got himself into some trouble," she said, taking another breath.

"What type of trouble?" Grace asked.

Auntie Mabeline began to tell Grace what happened in the emergency room.

"Well, let me finish where I left off earlier …. After I got the missed call, I dialed the number back and got Anna Mae's husband. He said that your sister didn't realize that she'd left her phone in the car. Rufus said he noticed the Georgia area code and answered it, because he knew it was me. He told me that Franklin was home from the army and had called Anna Mae to come up to the hospital. I asked him, for what?

"So, what else did he say?" Grace asked.

"That man is just as brainless as a jellyfish! After that, he said a bunch of nothing," Auntie Mabeline said.

"You said that Franklin didn't tell her why he asked her to come up here?"

"Rufus said they didn't know why."

"So . . . Anna Mae didn't know that I was pregnant?" Grace said, questioning herself.

"It's possible. Only Franklin can answer that. After I hung up with your sister's husband, I got a call from David."

"DAVID?" a shocked Grace said, listening intently.

"Yes, David. I could tell something wasn't quite right by what he was saying. That boy was talking all 'off the wall;' I thought he was Michael Jackson reincarnated."

"What did he say?" Grace asked, looking disgusted.

"I couldn't tell you! There was so much noise in the background, like he was walking in the rain. All I could make out was that Anna Mae had called him and told him to call me," Auntie Mabeline said. "I asked him if he needed me to come up here. He said he didn't know what was going on, because he'd been handling his own business and staying out of everyone else's. Whatever that means! I said to myself, there's some craziness going on here. I couldn't get hold of you and I hadn't heard from Anna Mae or David since I returned back to Georgia!"

"Auntie, you cannot tell David where I'm at," she said.

And why not?" She asked.

Grace wasted no time with telling her aunt the details surrounding her pregnancy. She wasn't worried about Old Man Joe knowing, because she knew there was an eighty percent chance that he would not remember what she said tomorrow. She told her aunt that she suspected that David was Justice's father, because she and Franklin discovered that David was not their blood brother. She shared everything with her aunt, just like she shared earlier with Macie.

"Since all that happened, I haven't seen anyone!" Grace

said.

Auntie Mabeline looked as if she'd been hit with a ton of bricks. She turned on the television, welcoming the distraction.

"Grace, I don't know what to make of all this," she said. "How do you know that David is not your brother?" She asked.

"I just told you! Are you calling me a liar?" She asked. "You're always protecting him, so I'm not surprised! I knew you wouldn't believe me. I shouldn't have told you anything either! The only thing that matters is that Franklin believes me!"

"No, no…. I'm just saying, it's a bit farfetched. That's a serious accusation. I just cannot imagine David doing this to you," she said. "You said you couldn't see the person's face, maybe you just thought it was David, since you were mad that he left the door open. That nurse said that they gave you some medication. Maybe it's making you hallucinate!"

"Now I'm crazy?" Grace asked, getting upset.

"Now, that is not true Gracie, but I want to see all the things that ya'll found in this safe," Auntie Mabeline said.

They were both interrupted by Old Man Joe's loud snores.

"He was just talking! He fell asleep fast!" Grace

commented.

"He told me that he hasn't been sleeping much. He's been suffering from migraines, and he's been unstable on his feet. That's why he uses the cane," Auntie Mabeline said, looking over at Old Man Joe.

"Is Big Tuna still in jail?" Grace asked.

"Yeah, he is. Joe misses him so much. He's accepted so many collect calls that his phone bill is close to five hundred dollars! He's struggling. I told him he better stop accepting those calls and teach that boy a lesson before his phone gets shut off for good!"

Grace looked at Old Man Joe with empathy. "I feel bad that he doesn't have anyone to take care of him."

"Yeah, he's having a tough time, but he wanted to come up here and see about you," Auntie Mabeline said. "He was really concerned about you."

"Oh," Grace said.

Auntie Mabeline reached out for Grace's hands. Grace reluctantly placed her hands inside of Auntie Mabeline's.

"What's going on Auntie. You're scaring me," she said.

"Gracie, I got to tell you something, and it's not good," she said.

"What is it? Just tell me."

"I know you're probably worried about Franklin," she

said.

"You know something? Where is he?" Grace asked, perking up.

All of a sudden, familiar music started playing in the background on the television, breaking Auntie Mabeline's concentration.

"What the heck!" she said. "They always interrupting some show and ain't got nothing important to say!" she said, sounding disgusted.

"Breaking News" flashed across the television.

"We interrupt this program to bring you breaking news," the local newscaster said. "Good morning everyone. We wanted to provide you with an update on the shooting that took place at the Lakewood Community Hospital."

"OH MY GOD! THAT'S HERE!" Grace exclaimed. A video of three men, with their faces covered, played on the news, showing them being led out to awaiting police cruisers.

The newscaster began to talk, "The three men who were arrested yesterday evening at the Lakewood Community Hospital are being held without ail, pending the investigation into the shooting that left a...""

Auntie Mabeline grabbed the remote, quickly shutting the television off.

"AUNTIE, WHY DID YOU DO THAT? MACIE KEEPS

TURNING THE TELEVISION OFF TOO! THEY WERE ABOUT TO TALK ABOUT WHAT HAPPENED HERE! WHAT DON'T YOU GUYS WANT ME TO KNOW??"

"I don't know how to tell you this but...."

"Tell me what?" Grace asked.

"Franklin was arrested," Auntie Mabeline blurted out.

"FOR WHAT?" Grace yelled, letting go of Auntie Mabeline's hands.

"Yeah, and he wasn't the only one," she said. "David and Rufus are in there, too!"

"OH MY GOD! WHAT HAPPENED?" Grace asked.

"I don't know all the details, but I know your brothers are not criminals. I can't speak for your sister's husband."

"DAVID IS A CRIMINAL! I TOLD YOU HE RAPED ME!" Grace yelled.

"Lower your voice little girl," Auntie Mabeline said.

"YOU CAN'T PUT A MUZZLE ON ME! I'VE KEPT QUIET LONG ENOUGH!" she yelled. "WHAT DID ANNA MAE DO? I KNOW THIS IS ALL HER FAULT!"

Auntie Mabeline sat on the bed, unable to calm Grace down.

"I don't know how much of this was her fault. I heard that they were arguing before she was shot, acting as if your Momma didn't raise them with good sense," Auntie Mabeline said, not holding back. "She must've called David up here!"

"DID YOU SAY … SHOT?" Graced exclaimed. OH MY GOD! SHOT BY WHO?" Grace asked. "IT WAS DAVID. I'M TELLING YOU IT WAS DAVID! WE HAVE TO CONTACT THE POLICE!" She blurted out.

Auntie Mabeline jumped to her feet.

"STOP TALKING THAT CRAZY TALK IN FRONT OF ME! THAT'S A SERIOUS ACCUSATION!"

"It's true … Auntie, I told you that David raped me when Momma was in the hospital," Grace said, feeling as if a burden had been lifted off her shoulders.

Grace began to tell Auntie Mabeline about the pictures that she and Franklin found in David's desk drawer.

Auntie Mabeline gasped, before starting to hyperventilate.

"This is too much for me!" Auntie Mabeline said, holding onto her heart. "I need to take me another pill!"

"I don't want to believe, as close as me and Leola were, I don't know why she would keep something like this from me. You know, I always knew that David was different. I just thought maybe he took more after your daddy's side."

Auntie Mabeline leaned her body up against the wall, as if all the air had been sucked out of her.

"Auntie, are you okay?" a concerned Grace asked. "Breathe, Auntie … just breathe."

"Breathe? Ya'll trying to kill me! I can't take no more," she said, looking up at the ceiling. "I don't want to believe this. It can't be true! I cannot believe that David would do such a heinous thing to you."

"Believe it!," Grace said.

"Well, it's true! He did it! You can even ask Franklin! He has a lot of nerve to assault me like that and then turn around and send me flowers!" Grace said.

Macie told Auntie Mabeline that she thought the baby's father sent the flowers, but she never mentioned David's name to Auntie Mabeline.

"Who sent you flowers?" Auntie Mabeline asked.

"David," Grace said. "I tossed them on the floor after I read the card from him."

Grace reached into the top drawer. She pulled out the card, handing it to Auntie Mabeline.

"Here, read it for yourself, since you don't believe me," Grace said, shoving the card in her aunt's face.

Auntie Mabeline stood in disbelief as she read the card.

"I think I'm gonna be sick," she said, as she sat back down on the side of the bed. "I know the good book says He'll never give us more than we can bear, but this is too much!"

"Tell me about it!" Grace said, continuing. "It's like he's taunting me. He knew that I would be having the baby around this time."

Grace shared with Auntie Mabeline the day she ran into Misty at the pharmacy, up to confirming her worst fears, finding out that she was pregnant.

"Running into Misty that day was heaven sent!" Grace exclaimed.

Auntie Mabeline was in complete shock.

"Gracie, I am so sorry that you had to go through this. I'm glad that Misty was there for you. Your Momma always spoke highly of her. I just wished I had ...."

Grace cut Auntie Mabeline off.

"We think that David had something to do with Momma's death!"

"We, who?" Auntie Mabeline asked.

"Me and Franklin," she said.

Auntie Mabeline looked as if she was holding something in.

"I think you feel that way, too, based on what you said at Momma's funeral," Grace added.

Auntie Mabeline held her head down in shame.

"Gracie, I'm going to be honest, when I heard what happened to your Momma, I smelled a skunk that's been skinned and left out in the hot Georgia sun. I must say, something wasn't adding up . . . so I had my doubts."

"He did it, Auntie! He killed Momma! I told Franklin what happened." Auntie Mabeline did not want to believe what she was hearing.

"I think we should go to the police!" Grace exclaimed.

"Hold on now, little girl. There you go, three blocks ahead of me, and I'm just now turning the corner. I will agree, that it is something to look into with everything that has happened. Now, I haven't been here for not even a day, and I have to deal with them knuckleheads in jail, your sister suffering from a bullet wound, and you just spat out a baby. So, your auntie here is gonna need some time to process all of this. As them kids say in my classroom, "pump your brakes little girl," Auntie Mabeline said, attempting to get Grace's racing thoughts off the imaginary speedway. "I just don't understand why he would want to hurt you ... or your Momma for that matter!"

"Because he's an imposter!" Grace said.

'Let's not go calling people names now," Auntie Mabeline said.

"Is Anna Mae going to be okay?" Grace asked, talking a mile a minute, feeling and sounding more at peace, now that her secret was finally out and she knew that Franklin was alive.

Auntie Mabeline looked at Grace intently, as if something came over her.

"Hidden within our soul is the life that we all try to hide, but in time, it will be revealed. All those secrets will be released, so before it ruins the life that you have, you must release them. Stories have been left untold, those very things that we don't want to unfold will soon come to light. Release them, for your struggle is over," Auntie Mabeline said, aloud in her trance.

Grace looked at Auntie Mabeline, as if something had taken a hold of her.

"Auntie, are you okay?" She asked. "I released my anger toward David. I'm not mad anymore. I'm just telling you what happened!"

Auntie Mabeline was in a stupor. Her blank stare said it all.

"Auntie ..." Grace said sharply, breaking Auntie Mabeline's trance.

"What did you say now?" Auntie Mabeline asked, snapping out of it.

"What did you mean by that?" She asked.

"By what?" Auntie Mabeline asked.

Grace looked intently. Auntie Mabeline was acting out of sorts, as if she didn't know what she had said.

"Where did Anna Mae get shot at? Is she going to be okay?" Grace asked.

"If I knew all the answers to the what, when and whys I would tell you," she said. "This whole situation has turned into one big question mark for me!"

"Macie called down to the ICU for me, and they said that she is still heavily sedated. I don't have no other details, Gracie. I thank God that the bullet did not take that girl's life," Auntie Mabeline said.

"That's all the praying that you and Momma did over us," Grace said.

"I know that's right! After burying your Momma, I couldn't see burying her child months later."

"So, is she gonna fully recover, or will she be in a wheelchair?" Grace asked.

"I don't know about that, but I know what needs to make a full recovery." Auntie Mabeline said.

"What?" Grace asked.

"Your relationship with her. Gracie, I know that child works your nerves. Lord knows she works mine too, but maybe this is the Man above's way of showing all of us that life is too short. At one time, you and your sister used to be thick as thieves," Auntie Mabeline said.

"Yeah, well that was before she turned into a witch! Auntie, she can just be so evil! It's unexplainable," Grace said.

"Well, we don't know what she is really going through with that husband of hers or behind that facade that she puts on. Something isn't too kosher there, but right now, I just can't think about all of that," Auntie Mabeline said.

"Yeah" Grace paused. "I hope Rufus don't leave her."

"Watch your mouth! Now that's just being cruel! You have more important fish to fry! I think you should get a DNA test done on Justice, while you are here in the hospital. I'm not saying that I don't believe you, but we have to be sure and very sure of who the baby's daddy is. This is the type of stuff that can destroy the very foundation of a family," Auntie Mabeline said.

"Well, I can ask Dr. Freelance if I can have one done while I'm here," Grace said.

"Good. I think that's the best thing to do. So, until we find out the results, don't accuse David or repeat this to anyone else," Auntie Mabeline said, sounding doubtful. "I think I need to get in contact with Pastor Fallback and ask him to pray for healing for this family . . . mentally and physically. I'm sure they have seen the news by now."

"Didn't you just say that we shouldn't repeat this?" Grace blurted out. "I'm sure Pastor Fallback has his own issues!"

"A little prayer doesn't hurt nobody," Auntie Mabeline said.

Grace folded her arms, in total disagreement.

Auntie Mabeline looked down at her watch.

"Anna Mae's doctor needed to speak to me about something. She was going to call the nurses' station up here once the doctor was available. I just cannot take any more bad news."

Auntie Mabeline put her head down. A great sadness fell on her.

"Are you okay Auntie?" Grace asked.

"Me and your Momma talked to ya'll so much about the danger of guns, especially knowing that's how your daddy died. I just don't understand it. I don't understand none of it! My head is about to explode with all of the things that I've heard today."

"Well we should have watched the news to see if there were any new developments. Auntie, who told you about the shooting anyways?" Grace said.

Auntie Mabeline knew that she needed to be honest with Grace, even if it meant throwing Macie under the bus. But she owed Grace the truth.

"That girl out there that has your baby told me what happened," she blurted out.

"MACIE?" Grace exclaimed.

"Yeah, her," Auntie Mabeline said.

"SHE TOLD ME THAT SHE DIDN'T KNOW WHERE FRANKLIN WAS!"

"Listen child. I'm just glad that you let this all out. I can only imagine how much stress this has been on you, but you've been stressing her out too! That nurse was so worried about you! You cannot blame her for not telling you what happened. She said you were acting as if you were on the verge of a nervous breakdown, throwing a vase like you done lost your ever-living mind! I have a better understanding now that you've explained everything to me. You've been through a lot! I get it. But Gracie, she was doing all she could do to support you, knowing that your siblings were in a messed-up situation. The poor child was working double shifts, running on that nasty coffee she was sipping on earlier, and adrenaline. Before me and Joe got up here, she was contemplating putting your butt in the psych ward, so you should be thanking her for looking out for you … and for that baby too!" Grace looked like a deer caught in headlights. She had no idea the amount of stress that she'd placed Macie under.

"I didn't know that Auntie. I didn't mean to stress her out," Grace said.

"I understand, Gracie. You've been through hell and back but always remember that you're a survivor, and you have people around you who generally care about you. They want to see you prosper," Auntie Mabeline continued.

"Macie told me that she heard on the news that all three have court tomorrow, to answer the charges. So, I'm gonna go to court in the morning and see for my own eyes what the devil is going on!"

"Charges!" Grace exclaimed. "What charges?"

"Yes…. charges. She heard, attempted murder," Auntie Mabeline said.

"DID YOU SAY ATTEMPTED MURDER?" Grace exclaimed.

"Yes, Gracie. I'll find out more tomorrow. I know your Momma must be rolling over in her grave." Auntie Mabeline shook her head. "From choir members to criminals! Shameful!"

"I think that if I hadn't been in this situation … none of this would have happened," Grace said, somberly.

'Now, don't go blaming yourself, Gracie. This is not your fault!" Auntie Mabeline said.

"I know it's not my fault, but I'm the reason why Franklin called Anna Mae," Grace said.

"The nurse said that they don't know which one of them brought in the gun. I know you pinning it on David, but I just don't know. Franklin had all that training in the army, so he would know how to use a gun. I hate to say it.

Who knows about your sister's husband? She jumped up and married him out of nowhere."

"I was with Franklin earlier. He wouldn't do that!" Grace exclaimed.

"He wouldn't do what?" Auntie Mabeline asked.

"He wouldn't intentionally hurt anyone, unless they tried to hurt him first. He just served our country. We should be thanking him! I know he'll be embarrassed to see you tomorrow, but he has nothing to hang his head down in shame for. He will always be my hero! I'm just glad that you will be there to support him," Grace said.

"I'll be there for the both of them!" Auntie Mabeline said.

Grace was in no mood to argue with her auntie, so she let it go.

"I'm trying to see if someone can go with me," Auntie Mabeline said.

"I'm waiting for Dr. Freelance to tell me when I can go home. Looks like it won't be tomorrow! How about Misty? She probably wouldn't mind taking you. We'd have to call the hair shop and ask her. The salon is closed on Mondays," Grace said.

Auntie Mabeline reached into her pocketbook and pulled out her cell phone.

"Now, don't forget to add her into my contacts,"

Auntie Mabeline said.

They both chuckled.

Grace called the shop and spoke to Misty. Misty was so delighted to hear that she'd delivered a healthy baby boy and that both mom and baby were fine, but she was shocked to hear about the shooting. She had seen the story on the news and couldn't believe it. She had no issues going with Auntie Mabeline to court the following morning, saying that she knew that Auntie Mabeline would appreciate her support.

Grace ended the call, just as Macie ran frantically into the room.

"Grace," Macie said with a worried look on her face.

"Child, where's the baby?" Auntie Mabeline asked.

"That's what I came to tell you," Macie said, looking frightened.

"I cannot find Justice," she said.

"What-chu say?" Auntie Mabeline said.

"WHAT? WHERE'S MY SON?" an upset Grace said.

"Ah . . . we don't know," Macie said.

"WHAT DO YOU MEAN, YOU DON'T KNOW!," Auntie Mabeline said, raising her voice.

Grace whipped the bedsheet back and began to get up

out of the bed.

"Grace, please get back in bed. We'll find him," Macie said.

"You better find him!" Auntie Mabeline yelled. "How can you lose a baby right up here in a secured nursey!"

"I'm so sorry! I don't know how this could've happened. Do you think one of your relatives would have come and taken him? You have to admit, your family has been the source of bad karma since you've been here!" Macie said.

"Now, how the hell they gonna come get him, when you already know that the guys are all locked up and that other one just come out of surgery!" Auntie Mabeline said.

"WHERE IS MY BABY?" Grace yelled.

The ruckus woke Old Man Joe up out of his sleep. He began talking out of his head.

"I got it . . . I got it . . . you should have been faster," he said, mocking the television comercial before falling back asleep.

"WHERE IS MY BABY?" Grace got out of bed against Macie's wishes and began to walk toward the door. Macie blocked the door.

"Child, get your butt back in this bed!" Auntie Mabeline exclaimed.

"NO! NOT UNTIL I FIND MY SON!" Grace began to

scream and cry.

"We just had a shift change. I'll check with the neonatal nurses again. Any time we take a baby out of the nursery, we have to check the baby out. They all know that's protocol."

"What kind of foolishness is that? You check the baby out and not even inform his mother?" Auntie Mabeline said, looking disgusted. "That don't make a bit of sense! Sounds to me like you are running a circus up in here!"

Just as Macie walked toward the door, the nurse casually walked in holding Justice.

"Here's mommy," she said. Grace recognized the woman as being the one who delivered the flowers to her earlier.

"WHAT ARE YOU DOING WITH MY BABY!" she yelled. Macie kept her cool as Sharmaine walked into the room, cradling Justice. Macie walked over, carefully taking the baby from Sharmaine and placing Justice in Grace's arms.

"Grace this is Sharmaine. She's one of the nurses who covers our breaks and shift changes in the nursery. I'm sure she didn't mean to take Justice and not inform anyone," Macie said, hiding her anger and attempting to save face for Sharmaine.

"She's the one who bought the flowers to me earlier," Grace said, looking at her aunt.

"I smell a fish," Auntie Mabeline said. "Something isn't right here."

Macie interjected, "Sharmaine, I had been looking for baby Johnson. Why didn't you check him out?"

Sharmaine looked at Macie as if she was appalled that she was asking her a valid question.

"Well, you'd went on break, so I couldn't tell you. I was covering the nursery and noticed this little fella was crying and seemed fussy, so I decided to take him for a walk. We only went down the hall," Sharmaine responded.

"You're trying to steal my baby!" an angry Grace yelled. "I don't want you near my son anymore!"

"Ah ... no Ms. Johnson. I was not trying to steal him. I have three younger siblings. The last thing I need is a baby," she said, unapologetically. "Plus, I knew that you were having a bad day today. Macie told me how you tossed the flowers that I bought in earlier on the floor."

Macie looked sharply at Sharmaine.

Grace couldn't make out the nurse's voice, but she'd seen this woman before.

"I know you from somewhere?" Grace said. Sharmaine looked at Grace.

"I'm sorry, you don't look familiar to me. I don't think we've met before today," Sharmaine said.

"Nurse ... whatever your name is ... don't you ever take off with my great-nephew again ... you hear?" Auntie Mabeline said. "Or else you are going to have me to deal with!"

"Yes ma'am," she said. Old Man Joe shot straight up in the chair, as if he was listening to the entire conversation with his eyes closed. "You can kidnap me anytime you want to!"

"Hush up you ole' goat!" Auntie Mabeline said.

CHAPTER 52

The courtroom started to fill up. They sat packed on the benches like sardines in a can. Auntie Mabeline looked around as the lawyers walked into the courtroom, one by one, greeting each other.

"This is my first time sitting up in a court room. The closest that I've seen a court room was when I used to watch Judge Joe Brown on TV. I like him, and he was easy on the eyes too," Auntie Mabeline said, as she smiled. "I'm so glad that you were able to come with me."

"Absolutely, Ms. Mabeline! I have so much respect for Ms. Leola. I love her and her kids as if they were my own relatives. I know that she would not want you to be here alone. This is still so unreal to me. I couldn't even imagine any of her kids getting arrested, let alone carrying a gun. Ms. Leola kept them all on a short leash!"

"Yeah, I helped her raise them kids," she said. "I don't know what got into them."

Auntie Mabeline reached into her pocketbook and pulled out her plastic baggy filled with peppermints.

"Would you like a mint?" She asked Misty.

"No, thanks," Misty said.

"Well, pass the bag down, and tell them to take one," Auntie Mabeline said, as if she was sitting in church.

Misty looked at the bag, dumbfounded.

"All rise!" the court officer said. Auntie Mabeline watched as everyone stood to their feet. She nervously tossed the bag of mints back into her pocketbook.

"Is it starting?" She asked Misty, as if they were about to watch a movie.

Misty chuckled as she whispered, "Yes, everyone has to stand when the judge enters into the courtroom."

"Oh," Auntie Mabeline said, as she held onto the bench in front of her, pulling herself up onto her feet.

"Good morning," the female judge said. She looked to be in her mid-sixties. "Let's get started. Please be seated."

Everyone sat down.

Auntie Mabeline and Misty sat and listened to five long cases.

"My hemorrhoids are hurting. When are they going to call David and Franklin's case?" She whispered to Misty.

"I don't know. Hopefully soon," Misty said.

They watched the court clerk fish through a host of files before standing up.

"Your Honor, this is case number 684879, the Commonwealth vs. David Johnson."

"David's case is about to be heard!" Misty exclaimed.

"Oh, okay. Good!" Auntie Mabeline said, speaking loud enough for the court officer to hear.

The court officer looked over at Auntie Mabeline, giving her a stern look.

Auntie Mabeline sat up straight, not knowing what was going on.

The judge looked down at the papers that the court clerk handed her.

"Is Mr. Johnson in lock up?" She asked.

"Yes, your Honor," the court clerk responded.

"Where's David?" Auntie Mabeline asked, looking at Misty.

The court officer looked over at Auntie Mabeline.

"No talking in the courtroom!" He exclaimed.

Misty's eyes bulged as she looked at Auntie Mabeline.

Auntie Mabeline watched the court officer walk over and slide back a panel that looked as if it was part of the wall, as the prosecutor read the charges against David. They couldn't see him from where they sat.

"I can't see. Can you?" She asked Misty.

Misty looked at the court officer, to make sure that he was not looking their way, as she shook her head no.

"They're not going to bring him out so we can see him,"

Auntie Mabeline said, looking confused.

"No," Misty answered.

The defense attorney began to speak.

"Your Honor, Mr. David Johnson was arrested with two others, one being his brother, on Saturday evening, at approximately 8:30 pm at the Lakewood Community Hospital."

"Okay, this is related to the shooting that took place at the hospital, correct?" the judge asked.

"Yes, your Honor," the DA said.

"Yes, I read the details while in the back," the judge said. "Go ahead," the judge nodded for them to proceed.

"Mr. Johnson entered the hospital. After signing in at the nurse's station, he was joined by a co-defendant. They proceeded to walk to the end of the emergency room, where the security guard on duty was arguing with the victim, who is Mr. Johnson's older sister. The security guard was trying to get her to leave the premises for disorderly conduct. She refused. Shortly after Mr. Johnson and the gentleman, who we have identified as the victim's husband, Mr. Rufus Payne, approached the victim and the security guard, a third gentleman, who turned out to be Mr. Franklin Johnson, the victim's eldest brother, exited the bathroom and attacked Mr. David Johnson from behind."

"What in the world would cause so much mayhem amongst siblings? They took sibling rivalry to a whole new level," the judge commented. "Do you know?"

"All we know is that a family member was hospitalized," the prosecutor said.

"Lord have mercy," Auntie Mabeline interjected.

"Wow, I always thought visiting the sick bought people together," the judge said, unaware that Grace had given birth. "Continue."

The prosecutor continued, "The security guard and the victim's husband broke up the fight."

"Yup, that was me!" the man exclaimed.

Everyone in the courtroom looked in the direction of where the voice came from. Leroy sat across from Auntie Mabeline and Misty. He was sharply dressed in a pin-striped suit, looking like a pimp, as he held his black hat on his knee.

Auntie Mabeline looked over at Leroy. She hadn't seen him since she was a freshman in high school. He was closer in age to Leola, but she remembered how she had a crush on him back in the day. All the girls did. He'd made a name for himself as a well-known boxer. Last she heard, he'd moved to Germany and was fighting over there before he went through a few divorces here in the States. Rumor had it, he had about 15 kids and possibly more over in Germany.

"QUIET IN THE COURTROOM!" The court officer yelled.

The judge looked sternly at Leroy, "Sir, one more outburst, and we will have to throw you out of the courtroom. Do you understand?"

Leroy shook his head yes.

"Please continue," the judge said to the prosecutor.

"Thank you, your Honor. After the security guard and Mr. Payne, the victim's husband, separated the Johnson brothers, the security guard asked the elder Mr. Johnson to come with him, in an effort to diffuse the situation. The elder Mr. Johnson walked away and then suddenly dashed back. Almost simultaneously, Mr. David Johnson reached into his pocket, at which time three gunshots rang out, and the victim fell to the floor with a gunshot wound to the stomach."

"I DIDN'T DO IT!" David yelled. "YA'LL ARE NOT GOING TO PIN THIS ON ME!"

Gasps could be heard from those sitting in the courtroom.

"David, shut up! Just shut up," Auntie Mabeline whispered, loud enough for the people sitting in front of her and Misty to hear.

"ORDER IN THE COURT!" The judged picked up her gavel, banging it three times. "MR. JOHNSON, WHAT

"YOU WON'T DO IS DISRUPT MY COURTROOM!"

"Yes, your Honor," David said solemnly. Auntie Mabeline tried really hard to see him but she couldn't. "What's the victim's status?" the judge asked.

"Your Honor, she had surgery on Saturday night and is recovering in the intensive care unit at Lakewood Community Hospital," the prosecutor said. The assistant prosecutor whispered in the ear of the prosecutor. "Your Honor, we have a message to call the surgeon. So, there's a possibility that the charges may be upgraded. We also have the officers here who responded to the call."

Auntie Mabeline and Misty saw the three officers sitting in back of the DA.

"What is he being charged with?" the judge asked.

"Your Honor, Mr. Johnson has a warrant for his arrest for evading the police when they attempted to arrest him for a DUI last year. That is the only thing on his record. He is being charged with attempted murder and held on bail, but again, the attempted murder charges may be upgraded."

Auntie Mabeline gasped. "I can't be dipping into my retirement. He's gone have to stay in here," she whispered to Misty.

"Okay. So, let's hold this case until we get a status update from the hospital," the judge said.

"Mr. Johnson, do you understand the charges against you?" the judge said.

"Yes," David responded.

"Sir, do you have a lawyer to represent you?" The judge asked.

"No," David responded.

The judge began to look around the court room. The public defenders were sitting along the wall.

"Attorney Pike, would you be able to take Mr. Johnson's case?" She asked.

"Do I have a choice?" He asked, looking disheveled, as if he'd just rolled out of bed.

"No, not really," the judge said, writing on the paper in front of her before looking up at David.

"Mr. Johnson, Mr. Pike will be your public defender. He will be in touch with you. This is your appearance. The next time you will be in court will be your preliminary hearing. This is after you meet with your attorney. During your hearing, you will enter in your plea of guilty or not guilty." The judge looked over at Mr. Pike.

"Will you be able to meet with Mr. Johnson today? If yes, we can hold his hearing tomorrow or Wednesday."

"Yes, I can do that," the attorney responded, as he scrolled through his phone. "Your Honor, I prefer

Wednesday for the hearing."

"That works for me," the judge said. The judge looked back over at David.

"Mr. Johnson, you're in luck. Attorney Pike will meet with you today. Your hearing will be held this Wednesday," she said.

"Do you have any questions for me?" the judge asked.

"No, your Honor," David responded.

"Okay," the judge said, looking at the court clerk. "Put this one on for Wednesday at 2 p.m." she said.

"You got it," the court clerk said.

"I need to take a 30-minute break," the judge said.

"ALL RISE," the court officer said.

"Stand up, Ms. Mabeline," Misty said, helping Auntie Mabeline up to her feet. The court officer whisked the judge out of the side door.

"Child, all this up and down has gotten me hot!" Auntie Mabeline said.

Chapter 53

Misty and Auntie Mabeline walked out of the courtroom and sat down on the bench in the long corridor.

"Ms. Mabeline, are you okay? I know this must be very difficult for you to hear," Misty said.

"Never in a million years would I have imagined that I would have my two nephews behind bars, and two nieces in the hospital at the same time, one with a gunshot wound and one with a baby that no one knew she was having. But I know I got to stay strong," Auntie Mabeline said.

Misty looked as if she had just swallowed a canary.

"Ms. Mabeline......I have a confession to make," she said.

WHAT?" Auntie Mabeline exclaimed.

"I knew that Grace was pregnant," she said.

"I know. She told me on yesterday," Auntie Mabeline responded.

"Whew!" Misty exhaled, placing her hand over her heart. I didn't want you to be mad with me. Anna Mae told me how you can set it off and go in on a person."

Auntie Mabeline grabbed Misty's hand. "Listen here child, my sister adored you, I just want you to know that."

"I adored her, too!" Misty said.

"I was so shocked to hear about Ms. Leola's fall." Misty said.

"Yeah, me too!" Auntie Mabeline said.

"Do you know how I met Ms. Leola?"

"Yeah. She told me when you were a teenager that she used to give you a ride to the bus station, when she saw you waiting at the bus stop," Auntie Mabeline said.

"Yeah! One day I was just waiting in the rain and she pulled up next to me and said that she has two daughters that I reminded her of and how she didn't want me to get sick standing in the rain. So, she would drop me off at the main bus terminal and wait for me to get on the bus. I never told my adopted mother. I knew she would try to report Ms. Leola or think she was trying to kidnap me but I knew she wasn't any danger to me. She told me that she'd noticed me a few times standing outside, when she was on her way to her doctor's appointments. She was one of a kind!" Macie said, reminiscing about Ms. Leola.

"Yeah. She was," Auntie Mabeline said.

Misty continued. "That's why that day I saw Grace in the drug store and she had a frightened look about her, I knew I had to be there for her, just like Ms. Leola was there for me. I was so shocked to find out that she was pregnant because Ms. Leola kept both Grace and Anna Mae on a short leash. Poor thing! I know she would have been there for Grace and her baby. Did you know, she didn't know that Grace was pregnant?"

"Well, I kind of figured that. None of us knew... but you," Auntie Mabeline said. "But...yeah...Leola would never turn her back on her kids, no matter what."

"No. Never! Her kids were so lucky to have her as a mom. She was like a second mother to me.

Auntie Mabeline grunted.

"Did she say who the father could be?" Auntie Mabeline inquired, waiting to hear if Misty knew about Grace's accusation against David.

"No, and I didn't even ask. I wonder if he attends the church. Maybe Pastor Fallback or Deaconess Franzine knows him. She comes in the shop all the time, running everyone's business but hers. She's always talking about somebody being pregnant by somebody's husband or who's getting divorced now. I just shake my head."

"Really? Hmmm.... I don't know," Auntie Mabeline said.

"Grace has never mentioned a boy to me, and I'd know if she had a boyfriend. Anna Mae would have definitely told it," Misty said.

"You got a point there," Auntie Mabeline responded.

"I knew that she was starting to get a little thick but never in a million years, would I have guessed that she was pregnant. I just figured that since she lost her Momma, she was depressed and eating more than usual. I'm so glad that you were there for her. You were at the right place, at the right time.," Auntie Mabeline said.

Auntie Mabeline shook her head, as if she was still in denial.

"I shared with Ms. Leola and her daughters that I wanted to find my birth parents, to see if I had any siblings. I'd hired an investigator, but he's taking so long to get back to me. It's been over a month. Ms. Leola had said that she was willing to help me, but sadly, she didn't get the chance to, so I'm kind of doing this for me and for her, too! She inspires me in death, just like she did in life," Misty said.

"What makes you want to find them after all these years? If your life is going so well, why would you want to disrupt it and theirs?" Auntie Mabeline asked.

"Well, I think I have a right to know who my birth parents are. I'm not angry at them for having me and giving me up. Well, I would never do that," she said.

"Do what?" Auntie Mabeline asked.

"Have kids and give them up. I think that's a cowardly act. My birth parents are a huge part of the reason why I don't want to have any kids. In the same token, I want to hear from them, the circumstances surrounding my birth and what led up to the decision to give me up. It's not like

I had a bad life, but I still want to know who they are. You know, it's my right. I think everyone wants to know where they came from," Misty said. "Wouldn't you?"

"Well, you have a good point, but if it was me, I would leave well enough alone. Why would I even care what they look like or who they are, especially if they gave me up? You know, but that's just with me," Auntie Mabeline said.

"Yeah, well, we are all different. But I also deserve to know their medical history. Like with your nieces and nephews, they know that Ms. Leola had leukemia, so they know what to look out for health wise. I have no idea," Misty said.

"Well, I have a good friend who is a genealogist. I can put you in contact with her," Auntie Mabeline said.

"Oh my God! You would do that for me?" Misty exclaimed.

"Why not?" She said.

Misty gave Auntie Mabeline the biggest hug.

"Thank you so much!" Misty said, reaching into her pocketbook for a pen and a piece of paper. "I'm going to have to write this down, since we cannot bring our phones into the courthouse."

Auntie Mabeline rattled off the number.

"I hope when you find out that I'm still in town. I would love to know who they are," Auntie Mabeline said.

"I hope they don't disappoint you, because you seem like you are high maintenance."

They both laughed.

"I am not high maintenance at all. My adopted mother instilled in me from when I can remember to always expect the best for myself. So, I don't look for people to take care of me. She reminds me daily that I am a queen," Misty said, looking at Auntie Mabeline.

"I admit, I'm a bit nervous. I hope your friend can track them down. I would love for you to be there when I find out the results. I know this may be asking too much, but can you come with me to meet my parents, if you're still in town? You remind me so much of Ms. Leola. It would feel as if she is still with me."

"Me? You want me to be there?" Auntie Mabeline said, placing her hand over her heart.

"Yes," Misty said, sounding excited.

"Well, I guess, I can be there, that's if I'm still here," Auntie Mabeline said.

"Oh great!" Misty exclaimed.

"I can see why my sister was so fond of you," Auntie Mabeline said.

"Why?" Misty asked.

"You are a special person. I know your parents are

going to be proud of the young lady that you've become," Auntie Mabeline said.

"I want them to see what they've missed out on all these years by giving me up," Misty said.

"Well, you don't know what folks face in life. I'm sure there's a good reason as to why they did what they did," Auntie Mabeline said. "My good friend should be able to help you out some."

"Thank you," Misty said, giving Auntie Mabeline a side hug.

"What do you think about my nephew, Franklin? He just got out the service. He's a good catch," Auntie Mabeline said, attempting to be a matchmaker.

Misty laughed.

"I've always seen Franklin and David as my brothers. Although recently David burnt me, but I'm trying to forgive him . . . you know ... for Ms. Leola."

Misty told Auntie Mabeline how David came in begging for a job, and how she paid him some money to take the towels to the laundromat, and how he washed them, placed them in the dryer, and forgot about them until after the laundromat had closed. She told Auntie Mabeline how she ran to Walmart as soon as they opened to purchase towels for the shop. She also shared how she allowed David to sleep at the shop on occasion, when he said he'd misplaced his key or it being too late to wake up Grace. She didn't know how true it was, but since she didn't have a burglar alarm installed at the hair shop, she thought it was a good way to get cheap security.

"I'm so sorry that happened to you. I wonder why in the world would he ask for a place to stay, when the boy has a warm bed at home. That is really strange," Auntie Mabeline said, thinking back on what Grace had said.

"Anna Mae called the shop one day looking for him. I didn't dare tell her that I had been allowing him to stay at the shop, but that's when she told me that he had been staying with her and her husband a few nights, and he left a bunch of dirty dishes in the sink. She was going off! She wanted him to come back and clean up after himself," Misty said.

"I cannot understand why David is making all these bad choices," Auntie Mabeline said. "He wasn't raised like that."

"Maybe he's taking Ms. Leola's death worse than the others. Although Grace is the youngest, she's been preoccupied dealing with her pregnancy. Anna Mae has her husband, and Franklin was in the Army. David has always seemed to be like a balloon just floating in the air, with nowhere to go. He lacks drive. He's just so different from the others," Misty said, continuing. "One thing he's consistent at is drinking! He loves to turn up. I've found a few half empty bottles that he'd stashed in the shop. I pour them out! You all should look into getting him therapy or encouraging him to go to Alcoholics Anonymous."

"Well, maybe so, but he doesn't need to see a shrink, no more than the others do," Auntie Mabeline said, quickly defending David. "Now, AA, yeah, he may be able to benefit from that!"

"I'm not saying that the others wouldn't benefit from talking to someone. Seeing a therapist is a good thing. My adopted mother took me to one when I was around 10," Misty said.

"Oh," Auntie Mabeline said.

Auntie Mabeline pondered.

"Well, a therapist is an option. His first therapist is going to be these four walls! I definitely don't have the money to get him out on bail, so he will have to stay his butt right in here. That goes for Franklin, too!" Auntie Mabeline exclaimed.

"As they say, if you did the crime you have to do the time," Misty commented, before changing the subject.

"You probably don't know Dalia, but she works for me at the shop. She was telling us that her sister Diamond was the secretary on duty the night that everything went down at the hospital," Misty said.

"Oh, really," Auntie Mabeline said, perking up. "What did she say?"

"Dalia said that her sister Diamond told her that everything was calm, until Anna Mae came in. Diamond said that's when all hell broke loose! Diamond had to send the security guard over to calm Anna Mae down. I heard that when the security guard went over there, she became loud and out of control. She had stirred up such a scene that people in the waiting area got scared and left before being seen by the doctor!" Misty said.

Auntie Mabeline's had blocked Misty out. She realized that she'd missed Leroy. He apparently left out of the courtroom before the judge finished David's case.

"Did you see that man who had the outbursts in the courtroom leave?" Auntie Mabeline asked.

"Who?" Misty asked.

"The older gentleman," Auntie Mabeline said.

"Oh, no," Misty said, looking down the long hall. "Oh, the security guard at the hospital. Do you know him?"

"Yeah, from back in the day. He used to be a well-known boxer," Auntie Mabeline said. "It's rare that I bump into anyone that Leola and I grew up with when I come into town."

"Oh . . . Well, maybe you will see him again," Misty said, continuing.

"He must've been the one that was trying to get Anna Mae to leave, but she wouldn't budge. More people came up to Diamond complaining about what was going on. Since her desk is at the opposite end, she could only read their body language. Then she said that David and this guy came in. She thought David signed them both in, but he didn't. She found out from the cop that the guy with David was Anna Mae's husband. She'd never seen him before. I don't remember seeing him at Ms. Leola's funeral," Misty said, looking puzzled. Auntie Mabeline reminisced back to the day of her sister's funeral, when Old Man Joe hit Rufus over the head with his cane as they rode to the church.

"Anna Mae's husband had a little accident on the way to the church, so he didn't make it," Auntie Mabeline said.

"Oh wow! That's horrible," she said. "Come to think of it, David wasn't there either."

"No. David had gotten into an altercation, and whoever it was with, they won! There was no way that we were going to allow him to come to my sister's funeral in the shape that he was in!" Auntie Mabeline said, remembering how drunk and beaten up David was.

"Well, you know that the barbershop is right next to my shop. Anna Mae's husband and David have come in to get haircuts together," Misty said.

"Since when did the barbershop start doing perms," Auntie Mabeline asked.

"Perms?" Misty said.

"Yeah. That child's husband had a jerry curl the last time that I saw him," Auntie Mabeline said.

Misty laughed. "Oh, he wears it cut low now. He looks totally different without all that long hair. I'd seen him before when I had to go over to the barbershop to tell them to keep their music down. They be over there blasting their music and cutting up. Rufus seems nice though. He always speaks to me."

Auntie Mabeline found it strange that neither Rufus nor David were at her sister's funeral. She wondered if it was just a coincidence or was there something to it?

"Well, they are brother-in-laws. I know them folks down at the shop like to gossip. That's why they have clients sitting there all day waiting to get their hair done," Auntie Mabeline said.

"I'm sorry," Misty said. "I know you have so much going on, and I shouldn't be telling you this. I'm sure you are stressed out enough."

"Mmmmhhh," Auntie Mabeline grunted.

"Have you heard how Anna Mae is doing?" She asked. "I heard on the news that she was shot in the stomach, but no one knows who shot her," Misty said. "Who do you think did it?"

"Child, I don't even want to think that one of her brothers would try to take her out. Her husband acts like he's so in love, and he looks too timid to hurt a fly," Auntie Mabeline said. "I don't know. That's why we are up here in court, to find out!"

"Is she going to be okay? Or is she going to have to go to rehab?" Misty asked inquisitively.

"I haven't seen her yet. That reminds me, I was waiting for her doctor to talk to me, but I guess he was busy. I'll check in with them when I go see Gracie later this evening," she said.

"I should go with you! I feel so bad that I haven't had a chance to go see Grace and her baby boy yet. I've been so busy at the shop. I've been working long hours. When is she coming home?" Misty asked.

"She was supposed to come home today, but the doctor decided to keep her an extra day. Her nurse told me that she had a nervous breakdown, so they want to make sure that she's stable enough to care for her son," Auntie Mabeline said.

"Oh, no! Poor Grace. That doesn't even sound like her, but I'm sure she's still reeling from the loss of her mom, and now this," Misty said.

"Yes. It's a lot," Auntie Mabeline said.

"You see Ms. Mabeline, therapy may benefit the entire family," Misty said. "You know that they're still looking for the person who killed that woman."

"What woman?" Auntie Mabeline asked, looking shocked.

"I'm surprised that Anna Mae and Grace didn't tell

you about the woman that the cops found dead in her house," Misty said.

Auntie Mabeline thought back to the day she flew in for her sister's funeral. She remembered that as Franklin turned onto their street, she noticed the faded yellow tape on the bannister that blew in the wind. She also remembered Old Man Joe's son, Big Tuna , passing by in the backseat of the police cruiser. She wondered why Grace didn't bring it up in conversation.

"Is she the one who lived at the top of my sister's street?" She asked.

"Yes. She lived on the corner, as soon as you turn onto their street. Her house is on the right." Misty said.

"Franklin and Grace told me about that. They still haven't found out who killed her?" Auntie Mabeline asked.

"Not to my knowledge. The police came into my shop and went over to the barbershop, asking questions. But you know that no one is going to say anything, even if they knew something. We all know that snitches get stitches," Misty said.

"What?" Auntie Mabeline asked.

"It's a saying that means if you tell the police what you know about a crime, you may end up with stitches or possibly DEAD!" Misty said.

"What kind of foolishness is that! No wonder there's so many unsolved crimes," Auntie Mabeline said.

The people in the hall began to file one behind the other back into the courtroom.

"Thirty minutes are up already!" Misty said, looking at her watch. "I think we better head back into the courtroom."

CHAPTER 54

Dr. Freelance walked into Grace's hospital room and stood at the foot of the bed.

"How's my favorite patient?" He asked.

Grace had a bit of an attitude with him because she hadn't seen him since she gave birth to Justice.

"I'm fine. When can I go home?" She asked abruptly.

"Are you not enjoying your stay here?" He asked.

"No. I am not! I am just ready to sleep in my own bed," she said.

"Well, I can understand that Grace. I feel the same way when I have to work a double shift. There's nothing like sleeping in your own bed," he said, agreeing with her.

"How are you feeling today?" He asked, being cautious, thinking back on what Macie mentioned and what he found out about her siblings being involved in the shooting. "I was told that the neonatal nurses fed Justice the other day. Are you not feeling comfortable with breastfeeding?"

"Now I am. At first I wasn't, but Macie explained everything to me," Grace said.

Dr. Freelance sat at the end of Grace's bed.

"Good to hear. Speaking of Macie, she was very concerned about you, and she told me that you were having a pretty rough day the other day. Are you feeling better?" He asked.

"I'm sleepy! I just wish the nurses would stop waking me up. As soon as I doze off, they wake me up to feed Justice," she said, sounding irritated. "Plus, I have a lot on my mind. I'm sure you heard about what happened in the emergency room with my siblings," she said, looking somber.

"Yes, I heard. Remember, we were bringing you into the delivery room when we heard the commotion," he said, continuing. "I know you have a lot going on in your head, but right now I need you to concentrate on Grace, and getting Grace in a good place, so that when you leave this hospital to go home, you are equipped with all of the knowledge needed to be the best Grace you can be while being the best mom you can be to your son," he said. "Okay?"

"Yeah," she said sadly.

"By the way . . . I'm a family practice doctor for all ages, so I can treat both you and your son.

"Okay," Grace said. "I feel better already."

"Good! You have to remember that right now Justice is totally dependent on you. So, he will need you to provide him with his daily source of nutrition. Remember, it won't be like this always," he said. "But right now, Justice needs to nurse between seven and nine times a day. Newborns are generally hungry between 1½ and 3 hours."

Grace looked exhausted, just listening.

"Do you have any questions for me?" He asked.

"When can I stop?" She asked.

Dr. Freelance chuckled, as he sensed Grace's frustration.

"You can stop breastfeeding at any time. However, I wouldn't encourage it. Most mothers will breastfeed for six months," he said.

"SIX MONTHS!" Grace exclaimed.

"Yes, six months. That means no water, juice or formula, just breast milk."

He continued.

"Breast feeding is not only good for your son, but it is good for you too! Breast milk provides the best nutrients for Justice. It has everything that your baby needs to grow strong and healthy. It's full of vitamins, protein, and good fats. Breast milk is also better for your baby's digestive system."

Grace hung on very word.

"Did you know that breast feeding will help your son fight off viruses and bacteria?"

"No, I didn't know that," Grace said, listening attentively.

"Yes. It also reduces the risk of baby Justice getting asthma or allergies. Now . . . you know that I would love a visit from you and your son, but it also reduces hospitalizations and trips to the doctor. Don't get confused about his vaccines."

"How am I supposed to know when he gets his vaccines?" She inquired.

Dr. Freelance smiled.

"Don't you worry. My staff will let you know when Justice needs to come visit me for his vaccines," he said. "You're not in this alone."

Grace looked relieved.

"Okay ... so how does breastfeeding help me?" She asked.

"Well, let me tell you, there's great benefits for mom, too! It helps you burn calories and shed excess weight," he said. "Not that I'm saying that you need to, but I'm just stating the facts."

Grace looked down at her body. "That's good to know. I need to do that," she said.

"Well, don't be so hard on yourself. You just gave birth two days ago," Dr. Freelance said. "Breast feeding allows your body to release a hormone that helps your uterus turn back to its pre-pregnancy size."

Grace seemed to perk up. "Oh."

"Oh, yes . . . I'm not done. It also helps ward off diseases like breast and ovarian cancer. One other major benefit is it's less expensive to breastfeed than purchasing formula, bottles, and nipples . . . at least for six months," Dr. Freelance said, smiling.

Grace hadn't thought about that. She looked into the resources that Misty had told her about the day she found out that she was pregnant.

"I like that," she said.

"Good. That's what I want to hear," Dr. Freelance said, looking intently at Grace.

"You look to be in deep thought. What is it?" He asked. "You can ask me anything."

"Is it possible to get a DNA test done on Justice?" Grace asked.

"Why do you want a DNA test done?" Dr. Freelance questioned.

"It's complicated," she said.

"Most people who ask for a DNA test are usually those who are not sure of who the father is," he said. "I don't mean to pry, but do you know who Justice's father is?"

Grace felt as if she was being victimized all over again

with the awkward line of questions, but she remembered what Auntie Mabeline said. She needed to find out for a fact that David was 100 percent Justice's father.

"Well, something very bad happened to me," she said, bravely.

Dr. Freelance listened closely. Although Macie had already shared with him about Grace's sexual assault, he wanted to hear it directly from Grace.

"Grace, I'm so sorry! I don't want to assume or put words in your mouth, but were you sexually assaulted?" He asked.

"Yes, I was," she said, courageously.

"I'm so sorry! Did you report it?" He asked.

Grace held her head down in shame.

"No . . . I was too afraid to!" she said.

Dr. Freelance stood up, walking toward the head of Grace's bedside.

"This is not your fault. Do you understand me?" He said, speaking to Grace as if he was talking to his own daughter.

"Sometimes I think that it is," she said, getting emotionally.

"Well, it's not! I don't want to pressure you, but I would suggest that you tell the authorities what happened, so that they can bring this perpetrator to justice," he said. "Especially if it is someone that you may know!"

"Is there someone who can go with you to report this?" He asked.

"Yes, my auntie is here. I told her what happened. She'll probably be willing to go with me," she said.

"Good. I'm sure an officer can come here or to your house so you can file a report. That's only if you feel like it's too overwhelming to go to the station. I want you to follow through on this. It's not only for your safety, but your son's as well," he said.

"I didn't think of that. Thank you, Dr. Freelance," she said.

"Now back to the DNA test . . . unfortunately, insurance does not cover it, since it's not a test that's medically necessary, and it is rather costly, but you have an alternative," he said. "However, if you inform the authorities, they may have some alternatives for you."

"Like what?" She asked.

"Possibly going through the court and inquiring about getting a court-ordered DNA test done on the father. You would have to reach out to them to determine that."

"In most cases, if the father is willing to determine paternity, a DNA kit can be picked up at your local pharmacy at a fraction of the cost!""

"Oh," she said.

"Grace, if you decide to contact the court, you may also want to seek advice on terminating this guy's parental rights, if you know who he is," he said.

"Okay, I hadn't thought of that, either," Grace said.

"Any more questions about that?" He asked.

"No. I don't have any," she said.

"Okay. Now, there is something that I want to speak to you about, that I think will help you while you are here and once you are home," he said.

"What's that?" Grace asked.

"Knock, knock," the male said, in sync with knocking twice on the door.

"Is this a good time?" the man asked.

"Yes! Perfect timing," Dr. Freelance said.

"Grace tried to peak around the privacy curtain but she couldn't see the man standing at the door.

"Grace, I want you to meet someone," Dr. Freelance said.

"Who?" Grace asked.

Grace could hear the footsteps walking toward where she and Dr. Freelance were.

"Howdy," the man said.

Grace looked up to see the handsome young man. He stood five feet, nine inches tall; his muscular arms popped through his suit jacket; and his dark skin was unblemished. His perfect wavy hair reminded her of Franklin's. He sported a diamond stud in his left ear that shone as bright as the sun. He was dressed in a navy-blue suit, with a crisp white shirt and a deep purple bowtie. He was fine! He stood tall next to Dr. Freelance, as he held a clipboard.

"This is the man with the plan," Dr. Freelance said. "Grace, I want you to meet Mr. Trevor Cooper. He is a grief and trauma counselor here. I'd spoken to him and asked if he could set some time up with you before you go home."

Dr. Freelance shook Trevor's hand.

"This young man has been very helpful to mothers who experience post-partum depression, mothers who suffer miscarriages or any type of loss, including relationships. I think that he would be a great resource for you, even after you go home, because Mr. Cooper here makes house calls." Dr. Freelance said, patting Trevor on his back. Grace and Trevor locked eyes, as she slowly pulled the blanket up covering her body, so close that it touched her chin.

Trevor flashed a Kool-Aid smile. His teeth were just as perfect as he looked.

"Oh my God, it's so good to see you!" He said.

Dr. Freelance looked at Trevor and then looked at Grace.

"Do you know each other?" He asked.

"Yes," Trevor said with excitement. "Of course, I know her. Grace and I went to school together! Oh my God, you had a baby. Congratulations on the birth of your baby!"

"Thank . . . you," she said reluctantly.

The last person that she wanted to see at this moment was Trevor.

"I'm so sorry to hear about your mother. You know that Ms. Leola was well-loved in the city. My cousin Diamond adored her and talks about her all the time. She is truly missed," he said.

Dr. Freelance looked surprised.

"Oh, Grace, I'm so sorry. I didn't know that you lost your mom," Dr. Freelance said.

"Yes, I lost my mother last year," Grace said.

"You poor thing," Dr. Freelance said, as he looked at Trevor. "Well, Mr. Cooper is the best grief and trauma counselor around! But if you feel uncomfortable, I can find you another one."

Grace fell silent. She wished that she could snap her fingers and vanish. She recalled how embarrassed she would get when Franklin would drive his ice cream truck in Dalia and Diamond's neighborhood, and without fail, Trevor would waddle out to the truck, just to gawk at her, as if she was a cherry bomb ice cream cone, while the other kids who had money would buy an ice cream. She recalled the day that Franklin noticed him. He felt so bad that Trevor didn't have any money that he gave him one of the orange-cream bars that used to make her sick. She remembered the day before Momma's funeral, when she was at the hair salon, Dalia mentioned her egg head cousin who had a crush on her. She could not believe that same pimply-faced little boy, who's head had finally grown into his body, was standing at the foot of her bed, looking like someone who'd just stepped out of a GQ magazine.

Dr. Freelance asked again.

"Grace . . . are you okay with meeting with Mr. Cooper?"

"Oh … yeah … I'm fine with him," she said.

"Great! You've made a good decision. If it's okay with the both of you, I'm going to step out of the room and let you two kids catch up. I have some more patients to check on," Dr. Freelance said. "Unless you have more questions," he said, looking at Grace.

"Ye-s," she said, still in shock. "When did you say I'll would get released?"

"I'm going to touch base with Mr. Cooper, later today. I'll let you know," he said.

"Cooper, take good care of her," he said.

"Absolutely doc," Trevor responded.

Dr. Freelance strutted out of the room.

"Grace, do you mind if I have a seat?" Trevor asked.

"No," she said.

Trevor was nothing like how Grace remembered him.

"Oh man, I cannot believe I am sitting in the same room as you. So, how have you been?" He asked, beaming.

"I'm okay," she said.

"It's been way too long," Trevor said.

"Well, it's only been about four years," she said.

"I remember you used to help your brother on the ice cream truck when we were teenagers. We were 15. I heard he went into the service," he said.

"Yes, but he's out now," Grace said.

"Oh yeah? I remember that your brother was always a hustler. He doesn't stay still," Trevor said.

"Yes, that's true," Grace said.

"Well, let me fill you in on what I've been doing," he said, as if Grace asked.

Grace didn't remember Trevor being this cocky.

"I ended up graduating from high school two years early, and I busted my butt going to day school and taking online classes to get my bachelor's degree from Northwestern University in grief and trauma counseling. So, I'm qualified," he said with a smirk. "I did an internship here, and they offered me the job! I'm the youngest counselor in my field in this area!" He said proudly.

"Congratulations. That's great!" she said.

She realized that's why she hadn't seen Trevor in the halls during those last two years of high school. She thought that he'd moved away. She remembered him being smart, but she never would have imagined that he was a brainiac and skipped two grades!

"So, what about you?" He asked. "What have you been doing with yourself?"

She knew that her life after high school was in total contrast to what Trevor experienced. She remembered her last years of high school, getting out of school for the day and rushing home to help out Momma. She felt as if Trevor was in the twilight zone. He was sitting across from her in the maternity ward. What did he think she was up to?

"Well, my life hasn't been as exciting as yours. Just look around. I just had a baby," she said. "After high school, I got a job working at a bank, but I've been out of work since Momma died. I have no plans of going back there!"

"Why not?" He asked.

"Because I don't want to," she said.

"Grace, just because you had a baby doesn't mean that you stop living or working," he said. "That is all the more reason to keep pressing on, staying the course to accomplish your goals."

"I don't have any goals," she said.

"Well, it's not too late to set some. Come on Grace, you're 19, right? We're the same age," he said.

"Yeah, but I don't know what I want to do," she said.

"That is totally fine. There's folks older than us that still don't know what they want to be when they grow up," he said. "You have to find your passion. What do you love doing? One thing that you can consider now that you have your own child, you can go back to school to become a childcare provider … or you can go back to the bank and work toward becoming the branch manager … or you can…"

Grace cut him off.

"That sounds great, but how am I going to do that with a baby?" She asked.

Trevor chuckled.

"Like many other moms in your position have done it," he said. "During my short career, I have met many people who have resources available that can help you succeed. I can put you in contact with them, and most of them, I might add, are working mothers. It's called work-life balance," he said. "Not only that, I saw my own single mother do it. Did you know that I was an only child? That's why I spent a lot of time at my cousin's house, because my mother had to work. My mother is now the CFO of Essence Bank Incorporated."

"Oh, wow! I didn't know that," she said. "That's awesome!"

"Yeah, my mother went to school and worked full time so that she could make a life for us. My auntie, Diamond and Dalia's mom, used to babysit me. It takes a village. I must say, they did a good job. Look at me now!"

Grace wanted to roll her eyes, but she could hear Momma's voice say, "they gonna get stuck one day!"

"Do you remember my cousin Diamond?" He asked, not allowing Grace to respond. "She's older than us. Well, she is the emergency room secretary here."

Grace reluctantly shook her head yes, as she thought about everything that he said, although he came across a bit braggadocio. She picked up on how successful Trevor's family was and couldn't help thinking about her own family. Franklin was the only one who really did something with his life by going into the army.

"Grace, I can see your mind racing, just like it used to in fifth period math class," he said, smiling. "Rome wasn't built in a day. Noah didn't build the ark in one day.

Everything that is worth it and is good for you, takes time. You have to believe in yourself. I believe in you!" He said.

Grace had to admit, although her expression read one way, talking to Trevor felt so empowering. She sat there thinking that Dr. Freelance may be right! Trevor seemed to be the man with a plan.

CHAPTER 55

Auntie Mabeline and Misty sat back down in the courtroom, this time in view of the window that David had stood behind.

"I don't see the judge up there," Auntie Mabeline said.

"I'm sure she'll come out soon," Misty said.

"Now, we'll be able to see Franklin when he comes before the judge," she said.

"Yes," Misty said, agreeing with her.

The two prosecutors sat in the chair, looking over the stack of files that they had in front of them.

The court clerk had his own pile of files that he was preparing for the judge.

The court officer was sitting at a desk, daydreaming until his walkie talkie started to buzz. He jumped to his feet, making his way to the door where the judge would enter.

"All rise," he said.

"My corns are going to be black and blue before this day is over, with all this up and down!" Auntie Mabeline said, as Misty helped her stand up.

Everyone in the court room stood as the judge entered

and sat at the bench.

"Please be seated," she said.

"I'm grateful for all this cushion I got back there," Auntie Mabeline said to Misty, referring to her voluptuous derriere. "I see you got a little something going on there yourself." She said, glancing over at Misty, who wore a fitted pink dress, with bell sleeves and a wide black waisted belt.

Misty chuckled.

"Who do we have next?" the judge asked.

The court officer poured over his files.

"Mr. Franklin Johnson," he said. "He's in lock up."

They all watched as the court officer walked over to the board that covered the glass, sliding it to the left.

"Oh my God! My nephew looks horrible," Auntie Mabeline gasped.

Franklin stood handcuffed, wearing an orange jumpsuit.

He looked into the courtroom, immediately noticing Auntie Mabeline and Misty. He had the look of shame.

"They roughed him up!" Misty exclaimed.

Auntie Mabeline began to tear up. She couldn't believe her eyes. Franklin looked disheveled.

"What did they do to my nephew?" She whispered, as tears rolled down her high cheek bones.

"They did something," Misty said. "He looks as if he was roughed up."

The prosecutor began to lay out the case, mirroring what she said when David went before the judge.

"I was told that the ballistics results from the gun just came back. Is that correct. Is the report back yet?" the judge asked.

The prosecutor looked at the paperwork, holding it up.

"Yes, I have it right here."

"And . . . what does it say?" the judge asked.

"Mr. Franklin Johnson's prints were not found on the gun," the prosecutor said, handing the document to the court reporter. The judge muted her microphone. The court reporter looked at the document, whispering to the judge as he handed her the document.

"I wonder what he's telling her?" Auntie Mabeline asked Misty.

"I don't know," Misty said.

The judge unmuted her mic.

"Mr. Johnson, how are you?" She asked.

"I've seen better days," Franklin said.

"Lord, me too!" Auntie Mabeline blurted out.

"Mr. Johnson, I understand that your tour of duty recently ended with the United States Army," she said.

"Yes, your Honor," Franklin said.

"Well, on behalf of me and everyone under the sound of my voice, thank you for your service," she said.

"You're welcome," Franklin said in a low tone.

"Now, onto the matter at hand. Mr. Johnson, I have some good news and some bad news for you. What do you want first?" She asked.

Franklin held his head down.

"Whatever order you want. I don't care," he said.

"Well, it looks like you can use some good news," she said. "Based on the ballistic testing report, there is not enough evidence for us to hold you. In fact, your prints were not found on the weapon. There is a zero probability that you were the shooter. So, we are going to have to release you, and I'm waiving your bail," she said.

Franklin had a relieved look on his face, as he looked up at the judge.

"I would never try to hurt any of my siblings," he said.

"Well, the evidence shows that you were definitely not the shooter," the judge said. "So, now for the bad news. You'll have to stick around until we get your discharge papers together before you can be released," she said.

"Thank you!" Auntie Mabeline blurted out with joy, as she dried her face with a Kleenex.

The court officer looked at Auntie Mabeline keenly, but this time he didn't say a word.

Misty hugged Auntie Mabeline.

"Finally, some good news, Ms. Mabeline. I think you are his good luck charm."

"Child, I put everything in the Master's hand," she said, looking up to the ceiling. "He did that! Not little ole' me."

The judge banged the gavel, hearing the chatter.

"Let's get some order, and let's move onto the next case," she said.

The court officer slid the partition back over the glass.

Auntie Mabeline started to stand up. Misty yanked on her arm.

"Ms. Mabeline, don't you want to stay to see how Anna Mae's husband fairs? I'm sure that his case is coming up soon," Misty said.

"He isn't any kin to me!" Auntie Mabeline said. "He couldn't protect his own wife! I don't have no time for him! Now let's go meet Franklin, so I can hug my nephew!"

Misty stood up and walked out of the courtroom with Auntie Mabeline, arm-in-arm. As Auntie Mabeline approached the last bench, she felt someone grab her hand. She looked down to see Leroy, flashing his crooked smile, revealing his missing tooth.

Auntie Mabeline pulled her hand away. She waved off Leroy and high-stepped out of the courtroom.

"That's the security guard. He must've remembered you from back in the day. There you go, Ms. Mabeline," Misty said, attempting to play matchmaker.

"Child, please. I am not studying that man!" Auntie Mabeline said.

Chapter 56

Trevor and Grace caught up from old times, reminiscing about their years in school. Trevor even admitted to Grace that he had a crush on her. Grace didn't mention that his big mouth cousin Dalia had inadvertently told her, while she was at the hair shop. She wondered if Trevor still had those same feelings. The two laughed like two old friends, something that they never did back in high school. She silently regretted not getting to know Trevor back then. She didn't realize he had this fun, quirky side about him.

"Well, Grace, I have a meeting with a patient at 11 o'clock," he said, looking down at his gold diamond encrusted Rolex. I didn't realize that I've been here for two hours."

"Oh, my gosh! It didn't seem that long," she said. "I have to get ready to feed my son."

"What's his name?"

"Justice," Grace said.

"Alright, I like that! You're thinking outside the box. He sounds like he's going to be a judge to me!" Trevor said. "What a unique name. So, how'd you come up with his name?"

Grace was expecting to get questions about Justice's name, but not so soon. She could see that inquiring minds would want to know. What she saw in her son was "peace," and no matter what, she was not going to allow the negative circumstances surrounding her pregnancy define the life that she wanted for not only her son but herself. Deep down inside, she wanted the perpetrator to be brought to justice!

"Well, you know that I've never been a drama queen or like to be the center attention," she said.

"You? No, never that! You were pretty quiet. Sometimes I forgot that you sat behind me. You never said a word. There were times that I asked myself, "does she have a voice?" He laughed. "Watch . . . your son is going to be the total opposite."

They both laughed.

"I do have a voice, and now that my son is here, I've found myself using it more. But as for his name, since my life has been kind of chaotic, not in a good way, I just wanted some peace; so that's why I named my son Justice. Giving birth to him has, in a sense, freed my mind, body and soul."

"That's deep, Grace," he said.

"I know," she laughed. "Wow, I haven't laughed like this in so long," she said.

"It's one of the best medicines, besides me, of course," Trevor said.

"So, are you a doctor?" She asked.

"Not yet. I'm working on my masters, but my goal is to get my doctorate," he said. Then you'll have to call me Dr. Cooper," he said, smiling. "You see, I have goals, too!"

"Yeah, yeah. I hear you," she said.

"You'll still be Trevor to me!" she said, as they chuckled.

"Well, I better get a move on it," he said. "Grace, I would like to set up an actual appointment with you before you go home. This was just a consultation. Well, only if that's okay?"

"Yeah, I would like that," she said.

"Great! I'll touch base with Dr. Freelance later, and we'll work something out that doesn't conflict with your breastfeeding schedule."

"Okay," she said. "You're so thoughtful, Trevor."

"I've always been that way. You never gave me the chance to show you," he said, flirting with her.

She knew Trevor was right.

"I'll see you soon," he said, as he headed to the door.

"Trevor!" Grace called out.

"Yes," he answered.

"Dr. Freelance said you did house calls."

"Yes, that's true," he said.

"After I'm home, would you be able to help me repair my relationship with my sister, Anna Mae?" She asked.

"Yes. We can make that happen," he said.

Grace smiled, "Thanks!"

Chapter 57

Auntie Mabeline and Misty waited on the first floor for Franklin.

"Do you see him, Misty?" She said, looking around.

"No. I don't see him yet," Misty said. "Let me ask the officer. I'm sure he'll be able to tell us where to meet him at."

Auntie Mabeline watched Misty as she sashayed over to the handsome officer, who sported short strawberry blonde hair, before quickly coming back.

"He said that an officer will bring Franklin through the secured doors down there, once they confirm that his bail has been waived," she said, pointing down the bright pastel yellow hallway.

"Okay," Auntie Mabeline said. "Well, I'm gonna sit down and rest my feet."

As soon as Auntie Mabeline sat down, the double doors opened. Auntie Mabeline and Misty watched as the officer escorted Franklin to where they were.

Franklin looked disheveled and exhausted, wearing the same clothes that he had on the day of the shooting.

"Franklin, baby, are you okay?" Auntie Mabeline said, jumping to her feet, waddling toward him. "Did this cop here rough you up?" She said, raising her pocketbook, getting ready to assault the officer who'd escorted Franklin out of the holding area.

Franklin put his hand up to block the blow.

The officer looked at Auntie Mabeline as if she was deranged, before turning back around and heading back through the double doors, where he and Franklin had entered.

"No, Auntie," he said, giving his aunt a hug.

"What are you doing here?" He asked.

"I'm sure you know why! Let's discuss that later. I want to get out of this place!" she said. "I need to get back up to the hospital and talk to your sister's doctors and figure out how I'm going to get Grace and this baby home."

"Hi Misty," he said, giving her a hug. "Thanks for coming up here with my auntie."

"Don't mention it. I'm glad that I was available," she said.

"How's Anna Mae?" He asked.

"She's a mess right now," Auntie Mabeline said. "She was heavily sedated on yesterday. So, I haven't seen her yet. I'm sure the poor child is hooked up to all them machines. I know it's not going to be a pretty sight."

"I just cannot believe how quick all this happened. Talk

about a nightmare," he said.

"Yeah, it sure is," Auntie Mabeline said. "I'm glad that you are out. Grace will be happy to see you. She's been asking everyone and their momma about your whereabouts. You know, I had to tell her before she drove me and all the folks at the hospital bat crazy!"

"How did she take it?" He asked.

"Well, she was right. She said that you didn't do it," she responded.

"I shouldn't even be here! I should be right by her side, supporting her," he said. "What did she have?"

"A big-headed boy, but he's cute," Auntie Mabeline said. "Joe and I went up to the hospital yesterday. She'll be happy to see you though!"

"Oh good. I'm glad that you were there for her." Franklin said, giving his auntie another warm embrace. "But how'd you know she was in the hospital?"

"Joe told me, but I'll get into that later," she said.

"How's Grace doing otherwise?" He asked.

"Not well. The child had a nervous breakdown yesterday. She threw a vase across the room, acting like she lost her mind! They were about to commit her but luckily Joe and I got up there just in time and talked some sense into her," she said, adding more to the story.

"Thank God! That would have devasted her!" Franklin said.

Franklin looked over at Misty.

"Misty, I appreciate you coming to court with my aunt," he said. Auntie Mabeline noticed the officer that Misty spoke with, standing nearby, watching them closely.

"Can I help you?" Auntie Mabeline asked him.

"Yes ma'am," he said.

"Well, whatever you got to say, you can say it in front of all of us. I need witnesses," she said.

"Okay, ma'am," he said as he walked closer to where they stood.

"Mr. Johnson, my name is Officer Collins. I was sitting in the courtroom, when the judge heard your case."

"I don't remember seeing you at the hospital," Franklin said, looking keenly.

"Oh, no. I wasn't there. I'd passed by you last year, after making an arrest on your street," the officer said. "I recognized your aunt. She was sitting in the front seat.

"I was one of the officers assigned to a homicide that happened at the top of your street. I wanted to see if you had time to come down to the station or perhaps, I can stop by your home and see if anything jogs your memory before the case grows cold."

"Well, I wasn't around when that happened, so I won't be of any help," Franklin said, quickly dismissing the officer.

"Well, maybe someone in your family saw something. This woman doesn't deserve to die in vain. Her death was senseless. If you don't know, maybe someone else in your family saw something odd and just didn't think that it would help us. At this point, any lead we get is moving in the right direction," the officer said.

The officer reached into his pocket and pulled out his business card.

"Please call me, if you hear anything," he said.

"Isn't that the woman that you were speaking about earlier?" Auntie Mabeline asked Misty.

"Yeah," Misty said, quietly, attempting to shut Ms. Mabeline up.

Officer Collins looked over at Misty.

"Aren't you the shop owner of Misty's Mane Cuts?" He asked.

Misty knew that everyone knew who she was, mainly from the enormous billboard with her picture on it downtown.

"Yes, I am," she said.

Officer Collins reached into his pocket and pulled out another business card and handed it to Misty. Misty squinted at the small writing, unable to read it.

"If anyone at the shop knows anything or if you do, please give me a call. We'd stopped in there around the time that the homicide occurred. We're hoping that people are willing to talk now," he said.

"Okay," Misty said. "But I can only speak for myself. I don't know anything. I work a lot!"

"Don't go handing me one of your cards! I ain't seen or heard nothing!" Auntie Mabeline said.

Officer Collins smirked. "We appreciate any help," he said and walked off. Just as Officer Collins walked outside, Leroy approached Franklin.

"Man, I'm glad things worked out for you. I was pulling for you!" He said.

"Thanks," Franklin said. "Leroy, this is my Auntie Mabeline and our family friend, Misty," he said.

"Hello," Misty said.

"Man, I know this beautiful lady. I'm a few years older than her but I knew her older sister Leola, really well," he said, looking at Auntie Mabeline.

"That was my mom!" Franklin said. "How'd you know her?"

"What? Get out of here," he said. "We went to school together."

"Oh, really? Mom passed last November," Franklin said.

"I know," Leroy said. "I went to her funeral."

"You were there?" Franklin asked.

"Yes, I was. I was shocked to hear about her accident. You know, there's not many of us still living in this area, so we tend to know what's going on with each other," he said.

Auntie Mabeline was so focused on Old Man Joe at the funeral, especially after he embarrassed her by passing out tracks, that she didn't see Leroy.

"Mabel, I see that you still have a voice of an angel," he said. "I enjoyed your solo."

"Thanks," Auntie Mabeline said, blushing, zoning in on Leroy's missing tooth. Leroy noticed Auntie Mabeline's blank stare.

"You know I lost my tooth boxing," he said, pointing to gap in his mouth, where a tooth once existed. Auntie Mabeline grunted. "The last time I was in church was your Momma's funeral."

"You can always go back, Joe," Auntie Mabeline said. "I mean Leroy."

Franklin looked at Auntie Mabeline, smiling at her Freudian slip.

"Joe? I haven't seen him in years! Is that cat still around?" Leroy asked.

"Oh yeah, he's still alive and kicking. He's getting migraine headaches now and is almost blind as a bat but yeah, he still in the land of the living," she said.

"He was the man back in the day!" Leroy looked at Franklin. "Bo-y he had all the women!"

"Whatever!" Auntie Mabeline said.

"He was smooth! He used to be down at the club, courting a different woman every week. Them women used to be fighting each other over him. Back in the day, he had class, style, and money! Last I heard all them women he was messing with took him to the cleaners! Woman will do that to you!" He said, looking at Franklin. "I wouldn't mind running into him!"

"Oh, he liv...." Franklin said, before Auntie Mabeline cut him off.

"We got to go! I have to use the restroom, and I don't use everybody's bathroom! Franklin, where's that gal that bought me up here!" she said, referring to Misty.

"She's right behind you, Auntie," Franklin said.

"Okay gal, let's go!" She said.

Franklin shook Leroy's hand. "I appreciate what you did to get my sister help and talk me down. I'll never forgive myself for what happened, but I will figure out who did this to her and make sure justice is served! I'm sure I'll run into you again at the hospital."

"Well, she is in my prayers. All of ya'll are. I told you, you remind me of myself in my younger days, when I was a boxer. I know you would have hurt that dude. I'll be at the job later tonight. Swing by to see me any time. You know I work part-time," he said.

"Yeah," Franklin said.

"Well, I'm gonna go back into the courtroom to hear that other cats' case," Leroy said.

"Who?" Auntie Mabeline asked.

"Rufus," Franklin replied.

"Oh, we ain't staying for that," Auntie Mabeline said. "Any man that's gonna allow his wife to take a bullet is nothing but a coward!"

"Well, Rufus didn't have a chance to help her. Everything happened so quick. You had to be there. I know you are not fond of Rufus. I just feel bad that he got arrested, too! David belongs under the jail! But I don't want to elaborate on anything here," Franklin said.

"Yeah, he's right. It happened so fast, I was just trying to save my own life," Leroy said, swaying left to right, showing off his boxing moves. "Good seeing you again, Mabel." Leroy walked back toward the courtroom.

"Bye!" Auntie Mabeline said, abruptly.

"Let's go! I want to get home, take a nice hot shower and put on some fresh clothes," Franklin said.

"Yes, you sure enough need one!" Auntie Mabeline said, turning her nose up.

"My car is still parked at the hospital. Misty can you drop me off there?" He said.

"Sure," Misty said.

"I need to go up there, too, and check on your sisters," Auntie Mabeline said.

"I'll stop by later to see both Anna Mae and Grace," Misty said.

"Okay. I guess I'll try to hunt down Anna Mae's doctor. The nurse told me he wanted to talk to me, since that ole husband of hers is in jail," Auntie Mabeline said.

"Auntie, you should probably wait until I come up there, so Anna Mae's doctor can speak to both of us together," Franklin said.

"You've been through enough, son. I'll fill you in on everything once you come up to the hospital," she said.

"Okay," he said. "Please get the doctor's contact information, in case I have any questions."

"You know this old mind is close to retirement. I'll have to write it down," she said.

As they walked to Misty's shiny white Jeep, they

approached the officer who arrested Franklin, as he spoke to Officer Collins. The officers stopped talking once they noticed Franklin, Auntie Mabeline and Misty pass by. Franklin could only assume that they were conversing about one or two things; the shooting in the hospital or the murdered woman who that lived across the street.

The officers watched them as Misty drove off. The three rode in silence for 15 minutes. Auntie Mabeline mulled over how she was going to share with Franklin all that Grace had shared with her. She knew that he had a lot on his mind already, but she knew it was something that they needed to discuss, especially before they saw Grace.

Franklin sat in the backseat, staring out of the window as if he'd been locked up for years and was now getting back into civilization. He contemplated sharing what he and Grace found out but didn't want to do it in front of Misty. He didn't want her to think that their family put the "d" in dysfunctional.

Misty looked in her rear-view mirror occasionally, gazing at Franklin, as he looked out the window. She could read his avoidance. She contemplated confessing about housing David in her hair salon, but didn't want to betray his trust, especially knowing how Franklin felt about him.

"Franklin," Auntie Mabeline said.

"Yeah, Auntie," he responded.

"I need to share some things with you before you come up to see your sister," she said. "I'm sure you already know most of it."

"Right now?" He asked, looking over at Misty.

"There's no perfect time, and right now seems like the most opportune time," Auntie Mabeline said.

"I know I can't turn back the hands of time, but I wish I never called her. None of this would have happened," he said, referring to Anna Mae. "I blame myself."

"Aww, hush up that foolish talk! You know your sister's head is harder than a cinderblock. She doesn't listen to no one but that husband of hers," Auntie Mabeline said. Misty was hesitant to chime in, but she couldn't remain silent any longer. She could see the pain in Franklin's face.

"Franklin, you had no idea that Anna Mae would get shot. Your sisters know that you love them, and you would never hurt them. I also know firsthand how irresponsible David is but I don't think he's that crazy to shoot his own sister!" Misty said.

"Anna Mae told me how he did you wrong with the towels," Franklin said. "That was messed up."

"I know I was really upset at the time, but he was very apologetic. He was even willing to give me my money back," she said. "I don't think he meant to put me out like that."

"Well, you don't know him," Franklin said.

"Wait? How'd did Anna Mae know about the towels? I didn't tell her!" Misty said.

"Rufus may have told her," he said.

"See how sneaky he is?," Auntie Mabeline said.

Misty thought for a minute.

"Oh, remember I said how he was coming into the barber shop with David, so maybe that's how he found out? I'm sure the guys over there gave David a hard time about it," Misty said.

"Oh, they hang together now?" Franklin said. "I thought it was odd that they would come up to the hospital together."

"I didn't realize how close he and Anna Mae's husband were," Misty added.

"Since when did they get so close?" Auntie Mabeline questioned.

"I don't know," Franklin said. "Anna Mae mentioned that Rufus cut his jerry curl out after Momma's funeral, so that would be my guess," he said. "He seemed to be making frequent visits to the shop." Misty pulled into the entrance of the hospital's emergency room.

"Maybe so," she said.

Auntie Mabeline looked at Misty.

"Aren't you going to tell Franklin that David was sleeping in your shop?" She said, catching Misty off guard.

"WHAT?" Franklin exclaimed.

Misty looked at Auntie Mabeline, a bit perturbed.

"I told your Aunt earlier that I helped David out a few times and allowed him to sleep in the shop on a few occasions. It wasn't a big deal. I'm sorry that I never said anything about it. I just didn't want to get in the middle, and I was only helping him out because I know that Ms. Leola would want me to."

"NO, SHE WOULDN'T! SHE WOULD TELL YOU TO TELL DAVID TO GET LOST AND GET A REAL JOB!" Franklin said. "YOU CAN'T ALLOW PEOPLE TO TAKE ADVANTAGE OF YOU, MISTY. YOU GOT TO GROW A BACKBONE!"

"Are you trying to say that I'm weak?" Misty said, feeling insulted.

"JUST REMEMBER THIS, YOU CAN PICK YOUR FRIENDS BUT YOU CANNOT PICK YOUR FAMILY!" Franklin said, sharing more than he'd planned to.

"What's that supposed to mean?" She asked.

"Just let me out here!" Franklin said, abruptly ending the conversation and attempting to avoid anyone seeing him in the same clothes as the day before.

"What does he mean by that?" Misty said, as she looked

over at Auntie Mabeline.

"I think that was a slip of his tongue," Auntie Mabeline said. "Don't pay him no mind."

Franklin opened the car door, and stepped out.

"I'll be back in about an hour or so," he said.

"Take your time. Looks like a nap could do you some good!" Auntie Mabeline said.

"Yeah," he said.

"Thanks Misty. See ya'll later!" He said, slamming the car door.

Misty was speechless.

Misty pulled up to the emergency room entrance.

"You are truly an angel, Misty," Auntie Mabeline said.

"Thanks. I guess, I'll see you later," Misty said, sounding confused.

"Don't you worry about what Franklin said. He got so much going on in that brain of his. You hear?" She said, looking at Misty.

"I guess," Misty said.

Auntie Mabeline slowly got out of the car, closing the car door. She watched as Franklin and Misty drove off separately, in the same direction.

CHAPTER 58

Auntie Mabeline signed in at the nurse's station. The nurse buzzed her through the secured doors that led into the intensive care unit.

"This place is more secure than a prison," she muttered.

"Excuse me, I am looking for my niece Anna Mae Payne's doctor."

The nurse raised her head up from the computer, looking closely at Auntie Mabeline.

"Are you her aunt?" She asked.

"Yes, I am Ms. Mabeline. I was waiting for the doctor to talk to me on yesterday. I stayed up here almost half the day, and no one came to get me."

"I apologize that no one got back to you. The doctor had two surgeries on yesterday," the nurse said, as she picked up the telephone. "Let me page him to see where he's at. He is expecting you."

Auntie Mabeline looked around at the other nurses moving around in the fast-paced, busy unit as she listened to the nurse's voice blare across the intercom.

"Dr. Flint, please dial ICU, Dr. Flint, ICU."

Immediately, the phone began to ring. The nurse picked it up.

"Dr. Flint, Mrs. Payne's aunt is here to see you," She paused. "Okay, 10 minutes . . . I will let her know," the nurse said, before hanging up.

"The doctor is on his way. He's on the other side of the hospital. He said, give him 10 minutes. You can have a seat in the conference room right there." The nurse said, pointing to the room with the glass window.

"Okay. How is Anna Mae doing today?" Auntie Mabeline asked.

"We still have her sedated because of the tubes, but the doctor will explain all of that to you," she said.

"What are you not telling me? Is she going to be a vegetable?" Auntie Mabeline blurted out.

"No, her cognitive skills are intact," she said.

"I have to sit down," Auntie Mabeline said, rudely interrupting the nurse and walking into the small conference room, taking a seat.

Auntie Mabeline noticed the tall lanky doctor dressed in blue scrubs and a long white jacket approach the nurse's station.

"She's in there," the nurse said, pointing toward Auntie Mabeline.

"Did you tell her anything?" He asked.

"No, I didn't," the nurse said.

Auntie Mabeline sat in the room, overhearing part of their conversation.

The doctor walked into the room.

"Ms. Mabeline," he said.

"Yes," Auntie Mabeline said.

"It's nice to meet you," he said, shaking Auntie Mabeline's hand.

"You too," she said.

"I'm Dr. Flint," he said, holding onto a clipboard and a pen.

"Okay, so what is going on with my niece?" She asked, anxiously. The doctor sat down.

"Well, as you know your niece suffered a gunshot wound on Saturday evening. The bullet nicked her stomach, bypassing the kidneys, pancreas, and her liver. It's still lodged in her stomach. I've seen worse in which it shatters the inside organs . . . and . . . well . . . the survival rate with that type of injury is very low, depending on the type of gun used; but your niece, she was really lucky."

"Why didn't you remove the bullet?" Auntie Mabeline asked.

"I didn't want to risk removing it and damaging her other organs," he said.

"So, she has to walk around with a bullet in her body,

for the rest of her life. She'll never be able to go through security at the airport!" Auntie Mabeline said. Dr. Flint, smiled. "Yes, she would be able to travel. We would provide her with a document that states that she has a bullet in her body. They used to require medical ID cards, but those are no longer required," he said.

"Oh, okay," Auntie Mabeline said. "So, what's her prognosis?"

"Mrs. Payne lost quite a bit of blood, so we had to give her a blood transfusion. We did an MRI. It showed that the bullet missed her organs but it did shatter her stomach. The stomach has a lot of acid that can burn other organs. Luckily for her, she got immediate medical attention, and we were able to remove the acid from her stomach before it damaged her other internal organs. I want to keep her here for another three weeks for precautionary measures. Once she's home, she may experience irregular bowel movements. This is expected with her type of injury. She'll need the support of a cane to walk but don't worry. We'll make sure that you have the folks to contact about that.

"Oh, my sweet Jesus," Auntie Mabeline said, gasping.

Dr. Flint grabbed onto Auntie Mabeline hands. "I know this is a lot to take in.

"Oh yes. The good book said, He'll give me what I can handle, but this is too much!" she said.

"It is. Oh, yes, and we'll provide you with a list of

gastroenterologists in the area," he said.

"Who?" Auntie Mabeline asked.

"A gastroenterologist physician specializes in the stomach and other organs."

"Oh, okay," she said.

"Now, what about her care once she goes home besides, seeing that gastro doctor?" She asked.

"Your niece will have a long road ahead. She will need to get up and take short walks, at least three times a day. This will prevent blood clots forming in her stomach. She cannot lift anything heavy. No more than 15 pounds. Anything more will put pressure on the wound, and we don't want that. We'll send her home with pain meds and an antibiotic to prevent infection, but if anything seems odd, she must come back to the emergency room, ASAP. We suggest physical therapy to strengthen those core muscles. Once she recovers – now, this will not be immediate – she will be able to resume her normal life activities, with restrictions, of course. And don't worry, I don't expect you to remember everything that I'm saying. It will be outlined in great detail, on her discharge papers."

"Yeah, we'll need that paper," she said. Dr. Flint smiled.

"Do you foresee any issues with her getting help at home?"

"I don't know . . . the kids are gonna have to cut their

foolishness and help out their sister. I cannot do it all!" Auntie Mabeline exclaimed.

"Well, that brings me to another important point. Support . . . this injury will be a shock to your niece. It's very common for patients who suffer significant trauma to become depressed, feel anxious, angry, and become afraid of something like this happening again. It's called PTSD, Post-Traumatic Stress Disorder. The hospital provides grief and trauma counseling. We have a young man who is phenomenal with working with patients who suffer traumatic events, such as your niece. Matter of fact, he's so popular that he extended his counseling to outside of the hospital. We'll make sure that we provide you with his contact information."

"I'll have to think about that one," Auntie Mabeline said.

"Mrs. Payne is going to need all the support she can get for both her physical and mental health," he said.

"Have you been in to see her yet?"

"No, I haven't," Auntie Mabeline said.

"Well, I want to forewarn you. Your niece has a nasogastric tube down her nose to remove air, fluid, and blood from her stomach. She also has an endotracheal tube down her mouth."

"What does that do?" She asked.

"Good question. The tube that's inserted in her mouth aids her in breathing and to keep her airway open. The loud noise that you will hear will be the respirator machine that allows her to breathe."

"Oh, my word," Auntie Mabeline said.

"She definitely has someone looking out for her," Dr. Flint said.

"Yeah, her Momma in heaven," Auntie Mabeline said.

"Oh, gotcha," Dr. Flint said.

"Can you be her proxy? We will need someone to make healthcare decisions for her, since she is incapacitated," he asked.

"Well, I reckon, I better. Her brother has way too much going on right now and his mind ain't right," she said. "I guess I'm going to have to move back up here and help take care of this girl," she said, looking perplexed.

"You're not from this area?" He asked.

"I was born and raised right here in this city, but once I got grown, I got tired of it and moved to Savannah, Georgia," Auntie Mabeline said.

"Oh, I see," he said.

"This is definitely going to be an adjustment. Initially, she will need round the clock assistance from her family," he said.

"I just don't know. Her husband may be getting out today," she said.

"I heard about her husband, and I hope that everything works out for the best. I know this must be tough for the entire family," he said.

"Yeah. I don't want to even say what I wish on that husband of hers, but thank you for the report. I have another niece up here that none of us knew was pregnant. She gave birth when all of this was happening, so I need to go see Anna Mae and then go see my other niece," Auntie Mabeline said, standing up.

"Okay. Now it makes sense. We didn't know why Mrs. Payne was up here at the hospital," he said.

"Yes, her older brother had called her up to see about their youngest sister. They don't get along, so I don't know how she gonna feel when she learns that her sister had a baby," she said.

"Well . . . there is something more that I need to share with you," Dr. Flint said, standing up, towering over Auntie Mabeline.

"I don't know how much more I can take," she lamented. Dr. Flint placed his hand on Auntie Mabeline's shoulder.

"Mrs. Payne was five months pregnant. She lost the baby. I'm so sorry!" Auntie Mabeline gasped!

Chapter 59

Auntie Mabeline walked toward Grace's room in a zombie-like trance. The news that Dr. Flint dropped on her was equivalent to an atomic bomb. She was shocked to find out that Anna Mae was pregnant and lost the baby. She didn't know how to share this information with Franklin and Grace, or if she should just keep it to herself.

The fact that both Macie and Dr. Flint mentioned the grief and trauma counselor had her contemplating if she should reach out to him or not. Maybe it was a good idea.

"Hey Ms. Mabeline. Is everything okay?" Macie said, noticing her melancholy mood. "You don't seem like your bubbly self."

Auntie Mabeline stopped and looked at Macie.

"I just got the report from Anna Mae's doctor," she said.

"How is she doing?" Macie asked.

"She's in stable condition, but I just found out that she was pregnant and lost the baby," she said.

"Oh, no! I'm so sorry. This is so devastating!" Macie said.

"I have to find a way to break the news to Franklin and Grace," she said.

"Well, Dr. Freelance had a counselor come and speak to Grace. He's awesome! I'm sure he can meet with you and your family to talk all of this through. You all are going through a lot right now, all at the same time. With, Grace having a new baby, the shooting, and now this devastating news of your niece losing her baby. Having a neutral ear is probably a good thing," Macie said.

"Yeah, and David is still in jail. They let Franklin go today," Auntie Mabeline said.

Macie remembered what Grace shared with her about David.

"Well, I don't know David, but I'm happy for Franklin! I know that Grace will be so happy to see him. Where's he at?" She asked.

"He went home to shower and change. He'll be up here later," Auntie Mabeline said. "I want to surprise Grace. So, don't you go telling her."

"My lips are sealed," Macie said, pretending as if she had a key, locking her lips shut.

"Good!" Auntie Mabeline responded.

"Well, there's a glimmer of hope!" Macie said with excitement.

"Yeah, the ballistic report showed that there was no way he could have been the shooter, because his prints were not found on the gun," she said. "I don't know about

David. They are still holding him. I found out that he had a warrant out for his arrest for a DUI. The report came out after he went before the judge. I don't think they will let him go. Lord knows, I don't have bail money just laying around. I would have to put my home up for collateral or dig into my retirement and . . . well . . . I love David, but I am not gonna do that. Luckily for Franklin, after the judge read that report, she waived his bail!" Auntie Mabeline said.

"Oh my God! That's good news, for Franklin anyways!" Macie said.

"Yeah, child. These kids are going to drive me to an early grave," she said.

"It will all work out! Well, I also have some good news to share," she said, sounding more upbeat than she'd been the last few days.

"What's that?" Auntie Mabeline asked.

"Grace is having a great day. I gave her some headphones, so she's been listening to music, which put her in a much better mood. Dr. Freelance came to see her earlier this morning, and she met the grief and trauma counselor. So, her spirits are up today! She'd gotten out of bed after she ate lunch and went down to the nursery to get her son, and she wheeled him back to her room for his feeding. She still has him. She's bonding well with him."

"Oh, good. When will she be ready to go home?"

Auntie Mabeline asked.

"Dr. Freelance will let her know later today. It will probably be tomorrow, since she's doing so good! I actually have a little surprise for her on the day she's discharged."

"What? A swift kick in the butt. I know she's worked your nerves," Auntie Mabeline said.

Macie laughed.

"Oh, no. Something more memorable. The other day she shared some things with me, so I have the perfect send off for her," she said, smiling. "We've all grown so fond of her, you know, considering what she's experienced. Most people her age could not handle what she's gone through. She is one strong young lady. I told her that I would love to keep in contact with her after she leaves," Macie said, cheerfully. "She's like my sister from another mother."

"Oh, that would be great. WE would love that! I appreciate you, Macie. Maybe you can help us out with Anna Mae," she said, attempting to recruit Macie.

"Ahhh . . . I am not trained in that type of injury, but I'm sure her nurses will provide you with resources. Maybe you can look into getting a visiting nurse or someone like a CNA who can help out," Macie said, just as Sharmaine passed by.

"Good day Ms. Mabeline, how are you?" Sharmaine said, pushing the food cart out of her way.

Auntie Mabeline gave Sharmaine the side eye, still salty from when she took her great-nephew out of the nursery without authorization.

"I overheard you both talking. You know that I am a member of this organization, rent-a-nurse. I work by the hour in my client's home. I will be more than happy to help your niece out, after she gets home."

"I don't know about that. I can't have you trying to steal my great-nephew again," Auntie Mabeline said.

Sharmaine smiled.

"I know it scared all of you, and I am so sorry for that. As I said, I was only trying to calm him down. He was cranky. I ran into Grace earlier this morning, and we had a heart-to-heart chat about it. She knows now that I am only here to help her and her son. That's my job. She trusts me," she said, smiling.

"Well, I need to talk this out with my niece and nephew, and I will get back to you," Auntie Mabeline said.

"Okay. I'll be around. Macie knows how to find me," Sharmaine said, as she proceeded through the double doors.

Macie could see that Auntie Mabeline had reservations.

"I don't know about her," Auntie Mabeline said to Macie.

"She's actually a good nurse. She comes from a family

who've devoted their life to caring for and helping others. Most of them work in the medical field. Trust me, I get it. I know after she took off with your great-nephew, you are hesitant and are probably questioning her motives. I would tell you if I didn't trust her, but I do. She's a great nurse. She's very attentive to her client's needs, and we're actually good friends outside of work."

"Well, I trust you Macie. So far you haven't steered me wrong," Auntie Mabeline said. "You may have withheld all the truth from me, but I know you have to follow hospital rules."

"Yes, and please don't judge me for that or for not telling Grace all of the truth about the incident that involved her siblings. I had to proceed with caution. We have to be very sensitive to our patient's overall needs and abide by the hospital policies," Macie said.

"Okay . . . we are definitely going to need some help once Anna Mae gets home," Auntie Mabeline said, thinking about everything Anna Mae's doctor had said.

"By the way, the awesome grief and trauma counselor that I mentioned to you, has Grace's vote! She cannot stop talking about him," Macie said smiling, as she and Auntie Mabeline walked toward Grace's room.

CHAPTER 60

"Hello sunshine! Look who I found," Macie said, as she and Auntie Mabeline entered Grace's room.

"Hey, Gracie," Auntie Mabeline said, reaching into her pocketbook and handing Grace her cell phone.

"Hi there! Oh, thanks Auntie! You remembered," Grace said, as she cradled Justice in her arms. "Say hi to Ms. Macie and Auntie Mabeline," she said, as if Justice could speak.

"You're quite chipper today," Auntie Mabeline said.

"Yes, I feel great! Dr. Freelance came to see me earlier this morning. He explained to me how important it is for me to take care of myself, so I can take care of this little cutie," she said, smiling, looking down at Justice. Justice began to coo, as if he understood what his mother was saying.

Macie and Auntie Mabeline looked at each other, pleasantly surprised.

"Well, I have to distribute afternoon meds, so I'm going to get back to work. Grace, press the call button if you need anything," she said.

'Okay, I will," she said, looking up at Macie.

"Bye ya'll," Macie said, rushing out of the room.

Auntie Mabeline couldn't believe her eyes. She didn't know what came over her niece, but this was a good sight to behold.

"Do you want to hold Justice? He's happy, full, and dry," Grace said.

"Yeah, give me the little rascal, but let me wash my hands first," she said, walking Grace to the bathroom. After she washed her hands, she carefully took Justice out of Grace's arms.

Auntie Mabeline stood by the side of the bed, just looking at Justice, as she held him.

"He's perfect," she said.

"Yes, he is," Grace said. "Auntie, have a seat. Stay a while."

"Yeah, I need to sit down. I've been on my feet all day," Auntie Mabeline said, sitting in the chair at the foot of the bed, admiring Justice.

'Auntie, Oh my God! You're not going to believe this," Grace said, looking exciting.

"What child? What did they put in your food today? You are very hyper," she asked.

"Nothing, I'm just happy," she said.

"So, what am I not going to believe?" Auntie Mabeline asked.

"I told you that Dr. Freelance came to see me today. Well, after he explained to me all of the benefits of breastfeeding, he told me about this grief and trauma counselor that they have here. He was talking about how the guy was so amazing, blah, blah, blah," she said, talking with her hands.

Auntie Mabeline listened attentively, wondering if this was the same councilor that Dr. Flint had mentioned.

"So, while Dr. Freelance was talking to me, someone knocked on the door. I couldn't see him because of this privacy curtain, but when he walked in and I saw him and my jaw dropped," she said.

"Why?" Auntie Mabeline said, remembering what Macie had shared earlier, of Grace being fond of the counselor.

"Why? Because the grief and trauma counselor is Trevor Cooper," she said.

"Who is that?" Auntie Mabeline asked.

"We went to school together. He used to have this crush on me back in the day," she said.

"Back in the day? You've been out of school for like two years," Auntie Mabeline said.

"I know right! But I haven't seen him in four years!" Grace chuckled. "Who knew that Trevor was this brainiac? He skipped the last two years of high school and went straight to college. Auntie he looks so good now!"

"Do I know him?" Auntie Mabeline asked.

"No, but he's such a good counselor! We spoke for two hours. He's so positive! I really enjoyed talking to him. He's gonna talk to Dr. Freelance and set up more sessions for me. He even does house calls! Do you believe it? I even asked him if he could come to the house and meet with me and Anna Mae. Maybe it will help our relationship," Grace said, talking a mile a minute. Auntie Mabeline sat in the chair holding Justice, feeling as if her prayers had been answered.

"Gracie, that is one of the best things I've heard all day," she said.

"Oh yeah, so how was court? I want to hear what happened? Did Misty go with you? Where's Franklin? Did you see him? When is he getting out of jail?" Grace asked, bombarding Auntie Mabeline with one question after the other.

"Slow down, little mama," Auntie Mabeline said, attempting to stall. She wondered what was taking Franklin so long to get to the hospital.

"Gracie, I think this baby sat up here and pooped. He smells like a grown man!" she said.

"Oh, I'll take him and change him," she said. Auntie Mabeline stood up, handing Justice back to Grace.

Grace lifted Justice's bottom up to her nose. "I don't smell anything Auntie. Maybe he passed gas. Did you pass gas little man?" She asked, looking at Justice affectionately.

"NO, I DIDN'T! DID YOU?" a masculine voice asked.

Grace looked up to see Franklin standing in the doorway looking fresh and so clean.

"OH MY GOD! FRANKLIN!" she yelled, as happy tears rolled down her cheeks, dripping on Justice's forehead.

Franklin walked over and gave Grace a huge hug.

"Stop crying, little sis. I'm here," he said. "I'm sorry that you had to go through this by yourself, but I am here now."

Auntie Mabeline pulled her handkerchief out of her pocket and dried her own eyes.

"Look at my handsome nephew," Franklin said. "Did you name him after me?"

"You know you're my hero, but I named him Justice," she said. Franklin looked at Grace with empathy, knowing that her son represented what she wanted deep down inside.

"I love it!" Franklin said.

"He can fit in the palm of my hand. How much does he weigh?" Franklin asked.

"He weighed six pounds, four ounces at birth, but we

weighed him today and he weighs 7 pounds since I've been breastfeeding. Do you want to hold him?" Grace asked, looking up at Franklin.

"You better wash your hands first," Auntie Mabeline chimed in.

Franklin listened to his aunt, and walked back over after he was done. He sat at the foot of Grace's bed. Grace carefully placed Justice in his arms.

"Here, you may need this, just in case he spits up. He ate not long ago," she said, tossing the burping pad over Franklins shoulder.

"He's so handsome Grace. He has a lot of hair," Franklin said, looking at his nephew.

"I was so worried about you, Franklin. What happened in the emergency room?" Grace asked, still not satisfied with Auntie Mabeline's account.

Franklin was in no mood to discuss the drama, but he knew that he had to share with Grace why he just vanished.

Franklin spent the next 30 minutes explaining to Grace from the time Anna Mae got shot in the emergency room to his, David, and Rufus's arrest, and his surprising outcome in court.

"So, there you have it!" He said.

"I'm sorry that happened to you Franklin. I hate that Anna Mae got shot, but I knew that you didn't do it,"

Grace said.

"Even though Anna Mae worked my nerves and got me so upset, I would never hurt her," he said.

"Gracie kept saying that you didn't do it," Auntie Mabeline said, finally in agreeance.

"I want to go see her," Grace said.

"Gracie, I don't know if that's a good thing. She got tubes going every which-a-way. It's not a pretty sight," Auntie Mabeline said.

"Auntie is right and if she sees you in a johnnie, it may traumatize her. She'll be wondering why both of you are wearing the same outfit," Franklin added.

"That's a good point," Grace said. "I didn't think of that."

"I'm trying to get my mind right before I go see her," Franklin said. "This is just crazy."

"Amen to that!" Auntie Mabeline agreed.

"I told Auntie Mabeline what David did to me. If he could do what he did to me, he could pick up a gun up and shoot Anna Mae. Besides, we all know that they never got along," she said.

"That's simply because they're so much alike!" Auntie Mabeline exclaimed.

"I hope that sick bastard never gets out of jail!" Franklin

said.

"I understand that you are upset, but I'm not gonna sit here and listen to you bad mouth him like that," Auntie Mabeline interjected, looking sternly at Franklin and Grace.

They both ignored Auntie Mabeline.

"I mentioned to Dr. Freelance earlier today what happened to me, and he told me that I should go to the police and tell them," Grace said. "Now that Justice is here, I don't want David nowhere near him. So, I want to talk to the police."

"Aren't you the little water faucet that won't shut off," Auntie Mabeline said. "Gracie, did you forget what we spoke about?"

"What did you all discuss?" Franklin asked.

"I merely suggested to Grace that she should confirm that David is the father before she goes and accuses him of something he may not have done. They have them DNA tests," Auntie Mabeline said. "Ya'll getting ahead of yourselves and getting my blood pressure up! I just cannot see this child doing anything to this girl, here."

"YOU'RE CALLING ME A LIAR!" Grace yelled.

"Hold up now!" Auntie Mabeline said, raising her hand in the air. "I think you're mistaken me for that baby boy right there," she said, referring to Justice. "Just because you popped out a baby, don't give you the right to talk to me any kind of way! You've been a mother for a minute!"

Franklin rose his voice, "STOP MAKING EXCUSES FOR HIM!"

"You both need to calm yourselves down," she said. "Now, I didn't come up here to be disrespected!"

"NO! I WILL NOT STAY CALM! YOU DIDN'T SEE WHAT WE FOUND IN DAVID'S DESK DRAWER! YOU DIDN'T SEE WHAT WE FOUND IN MOMMA'S CLOSET! DAVID GOT YOU FOOLED!" He said.

"I'm starting to think that talking to that shrink is not a bad idea!" Auntie Mabeline said.

"Shrink? I don't need no shrink!" Franklin exclaimed.

"Trevor is not a shrink. He's a grief and trauma counselor," Grace said.

"Why does that name sound familiar?" Franklin said.

"He's Dalia and Diamond's cousin. Remember when you used to drive the ice cream truck. He's the kid who never had any money," Grace said.

"Oh! Yeah. Diamond's cousin! She mentioned when I saw her the other day that he's a counselor. Wow!" Franklin said. "Good for him!"

"He's going to be our counselor," Grace asked.

"Macie and Dr. Flint, Anna Mae's doctor, told me that

he's good. Ya'll crazy kids need to talk to someone. Lord knows, everything that I am saying is going in one ear and out the other!" Auntie Mabeline said, sounding frustrated. "You're trying to send me to an early grave, like your Momma."

"Auntie once you see what we found, you can make your own mind up," Franklin said.

"Well . . . maybe so," she said. "As of right now, I cannot go off of hearsay."

Grace highjacked the conversation.

"Dr. Freelance told me that the DNA test that's done at the hospital is pricey. But he suggested that I get one at the drug store or even WalMart," Grace said.

"How are you going to test David. He's in jail?" Auntie Mabeline asked, looking perplexed.

"If she files a police report, maybe they can order the test while he's in jail," Franklin said. "We won't know until we ask."

"Dr. Freelance said I should go through the court. Maybe I can get a judge to issue a court ordered paternity test and have David's parental rights removed," Grace said.

"Well, he didn't sign the birth certificate. So that makes no sense," Auntie Mabeline interjected. "That's a waste of your time and energy."

"Maybe I can ask that cop that was talking to us earlier," Franklin said, looking at Auntie Mabeline.

"What cop?" Grace asked.

"The cop at the courthouse who's working on the woman who was murdered at the top of our street case. He was looking for leads. I guess the case had gone cold because no one saw anything," Franklin said.

"I know something," Grace blurted out.

"WHAT?" Auntie Mabeline and Franklin said in unison.

"She helped me after the assault," Grace said, solemnly.

"And when were you gonna tell us that?" Auntie Mabeline said.

"Well, you just said I run my mouth a lot," Grace said sarcastically.

"But that's something that you should tell us about," Auntie Mabeline said.

"What do you know?" Franklin asked.

"I told you both before, I had fallen asleep after dealing with David blasting music in Momma's house. David left the door open, and then he came back in and assaulted me. I remember him dragging me down the stairs after he punched me in my face. I tried to get up, but I stumbled and fell to the ground," Grace said.

"I don't want to hear no more because it's getting me pissed," Franklin said.

"Franklin, we need to let her get it out! This is part of her healing. It's not all about you," Auntie Mabeline said, contradicting her earlier statements. "I'm trying to figure out how she knew it was David."

Grace took a deep breath and continued.

"Well, after I got assaulted in the house, he dragged me down the steps, and I remember being blinded by this bright light. Well, it was the woman's headlights. She was coming home. When David noticed the car, he dropped me right in the street. He left me to die! She almost ran over me," Grace said.

"Oh, my God!" Auntie Mabeline said, holding onto her heart.

Grace continued.

"I remember hearing the car door opening and her standing over me asking me if I was okay. She was about to take me to her house and call 911, but I asked her if she could just take me home and I'd have David take me to the hospital. Well, this is before we found out that he did this to me!" She said.

"So, where did David go? Did you see what direction he ran off in?" Franklin asked, as Justice slept in his arms.

"I don't know! I just remember him dropping me to

the ground and the woman scaring him off. I was hit so hard, that my eye was practically swollen, and you know how dark our street is. It was hard to see anything," Grace said.

"I know. It's definitely not well-lit. It's no wonder that she almost ran you over," Franklin said.

"I can't believe this. You poor child," Auntie Mabeline said, casting doubt on Grace's account of events.

"The lady helped me in the house but it was strange," Grace said.

"What was?" He asked.

"After she helped me upstairs, she began walking through the house, but it seemed like she had been there before," she said.

"What do you mean?" Auntie Mabeline said.

"Well, she asked me who did I live with. I told her my Momma and my brother, David. I told her that he'd went out and should be back soon. She started walking through our house, like she lived there. I could see her shadow walking toward David's room. She even said she checked his closet to see if he was in there. It was strange," she said. "After she came out of his room, she told me to see about my bruises and she hurried out the door."

"She sounds crazy! I wonder if she knew David?" Auntie Mabeline said.

"I cannot believe that you didn't tell us this, Grace. You don't know who she was. She could have killed you!" Franklin exclaimed. "It's all just really strange! I'm wondering why she didn't call 911 after she bought you upstairs. That would have been the right thing to do. If I found someone beat up and battered in the street, I'm not just going to bring them home and leave them there. I'd call 911 and stay with them."

"Because she's a battle-like fool! That's why!" Anna Mae said, shaking her head in disgust, taking it personal.

"Very strange. Then the next day she ends up dead? All the things that David has done, could he be capable of murder?" Franklin said, questioning himself. "I think so!"

"Hush up that talk! I don't care what you and Gracie think, your brother is no murderer!" Auntie Mabeline exclaimed.

"Keep thinking that!" Franklin exclaimed. "And...he's not our brother!" Grace continued.

"The next morning when I got up, David was drunk on the couch. Then I heard all this commotion outside and saw the lights flashing through the curtain. When I went over to the window and pulled back the curtain, I saw the cops taking her body out. One of them was talking to Old Man Joe."

"It was probably the medical examiners," Franklin exclaimed.

"Joe didn't tell me none of this!" Auntie Mabeline said.

"Didn't you say he can be absent-minded?" Franklin questioned.

"Maybe so but that's one of the reasons I had to get up out of this city and move to Savannah! Everybody got secrets!"

Auntie Mabeline and Franklin looked at each other.

"Have you seen the woman before Franklin?" Auntie Mabeline asked.

"No. I've never seen anyone come out of that house. I've noticed a SUV parked outside sometimes, but never anyone getting in or out of it. I wonder if she worked nights," Franklin said.

"I think so because I swear, I never saw her either," Gracie said.

"What type of truck did she drive?" Auntie Mabeline asked.

Gracie responded, "Jeep Cherokee."

Auntie Mabeline grunted.

"I don't know . . . I think we should go to the police," Grace said.

"Well, knowing this, I think we have to," Franklin said.

"But how can you be sure it's the same woman who

helped you?" Auntie Mabeline said, casting doubt.

"There's something else that I remember," Grace said.

"What?" They asked.

"Her perfume smelled like oranges, and I'll never forget her shoes, because they made so much noise when she left. I know my head was killing me from the assault, and my mind was a blur, but her shoes were bright orange and the dead lady's shoes were the same color. I saw them! They weren't covered up by the sheet! I think they were crocs," Grace said.

The three were startled by a knock on the door.

"Surprise! I found you!" Misty said, smiling, as she walked in carrying wrapped gifts. Auntie Mabeline, Franklin, and Grace were stunned in their gaze at Misty.

Chapter 61

Is everything alright? Should I come back at a later time?" Misty asked.

"No, Child,' come on in. You're like family," Auntie Mabeline said.

Misty proceeded with caution.

"Okay, it seemed as if you all were busy," she said.

"No, we were just talking," Auntie Mabeline said. "Come on in."

"Misty, I'm so happy to see you," Grace said. "I haven't seen you in a long time."

"I know," Misty said.

Misty looked at Franklin, still wondering why he made the comment earlier.

"I'll take these off your hands," he said, standing up, taking the gifts from Misty, and placing them on Grace's tray. He turned around and grabbed the chair near the other bed.

"Don't drop my baby!" Grace exclaimed, watching Franklin hold Justice in one arm.

"I got this! Here you go," he said, with a warm smile, placing the chair next to where Auntie Mabeline sat.

"Aren't you the gentleman," Misty said, noticing a clean-shaven Franklin. "And you clean up well."

They both smiled.

"So, Miss Grace, how are you and your beautiful son?" She asked, as she gave Grace a huge hug.

"We're great!" Grace said.

"I haven't seen you in . . . what . . . six months?" Misty said, thinking, as she sat in the chair that Franklin bought over. "Yeah . . . the last time I saw you was at your mother's funeral."

"Yeah, that's right!" Grace said.

"Grace, he's gorgeous!" Misty said, admiring Justice.

"Thank you," Grace said.

"What did you name him?" Misty asked.

"His name is Justice."

"Oh ok . . . that's nice but different," Misty said.

"How much did he weigh?" She asked.

"Six pounds and four ounces," Franklin and Auntie Mabeline said in unison.

They all laughed.

"Now he's seven pounds. He grew since I've been breastfeeding," she said.

"Oh good. Some babies lose weight after birth. You have some good breast milk!" Misty said, smiling.

"Okay, TMI," Franklin said. The ladies laughed.

"Is he asleep?" Misty said, peeking over at Justice.

"Yes, Uncle Franklin rocked him to sleep," she said.

"Okay. I'll hold him when he wakes up. I don't want to spoil him," Misty said. "Open your gifts, Grace! You know I can't go nowhere empty handed."

"Look at you! A pro already," Misty said, observing how confident Franklin was holding his nephew.

"Let's see how much he's a pro once he has to change a pamper!" Auntie Mabeline said. They all laughed.

"Misty, this is wrapped so nice," Grace said, admiring each box wrapped in multicolor metallic wrapping paper with baby pampers splattered all over it and a large baby blue metallic bow.

"Aww, thanks," Misty said.

Grace ripped open the smaller box.

"Oh, Misty these are so cute!" She said, showing the silk christening shoes to everyone.

"I knew that you'd be getting him dedicated soon, now you don't have to worry about shoes."

Grace ripped open the larger box. She pulled out the

four-piece silk christening outfit.

"Oh, my gosh! I love it!" she exclaimed. "Thank you so much!"

"You are so welcome," Misty said.

"I haven't decided when I'll get Justice dedicated yet," she said.

"Well, you better do it before he gets in first grade. I see some parents wait so late to dedicate their kids . . . the kids 'bout near as big as the momma and daddy," Auntie Mabeline said. They all laughed.

"Well, most people do it before the child is one," Misty said.

"I'll call Pastor Fallback's secretary in a month or so and see when he's available. I definitely don't want him to outgrow this outfit," she said, admiring the silk outfit.

"I got size 1 to 3 months, so it should fit him with no problem, when you're ready," Misty said.

"That's really nice of you, Misty," Franklin said. "Grace mentioned that you were there for her when she found out that she was pregnant. I can't thank you enough for being there for Grace when she needed support." Misty looked relieved.

"Oh, don't mention it," she said. "Grace is like my little sister. I had told Auntie Mabeline, I hope that you all are not mad at me for keeping her secret, but I wanted Grace to know that she could trust me," she said, looking over at Grace smiling.

"Thanks, Misty," Grace said. "I know that I never said this to you, but you're like the older sister that I wish I had."

"Well, you already got one . . . Anna Mae," Auntie Mabeline said, snidely.

"Oh, that's so sweet," Misty said, ignoring Auntie Mabeline.

"I wish that Anna Mae and I had the same type of relationship," Grace said, somberly.

"Well, I hate to say it, but sometimes it takes a tragedy like this for people to wake up and realize that life is simply too short. I wish I had sisters," Misty said, chuckling.

"Well, you can look at us as your family," Franklin said. "We all appreciate you," he paused. "And about what I said earlier, just forget that I said that. I said it out of anger."

"O-kay," Misty said.

"Have you thought about godparents yet?"

"I have two people in mind, but I'm gonna wait," she said, looking up at Franklin, remembering that he suggested Misty, as the god-mother.

"Well, that's something that you really want to think

about and make the right decision for you and your son. You don't want to pick just any ole' body. You want someone who is going to look out for his best interest as you would," Misty said.

"Yeah, you're right," Grace said.

"Ms. Mabeline, did you get a chance to speak to Anna Mae's doctor?" Misty asked.

"Yeah, I sure did. They still have her sedated and are giving her pain meds. She'll have a long road ahead, but I'm gonna see if we can get some help taking care of her," she said.

"Yes, you'll need it. Plus, who knows when her husband will get out of jail," Misty said.

"Well, he can thank David for that!" Franklin said, sounding abrasive.

"Grace's nurse said that she can come by the house and help us out," Auntie Mabeline blurted out.

"Macie?" Grace asked, with excitement.

"No, that other one, who took your baby out the nursery," Auntie Mabeline said.

"Oh, Sharmaine. She's actually nice, auntie. She came in earlier and was telling me different things to do once I get home for me and Justice. She apologized again for taking Justice, but she said that she was only trying to help," Grace said.

"Well, she told me that she can help us out after Anna Mae gets home," Auntie Mabeline said. "But I told her that I had to discuss it with you and Franklin. We have to face the facts . . . she can't go back to her apartment by herself, unless one of ya'll move in with her." Franklin and Grace looked at each other, pointing the finger at each other.

"I have to meet this nurse first," Franklin said.

"I spoke to her earlier before I came in here, so, she must still be here somewhere," Auntie Mabeline said.

"That would be great if you can get her to come a few days out of the week and give you all a break. I wish I had a family like ya'll," Misty said, sounding somber. "You really pull together during tough times."

"You're the only child, right?" Franklin asked, knowing the answer already, after his and Grace's discovery.

"Yes and no. I'm my adopted mother's only child but she told me that my birthparents may have other kids. She mentioned that once I turned 18, she didn't care if I looked for my birth mother. In fact, she encouraged me to."

"Aren't you over 18? I thought you were older than Grace," he asked, knowing the answer. Misty chuckled.

"Yes, I am. I'm 21. I'm the same age as David."

"Don't even bring his name up to me," Grace said, rolling her eyes.

"Have you started looking for your family?" Franklin

asked.

"Boy, stop asking the girl 20 questions," Auntie Mabeline interjected.

"No, it's okay. I don't mind talking about it. While we were at the courthouse, I mentioned it to your auntie, that I wanted to find my family. Ms. Mabeline was nice enough to give me the number of a genealogist that she knows," Misty said, looking over at Auntie Mabeline. "You gave me the number but I didn't catch the name?"

"Oh, child, her name is Bessie," Auntie Mabeline said.

"That's your church friend, right?" Grace asked.

"Yeah, the one I mentioned the other day," Auntie Mabeline said.

"Oh wow! That's cool," Franklin said.

"Yeah, I'm so excited! I can't wait to call her. I hope she can give me some good news! Since my birth mother had me here . . . actually, at this very hospital, I am hoping that it doesn't take long for me to find out. I just want to see who I look like and to meet my siblings, that's if I have any out there. I wonder if they are like me . . . successful and all."

"What if they're crazy!" Grace blurted out!

"GRACIE! WATCH YOUR MOUTH!" Auntie Mabeline said.

"Well, we wish you the best of luck with that," Franklin said. "I hope you're not disappointed. You know . . . you're such a good person."

Grace looked at Franklin keenly.

"I know, right! I think I'll embrace all of them. As we know, there's fruits and nuts in every family," Misty giggled. "Except mine, since I'm an only child. Well at least until I find out my results. You know me, I'm drama-free."

"Good luck!" Franklin said. "Keep us posted!"

"Grace, remember that conversation we had when your mom was going to help me look for my biological family?" Misty asked.

"Yeah . . . I remember," Grace said reluctantly.

"Well, I have the next best woman! Your Auntie said that she would be there with me when I read the results!" Misty said, reaching out for Auntie Mabeline's hand, taking Franklin and Grace by surprise.

"Right, Ms. Mabeline?" Misty questioned.

"Child, I say so much stuff, but if I said that, I guess, yeah, I'll support you," Auntie Mabeline said, with a side of a foot in her mouth.

Grace and Franklin looked as if they swallowed the canary AND the cage! Misty directed her attention to Franklin.

"Franklin, what did you think about what that cop said? The one who gave us his business card. What's his name?" She said thinking. "Oh, yeah, Officer Collins. The one who is working on the case of your murdered neighbor."

Auntie Mabeline, Franklin, and Grace tried to act as normal as possible after hearing that Grace had an encounter with the murdered neighbor.

"Oh, I haven't really . . . ," Franklin said, before a calculated Grace cut him off, diverting the conversation from the woman who saved her to Justice.

"Misty, do you want to hold Justice before I bring him back to the nursery?" She asked.

"Isn't he still asleep?" She asked, looking puzzled.

"If ya'll continue to keep holding that baby while he sleeps, he's going to grow up to be a spoiled brat!" Auntie Mabeline said.

"Oh, it's okay," Grace said.

"Well, I guess . . . yeah," Misty said, looking puzzled.

"Can you please wash your hands first?" Grace asked politely.

"Of course," Misty said, walking over to the sink.

Franklin looked at Grace, taking a sigh of relief.

Auntie Mabeline didn't make eye contact with either

one. Their attention turned toward the voices coming from the hallway.

Sharmaine rushed into the room.

"I'm so sorry to interrupt, but Ms. Mabeline, I thought you may have left already. I'm so glad I caught you!" Sharmaine said.

"What happened? Is Anna Mae okay?" She asked.

"Yes, she is. One of the nurses who works for Dr. Flint called up looking for you. He needs to meet with you again." Sharmaine said, looking worried.

"What happened?" Franklin asked.

"Are you one of her nurses?" Franklin asked.

"No, she's mine," Grace responded.

"Sharmaine, this is my brother Franklin and Misty. She's a friend of the family," Grace said quickly.

"Oh, hi! Nice to meet you both," Sharmaine said. Franklin was struck by Sharmaine's beauty. Auntie Mabeline wrestled out of the chair, attempting to stand up.

"What is going on? My heart can't take this," she said. They all gazed at Sharmaine.

"I was told that you are your niece's proxy. Her nurse called up here and said they needed to talk to you. I'm not supposed to tell you this but Anna Mae needs blood. They have no more of her blood type, which is O positive," she said.

"Proxy? I didn't know that!" Franklin said, looking at Auntie Mabeline as he handed Justice back to Grace.

"Well, it's not like I had time to ask you," she said, looking at Franklin.

"Her nurse said that they only need a pint," Sharmaine said.

"I'm B positive," he said.

"It ain't like I go around checking my blood type," Auntie Mabeline said.

"Well, can they test her?" Misty said, pointing to Ms. Mabeline.

"Child, what do I look like, a guinea pig?" Auntie Mabeline said. "I was starting to like you!"

"I'm sorry to volunteer you, Ms. Mabeline, but if I can save a life, I'm going to do it," Misty said.

"Well, it's to save your niece's life," Sharmaine said. "The ABO test is pretty quick. They'll just need a sample. If you are a match, they'll need you to come back for the procedure."

"What about me?" Grace asked. Everyone had a surprised look on their face as they turned their attention to Grace.

"Don't you think you've been through enough?" Auntie Mabeline asked.

"Well, if Anna Mae needs blood to live, I don't mind giving it to her," she said to Sharmaine. "Since we're sisters, chances are we may share the same blood type."

"Just because we're siblings, don't mean we have the same blood type. I don't know about this Grace," Franklin said, looking over at Sharmaine. "Can she give blood, seeing that she just gave birth?"

"Technically she can. Doctors like to wait at least six weeks, but we can always ask Dr. Freelance."

"Well, let's hold off on that for right now. I guess you can start with me first!" Auntie Mabeline said, reluctantly. "Lord help me!"

"The test takes less than five minutes to check to see if you're a candidate. I can walk you down to where Anna Mae's nurses are. They can guide you from there," Sharmaine said.

"Okay," Auntie Mabeline said.

"I'll go with you," Misty said, feeling bad.

CHAPTER 62

A quietness fell on the room, as Grace and Franklin waited patiently for Auntie Mabeline and Misty to return. Franklin sat in the chair, dozing in and out of sleep.

"Grace, do you mind if I step out to go talk to Leroy?" Franklin asked, stretching his arms in the air as he yawned.

"Who's that?" Grace asked.

"He's the security guard who was on duty when the shooting occurred. We saw him earlier at court. I want to know what he found out about Rufus' case. Auntie Mabeline didn't want to stick around for it. She said, he ain't no kin to me," Franklin mocked his aunt, in a high-pitched voice.

"Oh. You should ask him if he heard anything else," she said, referring to David.

"Yeah, I'll ask," Franklin said, reading between the lines.

"If they let him out, I don't know what I'm going to do," Grace said.

"I think the only option that we have is to go to the police. Although, it's not what I really want to do," he said.

"It's the only way to keep him behind bars, so he can't do this to anyone else," Grace said.

Grace noticed that Franklin looked hesitant to say something.

"What? I can tell you want to say something," she said. "Just say it."

"Well . . . I'm not trying to upset you, but are you sure it was David?" He asked.

"YES! I'M NOT LYING!" She yelled.

"Grace . . . Shhhh! Keep it down! I'm just saying, could it have been someone else? The more I think about this, I don't know . . . Auntie Mabeline may be right. Is David capable of doing something so heinous? Just think about how scary he was growing up."

Grace looked mad.

"You can say that, because he didn't bully you growing up! Besides, who else could it be?" She asked.

"Maybe Big Tuna ? I don't know," he said.

Grace sat in the bed thinking back to the day she and Old Man Joe came back from Fifi's Finger Lickin' Fried Chicken, and she noticed that Big Tuna had on Timberlands, similar to the perpetrator. She wondered, could she be wrong?

"Was Big Tuna in jail when this happened to you?" Franklin asked.

"No . . . he was out. I remember when I came home from

the hospital. David was being so disrespectful, blasting music in Momma's house, that I went out on the front porch to get some air. I remember hearing him talking to a female. I just heard her laughing," she said.

"Well, that dude hangs out with a cast of characters from what Momma told me, so no telling who it was he was taking to," Franklin said.

"I remember him saying something about he was gonna get him some tonight," she said.

"WHAT?" Franklin yelled, jumping up to his feet. "THAT DUDE IS LUCKY HE'S IN JAIL, OR ELSE!"

"Franklin, you're gonna wake up Justice. Please lower your voice," Grace cut him off in a whisper.

"I don't know . . . I hate to go to the cops, but in the same token, as your brother, I have to do what I couldn't do before," he said.

"What?" Grace asked.

"Protect you!"

"I want David to rot in hell if he did this to you, but in the same token, even if he's not our brother, I can't send an innocent man to prison for a crime that he didn't commit. I wouldn't be able to live with myself," he said. "In spite of everything we hear about how some cops view us black men, I just can't stay silent. I'll call that cop to see if he can help us. Hopefully he's not crooked."

"But what about the stuff in the safe that we found?" Grace asked.

"Well, since Momma is not here to answer our questions, I think we should lay it all out and see if Auntie Mabeline can shed any light on any of it. I just find it odd that she didn't know none of this," he said.

"I know. I asked her and she said Momma never told her. I find that odd too," Grace said.

"I mean, she has to know something. She was very close to Momma. So maybe she'll be able to make sense out of what we are still puzzled about," Franklin said.

Graced looked deep in thought.

"Yeah . . . maybe. I wonder if she knew Ms. Purlie, Momma's best friend. I mean, she had to. She lived here for several years before moving to Savannah. Unless she lived her life under a rock! She has to know her. Momma was around Ms. Purlie all the time. Come on now, she had to have met her at least once. She grew up here. I know she didn't block that much out," she said.

"Momma used to share a lot of stories with me about them growing up, but I don't recall her going into detail about them as young girls. You're right though, she used to mention Ms. Purlie a lot," Franklin said.

"Yeah, up until the day that Ms. Purlie called. Whatever she said got Momma hot as fire. I wondered what Ms. Purlie did? Yeah, dropping your kid off on someone's doorstep would make anyone go off, but that was years ago," Grace said. "But Momma wasn't forgiving or forgetting!"

"Please, you try and drop Justice off and run off. I will come find you," Franklin said.

They both laughed.

"The only way to find out more is to ask Auntie Mabeline," Grace said.

"Wait . . . Ms. Purlie met Old Man Joe around the same time Momma did," Franklin said.

"Yup! I wonder if she had kids by him?" Grace asked.

"It wouldn't surprise me. I don't know if it's a good idea to let Auntie Mabeline know of our plans to reach out to her," Franklin said.

"Why not?" Grace said.

"Well . . . she's been spending a lot of time with Old Man Joe. Now, I love Auntie Mabeline ... but she is a little on the jealous side," Franklin said.

"Hmmmm .... maybe you're right. Or .... we could talk to Old Man Joe," Grace said.

"Okay, now you got jokes," Franklin said, as they both laughed.

"Ya'll are underestimating Old Man Joe," Grace said.

"How so?" He asked. "He is not the same man that

he used to be when he was in his 60s, when I helped him around the house. Besides, you all have mentioned how absent minded he is. You see how he kicks that son out, then forgets, and lets him back in! I don't need to talk to him. Besides, he doesn't even remember that I was the one who helped him out all those years, before Big Tuna came to live with him."

"I used to think that, too, but I don't think Old Man Joe is as senile as we think!" Grace said.

"Why do you say that?" Franklin asked.

"He came to see me the other day." Grace said.

"What? Really?" He questioned.

"Yeah. The day that I went into labor, he called Auntie Mabeline that evening and told her how he heard a lot of noise above his head. Apparently, we had interrupted his nap, which he'd started in his bedroom. He said it was too noisy, so he went into the living room. That's when he heard more noise coming from the hallway, and he cracked his door open and saw the EMT's taking me out. But he told Auntie Mabeline that they were taking me to the crazy house," Grace said.

Franklin laughed.

"Really?" Franklin said.

"Yup," Grace responded.

"I know Anna Mae told me that she'd called her, but

she didn't leave a message. She couldn't," he said.

"Auntie Mabeline saw the missed calls and called the number back and got Rufus," Grace said.

"Rufus?" Franklin said, pondering. "Oh! Anna Mae was looking for her phone but couldn't find it. She must've left it in the car. I remember seeing a phone on the floor after the shooting. It must've been hers. The case was hot pink and I can't see Rufus walking around with that!"

"Yes, that's what Rufus told Auntie Mabeline, but at least Old Man Joe had sense enough to call her and tell her that something seemed off. I told them the noise was likely when you dragged the safe," she said.

"Well, if he's nosy like that, why didn't he hear or see something the night that you were assaulted? Oh, maybe because it could have been his son!" Franklin said, intentionally answering his own question. "So, we're back at square one. It could be David based on what we found out, or it could be Big Tuna ."

"Maybe we should talk to Old Man Joe," Grace said.

"I think we're better off sticking to our original plan," he said. "Let's start with Auntie Mabeline. We'll show her the things we found. Find out what she knows. Then you and I can try to contact Ms. Purlie and see what she knows," he said.

"Then go to that cop," Grace added.

Franklin reached into his wallet pulling out the card that the officer gave him.

"Officer Collins," he said, looking down at the business card.

"I think that's our best bet before we even think about going to the police. The fact that David is not out of jail leads me to believe they had enough evidence to hold him," he said. "So, don't worry about that."

Grace looked down at her son, who was fast asleep. "I simply want justice."

"Me, too," he said, standing up. "I'm gonna go track down Leroy to see what he found out at court, after we left."

"Okay," Grace said.

Franklin and Grace could hear Auntie Mabeline and Misty talking.

"They're on their way back. Don't say a word about what we just discussed," Franklin said, in a low tone. "Let me handle it."

"Okay," Grace said.

Auntie Mabeline and Misty walked back into the room looking somber; their expression spoke louder than words.

"So, what happened?" Franklin asked.

"She's no match!" Misty said blurting it out.

Chapter 63

Well, Auntie, you tried, and I'm sure Anna Mae will appreciate that." Franklin said. "Is she still sedated?"

"Yes," Auntie Mabeline said, looking weighed down with worry.

"We visited her after your aunt's blood test. Poor thing. She has all these tubes coming out of her. I felt so bad that I asked the nurse to check my blood type, but I wasn't a match either," Misty said.

"That was nice of you, Misty," Grace said.

"Yeah, you didn't have to do that," Franklin said.

"I know. I felt bad volunteering Ms. Mabeline," she said.

"You should feel bad! Just don't do it again," Auntie Mabeline said, looking at her intensely. "But at any rate, there is a glimmer of hope."

"What's that?" Franklin and Grace said in sync.

Auntie Mabeline looked at Grace.

"I told Anna Mae's nurses that you were willing to donate blood, but you'd just given birth," Auntie Mabeline said. "She said that your doctor would have your blood type on file. If you are O positive, they can set up an appointment and have you come back."

"That girl Sharmaine, sounded as if Anna Mae needed blood, like now," Franklin added.

"I don't know about that child coming to help us. She would drive my blood pressure through the roof. With her ole, worrisome self!" Auntie Mabeline said. "But Anna Mae's nurse said that they could get by with the blood they have in the bank until Grace can come back."

"Well, Sharmaine is not Anna Mae's nurse, and she was only trying to get her help as soon as possible. I wouldn't blame her. If giving blood is going to help Anna Mae, I'll do it," Grace said, without hesitation.

"That is odd that nurse Sharmaine didn't tell us that before they poked you?" Franklin said.

"We saw her at the desk just a few minutes ago, and Ms. Mabeline laid her out. She reminded me of myself," Misty giggled.

"You?" Grace asked.

"Oh yes. Don't let my classiness fool you. Girl, please, I will set it off in a minute. Ask Dalia. She knows," Misty said.

"Yes, that's true," Grace said, remembering back to the day, when Dalia and Vonda's behavior changed as soon as Misty went to the store with Anna Mae. "They only cut up when you're not around."

"Uh, huh," Misty said.

"I'll be back," Franklin said, walking to the door.

"Where are you off too? To get us something to eat, I hope. I'm past hungry. I'm hangry, and I don't want none of this nasty hospital food," Auntie Mabeline said.

They all laughed.

"It's really not that bad," Grace said.

Auntie Mabeline smirked.

"I was going downstairs to see Leroy," Franklin said. "But I can bring you some food first. What do you want?"

"I want a fish sandwich from McDonalds with extra tartar sauce," Auntie Mabeline said.

"Can you get me a Big Mac?" Grace asked.

"Woah! Since when did you start eating Big Macs?" Franklin asked.

"You'll be wearing elastic waist pants at 19 like me, keep on," Auntie Mabeline said, lifting up her shirt, revealing her stretch marks. "You see this?" She asked. "This is what happens when your eyes are bigger than your stomach. You see all them ribs, cornbread, potato salad, and lemon pound cakes, I've eaten through the years."

Grace, Misty, and Franklin looked at her stomach.

"Auntie, you look good. I just see southern comfort," Franklin joked.

"Get out of here," Auntie Mabeline said, pretending to throw her pocketbook toward Franklin.

They all laughed.

"Every time I go to the doctor, he talks about putting me on some other kind of medicine. I told him I'm already taking medicine for my arthritis and my hypertension. I ain't taking another pill for nothing else!" Auntie Mabeline exclaimed.

"Okay, do you still want the fish sandwich," Franklin said, looking at Auntie Mabeline, as he pulled out his phone.

"Yes, I do! I am still going to eat it," Auntie Mabeline said.

"I'll get what she's having!" Grace said.

"All that sodium is not good for you," Misty said.

"Child, we're all gonna die from something." She looked Misty up and down. "You look like you could benefit from some fries and a shake yourself."

Misty laughed. "I'm not judging you, Ms. Mabeline, I'm guilty too . . . but I eat junk food in moderation. If you know you have hypertension, you should reduce your salt intake."

Auntie Mabeline looked at Misty sideways.

"Okay … anything else?" Franklin asked, looking at

both Auntie Mabeline and Grace.

"Can you get me a hot fudge sundae?" Grace asked.

"Is that it?" He asked.

"Oh, and nuts. That's it for me!" Grace exclaimed.

"Nothing more for me," Auntie Mabeline said.

"Misty, can I get you something?" He asked.

"No, thanks. I'm about to leave. I'm going to make a salad and lemon pepper salmon when I get home," she said.

"That's sounds so delicious," Auntie Mabeline said, facetiously.

"Call me if you need me," Franklin said.

"I guess I'll walk out with Franklin. I have an eight o'clock client coming in the morning." she said, walking over to hug Auntie Mabeline.

Auntie Mabeline reluctantly hugged Misty back.

Misty walked over to the side of the bed. She leaned down and kissed Justice on his forehead before hugging Grace.

"Nice to meet you, my little nephew," she said jokingly. "When are you going home Grace?"

"I'm hoping tomorrow. I'm waiting for Dr. Freelance to come back in," Grace said. "I hope I can finish my counseling with Trevor at home."

"Oh, Trevor … He's Dalia's cousin, right?" Misty said.

"Yeah," Grace said. "Do you know him?"

"No, but she talks about him all the time. I guess he's pretty popular. You're lucky to have gotten him. Dalia said there's a long waiting list of people waiting for him."

"Oh, wow!" Grace said.

Misty looked at Franklin. "Do you know that she has a crush on you?" She smiled.

"She sure does," Grace chimed in, smirking.

"I heard," Franklin said. "Anna Mae told me. She's too young for me!"

"And immature!" Misty added.

"Probably so. I'm going to see if Leroy is working. I'm curious to see what happened at court, after we left," he said, eager to end the conversation.

"Have you all thought about what you plan to do if he is not out by the time Anna Mae is discharged? She obviously can't go home solo," she asked, looking around at the three of them.

"We'll have to take her home with us. We have no other choice," Franklin added.

"That's for sure," Auntie Mabeline said.

"With an injury like hers … most definitely. Thank God she has all of you," Misty added.

"Yeah," Franklin said.

"Okay, I'll be back with your food," he said as he and Misty exited the room. "Bye ya'll!" Misty exclaimed.

CHAPTER 64

Who do we have here?" Dr. Freelance said, entering the room as Auntie Mabeline and Grace were eating the food that Franklin bought, before going back to catch up with Leroy.

"Hi, Dr. Freelance," Grace said, with a mouthful, attempting to hide her hot fudge sundae behind the boxed gifts that Misty bought. "This is my Auntie Mabeline. She's from Georgia."

"How are you doing young lady," he said, shaking Auntie Mabeline's hand.

"Hello," she said. "Has anyone ever told you that you look like that singer, Lionel Ritchie?" She asked.

Dr. Freelance laughed.

"Yes, I get that all the time," he said.

"Uh huh. Ya'll could pass for brothers. So, when can Grace go home?" She asked, abruptly.

"That's what I came in to discuss," he said, looking at Grace. "Grace, is it okay to talk in front of your aunt?"

Auntie Mabeline cut her eyes at him.

"Oh yes, it's fine," she said.

"Well, I touched bas with Mr. Cooper. He told me that

your preliminary meeting went well. He would like to set up 12 meetings with you."

"So, I have to stay here?" She asked.

"No, no. He initially wanted to meet with you before you went home, but he's fine with resuming your meetings after you get home," he said.

"That's great!" Auntie Mabeline chimed in.

"Oh, okay," she said.

"I checked with the nurses, and they told me that you had Justice pretty much all day with you," he said.

"Yes. I bought him back to the nursery not long ago. I feel more comfortable now," she said.

"Good. We're satisfied that you know how to care for Justice after you get home, and that you have support at home, if needed," he said, looking at Auntie Mabeline. "Do you have any questions before you leave us?" He asked.

"No. Macie and Sharmaine told me everything that I should expect," she said.

"Good," he replied.

"So, with that being said, I am going to have the nurses get your discharge paperwork together, so you can get out of here tomorrow," he said. "My office secretary will get in contact with you to schedule Justice's first appointment. Remember what I told you, that you don't have to remember Justice's vaccination schedule all by yourself. We will be there with you, every step of the way. Okay?" He said.

"Yes!" Grace said, her mind going back to Trevor.

"So, how do I get in contact with Mr. Cooper?" She asked.

"Don't worry. His contact information will be in your discharge packet," he said.

"Okay," she said.

"Well, young lady, if you have no other questions for me, I will see you soon," he said.

"Actually, I do," Grace said.

"My sister Anna Mae needs a blood transfusion. Will I be able to give her some blood?" She asked.

"The rule of thumb is anyone over the age of 16 who is healthy, and preferably one who eats healthy, can give blood," he said, looking down at the hot fudge sundae.

He continued.

"For patients like yourself, who just gave birth, we approve blood donations after the baby is six-weeks old. Let's talk about it when you come into the office in a few weeks."

"That's good," Auntie Mabeline said.

"You can continue to breastfeed after," he said.

"Okay," Grace said.

"Is there anything else?" He asked.

"No. I can't think of anything else," Grace said.

"If you do, please call my office. Tomorrow is my day off. I'll see you next at Justice's first appointment," he said.

"Okay, thank you Dr. Freelance," Grace said.

He smiled.

Dr. Freelance looked at Auntie Mabeline.

"It was nice to meet you," he said.

"You too, Lionel," she said jokingly. "Take care."

Dr. Freelance walked out of the room.

Grace had a serious look on her face.

"What now Gracie," Auntie Mabeline said.

"I don't even have a car seat or anything to dress Justice in!" she exclaimed.

"Well, they definitely won't allow you to bring him home without it!" Auntie Mabeline said. "Call Franklin. We're gonna have to go pick up one!"

"And a newborn outfit!" Grace added.

CHAPTER 65

The elevator opened into the emergency room area. Franklin observed Diamond checking in a patient at the front desk. Diamond looked up, noticing Franklin. She quickly rushed the patient through the check in process before directing her to sit in the waiting area.

"Hey, Franklin!" she said, waving him over. "I'm glad that you're out of jail," she said, loudly.

Franklin looked around at those in earshot, as he whispered, "Yeah, remember I said I didn't do it."

"I know, I saw it on TV. I was on there too!" she exclaimed.

"For what?" Franklin asked.

"After the shooting, the local news reporter came in and asked if I wanted to be interviewed about the shooting. My boss said I could, as long as I stood outside and didn't throw any of them under the bus."

"What did you tell them?" Franklin said, inquisitively.

"I just told them that I knew all of you, except Anna Mae's husband, and that you came from a good home. I told them how Ms. Leola was like a mother to all of the kids she knew, and how she treated us like her own, and she would be shocked to see ya'll caught up in something like this!" Diamond said, not mincing her words. "The reporter asked me how was Anna Mae doing. I was like, good question, I can't really speak on that, but I heard through the grapevine that she survived the gunshot wound!"

Franklin looked at Diamond visibly annoyed.

"Oh, and I told them how I helped save her life by pointing to where she was on the floor when the doctor and nurses arrived on the scene," Diamond said.

Franklin didn't want to hear anymore of Diamond's five minute of fame.

"Have you seen Leroy?" Franklin asked.

"Yes. He's down there," she said pointing to the end of the emergency room sitting area. "They changed his post, after the shooting. He got written up for falling asleep on the job. So, they have a more alert security officer at the entrance, and they changed his post. He's at the far end, so they can watch him on the security camera."

"Thanks," Franklin said, walking in the direction of where Leroy sat, which is the same location of where the shooting happened.

Franklin could see Leroy dozing off to sleep in the distance, as he sat in the chair, slowly leaning to the left. Franklin did a slow trot towards Leroy, narrowly saving his head from slamming against the wall.

"Hey Leroy!" He yelled.

Leroy nearly jumped off the chair.

"Oh shoot! You scared me! I was watching my eyelids! I wasn't asleep!" Leroy blurted out, surprised to see Franklin.

"Hey man! It's you. I thought you were someone that worked here. You know, they got me on their radar after that incident happened. They tried to fire me, but I threatened them with IDA."

"Who's IDA?" Franklin asked.

"You know, that law that says they can't discriminate against me for my age," Leroy said.

"Oh, you mean the A-D-E-A," Franklin said. "The Age Discrimination in Employment Act."

"Uh huh," Leroy said.

"So, what happened in court after we left?" Franklin asked.

"Oh yeah, I stayed there practically all day. The lawyer told me that I didn't have to testify, since they saw everything on the surveillance," Leroy said.

"Good ... but did they call the other case?" Franklin asked, inquisitively.

"Oh yes. They called him up. He ain't getting out no time soon."

Franklin was puzzled, thinking that Leroy got David

and Rufus mixed up.

"What did he look like?" Franklin asked.

"He was about my height, with short wavy hair but he didn't have no belly like me," he said.

"Did they say his name was Rufus?" Franklin asked.

"Yeah, yeah, that's what they said, uh huh," Leroy said. "A buddy of mine got the same name."

"So, why are they holding him?" Franklin said.

"He had a warrant out for his arrest. So, he ain't going nowhere soon," Leroy said.

"Did they say what the warrant was for?" Franklin asked.

"I dozed off. When I woke up, they had a woman up there who got arrested for stealing a bar of soap out of the dollar store 'around the corner there, near the carwash. The stench in the court room woke me right up!" Leroy said.

"Did they say anything else about the other dude?" Franklin asked.

"Oh, your brother?" Leroy asked.

"Whatever," Franklin said. "Yeah, him."

"No. They didn't mention anything else about him … that I can remember," he said.

Franklin looked puzzled. He wondered what on earth could Rufus have done to have a warrant out for his arrest. He wondered if Anna Mae knew this.

"Okay, man. Well, I appreciate the update," Franklin said, as he walked toward the elevator, deep in thought.

"Hey," Leroy called out.

"How long is your Auntie gonna be in town for?" He asked. Franklin looked at him strangely.

"I'm not sure," he said. "Why?"

"Well, tell her, I would love to take her out to dinner. We can go over there to the wharf and get us a fish sandwich or something," he said, flashing his crooked smile. "I would love to catch up on old times."

"Okay, I'll tell her," Franklin said. The elevator door opened right on time.

Franklin took a detour and got off on the third floor. He proceeded to the busy nurse's station.

"Hi, I wanted to see if I could see Anna Mae Payne," he said.

"Are you her husband?" the middle aged nurse asked.

"No, I'm her older brother," he responded.

"Oh, okay. Silly me . . . I shouldn't have assumed," the nurse chuckled, placing her hand over her heart.

"I met your aunt earier. Boy, was she disappointed that she did not share the same blood type as your sister. She mentioned that there may be another family memer who may be a match. Did you come to get checked?" She asked, as she buzzed Franklin in.

"No. My sister's blook type is O positive. My blood type is B positive. I'm definetely not a match!"

"You're right about that! You can only donate blood to a person who is B positive like yourself or AB positive," the nurse said.

"My younger sister wants to check with her doctor to see if she can donate."

"Well, anyone who wishes to give blood, should consult with their physician first."

"Understood," Franklin said. "We got some good news after your aunt left."

"What's that?" Franklin asked.

"There's enough blood in the bank, in the event that she needs a blood transfusion, to buy us some time until we can get blood from a matching family member or a donor," the nurse said.

"Yeah, my aunt shared that. Okay, good to know," Franklin said.

"I can take you to go see your sister. I'm sure your aunt told you that she's heavily sedated because of the pain," she said.

"Yes, she did. Is this similar to being in a drug induced coma?" He asked.

"Not exactly," the nurse said. "I don't mean to be so blunt, but if she had gotten shot in the head, but thank God she didn't, then we would have placed her in a drug induced coma to reduce the swelling of the brain.

"Our intent is to get the swelling in her belly to go down; therefore, we want to reduce her pain as much as possible. We are also monitoring her to make sure that infection does not set in. She'll be on a few antibiotics after she goes home."

The nurse stopped at the door, looking at Franklin with sympathy.

"I just want to warn you that your sister has a lot of tubes going every which way. I don't want you to be alarmed. Your aunt was a bit shook up when she saw her."

"Will she be able to hear me?" He asked.

"Yes, she can hear you, but she cannot respond. Do not say anything that is going to upset her," she said.

"Okay," Franklin said.

"We have to watch her closely on the monitor at the nurse's station for any changes, so we'll know," she said.

"Okay. I got it," Franklin said.

"I just hate that this happened to her," he said, sounding somber. "I wish I could have stopped the bullet."

"Oh? You were the one in the emergency room with her?" She asked.

"Yes," Franklin responded.

"I knew you looked familiar." She said, looking at Franklin closely. "Yes, I saw on the news that you were exonerated! Thank God for ballistic testing, huh?"

"I'm truly grateful," he said looking surprised.

"My husband works in that field. He tells me all the time that the testing has saved a lot of innocent people from wrong convictions," she added.

"I bet," he said.

She paused, placing her hand on the door. "Are you ready?"

"Yes, I guess. As ready as I'm gonna get," Franklin said.

"Oh, and please don't mention the baby," she said. Franklin looked at the nurse. "No worries. I didn't get a chance to tell her that our little sister had a baby," he said.

"I'm referring to her baby," the nurse said.

Franklin's jaw dropped.

"WHAT?" Franklin yelled.

"Your aunt didn't tell you? Your sister was pregnant.

She lost the baby when she was shot in the stomach."

"How many months was she?" He asked.

"By our assessment, she was in her second trimester," she said.

"And that means?" He asked.

"The test revealed she was four months," she said.

The nurse covered her mouth. "Oh my God! You really didn't know?"

"Heck, no!" He replied.

"I'm so sorry," she said.

Franklin placed his hands on his head, wondering why Auntie Mabeline withheld this information from them.

CHAPTER 66

Franklin had sat silently at Anna Mae's bedside for 30 minutes before going back to Grace's room.

He walked into Auntie Mabeline and Grace watching Wheel of Fortune on the television.

"I don't know why they buy a vowel instead guessing one of the other twenty-one letters in the alphabet. I just don't understand it," Auntie Mabeline said, shaking her head, as she spoke to the television.

"Oh, look who the cat dragged in," Grace said, jokingly, before noticing Franklin's serious look.

"What's wrong with you?" Auntie Mabeline asked. "What did Leroy say now? As long as I've known that man, he's always stirring up some foolishness!"

"Well, Leroy shared more than some folks," he said, taking a dig at Auntie Mabeline that went right over her head.

"What did he say?" Grace asked.

"I don't really feel like talking about that right now," he said, before changing the subject. "Did the doctor come to see you?"

"Yes," Grace said with excitement, as she danced in her bed. "He said I can go home tomorrow!"

"Good," Franklin said. "I know you're happy about that, little sis."

"I'm over the moon," she said. "But I was telling Auntie Mabeline that we have a problem."

"What's that," he said, leaning against the wall.

"I don't have a car seat, nor do I have clothes to bring Justice home in."

"What are you talking about? You have something for that baby to wear!" Franklin exclaimed.

"What?" Grace asked.

"That outfit that Misty bought you. He's not going to know the difference," he said.

"Ah, no," Grace said, zoning in on Franklin. "That's for his dedication." She said, rolling her eyes, before looking back at Auntie Mabeline for reinforcement.

"They gonna get stuck one day. Just watch," Auntie Mabeline said.

"So, are you saying that you need me to go get you a car seat?" He asked.

"I don't know what got into you from the time you left, but yes, that's what she's saying," Auntie Mabeline chimed in. "We better get going. It's going on 7:30 now," she said, looking up at the wall clock.

"I tried to call and tell you earlier, but my call didn't go through. It said all circuits are busy," Grace said.

Franklin took out his phone and began scrolling through his call log.

"Oh, I didn't know that. It may have been when I was in the elevator, or when I went to see Anna Mae. There's so much electrical equipment in here, I'm sure there's parts of the hospital where the reception is bad," he said.

"How's Anna Mae doing?" Grace asked.

"There's no real change from what Auntie Mabeline told us," Franklin said, looking at Auntie Mabeline.

"Will she be here for a while?" Grace asked.

"I didn't even ask her nurse, but we did have a long chat about what Anna Mae had gone through," he said, waiting to see if Auntie Mabeline was going to say anything about Anna Mae's pregnancy.

"Well, Dr. Flint told me that they were keeping her for another three weeks, and that she'll have a long road ahead of her," Auntie Mabeline chimed in. "She may need some physical therapy, too."

"What else did Dr. Flint share?" Franklin asked.

"That's mainly it," she said, pondering. "Yeah, I can't think of anything else." Franklin had never doubted Auntie Mabeline before, but he couldn't help but notice that she was not being forthcoming.

"Oh, he did say something else," Auntie Mabeline said.

"What?" Grace asked.

"He said that she will need all of our support because she won't be able to do much of anything once she gets home."

Franklin was starting to have second thoughts about sharing what he and Grace discovered in the safe with Auntie Mabeline. He looked across the room at Grace, who seemed to be getting stronger mentally and physically. He needed to tell her in private that Anna Mae was pregnant. Grace broke his concentration.

"I don't have anything to wear home either," Grace said, sounding like a chatty Kathy. "I don't want to wear what I wore in here. Matter of fact, I am tossing it in the garbage." Franklin interrupted her.

"I can bring you back some clothes in the morning," he said. "Don't worry."

"Thanks, Franklin," she said. "Can you bring my jean dress? It's hanging in my closet, to the left."

"Sure," he said.

He looked at Auntie Mabeline, who was glued to the television.

"Auntie, we better head out, so we can stop and get the car seat," he said.

"Don't forget a cute outfit for Justice," Grace said.

"Oh, can you please pick up a cute matching blanket, too! He got to look stylish on his first debut out into the world!"

"Okay," Franklin said. "Just call me if you think of something else."

"You know I will," Grace said, sounding giddy.

"What time should we come get you?" He asked.

"I don't know. Macie will come and tell me. I'll let you know," she said, finishing her sentence, just as Sharmaine knocked on the door.

"Hey, everyone," Sharmaine said, walking past Franklin.

Auntie Mabeline looked her up and down, not acknowledging her.

"Hi," Franklin said, clearly mesmerized by her beauty, as she sauntered over to the bed with a packet in her hand for Grace.

"Grace, these are your discharge papers. Macie's busy, so she asked me to go over them with you," she said, taking the papers out of the envelope.

"Excuse me," Franklin said, interrupting Sharmaine.

"Yes," she said. "It's Franklin, right?" She asked, looking at Franklin intently.

"Yeah," he said, smiling, impressed that she remembered his name.

"What time should we be here in the morning to pick her up?" He asked.

"You should be here by 8:30 a.m.," responding to Franklin before looking back at Grace. "We will make sure that you're up, so you can breast feed Justice. We'll have him bathed early. While we are bathing Justice, you can get showered. If you need help, just let us know."

"Okay," Grace said.

"Cool, thanks! Is there anything else that I need to know, before I head out?" Franklin asked, looking worn out. "I need to make it to the store and buy this car seat, or else she'll really be here one more day."

"Oh!" Sharmaine said. "I'm glad that you mentioned that. Macie bought one for you!" she said, looking at Grace.

"SHE DID?" Grace said, looking surprised. "Oh my gosh! That's so nice of her. I have to thank her!"

"WOW! That's nice!" Auntie Mabeline said, holding her pocketbook close. "Franklin now you can keep your money in your pocket!"

"But I still need an outfit for Justice," Grace said, directing her comment to Auntie Mabeline.

"No, you don't," Sharmaine said. "I felt so bad about the other day, that I went out and bought a few outfits for him. You can think of it as a peace offering," she said, smiling. "Just don't tell anyone here what Macie and I have done," she whispered. "We don't want people to think that we are playing favorites or we could lose our jobs."

"I won't," Grace said. "Thank you so much Sharmaine. You didn't have to do that."

"Don't mention it. You've kind of grown on me," she looked at Franklin and Auntie Mabeline. "I can tell that you all are a good-loving, close-knit family."

"Yeah, that's how me and their Momma raised them to be, good-loving, close, and honest," Auntie Mabeline chimed in.

Franklin smirked as he looked at Auntie Mabeline.

CHAPTER 67

The day that Grace had been looking forward to had finally come.

She surprised the nurses. She'd woken up on her own at 5 am, showered, and threw on two hospital gowns, making sure that she was fully covered. By 5:30, she'd walked down to the nursery and breastfed Justice, after calling the housed to remind Auntie Mabeline of her change of clothes.

After she fed Justice, she came back to her room and packed her few belongings.

Grace sat in the chair, as she looked out the window, daydreaming. It had been three days since she'd been outside.

"Well, good morning Sunshine," breaking Grace's concentration.

Grace turned her head toward the door.

"Good morning Macie! Oh, before I forget, I have something for you," she said getting up from the chair.

"What's that?" Macie said.

"The earphones that you let me borrow the other day," Grace said.

"Oh, you can keep them. I have three others, just like

it," she said.

"Thank you so much, Macie," Grace said, rushing toward Macie and hugging her. "I'm happy to be going home, but I am really going to miss you and Sharmaine."

"Well, you won't be getting rid of us that quick. We plan to check in on you and Justice from time to time. Sharmaine volunteered to help out with your sister, once she gets home," Macie said.

"Oh yeah, my aunt mentioned that. She seemed a bit skeptical about Sharmaine, but I told her, after she came and spoke to me after taking Justice that day, I feel more comfortable with her now."

"Oh good," Macie said, looking around, noticing Grace's partially packed bag. "So, do you have everything?"

"Well, I didn't come here with much, but I think so," Grace said.

"Sharmaine told me that she ruined the surprise last night," Macie said, referring to the car seat.

"Yeah, my brother was about to leave and go buy one. She happened to come in at the right time," Grace said. "Franklin appreciated that, as much as I did. I really appreciate everything that you both have done for me and Justice."

"You're more than welcome, Grace," Macie said. "Let me go get it and the bag of clothes from Sharmaine."

"I'll come with you, so I can dress Justice and say bye to the neonatal nurses," Grace said.

"We got that covered. Yeah, Sharmaine washed one of the outfits. She gave it to the nurse last night, and they dressed Justice for you already," Macie said.

"Oh, I can't wait to see him," Grace said.

"He looks so cute!" Macie said. "We're going to miss him, just as much as we're going to miss you."

"Don't make me cry," Grace said.

"No crying allowed, remember, you're phoenix rising," Macie said, smiling.

"True, that," Grace said, laughing.

"I called Franklin earlier. He said that he and Auntie Mabeline would be leaving the house around 7:30 to come pick us up," Grace said.

"Okay, when he comes, he can park in the front. We have someone downstairs who checks to ensure that the car seat is installed correctly," Macie said.

"Let me call him back now and tell him," she said.

"Okay, I'll be right back," Macie said, as she exited the room, closing the door. Grace called Franklin and relayed the message.

Macie returned 10 minutes later, carrying the dark blue, grey, and teal car seat.

"Oh, that is so cute!" Grace said. "I love it!"

"Isn't it cute," Macie said. "Now, when Justice falls asleep in the car, his head may slump. Just roll up a cloth diaper, just like this, and place it alongside his body," Macie said, demonstrating.

"Okay," Grace said.

"What time is it?" Macie said, looking at the clock.

"It's 7:15," Grace said.

"Okay, I'm gonna have to run. I have to take care of some things. It's customary that we take you out in a wheelchair, so I have to make sure we have one up here," she said.

"Okay," Grace said.

"Anything else, before I go?" Macie asked.

"No," Grace said. "Oh yeah, I called Franklin, and I gave him the message."

"Okay. Good! Time is moving along. I'm getting sad now," Macie said, pretending to shed a tear.

"Well, you're not going to be able to get rid of me either," Grace said, as she watched Macie walk out, laughing and closing the door behind her.

Grace sat on the side of the bed, looking at herself in the mirror. She reached into the drawer. She picked up the card from the flowers and tossed it in the trash, before reaching for the comb in the plastic bag. She looked at the comb as if it was a foreign object.

"What am I going to do with my hair?" She said, talking to herself.

A knock on the door broke her concentration.

"Come in," she said.

"Hey there, Grace!"

"What are you doing here? I thought you had an eight o'clock client coming?" Grace asked, looking pleasantly surprised to see Misty.

"Well, just as Franklin and I got off the elevator last night, my client called and cancelled. So, I told Franklin that I will surprise you and come back up and do that head of yours, since my next appointment isn't until 10 o'clock," she said. "We cannot have you leaving out looking any kind of way, now can we?" Misty smiled.

"Thank you, Misty," Grace said.

"Now, give me that, and let's see what I have in my bag," she said, taking the plastic comb from Grace and tossing it in the trash. She took out her wide tooth comb and hard thistle brush.

"Hmmmm," she said, looking at Grace's hair, trying to figure out what she was going to do.

"She looked back in her carrying case and pulled out

her flat iron, plugging it up near the foot of the bed.

"Okay, come sit in this chair here, so I can work my magic," she said.

Grace sat in the chair as Misty began to comb the kinks out of her hair. Misty parted Grace's hair in the middle, trimming the dead ends before she began to flat iron it into a cute bob, with a swooping bang.

"Okay, Miss Grace, go look in the mirror," she said, proud of her simple creation.

Grace stood up and walked over to the mirror.

"I love it!" she said, carefully running her fingers through her hair. "It grew a lot!"

"Well, those prenatal pills will do that," Misty said, packing up her hair products and tools, placing them back in her carrying case.

"Let's add a little blush to those cheeks," Misty said, walking over to Grace as she stood primping in the mirror.

"I have my own gloss."

"Okay," Misty said.

Grace and Misty could hear Auntie Mabeline and Franklin outside the door.

"Oh, they're here," she said.

"Yeah, I can hear them talking to the nurse," Misty said,

as she dabbed the last bit of blush, in an upward stroke on Grace's high cheekbones. "Okay, cherry cheekbones for the new mom."

"I love it," Grace said. "I've never worn makeup. Well, only the time after my assault when I used Anna Mae's makeup to cover up my bruises," Grace said.

"You're what? What assault?" Misty exclaimed.

Grace realized that Misty was unaware about her assault or that David was the person who assaulted her. She was not going to allow any talk of David kill her good mood.

"Did I say assault? I meant when I fell flat on my face on the asphalt!" Grace said, interrupting the truth with the lie she told.

"Well, you got to be more careful. We are not going to live in the past. From this day forward, we are going to look toward your bright future, that don't include falling flat on your face," Misty said, sounding optimistic.

Grace smiled. "Thanks for being here for me, Misty."

"Of course,," Misty said.

"I wanted to ask you something," Grace said.

"What's that?" Misty questioned.

"Would you be Justice's godmother?" She asked.

Misty placed her hand over her mouth.

"Oh my God! Me?" She asked.

"Yes, you," Grace said.

"I would be honored too!" Misty said. "Who's the godfather going to be?"

"He doesn't know it yet, but I'm going to ask Franklin. I think you both would be great godparents for my son," Grace said.

"Thank you," Misty said, pulling Grace in for a hug.

"Oh, this feels familiar but different," Grace said, laughing, referring to the day back in the pharmacy.

Auntie Mabeline busted through the door, abruptly closing it behind her.

"Well, good morning," she said, holding Grace's jean dress up, eye level.

"You found it!" she said.

"It wasn't hard," she said.

"Where's Franklin?" She asked.

"He's out there talking to Macie. She's talking to him about the car seat," Auntie Mabeline said.

"Okay," Grace said.

"He'll be in shortly," Auntie Mabeline added.

"Misty, how are you doing today?" She asked.

"I'm fine. You?" Misty asked.

"I'm blessed. Gracie, I love the hair," she said, touching Grace's hair.

"Thanks. Misty surprised me. She just did it," Grace said.

"I thought you had to work?" Auntie Mabeline placed her hands on her hips, still holding onto her attitude from the day before.

"My client cancelled out, so I told Franklin that I would come up and surprise Grace," Misty said.

"Hmmm . . . he didn't mention that," Auntie Mabeline said.

"Auntie because it was a surprise," Grace said. "Well, I'm going into the bathroom to change."

"Yes, it's 7:50, so you have to put a move on it. Your undergarments are on the hanger and the baby's blanket. I was up all night washing that thing," Auntie Mabeline said.

"I appreciate you, Auntie," Grace said smiling, disappearing into the bathroom. Auntie Mabeline and Misty stood in silence, until Franklin knocked on the door.

"Is it safe to come in?" He asked.

"Come on in," Auntie Mabeline said.

Franklin walked in the room, as if he was in a rush.

"Hey Misty. I'm glad you could make it back," he said.

"Me, too," she said.

"Where's Grace?" He asked.

"She's in the bathroom changing into her dress," she said.

"Okay, well, I'm going to go put the car seat in, and I'll be back. Macie said to keep this door closed. She'll be coming in shortly with Justice," he said.

"Why does she have us cooped up in this hot room? What in the world is going on?" Auntie Mabeline said. Franklin ignored her questions as he grabbed the car seat and Grace's bag that she had packed, closing the door behind him, just as Grace came out of the bathroom.

"My dress is so tight," she said, looking sad.

"You're going home, and Macie has the wheelchair out in the hall, so ain't nobody gonna notice that," Auntie Mabeline said.

"You look fine, Grace. Remember, you just had a baby. Don't be so hard on yourself," Misty said.

"Where's Franklin?" She asked. "I thought I just heard him."

"You heard right. He went downstairs to put the car seat in," Auntie Mabeline said. "He took the bag you had on the bed with him."

"Okay," she said.

"Knock, knock," Macie said, as she opened the door, rolling Justice in the bassinet.

"Oh my gosh! He looks so adorable!" Grace exclaimed.

Justice laid asleep in the bassinet, dressed in a little dark blue and white sailor suit with a crisp white hat and little white booties.

Grace started to cry. "I love what Sharmaine picked out for him."

"Gracie, stop that crying. You got a whole lifetime for this boy to make you cry!" Auntie Mabeline said.

"Oh, Grace, I know those are happy tears," Macie said.

"Yes, they are," she said.

Fifteen minutes had gone by when Franklin returned to the room.

"That was fast," Macie said.

"Yeah, the male nurse that you told me about, was already downstairs. He helped me put the car seat in. The car is downstairs in the front," he said. "Let's roll out."

Macie looked at Misty.

"I don't believe that we met," Macie said.

"I'm so sorry," Grace said. "Macie, this is Misty. She's Justice's godmother."

Franklin looked at Grace, closely. He realized Grace changed her mind, after having reservations about David being Misty's brother.

"Who's the godfather?" Macie asked, with enthusiasm.

Grace looked at Franklin. "Well, there's only one person that I would want to be Justice's godfather, and that's you, Franklin."

Franklin looked shocked. "Really, are you sure about that?"

"Yes, I am sure," she said.

"I'd be honored to," he said. "He's going to be playing soccer, baseball, football…"

"Okay, okay, let's not rush it," Grace said, interrupting him.

They all laughed.

"Okay, let me go get the wheelchair," Macie said, returning quickly, closing the door behind her.

"Okay, be careful sitting down," Macie said.

Grace carefully sat in the chair, draping the colorful blanket that Auntie Mabeline bought on her lap.

"Okay, now for Justice's first ride in a wheelchair," she said, picking up Justice and carefully placing him in Grace's arm.

"Mine too!" Grace added.

"Are you ready?" She said, bowing down looking at Grace closely.

"Yes," Grace said, looking around at the room.

"Okay, Miss Grace. I'm going to wheel you to the elevator, and Franklin will take over from there," she said.

"Okay," Grace said.

"Franklin, can you get the door for us," Macie said.

"Sure," Franklin said, walking over to the door.

Just before Franklin opened the door, the music began to play.

"Wait! That's my song," Grace said, with excitement. "Andra Day!"

"Yes, it is, phoenix rising" Macie said, kneeling down next to Grace.

"Grace, during your short stay, you shared a lot with me. You are one of the strongest young ladies that I've ever met. You have taught me so much about self-discovery, perseverance and never giving up, even when you felt that the odds were stacked against you. You came in here one way, and you are leaving out recognizing that your voice counts. We, your many sisters, and Franklin honor you today, and we want you to know that we stand with you, not just today, but forever. We hear you! We see you!"

Macie said. "Not everyone needs to know your story, all they need to know is that you are a survivor with a story to tell."

Franklin opened up the door widely, clearly being in on the secret.

To Grace's amazement, the hospital corridor was lined with women from every part of the hospital. There were nurses, doctors, janitors, and paraprofessionals, who dropped what they were doing to come and join in solidarity with Grace.

"Best of luck to you, Grace," a few said, as Macie slowly pushed her down the hall, with Auntie Mabeline, Misty, and Franklin following closely behind.

"We love you Grace and baby Justice!" one nurse yelled as she rolled by.

Tears fell from Grace's face. She never felt so much love before.

"Keep your head up, my sister," a woman with long flowing locks said.

"Thank you so much," Grace said.

"Best of luck to you, Grace," the doctor with the messy blond bun and blue scrubs said.

"Thank you," Grace said.

"Justice, we love you," one of the neo-natal nurses who

took care of Justice shouted out.

Each of the women reached out, touching, and agreeing with Grace, as Macie slowly wheeled her by down the long corridor. Just as they approached the elevator, Sharmaine stepped out of formation.

"I love you girl," she said, handing Grace a bouquet of pastel-colored flowers. "Now don't go throwing these on the floor!" they both laughed. "See you soon!"

Macie turned Grace around as the woman crowded the long hallway, waiving to Grace. Auntie Mabeline and Misty stood in the elevator, unable to shut off their flowing tears.

"Just beautiful," Auntie Mabeline said. "I wish your Momma was here to see this."

"Good luck, Grace! We'll miss you!" they said in unison.

Grace looked up at Macie, "Thank you so much Macie. You're the best nurse ever!"

Macie held back her tears, as she gave Grace a warm embrace.

Franklin was all choked up, trying his best to hold his emotions in.

"We love you, Grace. Remember, you are never alone. Take care of yourself and Justice. I'll see you soon," she said.

"I love you all, too! Okay, I will. See you soon," Grace said, as Franklin wheeled her into the elevator, clearly moved by the outpouring of support.

Grace continued to wave until the doors closed.

CHAPTER 68

It'd been two weeks since Grace and Justice had been home.

After the emotional surprise departure from the hospital, being home had been a total contrast.

Auntie Mabeline was so hands off when it came to Justice. The few times that Grace had asked for help, she would lash out at Grace and tell her how Justice is her baby and her responsibility. She would tell Grace to "woman up" or tell her to "put on your big girl panties" and "if your Momma could raise four kids by herself, after losing your daddy, then you have no excuse with raising one!"

She'd put in all the vacation and sick days she could. She said she'd stay long enough to help out with Anna Mae until she could get back on her feet, which meant that she would be around until the end of August. Franklin and Grace didn't know why, because Auntie Mabeline spent most of her time downstairs with Old Man Joe. On a few occasions, while Grace was up feeding Justice, Auntie Mabeline would tiptoe past her bedroom door and slide into momma's bed, pretending as if she'd been asleep the entire night. If Grace didn't see her, she heard the funk music coming from Old Man Joe's apartment, and the both of them keeping up a lot of racket. They obviously didn't realize that the floors, just as the walls, were paper-thin.

Franklin had become a recluse. He was spending most of his time alone. He appeared to still hold onto some of the guilt for calling Anna Mae up to the hospital. He wasn't saying much of anything but shared with Grace that Anna Mae was pregnant and had lost the baby as a result of her injury. Grace was in total shock, to find out that she and Anna Mae were pregnant at the same time.

Whatever bothered Franklin, kept him up most of the night. There were many nights where he'd creep into Grace's room and remove Justice from the crib. Grace would find him fast asleep in the living room, with Justice, sweaty and nestled on his uncle's chest. There were a few times when Grace would lay wide awake, watching Franklin take her son but she never mouthed a word. Franklin seemed depressed. His thoughts seemed to be held hostage. If Justice was the source to eliminate Franklin's dejected attitude, Grace was for it.

Everything that Franklin and Grace had discussed in the hospital; from showing Auntie Mabeline the contents of the safe, to going to the police, was essentially put on ice. Grace kept busy with Justice and just left it alone.

Anna Mae still remained in the hospital. The doctor said that she was awake, talking and asking for Rufus. The hospital staff felt that it was best for the family to break the news that her husband still remained in jail. As for the blood transfusion, Anna Mae was doing so well that she didn't need one after all, although Grace was willing to donate. Dr. Flint confirmed that she would be able to come home in one week.

Misty had promised to come to the house to do Grace's hair twice a month, but she'd gotten so busy at work, with the young ladies coming in to get their hair done for semi-formals, debutantes, and proms.

One day, out of the blue, she called Grace to tell her that she had a minor setback, after calling the woman that Auntie Mabeline referred her to. The number had been disconnected! So, she reached out to a background investigator, who was searching for her family.

If there was a light at the end of the tunnel, Justice was a good baby and didn't cry much, only when he was wet or hungry. Grace continued to breastfeed. She had shed a few pounds and was inching back down to her prebaby weight. She had embraced motherhood and did what Momma taught her to do at an early age ... that was to pray about everything and worry about nothing! She wanted to be the best mother that she could be, since there was no handbook for motherhood or family support! One other thing that Grace was happy about was that Justice was looking more and more like her and didn't favor David ... yet!

Trevor's secretary had called and set up Grace's first in-house appointment the week that Anna Mae was coming home and Justice's first-month appointment. Grace was looking forward to healing their relationship and not reverting to the way that they used to be. She was also hoping that Trevor could help out with whatever was going on between Franklin and Auntie Mabeline. At times, the tension could be cut with a knife.

As for David, he was still in jail for a second DUI that no one knew about. A few weeks prior to the shooting, he apparently had hit a car and fled the scene. Momma's car didn't have one scratch on it, so we don't know whose car he was using. A huge part of Franklin's issue was that Auntie Mabeline was secretly accepting David's calls from jail and not filling anyone in on what was going on. She would only say that he would be going back in front of the judge.

Much to Grace's surprise, First Lady Fallback and Deaconess Franzine had gotten together with the ladies on the women's board at church and surprised Grace with two garbage bags full of pampers, from zero to six months. Pastor Fallback and First Lady dropped the bags off the day she came home with Justice. Apparently, Auntie Mabeline had called down to the church and left a message with the church secretary for Pastor Fallback, telling him that Grace was up in the hospital having somebody's baby and asked if he knew who the daddy was! She also told him that the other kids (Franklin, Anna Mae, and David) had lost their ever loving-minds, acting as if they were gun toting gangsters, and that she needed for the church to pray for all of them. Pastor Fallback said that he had no idea that Grace was pregnant, and he didn't know who the baby's daddy was, all he knew was that it wasn't him because he shoots blanks! First Lady Fallback had already given him the third degree and told him he wasn't allowed to come by our house unless she was with him! He suggested that Grace get in contact with the church secretary, so that they could set a date for Justice's dedication.

If there was anyone who remained consistent, it was Macie and Sharmaine. They'd called Grace every week, checking up on her and Justice. Grace was able to ask questions that she had. They were both so helpful. They both promised to stop by soon. That gave Grace something to look forward too!

CHAPTER 69

Franklin walked in the house, dropping the mail on the coffee table as he sat down in the recliner.

"Hi, to you, too!" Grace said, as she rocked Justice in her arms.

"Hey, Grace," he said.

"Is everything okay? You've been acting really weird for the past couple of weeks," she said.

"I just got things on my mind," he said.

"Anything that you want to talk about?" She asked.

"No," he said.

"Well, Macie is stopping by this evening. I hope you are in a better mood."

"Cool," he said, staring at the television.

Grace laid Justice down on the couch and picked up the mail.

"I'm waiting for Justice's appointment card for his doctor's appointment next week," she said, looking through the mail.

"OH, MY GOSH!" she said, looking as if she'd seen a ghost.

"What?" He asked.

" Big Tuna wrote me a letter from jail," she said.

"WHAT?" He said, quickly sitting on the edge of the recliner. "WHAT DOES HE WANT? GIVE ME THAT!" Franklin yelled.

Franklin grabbed the envelope out of Grace's hand.

"What is wrong with you!" she exclaimed.

Franklin ripped the envelope open, reading it in silence.

"AWWW, HELL NAW! YOU AIN'T DOING THAT!" He yelled.

"WHAT DOES IT SAY?" She exclaimed.

Auntie Mabeline hurried from the kitchen into the living room.

"What in the world are you in here yelling about?" She asked, looking sharply at Franklin. "What is going on?"

"Old Man Joe's son wrote me a letter from prison," Grace said. "Franklin just snatched it out of my hand, like he ain't got good sense!"

"He did?" Auntie Mabeline asked inquisitively. "Well, what in the world does he want?" She asked, looking at Grace.

"I don't know," Grace said, looking at Franklin. "What does it say?"

Franklin tossed the letter at Grace and walked into the kitchen.

"The disrespect!" Grace said. "I don't know what is going on with you, but this is not like you!"

"What does the letter say, Gracie?" Auntie Mabeline asked.

Grace read the letter out loud.

"Hey Shorty,

How you doing? I hope you good. I've just been chilling and working out, waiting for my court date. I'm looking to getting up out of here soon. You probably wondering why I'm writing you. I like the way you move, Shorty. You the only one I trust. I need you to go down and check on my pops when you can and make sure he takin' his meds and doing alright. Moms moved back to help me take care of him, but he probably thinks she trying to take his check, so he probably not opening the door for her. I ain't heard from her in a minute, but that's like her.

My pops told me that you went crazy and the ambulance took you to the looney hospital. I called the hospitals but couldn't find you. Then I found out from my dude, who works up at memorial on food tray duty that you had the baby. If you ain't busy, you should come up to see me. If you can't, when I get out, let's go out for a bite or something.

Oh yeah, I heard about your brothers. David betta hope

I don't run into him. I remember that day he disrespected me in the hallway in front of you.

Write back shorty. Let me know what's good.

I hope you got the flowers that I sent.

Big Tuna

"Oh, my God? I thought the flowers were from David," Grace said.

"Sounds suspect to me!" Auntie Mabeline said. "How convenient for him to contact you now, after you had the baby," she said, cutting her eyes at Grace ... "and you were accusing David. That's why I told you to get your facts straight first, before you start accusing innocent people!" She said.

"Just because David didn't send the flowers, doesn't mean that he did not assault me!" Grace said.

"It could be that big can of tuna! You said yourself that the person was big," Auntie Mabeline said.

"Everyone looks big to me!" Grace exclaimed.

"Well, now I know how he knew I was in the hospital!" Grace exclaimed.

"Well, you know that daddy of his tells him everything," she said.

"Well, Auntie if you knew that, maybe you shouldn't have bought him up to the hospital. There's no telling what else he's told him!"

"Joe? He just as nutty as a snickers bar!" Auntie Mabeline.

" You seem to like nuts, Auntie!" Grace said.

"GRACIE, YOU GETTIN' BESIDE YOURSELF NOW! WATCH YOUR MOUTH!" Auntie Mabeline yelled. "YOU BETTER PUMP YOUR BRAKES, LITTLE GIRL!" she exclaimed.

Franklin returned back to the living room carrying his can of soda. He sat down and cracked it open.

"Why is Big Tuna writing you from jail?" Franklin asked, looking intently at Grace.

"Is there something that I need to know?"

"What?" Grace said. "You are crazy!"

"Seriously. Is there something you want to share?" He asked.

"What are you talking about Franklin?" Grace asked.

"I don't know Grace ... this dude has been in jail since last November. Five months later, after you give birth, he just decides to write you?"

"What are you trying to say?" She asked.

"I think you know," Franklin said.

"Gracie, have you been lying to us? Is this boy this

baby's father?" Auntie Mabeline asked, pointing to Justice.

"NO! I DON'T KNOW! I TOLD YOU BOTH THIS!" Grace said angrily.

"Just seems odd to me. Have you been seeing this dude on the low?" Franklin said.

"What? Are you joking right now? Franklin, I'm shocked that you would even say something like this," she said, picking up Justice.

"It seems kind of odd to me too, Gracie," Auntie Mabeline said. "If you've been sexually active with that boy, just say so. The baby is already here. This family can't take no more secrets. We need to go to the police and ask them to have him submit to a DNA while he's in jail."

"I can't believe you are calling me a liar, too!" Grace said. "If that's what you want to do! I'll do it! I'm the victim, and you're making me out to look as if I asked for this!"

"I'm just saying that something is not adding up," Auntie Mabeline said.

"I agree with Auntie Mabeline. Yeah, we should ask for a DNA test ... along with David," Franklin said, looking over at Auntie Mabeline, who looked as if she swallowed a canary.

"I'm surprised you're saying that," Franklin said, under his breath.

Auntie Mabeline looked at Franklin.

"You talking to me?" Auntie Mabeline asked. "I've noticed you've been very quiet, walking around here like you have an attitude. If you got something to say to me, just say it."

Franklin looked as if he was about to blow a gasket.

"Why didn't you tell us that Anna Mae was pregnant?" He blurted out.

Auntie Mabeline looked appalled, placing her hand over her heart.

"Is that why you've been walking around here like you got a hair across your behind?" She asked.

"Well, I'm just saying, you can't accuse Grace of lying but you're keeping secrets," he said. "Auntie, I'd asked you to wait until I got back to the hospital, so we can go see Anna Mae together. But no, you insisted on going to see her, and you said that you would tell me what her doctor said, since he needed to share something with you. Was that it?" He asked.

"Yeah, he told me that Anna Mae was almost four months pregnant and that she lost the baby when she got shot in the stomach," she said. "I was gonna tell ya'll in time, but I know you would only blame yourself."

"Really, Auntie. In time? Or deep down did you think I shot my sister?" He asked.

Auntie Mabeline was appalled.

"Where is all this coming from?" She asked.

"It just seems like you are here for the wrong reasons," he said.

"I don't appreciate the way you are talking to me, Franklin. I understand you are grown, but I'm not liking this," she said.

"I'm just saying, since you've been here, you've spent more time downstairs with Old Man Joe than you have up here. You know that I have mad respect for you, but it's just messed up. Don't get me wrong, I appreciate you staying here to help us out with Anna Mae, but you can't help us if you're down there helping yourself to Old Man Joe!" Franklin said, getting it all off his chest.

"WATCH YOUR MOUTH!" Auntie Mabeline yelled. "You waited all this time to tell me all of this?"

"That's just it . . . I shouldn't have to tell you anything," he said.

Auntie Mabeline looked over at Grace.

"Do you feel the same way Gracie?" She asked.

"Well, yeah, kind of. You really haven't been any help since I've gotten home. I could really use your help with cooking and cleaning, especially if you are not going to help me with Justice," Grace said.

Auntie Mabeline looked down, pondering on what her nephew and niece were saying.

"Well, I'm sorry if you both feel that way, but you have to remember, I am still your aunt," she said, looking back and forth from Franklin to Grace.

"Grace, just let it go," Franklin said.

"No, I won't let it go, Franklin. You both have no problem with accusing me of being with Big Tuna , even after all the stuff that we found out in Momma's safe, that you still have not showed Auntie Mabeline. You said that you would call that officer, so that I can talk to him about the assault, and tell him what I know about the murdered lady that helped me. You are not being honest yourself," Grace said to Franklin, sounding frustrated.

"I'm sorry," Franklin said. "I've just been so stressed with everything that's going on. Anna Mae will be home next week. I don't even know how we are going to care for her."

"Remember, I told you that nurse said that she would be willing to help us out with Anna Mae's care," Auntie Mabeline said.

"Yeah, Sharmaine," Grace said.

"Yeah, I remember," Franklin said, "but how are we going to pay for her care?"

"That child ain't said nothing about money," Auntie Mabeline said.

"Well, we can ask Macie when she comes over later,"

Grace said.

Auntie Mabeline sat down on the couch next to Grace as she looked at the both of them. She placed her hand on Grace's knee.

"Well, I'm sorry. I didn't know that ya'll were caught up in your feelings," Auntie Mabeline said. "I should have been more in tuned to how ya'll were feeling, but you need to start speaking up. Now, I don't know if I'm going to stop going down to see Joe. He down there by himself and, well, someone need to look out for him." She looked over at Grace, "and not you!"

"Grace, why don't you write Big Tuna back and tell him that Auntie is on it!" Franklin said. He shook his head as he got up and walked back into the kitchen.

"Since when did you become so sensitive?" Auntie Mabeline yelled.

Grace's phone started to vibrate on the coffee table. She looked over to see who it was.

"It's Macie," she said, picking up the phone, as Auntie Mabeline sat back on the couch.

"Hi, Macie," Grace said, pausing. "Yes, I am home ... okay . . . we were just talking about her. I'm sure they won't mind . . . okay . . . hold on and let me check."

Grace placed the phone on mute.

"Auntie, do you have a problem if Macie brings

Sharmaine over with her, so she knows where we live at before Anna Mae comes home?" Grace asked.

"No, I don't mind, but you better ask your crazy brother in there," she said.

Franklin was heading back into the living room just as Grace began to yell for him. "FRANKLIN!"

"WHAT?" He said. "Why are you screaming?"

"Macie is on the phone. She wants to know if it's okay if she brings Sharmaine over later, so she knows where we lives at?" Grace asked.

"I don't care," he said.

Grace took the phone off mute. "Hey Macie. They don't mind . . . okay . . . no, I'm all set, but thanks . . . okay . . . 6:30? . . . okay, see you then," she said, before hanging up.

"They'll be here by 6:30 p.m.," Grace said.

"We don't have nothing in there to offer them," Auntie Mabeline said.

"We did, until you bought it down to Old Man Joe's," Franklin said, still perturbed.

Chapter 70

Franklin went into his room and closed the door, intentionally putting some space between him and Auntie Mabeline.

Auntie Mabeline was in Momma's room taking a cat nap, probably worn out from her late-night rendezvous with Old Man Joe.

Grace sat in the living room playing with Justice. She was interrupted by a knock on the door.

She looked through the peep hole to see Macie. She opened the door.

"Hey, Macie," Grace said, giving her a warm embrace. "Come on in," she said, looking down the steps.

"Hi, Grace." Macie said. "Hi, Justice," she said, in a baby voice.

"You're looking well," Macie said.

"Oh, thank you," she said.

"Where's Sharmaine? I thought she was coming with you," Grace asked.

"Everything with Sharmaine is a long story, so I'll keep it short. She couldn't make it," Macie said, sounding drained.

"Can I hold him?" Macie asked, reaching into her pocketbook for her sanitizer. She doused her hands, rubbing them together, before reaching out for Justice.

Grace handed Justice to Macie.

"I miss you, little pumpkin. It's just not the same in the nursery without you," Macie said.

"Thank you so much for that beautiful send off. That made me feel so special," Grace said placing her hand over her heart.

"Well, when you told me about what happened to you, I had to do something to let you know that we support you," she said.

"But how did all those ladies know about me? Did you tell them what happened to me?" Grace asked.

"Of course not! I didn't have to," Macie said.

"So how'd they know?" Grace asked, curiously.

Macie took a deep breath.

"I had a very bad accident two years ago, that put me in the very same hospital. I went from being the nurse to needing a nurse. Many of those women that you saw rallied around me. It was incomprehensible the amount of support they gave me. They were instrumental in my recovery.

"Are you okay now?" Grace asked.

" I am. I take one day at a time and try not to relive that dark part of my life," she said.

"I'm sorry," Grace said.

"Don't be! So, when I sent an email and told a few of the ladies how I met an extraordinary young lady who needed the same support that they gave me . . . they didn't need to know why . . . they just showed up!

Misty smiled.

"I didn't know most of them but this is what we do. We support one another. We don't need to know what happened, we just show up."

"WOW!" Grace said. "I was so honored. After momma died, and then the lady who helped me," Grace said before Macie cut her off.

"What lady?" Macie asked.

"Oh, I didn't tell you about the lady across the street?" Grace asked.

"No, you didn't," Macie said.

"Well, after I got assaulted. That criminal dragged me down the stairs and into the street. Since I was punched on the right side of my head, I couldn't really see. The lady who lived over there," Grace said, pulling back the curtain and pointing to the house on the corner, "was coming down the street. She almost hit me with her car. Well, when she got out of the car, I was trying to get up, but I stumbled back to the ground!"

"Oh my God!" Macie gasped. "He could have killed you!"

"I know. He left me for dead!" Grace said. "The lady jumped out the car and ran over to help me. She wanted to call the police, but I told her that I just wanted to go home, and I would ask David to take me to the hospital. I didn't know at the at the time that he was the one who did this to me. Well, she helped me back into the house. The very next day, when I woke up, I heard so much noise outside, and I noticed flashing lights through the curtain. I looked out the window to see an ambulance and five police cruisers at the woman's house."

"What happened to her?" Macie asked.

"She was murdered," Grace said.

"WHAT? OH NO!" Macie exclaimed. "Did they find her killer?"

"Not that I know of. The police came around after it happened and asked people if they knew anything, but I was so scared, I didn't open my door. I thought that whoever did this to her would come back and kill me, too," Grace said.

"But don't you think you should go to the police. I mean, the killer could still be out there, and especially if he did this to you, you don't want him to come after you and Justice," Macie said. "It's not just you anymore."

"The only reason why I am not too worried is because David is still behind bars. I spoke to Franklin and my Auntie about going to the police. Franklin met an officer the day he was released from jail. He said he would call him so I can talk to him, but he hasn't done it yet." Grace said, sounding disappointed. "He's said a lot of things that he hasn't come through on."

"Well, if you need me to go with you, I will do it!" Macie said. "You have to protect this baby at all cost. It's not just about you!"

"You are so right," Grace said looking over at Justice. "Thanks Macie. I will let you know if Franklin does not take me."

"Okay," Macie said. "You better!" Grace looked down the hall to make sure that Auntie Mabeline or Franklin were not in earshot.

"Do you remember Old Man Joe? He was the old man that came up to the hospital with my Auntie to see me," Grace said.

"Oh yeah. The one with the walking stick. He was asleep in the chair," Macie said.

"Yes, him," Grace said. "Well, his son is in jail for locking this girl in the trunk."

"Oh, my God! What kind of people are you around?" Macie asked. "Is this a bad neighborhood?"

"No. We've lived here since I was a baby. We know everyone in the neighborhood," Grace said.

"O-kay," Macie said.

"Let me tell you before my aunt and Franklin come in here. Well, he sent me a letter from jail."

"Saying what?" Macie asked.

"His dad lives on the first floor. He's known my parents way before I was born. Well, Big Tuna asked me if I could go downstairs and check on his father, but Auntie Mabeline is not having none of that," she said. "But the strange thing is, he knew that I had a baby, and remember those flowers that I received in the hospital?"

"Yeah, do I," Macie said, smirking.

"He was the one who sent them to me. Not David," Grace said.

"No way!" Macie said. "Speaking of that, I've been thinking about what you said . . . I understand that David is not your brother, but do you think he is capable of assaulting you? I mean . . . it's just sick! I don't know Grace . . . I didn't want to say anything, but I just cannot see that happening. I don't know him but it just doesn't make any sense."

"You're ..." Grace said, before Macie cut her off.

"I am NOT saying that I don't believe you. I'm only saying that if you think that it could be someone else, you need to go to the police and tell them," Macie said, as she rocked Justice. "How do you know it wasn't this Big Tuna dude, who sent you the flowers? Don't you think it's odd that he would send you flowers in the hospital. How did he know you gave birth?"

"His father told him, and he told me he confirmed it with some friend of his who works in the hospital's kitchen," Grace said.

"But just look at the timing. When did the assault happen?" Macie said, sounding more like a detective than a nurse.

"Last July," Grace said.

"Last July, and when did he go to jail?" Macie asked.

Grace began to think.

"It was the day we picked up Auntie Mabeline from the airport ... after Momma died ... so November," Grace said.

"Okay, so he's been sitting in jail since November, and it's almost the end of April. Did you hear from him between November and April?" Macie asked.

"No," Grace said.

"Do you see what I mean? There's some doubt that it was David ... and I'm just saying, while this dude is in jail, you need to get the cops to get a DNA test done," Macie said.

"Well, if David was innocent of shooting my sister, he would be out like Franklin, but he's not getting out any time soon. Especially since we found out about his other DUI," Grace said.

"I understand where you're coming from. But you don't want to accuse an innocent man for something that he didn't do to you," Macie said.

"You sound like Auntie Mabeline," Grace said. "She keeps defending David."

"Well, you were the only one there. You're going to have to speak up. Let's say that David was the one who did this to you and say hypothetically, he gets released... do you really want him living here with you? What are the chances that he'll do it again?" Grace stood silently.

"Isn't your sister's husband still locked up too, right?" Macie asked.

"Yes. We don't really know what's going on with him. Auntie Mabeline said that since he's no kin to us, it makes no difference to her if he stays in there or gets out. Especially now that we have to take care of Anna Mae. Rufus is the last person she wants to see," Grace said. "Auntie Mabeline keeps saying that she doesn't know why he didn't step in front of his wife and take the bullet."

"Well, I don't know if I would even do that," Macie said, grinning. "It may not matter to them what his outcome is, but it will matter to your sister. That's her husband. More importantly, if Franklin was released and your sister's husband and David weren't, in my opinion, they are both suspects! I know if it was my sister, I would want to know who shot her."

"Of course, I do, but it's just too much!" Grace said.

"It is. It seems like your family has a bad cloud floating above their heads," Macie said, nervously laughing. "Something is always going on with ya'll. I think I would lose my mind."

"Yeah, I'm almost there," Grace said, looking stressed.

"Grace, just see if your brother is going to take you to talk to the police."

"Well, Misty mentioned when I was in the hospital that the officer gave them his business card," Grace said. "He's one of the officers investigating the lady's murder."

"Then get his name from Franklin," Macie said.

"Franklin? Please … he's been in such a funk lately. I don't want to ask him anything," Grace said.

"Well, you got to do, what you got to do," Macie said. "I'm sure if you don't feel comfortable going down to the police station, I'm sure you can call and ask if he could come here to the house. Or you can talk to him at my place," Macie said.

"Dr. Freelance also encouraged me to speak up," Grace said.

"That doesn't surprise me. He's that dude! He always encourages us to stand up for ourselves," Macie said, smiling.

"Well, I definitely don't want to take Justice down to no police station!" Grace said.

"True! But don't wait too long. They need to know what happened to you. They can check and see if they have any leads, or if it's connected to the murder of that woman. Tell him everything girl. Let him know that you think it could have been David or that Tuna guy, who sent you flowers and a love letter," Macie sneered.

"I know you meant, Big Tuna ," Grace said, smirking.

"Whatever his name is. I just know from the sounds of it, he sounds crazy! Locking a girl in his trunk? You need to stay far away from him! Between that, the assault, the murder, and the shooting ... I don't know ... it may all be tied together. I don't know. For the officer to mention it to Franklin, they are obviously working on the case," Macie said.

"I mentioned to you that my mother was in the hospital, but I didn't tell you about her fall," she said.

"What?" Macie said.

"The day I got assaulted is the same day that Momma fell in the bathroom and went into a coma," Grace said.

"I'm so sorry. Your mom passed away last November,

right?" Macie said.

"Yes, how'd you know?" Grace said.

"Leroy told me earlier. I'd mentioned to him that I was coming over here to see you, and that you were Franklin's sister, and that's when he told me that he knew your mom and your Auntie."

"Yeah, I heard," Grace said.

"Dang, should I be afraid to be around ya'll? Tragedy is all around your family!"

Grace gave Macie a look.

"I'm kidding. Girl, I carry my mace wherever I go!"

"Anyways, Momma had leukemia, that made her bones fragile. The day of Momma's fall, I was making breakfast, and Momma rang her bell, like she always did when she needed help. I asked David to get up and go help her into the bathroom. He did but then I heard Momma yelp. I ran right into the bathroom to see David standing over her. Momma had hit her head on the bathroom tub and was bleeding from the back of her head. David was just stone-cold. I called 911 and got Momma to the hospital, but she ended up going into a coma on the way."

"Did she ever come out of the coma before she passed?" Macie asked.

"No. The doctor spoke to us and we ended up taking her off life support last November," Grace said sadly.

"Momma never had a chance to tell us what happened."

"Grace, that is so tragic! No wonder why you are strong as an ox! You've suffered so many losses," Macie said, sympathizing with Grace. "And, now I see why you feel the way you do about David. I don't know him, but if my mother was in the bathroom and she fell, the first thing I would do is yell to get help or call 911 myself."

"Exactly," Grace said.

"Wow," Macie said. "Now I see why you suspect David did this to you. How do you know that David didn't assault your mom in the bathroom?"

"Exactly," Grace said. "I don't."

"And you've shared all of this with your brother and Auntie?" Macie asked.

"Yes," Grace said.

"If they are not going to take you seriously and support you, you're gonna have to forget about them!," Macie said. Macie looked at Grace affectionately. "You definitely have an angel watching over you."

"Yeah, I do. My Momma," Grace said.

"Oh yes," Macie said. Auntie Mabeline could be heard singing and walking toward the living room, where Grace, Macie, and Justice were.

"Please don't say anything to them," Grace said,

whispering.

"I won't," Macie said.

"Hi Macie. How are you?" Auntie Mabeline asked. "I didn't hear you come in."

"Hi Ms. Mabeline. Yeah, I came in a few minutes ago," Macie said, giving Auntie Mabeline a halfhearted hug.

"Child, that was some surprise that you gave Gracie when she left the hospital. With my birthday coming up, I would be open to something that grand," Auntie Mabeline said, dropping a hint.

"When's your birthday?" Macie asked.

"Oh, its August 11th," she said.

"Will you still be here?" Macie asked.

"Yes, until these kids run me out," she said, giving Grace the side eye. "I was able to use all the vacation and sick time that I had stored up, so I'll be here until August."

"Nice!" Macie said. "I'm sure Grace and Franklin appreciate your help around the house and your support," she said, being facetious about the latter, after hearing everything that Grace shared.

Auntie Mabeline grunted. Macie looked at Grace.

"How have things been since you got home?" Macie asked.

"Oh, don't ask her that. She already laid-me out earlier. Her and Franklin both," Auntie Mabeline said, looking for sympathy.

"What did you do, Ms. Mabeline?" Macie asked, acting dumbfounded.

"Nothing . . . that's their problem with me. They said that I ain't helping out enough. Heck! I'm on vacation!"

Macie smirked.

"So, where's Franklin?" Macie asked.

"He was in the shower when I walked past the bathroom. I heard the water running," she said. "Now that their Momma is gone, they run water, like it's free!"

Grace interjected.

"Yeah, he ran and got in the shower after I told him Sharmaine was coming over," Grace said.

They laughed, as they sat down.

"Where's she at? I needed to talk to her," Auntie Mabeline asked.

"It's a long story," Macie continued. "She was planning to come with me, so that she could see where you all lived before Anna Mae came home, but the body shop called and told her that her car was ready, so I dropped her off, to pick it up. I'm glad about that!"

"Why?" Grace asked.

"I've been giving her a ride to work for the past few months. Well, only when we've worked the same shift," Macie said.

"Did she have a car wreck?" Auntie Mabeline asked.

"She just told me that her car was in the body shop. Apparently, one day when she was leaving work, she backed into a pole and got the yellow paint from the pole all over her car. That's what she said, but she's known for telling a little white lie."

"You hear that now, Grace. That's why I don't care for that girl. I don't know if I can trust her!" Auntie Mabeline said.

"Ms. Mabeline, I don't mean to talk bad about her, but I will say this, she takes her job seriously. It's just her personal life that's shrouded in mystery. She's pretty private. You would think, as close as we are, she would share more with me … but she doesn't. I respect that."

Franklin slowly opened the bathroom door. He stood out of sight, eavesdropping. He had an instant attraction to Sharmaine the day he met her and was curious to see what Macie had to say about her. She was definitely the type of woman that he would date.

"One thing I know for certain is that Sharmaine has a thing for bad boys. I know I shouldn't be talking about her, but she likes these dudes who cannot do anything for her and who are definitely not on her level. She works so hard, but then she links up with these guys who have bad credit, live at home with their parents, or have nothing to offer," Macie said. "She recently bought a townhouse, and this dude that she was dating asked her if she could add his name to her deed."

Franklin listened, thinking that he would never be that low to ask a woman to add him to anything that she worked hard for. He wondered, what kind of corn balls was she dealing with?

"Oh no," Grace said. "I hope she said no!"

"Well, she told her parents, and her father set the dude straight," Macie said. "She comes from a good family. They don't play when it comes to her. Her dad is overprotective. He's an engineer and her mom's a retired nurse. She really needs a good man."

"Franklin is single," Auntie Mabeline blurted out, "and he can use some business of his own, so he can stay out of mine!"

"I can hear you," Franklin yelled.

"Hey, Franklin," Macie said, unable to see him.

"Hi Macie. I'll be in there in a minute," he said.

Franklin hurried into his bedroom, and threw on his silk boxer briefs, a black tank top that exposed his muscles with red, black and white knee length short pants, striped tube socks and his Nike flip flops, before joining the others in the living room.

He reached over Grace to give Macie a hug.

"Excuse you!" Grace said.

"My bad," he said.

"How are you, Macie?" He said.

"I'm good," she said.

"I have to give it to you, that was really nice what you did for Grace when she left the hospital," Franklin said. "You had me all choked up!"

"I still get teary-eyed, just thinking about it," Grace said.

"Well, it was easy to do because we all fell in love with Grace," she said, responding to Franklin.

Franklin quickly turned the conversation.

"I heard you talking about Sharmaine. What's her story?" He asked.

"What do you mean?" Macie said, smiling.

"You know what I mean," Franklin asked.

"Is she single?" Franklin asked.

"I try not to get into her business," Macie said.

"Well, you sure could have fooled me," Auntie Mabeline said.

"I know she was dating this dude that she met at the hospital. I'm not sure if they are still together," Macie said. "But I can find out for you."

"Uh huh. I knew it. I knew you liked Sharmaine," Grace said. "I noticed how you looked at her, that time she came into my room."

"Be quiet Grace!" Franklin said.

Macie and Grace laughed.

"I'd appreciate if you could find out for me," Franklin said. "I was looking forward to seeing her tonight. Grace mentioned that she was coming."

"I bet you were," Auntie Mabeline said under her breath.

"That's why he bathed," Grace said, taking a cheap shot at Franklin, as she laughed.

The conversation was interrupted by Macie's ringing cell phone.

"I'll take Justice back so you can get that," Grace said, taking Justice out of Macie's arms.

Macie grabbed the phone out of her pocketbook, looking at the caller ID.

"Speaking of the devil. It's Sharmaine. Maybe she changed her mind, and she's swinging by after all," Macie said answering the phone.

"She'll need our address," Franklin said, smiling.

"Put your teeth back in your mouth," Auntie Mabeline said.

"Wow! I haven't seen that smile in a while," Grace said.

"Excuse me ya'll ... Hey girl," Macie said.

We could hear Sharmaine talking a mile a minute, but we couldn't make out what she was saying. The expression on Macie's face, looked serious.

"Okay . . . yeah, I'm here. It was easy to find. Okay . . . I'll see you tomorrow ... oh by the way, Franklin is interested in you! Can I give him your number?" Macie said, sneaking it into the conversation.

"Macie, that's wrong," Franklin said, although deep down he was elated.

Macie laughed.

"Okay girl . . . I will," she said, hanging up.

"She won't be able to come by tonight," Macie said. "She apologized, but said that she'll swing by another time, before Anna Mae comes home."

"Okay," Grace said.

"Franklin, she said it was okay to give you her number," Macie said smiling. "Can I write on this?" She said, pointing to the envelope that Big Tuna sent.

"Sure," Franklin said. "It's trash," he said, looking at Grace.

"Didn't you say she had a man?" Auntie Mabeline asked. "Don't be getting my nephew caught up in no bull!" she exclaimed.

"Well, obviously he's not relevant anymore because she said it was okay for me to have her number," Franklin said.

"Ms. Mabeline, you're not the only one that someone is trying to holla at?" Macie said.

"What are you talking about?" Auntie Mabeline asked. "I know Gracie is not running my business."

Grace widened her eyes, as she looked at Macie.

"I bumped into Leroy and mentioned I was stopping by, and he asked for you," she said.

"It's no wonder why you and Grace bonded, you are a little faucet too," Auntie Mabeline said, referring to Macie running the business.

"Yeah. I forgot to tell you, he also mentioned that to me the day I went looking for him that he wanted to take you out," Franklin said.

"And you just now telling me?" Auntie Mabeline said, looking at Franklin.

"Well, you seemed disinterested, when he spoke to

you at the courthouse," Franklin said.

"Auntie, you already got a boo!" Grace added.

Auntie Mabeline cut her eyes at Grace.

Macie continued, looking at Auntie Mabeline. "He was telling me that he knows you and your sister. He said that he saw you singing at your sister's funeral. He seemed bummed that he didn't get a chance to talk to you, but then he'd ran into you at court. He was saying how good you looked the other day. Looks like you got yourself an admirer, Ms. Mabeline."

"I am all set!" Auntie Mabeline said, "and please keep my name out of your mouth when you're talking to that man."

"Oh, I'm sorry," Macie said, handing Franklin the envelope with Sharmaine's number on it.

"Sharmaine said she's off tomorrow night, so if you want to get together, she said you should call her. We work six days straight before we get a day off, so you may want to jump on it! Grace, I'll take Justice back," she said, reaching out for Justice.

"Okay, thanks Macie," Franklin said, looking down at the envelope, beaming from ear to ear.

"Don't even think about bringing no more babies up in here," Auntie Mabeline said, looking at Franklin. "One is enough!" She looked across at Justice.

"Really, Auntie," Franklin said, smirking.

They all laughed.

"So, Franklin, where are you going to take Sharmaine out to?" Grace asked.

"None of your business," he said. "I don't need you and Auntie staking out the place." Grace and Macie laughed.

"Well, if you really want to impress her, she loves that Sushi restaurant on Lincoln Boulevard," Macie said.

"She eats that raw stuff?" Auntie Mabeline said, looking at Franklin. "Franklin, do you eat that stuff?"

"Yeah. I've been to a few sushi spots when I was in the army," he said.

"I used to think like you Ms. Mabeline, until Sharmaine took me there. I fell in love with the food . . . and that wasabi . . . Mmmmhhh . . . Mmmmhhh! So spicy and good!" Macie said.

"No, thanks." Auntie Mabeline said. "If it ain't been dropped in some hot grease, I don't want it!"

"Not all of it is raw. You'd like the shrimp tempura!" Macie said to Auntie Mabeline. "It's coated in a light batter and deep fried."

"Hmmmm .... that sounds good," Auntie Mabeline said.

"My favorite is the California roll. It has cucumber,

crab, and avocado. Simply delicious!" Macie said.

"Grace, have you tried it?" Macie asked.

"No," she said. "Is it good for Justice, since I'm breastfeeding?"

"Are you serious? Sushi is safe to eat while breastfeeding, as long as you eat it from a reputable restaurant that uses high-quality fish from reliable sources. This place is on the high end," Macie said.

"You hear that Franklin? That child is gonna eat up your check," Auntie Mabeline said, taking a dig at Sharmaine.

Macie continued talking to Grace.

"But you should avoid eating any fish that contains high levels of mercury, regardless of whether that fish is raw or cooked."

"That's good to know," Grace said.

"Maybe Franklin can bring you some back from his date, if they decide to go there," Macie said, looking at Franklin.

"Yeah, I can do that," he said, looking at Grace as if it was a peace offering from their spat earlier about Big Tuna's letter.

"Thanks," Grace said.

"Macie," Franklin said hesitating.

"Yes," she answered.

"I don't know if I should mention this while I'm on our date, but we were talking earlier about Sharmaine coming to help out once Anna Mae comes home. She'll actually be home next week. Although we welcome the help, we're not sure if we can afford her services," Franklin said.

"Sharmaine actually works for a separate company that is not through the hospital. So, I don't know the rates, but I'm sure if you treat her right, she'll hook ya'll up. Another thing that she loves to do is shop until she drops, so taking her to a mall would put her in heaven," Macie said.

"I'm not balling like that," Franklin said. Grace quickly changed the subject.

"That reminds me, I want to invite you and Sharmaine to Justice's dedication," Grace said.

"When is it?" Macie asked.

"I'm not sure yet but I'll let you know," Grace responded.

"Okay. I'll tell Sharmaine. You know if we're off, we'll be there!" Macie said.

"When are you meeting with Mr. Cooper?" She asked.

"Oh, Trevor?" Grace said. Macie shook her head, yes.

"He's coming next week after my sister gets home. It will be our first in-house visit," Grace said, sounding exited.

"That should be interesting," Macie said, thinking about all of their family drama.

The house phone rang.

"Excuse me," Franklin said, rushing into the kitchen.

Out of the blue, they could hear Franklin yelling at the caller.

"NO! I WILL NOT!" He said, slamming the phone down, before storming back into the living room.

"Maybe Trevor can come sooner than next week," Macie said, after overhearing Franklin.

"Who are you yelling at now?" Auntie Mabeline asked Franklin.

Franklin looked irate.

"GRACE'S BOYFRIEND!" He said yelling.

Everyone looked a Grace.

"WHAT ARE YOU TALKING ABOUT?" Grace asked, looking shocked!

"NOW YOU WANT TO PLAY INNOCENT?" Franklin asked. HOW DID **BIG TUNA** GET OUR HOUSE NUMBER!" He yelled.

Macie and Grace looked at each other, thinking back to their earlier conversation about going to the police.

Grace looked fearful all over again. "WHAT? HE

CALLED?" She said.

"WHY ARE YOU TRYING TO ACT SURPRISED?" He yelled.

"BECAUSE I'M JUST AS SURPRISED AS YOU ARE!" she said.

"HE'S SENDING YOU FLOWERS; HE'S WRITING YOU LOVE LETTERS, AND NOW HE'S CALLING OUR HOME!" Franklin yelled.

Macie looked back and forth at the siblings, as if she was watching a bad tennis match. She slowly reached for her pocketbook.

"IF YOU DIDN'T GIVE HIM OUR NUMBER, THEN HOW DID HE GET OUR NUMBER?" Franklin yelled. "EXPLAIN THAT ONE!"

"HOW DARE YOU DISRESPECT ME LIKE THAT!" Grace yelled. "HOW WOULD I KNOW?"

Justice busted out crying, with all of the chaos going on around him.

"Excuse me," Macie said, trying to gain some order as she consoled an upset Justice. They all looked at Macie. "All this yelling has gotten Justice upset," Macie said, rocking Justice, in an effort to comfort him.

Franklin ignored Macie and had no sympathy for his nephew.

"GRACE, WHY DID YOU GIVE THIS DUDE OUR NUMBER?" Franklin continued to yell.

"I DIDN'T!" Grace yelled back. "THINK WHATEVER YOU WANT TO!"

Whatever had Franklin boiling these past couple of weeks had him exploding like a raging volcano.

"STOP YELLING AT THE GIRL. SHE DIDN'T GIVE HIM THE NUMBER," Auntie Mabeline said. "I GAVE THE NUMBER TO OLD MAN JOE! HE MUST'VE GAVE IT TO HIM! I TOLD YOU, HE SHARES EVERYTHING WITH HIS SON!"

"WHAT?" Franklin said, looking surprised.

"The other night while I was down at Old Man Joe's, he asked for the house number after not being able to reach me on my cellular phone. He said he was trying to call me to come down to help him. So, I gave it to him. I didn't think it was an issue. I'm sure he gave it to him by mistake."

"You what?" Franklin asked.

"Yeah, I gave it to him! I didn't tell him to give it out! You know his mind ain't right!" Auntie Mabeline said.

"See that! You're accusing me for no reason!" an angry Grace said.

"I'm sorry, Grace," he said. Grace stood up and stormed into the kitchen. Macie followed her with Justice.

Macie pulled on Grace's arm.

"Grace, you got to go to the police," she said, whispering. Grace began to cry.

"Just remember what I said," Macie said, comforting Grace as Justice lay asleep on her shoulder.

Grace and Macie walked back into the living room.

"Please stop sharing so much with Old Man Joe," Grace said, pleading with Auntie Mabeline.

"You are not the boss of me!" Auntie Mabeline said.

Franklin hugged Grace.

"Grace, I'm really sorry. You have to realize as your older brother, I'm very protective of you and I don't want no one to hurt you ever again."

Grace flicked his hand off of her shoulder for embarrassing her in front of Macie.

"Well, I better get going. My shift starts at seven in the morning," Macie said, carefully handing Justice back to Grace.

"Macie, I'm sorry to blow up in front of you," Franklin said. "It's just that I don't want to see my sister hurt by no knucklehead."

"Yeah, I feel the same about my friend," Macie said, smirking, referring to Sharmaine.

"Have fun on your date!" She exclaimed.

"Just do me one favor?" He asked.

"What's that?" She said.

"Please don't mention this to Sharmaine," he said.

Macie grunted.

"Well, I'm going to chop this up as an overprotective brother, but I hope that you are not always this explosive! I wouldn't want that for my friend. Besides, Sharmaine would drop you in a minute, that's if her daddy don't get to you first!" Macie said, giving Franklin a fair warning.

"See ya'll later," she said. "Grace, I'll be in touch!"

"Thanks for coming by Macie," Grace said.

"Don't mention it, Grace," Macie said.

"I'm sorry that you had to hear this," Grace said, looking at Franklin, as he held the door open.

"You have nothing to be sorry for. I'll be in touch," Macie said, as she made her way down the stairs.

CHAPTER 71

Franklin didn't waste any time calling Sharmaine, after Macie left. The following evening his Giorgio Armani cologne filled the air as he got ready for his big date with Sharmaine. Grace had given him the silent treatment all day after embarrassing her in front of Macie.

Grace waited until she heard Franklin close the door. She knew that he would be out with Sharmaine for a while, so it was time to make her move.

Auntie Mabeline had snuck downstairs earlier in the day to shack up with Old Man Joe, and Justice was fast asleep in his crib.

Grace tiptoed in Franklin's room, hoping that Auntie Mabeline or Old Man Joe didn't hear her movements from downstairs.

"Where is it?" She murmured, as she looked for the police officer's business card. Franklin's room was in total contrast to David's. It was neat. Everything on his dresser was set up in an orderly fashion.

Grace stood in Franklin's bedroom, looking around.

"Maybe he has it with him in his wallet," she said. She walked toward Franklin's dresser, where he had his military badges placed neatly in a row. She noticed a jewelry box that was placed on top of his razor kit.

"What's this?" She said, carefully picking up the box. She opened it up to find several business cards that Franklin had collected.

"Jelly Belly's Jungle Gym," she said, looking at the card with the half-naked lady, striking a pose. "Hmmmm … and he's getting on my case!" she uttered. "Looks like he's the one with secrets."

Grace began to look through the rest of the pile of cards. She came across a card for car detailing. She turned it over, reading the large print, call me for a discount, signed Shea. "I bet, Ms. Shea," she said, under her breath.

She kept going through the business cards one after the other before stopping in her tracks. The crisp white card with the dark blue writing stood out. It was from Officer Collins. "Oh, my God!" she said. She grabbed a pen from Franklin's desk drawer and wrote down the number on her palm. She carefully placed everything just like she found it and tiptoed out of the room.

"Success!" she said, smiling.

Chapter 72

Franklin sat across from Sharmaine, trying not to stare at her too hard. He was mesmerized by her beauty. Sharmaine had on a low-cut black fitted shirt, white leggings and peep toe heels. Her auburn hair color perfectly matched her heels and her pocketbook.

Franklin sat across from her in a plaid blue and white pin-striped shirt, blue jeans and red sneakers. His bulging biceps popped through his short shirt sleeves, like blazing guns.

"I'm really glad that you called me," she said.

"I was a little nervous at first," he said, taking a large gulp of his water.

Sharmaine noticed his nervousness. She reached under the table and placed her hand on his knee.

"Relax, Franklin," she said.

Franklin's manhood bounced, as if it was going to bust out of his blue jeans.

"So, how did you know that I love this restaurant?" She asked, smiling seductively.

Franklin didn't want to throw Macie under the bus or risk her telling Sharmaine about his outburst, during her visit.

"Ahhh, I assumed that ..." he said, struggling to think of something.

"I know Macie told you," she blurted out. "She knows how much I love sushi."

"Yeah, I like it too," Franklin said.

"So, we have one thing in common," Sharmaine said, smiling. "So, why don't you tell me about yourself," she said, trying to get a dreamy-eyed Franklin to look at her eyes and engage in conversation, after sitting in silence since they'd arrived at the restaurant. "What do you like to do for fun?"

"Well, I really haven't been out in a long time. I was in the army for a few years, and I recently finished my tour of duty," he said.

"Didn't you go out on the weekends while in the service?" She asked. "I have friends in the army, and they said they turn up on the weekends."

"Well, I wouldn't call it turning up, but yeah, me and my military friends got together. We went to the club a lot," he said.

"So, you think you can dance?" She asked, smiling.

"I know I can dance," he said, flashing a Kool aid smile.

"Let me be the judge. We have to go dancing soon," she said. "So, what did you do when you were in the service?"

Franklin didn't want to make the evening about him, so he reluctantly answered Sharmaine's questions.

"I was part of the artillery troop," he said.

"Oh, so you know how to use a weapon," she said.

Franklin's mind reminisced back to the shooting at the hospital. He knew that Sharmaine must've heard about it. He quickly changed the subject to something lighter.

"Yeah, but I like to bowl and play a game of pick-up basketball, when I can," he said.

"That sounds like fun. I like to bowl, and I played basketball in high school. We should play one-on-one," she smiled. "When was the last time you bowled?"

Franklin almost lost his train of thought.

"Uh, probably about seven years ago," he said.

Sharmaine looked perplexed. "Oh, I thought maybe it was more recent."

"No," he said.

"You seem as if you don't get out much," she said. "You seem very reserved."

Franklin didn't want to go into his family history. He felt it was too premature to tell Sharmaine why he lived such a humdrum life.

"Not while home on leave. I had a lot going on, so no,

I haven't been going out much," he said.

"That's good! That means you don't run the streets," she said.

"Well, I like to have fun, but no, I've never been that type of guy," he said.

Sharmaine changed the subject to something that she thought would allow Franklin to open up more.

"So, how's Grace and Justice doing?" She asked.

"They're doing good," Franklin said.

"I miss seeing them. I know all mothers have to go home after giving birth, but your sister grew on all of us," she said.

"Yeah," Franklin said. "She has that effect on people."

"How's your auntie doing?" She asked, giggling.

"She's fine," he said, knowing that he's kept his distance from Auntie Mabeline for not being forthcoming about Anna Mae.

"Your auntie is a trip! She laid me out a few times while Grace was in the hospital. I'd mentioned to Macie that I am staying out of her way," Sharmaine said, snickering. "I don't think she likes me."

"She's like that with everyone," Franklin said. "Don't take it personal. If she didn't like you, trust me, you would know."

Sharmaine and Franklin sat in awkward silence searching for something else to say.

Franklin had gulped his glass of water down, placing the empty glass on the table. The attentive waiter noticing, rushing back over to refill his glass.

"Well, do you want to know anything about me?" Sharmaine asked.

Franklin straightened up in his seat. "Yeah," he said. "How old are you, if you don't mind me asking?"

Sharmaine smiled.

"Most people think that I am much older than my age. Maybe because of the way I carry myself, but I turned 25 in February," she said.

"Oh, okay. Yeah, I would have guessed late 30s or early 40s," Franklin said.

Sharmaine chuckled. "I get that all the time ... and you?" She asked Franklin.

"I'll be 26 in October," he said.

"Oh, wow!" she said.

"So, where are you from?" He asked. "I know a lot of people, and I've never seen you around before."

"I'm originally from Detroit, but I came this way for nursing school and never left. My mother is a retired nurse, so I followed in her footsteps, and my dad is an engineer. He's about to retire in two years."

"Are your parents still in Detroit?" He asked.

"Yeah, they are. I have three younger siblings, ages 19, 15, and 10. My parents aren't going nowhere, and I definitely ain't moving back to Detroit. I had to help raise my brothers and little sister while my parents worked," she said.

"Yeah, I know that feeling. My sister and I had to do the same thing," he said.

"The one in the hospital?" She asked. "Macie shared with me that your sister was the one who was shot and I had a brief conversation with your auntie."

"Yeah, Anna Mae," he said.

"How is she doing?" She asked.

"She's doing okay. She's coming home next week," he said.

"That's good news! I told your auntie that I could come by and help out," she said. "Did she tell you?"

"Yeah, she did. I'm glad that you bought that up. I know we're on a date, but I wanted to discuss it with you."

"Go for it!" she said.

"Well, since I just got out of the service, I don't really have a lot of money to ... you know ... pay for your services," he said.

Sharmaine laughed.

"I don't know if my sister has insurance. It's not like I could ask her or her husband, for that matter," he added.

"We can work something out. I work for a company, but I don't need to go through them," she said.

"Oh good," he said, looking relieved.

"I was simply volunteering because you all seemed as if you could use some help."

"We could use all of the help that we can get, once my sister comes home next week."

"Oh, don't mention it! I really like your family. You all seem so close knit, and I know how worried your auntie looked the day she was talking to Macie about your sister's situation," she said.

"Yeah, I guess we are all a bit stressed, in our own way. You know... it's the fear of the unknown," he said.

"Well, you can just keep bringing me here and that will be payment in full," she said, smiling.

"I can do that," he said grinning.

"I don't mean to be nosy, but I heard your brother was arrested along with you," she asked, catching Franklin off guard. "Is he still in jail?"

"Yeah ... I guess ... I really don't want to talk about him," Franklin said.

"Oh, I'm so sorry," Sharmaine said.

Franklin stared at Sharmaine, intensely.

"You seem as if you want to ask me something," she said, attentively picking up on Franklin's expression.

"Well … I'm just wondering, how can someone so beautiful be single?" He asked.

"It's easy when you continue to date losers," she said, poking fun at herself.

"Where are you meeting these guys?" He asked.

"I meet guys everywhere, but mainly at the hospital, since I spend most of my time there. By the time I get home, I shower, eat, and crash! I cannot tell you the last time I watched television. I go out on occasion, or if I am dating, but I'm really a homebody," she said. "But once I meet Mr. Right, I'll know."

"So, how many men are you dating now?" He asked, looking around. "I'm sure they've taken you here, and I don't want any problems."

"None of them have brought me here, because they can't afford it," Sharmaine said, laughing. "So, you have nothing to worry about; but I'm dating two right now. I was dating three, but I dumped one. Not including you," she said.

"So, what's up with the guys that you're dating, and did you tell them about me?" He asked.

"Well, I'll answer your last question first. No, I didn't, because I have to see if we have chemistry. I consider this a meet and greet," she said, smiling. "To answer your first question" … she deliberated. "Where do I began?" She said, looking drained.

"I met the first guy in radiology. He was there to pick up his x-ray films, and we struck up a conversation."

"What happened to him?" He asked.

"Oh, we're still dating, but he's on parole, so he can only go out at certain times, and those times don't always work with my schedule at the hospital. Plus, he has to wear his GPS ankle bracelet. You know, I don't have a problem with it, but he acts like he has no curfew! A few times we've caught a late-night movie and have been at a nightclub when that thing has gone off, like a fire alarm! I just can't!," she said, rolling her eyes.

"What on earth did he do?" He asked.

"Well, he told me that he was taking an Uber to the bank, but then he wanted the driver to go to his brother's housed to pick up some bootleg movies that he'd planned to watch. The driver refused until he reentered the new trip, since it was a different location. He said no. He wasn't doing all that. Well, the driver told him to get out. He tried to choke the driver out, and then the driver picked up a wrench that he had under the front seat and busted him on his hand. That's why he was picking up his x-rays from radiology. He told me he's trying to sue Uber, and then he'll be able to take me to more expensive places."

Franklin looked like a deer caught in headlights.

"I just cannot see you dating a man like that," he said. "You don't seem to suffer from self-esteem issues."

Sharmaine laughed. "Mommy said that I have a sign on my forehead that says, "I work on projects," she said, laughing.

"Your mother is right," Franklin said.

"Aren't you concerned that one day he'll put his hands on you?" He asked. "He seems explosive!"

"Daddy said he would kill any man who ever put a hand on me," she said.

"Yeah, but your father is in Detroit. For your father to say that, I'm sure he's thinking the same way I am," he said.

The waiter placed their food on the table, interrupting their conversation.

"This looks so delicious," she said, quickly changing the subject. "I just love sushi, and it loves me back," she said, patting her hippy hips as she picked up her chopsticks.

Franklin was more intrigued with her stories. One thing he knew was that Macie was partly right. Sharmaine not only dated bad boys, but rejects!

"Do you know how to use chopsticks?" She asked,

noting that Franklin was not partaking in dinner.

"Yeah, I know how to use them," he said.

"Well, dig in," she said.

"What about the other guy?" He asked.

Sharmaine chuckled.

"You want to hear all about them, huh?" She smiled, not waiting for a response. "Well, I met him in ICU," she said. "I had to pick up a patient's medical records, and I saw him leaving. He was there visiting a family member. His physique was just how I like it," she said.

"How's that?" He asked.

"Like yours, muscular and big. Well, he had a little more weight to him, but I don't discriminate," she smiled.

"What happened with him?" He asked, being curious.

"Things were going great between us. We would hang out after I got out of work. He would come to the hospital to pick me up every day," she said.

"Oh, so that's good, at least this dude had a car," he said.

"Oh, no. I let him use my car while I was at work," she said.

Franklin couldn't believe what he was hearing.

"You're so generous," he said.

"Yeah, to a fault," she said, chuckling. "Well, anyways, he was a lot of fun."

"In what way?" He asked.

"He loved to shop as much as I did," she said.

"Well, I hate shopping. I grew up with two sisters. One loves the malls, the other one is just like me," he said.

"Well, he loved going with me. He would drive me and stay with me the whole time. He would carry all my bags and help me pick out outfits to wear on our dates," she said.

"Well, outside of him not having a car, he sounds much better than the other dude. At least he treated you like you should be treated and bought you things," he said. "I know you woman love pocketbooks, shoes and ..."

Sharmaine cut Franklin off.

"Oh, he was broke! I bought my own clothes. He just helped me decide on what I should buy. There were times that I gave him money, like a stipend, if he helped out around my apartment," she said.

Franklin held his head down. "What?" Sharmaine was turning him off like a carbonated soda that lost its fizzle.

"And you still talk to this dude?" He asked.

"Well, I was mad at him for a while. He had a wreck in my car last year, and then he had another one and refused to help me pay for it," she said. "He was nice enough both times to drop my car off at a friend's body shop."

Franklin remembered what Macie had said the night before, about Sharmaine getting her car out of the body shop.

"Well, he's a loser then!" Franklin said.

"Yeah, he turned out to be! I haven't called him in two months," she said, sounding proud of herself.

"Maybe you should stop meeting men at the hospital," he said. "It's bad luck."

"Maybe … but the other guy that I dumped, I met him in church," she said.

"I'm afraid to ask what happened with him.

"Well, he was an usher at the door. He would always check me out when I came into church. If he wasn't on the door that I came in, he would run over and walk me to my seat. He wasn't really my type, but I felt that since he was right with the Man above, what issues would I have with him, right?" She said.

Franklin remained silent, waiting for the other shoe to drop.

"WRONG! Well, he took me out to this very nice steak restaurant. The steak melted in my mouth," Sharmaine said, looking as if she was making love with the food.

"Well, I know you like to eat," he said.

She laughed. "Who doesn't like good food?" She asked.

"True," he said.

"So anyways, then we started going to church together. One weekend my parents came in town, and he insisted on meeting them. I told him that I thought it was too premature, but he was bent on meeting them. I thought he may be the one. Well, he met mommy and daddy, and you know, that went fine. At the end of the night, he took daddy aside and told him that he wanted to take care of me for the rest of my life."

"How long did you know him for?" Franklin asked.

Sharmaine looked up to the ceiling, as if she was counting. "Oh, five months," she said.

"WHAT?" He asked. "WOW!"

"Oh, he was older than me and seemed mature," she said.

"That means absolutely nothing," Franklin said.

"That's what daddy said," she said.

"What did your father say? Did he approve?" He asked.

"I may be the oldest child, but I'm still daddy's little girl. Daddy made it crystal clear to him that he couldn't say yes to him just yet, since he had only met him once. Daddy told him that he needed to see what he was working with before he would approve a lifelong commitment of him being with his princess. Daddy took me aside and told me that he knows a lot of men like him, and they all run game. He warned me to be careful and to take it slow."

"Well, was he running a game?" Franklin asked.

"Was he? He tried to run a marathon!" she said, figuratively.

"Come to find out, he was the church whore! He had slept with most of the women on the usher board. I also found out that he had bad credit, and he was in so much debt. His debt collectors and the IRS were after him for nonpayment. Apparently, he and his ex-girlfriend invested in a cigar bar, and it went belly up, and he was in debt up to his eyeballs. The kicker was, he'd asked me if I could help him pay his debts off. In turn he would move into my townhouse and help me pay my bills, after I add him to my deed."

"WHAT?" He asked. "WHAT AN IMPOSTER!"

"Tell me about it!" she said, devouring the sushi on her plate.

"Did you tell your father?" He asked.

"I sure did. Daddy surprised me and jumped in his truck and drove 12 hours to get here. He went straight to the church and set it off," she said. "The pastor had to call the police and put daddy out. I heard that the guy doesn't even go there anymore, because he's too embarrassed. He'd been lying to all of them, too!"

"I think you should take some time to regroup and get to know yourself!" He said.

"Yeah, mommy said that my picker is off," she said.

"Picker?" He questioned.

"Yes, my men picker," she said, smiling.

Sharmaine rubbed her stomach. "I am so full! You didn't even touch any of your food."

"Yeah, I kind of lost my appetite," he said. "I promised Grace that I would bring her some food home. I'll order her something before we go," he said, waving down the waiter.

"You can take this. I don't eat day old sushi," she said.

"Are you sure?" He asked. "I don't want to fall into your category of losers."

Sharmaine laughed, not responding to Franklin's comment.

"I'm positive," she said.

Franklin couldn't get the information about the three men out of his mind.

"Wow, loser one, two, and three!" He muttered. "I look like a saint compared to them!"

Sharmaine laughed. "Well, out of Ramon, David, and Paxton, I miss David the most because we had the most fun!"

"Who?" He asked, looking intently.

"David. He's the one who would pick me up every day from work. I just mentioned that," she said.

"Yeah, but you didn't mention their names," he said.

"Well, David is the one who would go shopping with me for hours. He's also the one that wrecked my car and refused to help me pay for it. I'm so mad at him that if I saw him, I think I would kill him! Never mind calling daddy! I haven't spoken to him in over two months!"

Franklin sat up and leaned into the table, thinking, it just cannot be.

"What's David's last name?" Franklin asked.

"Oh, Johnson," she said.

Franklin's eyes bulged out of his head.

CHAPTER 73

Franklin returned home after his date with Sharmaine, shocked beyond belief, to find out that the David that Sharmaine was dating was the same low-down dirty scoundrel that they called a brother.

Franklin busted through the door.

Grace noticed him walk past her bedroom toward the kitchen.

"Your food will be in the refrigerator!" He exclaimed.

Grace could hear him open the refrigerator door, tossing the bag of sushi in it, before slamming it shut. He headed back down the hall, startling her, as he banged on her partially opened door as she sat on the bed rocking Justice to sleep.

"What is wrong with you?" She asked. "Don't you see me trying to put Justice to sleep?"

"I put your sushi in the refrigerator," he said.

"I heard you yell that as you walked on by . . . okay, thanks," she responded.

"Where's your aunt?" He asked.

"She's your aunt, too! Where do you think!" she responded, following him out of her room.

Grace watched as Franklin headed toward the living room. He flung the door open so wide that it hit the wall with a loud bang. She could hear him as he stomped down the steps.

"Dang, that must've been some date," she muttered.

Grace could hear Franklin pounding on Old Man Joe's door, demanding that Auntie Mabeline come back upstairs.

Auntie Mabeline followed Franklin up the stairs, fussing at him for disrespecting her in front of Old Man Joe. She could be heard cursing Franklin out, saying she knew that going out with Sharmaine was going to make him bat crazy. Contrary to what she assumed, Franklin spent the entire evening filling Auntie Mabeline and Grace in on what he found out from Sharmaine.

Franklin had shared that after discussing the timeline with Sharmaine, she confirmed that she'd met David the day Momma was admitted into the hospital. They began dating shortly after that. David expressed to her that he'd blamed himself for Momma's fall. She said how she felt so bad for him, because he said he had nobody, as if he was an orphan with no family. He'd been depressed and hitting the bottle a lot. She'd taken him out shopping a few days before Momma's funeral, but when she volunteered to drop him off at home, he said that one of his boys was waiting out in the parking lot to pick him up.

Grace realized that Sharmaine was the woman who

she saw David with the day she waited for him outside of the mall and the day she came to pick him up in her red BMW. That was the last time she'd seen him.

Franklin and Grace remembered that the day that Auntie Mabeline flew in, she'd inquired about David's whereabouts. Sharmaine mentioned that David said his annoying auntie was coming in for the funeral, and he wanted to be anywhere but home! So, she allowed him to chill at her place. That comment did not sit well with Auntie Mabeline, who folded her arms in disgust. Sharmaine said that David had left to go pick up Chinese food around eight o'clock that evening. She'd fallen asleep on the couch. She woke up at five o'clock the next morning to David coming in empty handed, smelling like moonshine. He told her he'd went to see his auntie before she put out an APB on him.

"That's the day he walked into the kitchen smelling like he fell in a bucket of homemade moonshine," Auntie Mabeline recalled.

"Yes, I remember that, too!" Grace said. "Did she know what happened to him the day before Momma's funeral? I remember he came in looking as if he'd been in a fight."

"I was getting to that. He didn't get into a fight. Apparently, the day before Momma's funeral, she said that she wasn't feeling well, so she let David use her car because he said he had to go get a haircut. He'd jumped on the highway and was speeding. He ended up hitting the guard rail and got banged up pretty bad. He lied to her and minimized the damage to her car," he said.

Franklin voiced how he couldn't understand why the cops hadn't arrested him, but Sharmaine said that she'd later found out that he fled the scene and had her car towed to an acquaintance from the barbershop, who has his own body shop. That guy helped David hide Sharmaine's car from the police. He didn't return back to her apartment, but told her he had to go somewhere and that he'd be back. She knew he'd been drinking because he was slurring his words on the phone. He apparently took a taxi here the morning of Momma's funeral.

"I told her that he'd come home looking as if he'd had been in a bar fight and reaking like alcohol. His eye was partially shut, and his clothes were ripped, but he'd lied to us and said someone had stepped on his shoe, and he got into a fight. I knew that sounded lame from jump!" Franklin said.

Auntie Mabeline shook her head.

"I cannot believe she still dealt with him. I don't know … I thought she was smarter than that!" Grace said.

"Remember, she's the one who took your baby out the nursery without your permission. I don't believe nothing that sneaky girl says!" Auntie Mabeline exclaimed.

Franklin continued.

"She'd threatened to break up with him, but he ended up sweet talking her and telling her that he had no one. She ended up picking him up last November, after Momma's funeral, and he moved in with her. She said he never mentioned that he had any siblings.

"But she came here to pick him up last November," Grace said.

"Yes, he lied and told her that he was living with a friend after his mom died, and they told him that he needed to move out because they were selling the place," he said. "She said, all she wanted was him to fix her car. He couldn't come up with the money, so her father helped her get her car fixed. She questioned him about his drinking after having a heart-to-heart talk with him. He'd confessed to getting arrested for a DUI after driving a friend's car. You want to hear the funniest thing?" He said.

"What?" they both asked.

"Anna Mae and Rufus had bailed him out."

Auntie Mabeline and Grace listened intently, shocked at what they were hearing.

"WHAT? Why am I not surprised?" Grace said.

Grace thought back to the night that she'd snuck out on the porch, the day the cop followed David home. She witnessed David taking the sobriety test given by the cop. She knew that he hadn't taken Momma's car since she hid the keys. Although she couldn't hear what the cop was saying, she saw the cops handcuff David and take him away.

"All this time, he was driving with no license," Franklin said.

"So, David has two DUI's," Grace commented. "He needs Alcoholics Anonymous."

Sharmaine mentioned that she didn't know where he was living at. She thinks that he may've been living with Anna Mae and Rufus. When she described the apartment building, it sounded like where they live. She hadn't seen or heard from David in two months."

Franklin continued. "Sharmaine had no idea that David was the same guy that she was dating, and the one who was involved in the hospital shooting. She was in denial and said that she could not fathom David doing anything to hurt anybody, since he was like a gentle giant to her."

"Really? She's crazy! David lied to her, as much as he lied to us," Grace commented.

Franklin continued telling them that David had mentioned to Sharmaine that word on the street was the woman across the street go sniffed for being a snitch.

"David probably knows what happened to the lady," Grace said, sounding more like a detective.

Auntie Mabeline looked in total shock.

"This boy needs help!" she said. "I cannot believe this!"

"He needs more than help," Franklin said. "He needs to get beat down, and who knew that Anna Mae and Rufus was enabling him like that!"

"I told you, I am not surprised," Grace said. "So, where does this leave you and Sharmaine?" Grace said.

"She's real cool, but she's not my type," Franklin said. "I told her that I enjoyed hanging out with her, but I can only see us as friends, especially knowing all this."

"Well, yes, after she was with your brother, I reckon so," Auntie Mabeline said.

Franklin cut his eyes at Auntie Mabeline, noticing her emphasis on "brother."

"The day that I saw her at the mall, I'd wondered what she saw in David, but now that you've mentioned all this, she really has bad taste in men. I see why she was stuck on stupid!" Grace said.

Auntie Mabeline looked across at her nephew, seeing that he was in deep thought.

"What are you thinking, child?" She asked Franklin.

"Well, if we don't act fast, there may be a chance that David will get out of jail if they find that he's not guilty of the shooting. He's not welcomed back at Sharmaine's, and he's definitely not staying here! Unless he stays at Anna Mae's, but that's not my call."

"Franklin, you would just let him stay on the street?" Auntie Mabeline said.

"Yeah, I would," Franklin said.

"I don't feel comfortable with David coming back here," Grace said.

"So, what's your bright idea?" Auntie Mabeline asked.

"He can move with you to Georgia," Grace said.

Auntie Mabeline was caught off guard.

"You know I only got a one bedroom. That won't work," she said. "Besides, grown folk need their own space."

"Then what?" Grace asked.

"We have to talk to the cops and let them know everything," he said.

"And tell them what? That girl is not gonna turn on David?" Auntie Mabeline asked, referring to Sharmaine.

"Never mind Sharmaine. Let's not forget what he did to me?" Grace asked.

"Ya'll just reaching now. They sure ain't gonna listen to hearsay, or what you think done happened," Auntie Mabeline said.

"Why are you being so negative?" Franklin asked.

"Right!" Grace exclaimed.

"I'm just saying," Auntie Mabeline said, turning her nose up. "Well, I'm gonna go back downstairs and sit with Joe. I've heard enough."

"Don't you think you need to leave him alone and help us figure out our game plan?" He asked.

"My plan is to go watch Jeopardy with Joe," she said, getting up and heading out the door.

Franklin stood up, placing his hands on his head. He walked to his room, clearly frustrated.

Grace knew that she needed to act and fast. Time was of the essence!

CHAPTER 74

The next morning Grace crept through the house. She peeked in Momma's room. She was surprised to see Auntie Mabeline fast asleep. She heard Franklin snoring, so she knew that he was out for the count. She'd just fed Justice, which knocked him back asleep, too!

Grace walked to the kitchen, carefully opening the back door that led downstairs, holding the phone to her ear as it rang. Macie answered the phone on the third ring. Grace told Macie everything that Franklin found out from Sharmaine. Macie was shocked! She had no idea that Sharmaine was involved with David. After listening to Grace, Macie agreed to go with her to the police station. She had plenty vacation time stored up so she could afford to take a day off. They both feared, with Sharmaine's unstable behavior toward men, she would possibly feel bad for David and bail him out of jail. Macie felt as if she was betraying Sharmaine's trust, but she knew that this would be in the best interest of Grace and Justice. They had to get to the cops before David's impending release.

Grace had showered and dressed by 6:30 a.m. She fed Justice again and changed him before going into Momma's bedroom to wake up Auntie Mabeline. Auntie Mabeline was cursing like a sailor, wondering why on earth was she waking her up at seven o'clock in the morning. It was like World War Three to get Auntie Mabeline to watch Justice. She used every excuse in the book as to why she couldn't watch Justice for two hours. She asked what was so important that Grace needed to leave the house at the crack of dawn. Franklin woke up to both of them speaking loudly. Out of frustration, he took Justice from Grace, saying only two words, "just go!"

Grace was reluctant to leave her son with him and his bad attitude, but she knew that she had no other choice. She could no longer wait on Franklin or Auntie Mabeline. She had to act now.

Grace stood in the living room looking out the window for Macie's car. She noticed a dark green Toyota corolla pull up, at 7:15. Macie looked up, noticing Grace peering out the window. Grace darted over to the coffee table; she grabbed the letter that Big Tuna wrote and placed it in her pocketbook. She opened the door, slowly closing it, before hurrying down the steps!

CHAPTER 75

Macie pulled into the parking lot of the police station, putting the car in park.

"Okay, we're here! Let's do this," Macie said with confidence; Grace, looking anything but.

Grace took a deep breath, as she and Macie walked through the double doors.

"You can do this Grace," Macie said, hugging her shoulders.

They walked up to the officer, who sat at the window, sucking on a lollipop while reading the newspaper.

"Excuse me," Grace said, her voice quivering.

The officer looked up, sliding the glass window to the left.

"How can I help you?" He said in a rough tone.

"I'm looking for Officer Collins," she said.

"What's the problem?" He asked.

"Umm, I wanted to talk to him about something," she said.

"Miss, unless you tell me the problem, I can't help you," he said.

Macie spoke up.

"Officer Collins asked her to come speak to him only. He's waiting for her," she said, telling half of the truth.

"Let me see if he's in roll call," he said, looking at the roster.

"Hold on," he said, dialing the extension before covering the mouthpiece.

"What's your name?" He asked.

"Grace Johnson. I'm Franklin Johnson's sister," she said.

The officer slid the door closed so that Macie and Grace could not hear him talking.

Macie instantly turned back into Grace's breathing coach, as when she was in labor, as she looked at Grace. "You got this, Grace. Just breathe."

Grace took a deep breath, inhaling and exhaling.

The officer slid the door open. "He just got in. He's on his way down. Have a seat," he said, pointing to the wooden bench.

Macie and Grace sat down, looking around the dingy police station. They watched as officers starting their shift were buzzed through the secure metal door.

Then the door opened and a nice-looking gentleman walked out, carrying a black binder under his arm. He had strawberry blonde hair, and his uniform hugged his body like a perfectly fitted glove.

"Miss Johnson," he said.

"Yes," Grace said, as she and Macie rose to their feet.

The officer extended a handshake and a warm smile. "I'm Officer Collins. It's nice to meet you," he said, shaking Grace's hand.

"This is my friend, Macie," Grace said nervously.

"Hello, Macie," Officer Collins said, also shaking Macie's hand. "Let's go in here," he said, directing them into a conference room with a small window. He walked into the room and closed the blind.

Grace and Macie sat down.

"Is Franklin outside?" He asked.

"No. He doesn't know that I'm here," she said, bravely.

"So, what brings you in today?"

Macie reached out and held Grace's hand.

Officer Collins looked surprised.

"He told me that he saw you the other day, when he was leaving court," she said.

"Yeah, I bumped into him," Officer Collins said enthusiastically, as he sat back in the chair, with his arms folded. "Yeah, I was in court the other day as a witness for another case. When they called his name, I was shocked to see him. I went to high school with your brother. I was really scrawny all throughout school, so I'm sure he had no idea who I was. Considering the circumstances of him just getting released from jail, I didn't think it was a good time to bring it up. He was one of the star basketball players. I remember he left the team. I'm not sure why, but the team suffered after his departure. They lost the remaining games of the season."

Grace remembered that playing basketball was Franklin's second love after his family. His dream of going into the NBA was dashed when he made the decision to leave the team to help Momma out around the house. He traded his Air Jordan's in for a pair of boots, and his basketball jersey in for a smock. In addition to working at the corner store, he helped Old Man Joe and some of the other older neighbors with running their errands and assisting them in whatever way he could. Franklin never regretted his decision, but it was something he didn't discuss.

"Oh, I didn't know that you played basketball with my brother," Grace said.

"Oh no!" He laughed. "I was one of the male cheerleaders who tossed the girls in the air."

Macie and Grace chuckled.

"If Franklin still has our high school yearbook, I'm Neil Collins," he said. "Look me up."

"Okay," Grace said.

"I also patrol in your area. You live on Rosehill Way, correct?"

"Yes," Grace said, pausing. "Wait, were you the one who arrested David last year?"

"Your brother, no. I worked the morning shift, but I heard about it. One of the other officers arrested David. We'd received a boatload of 911 calls of a car swerving down side roads. By the time, he caught up with your brother, he was on foot. He told the office that he lived upstairs, but he could tell he was drinking, plus the callers all described him to the "T"! He failed the breathalyzer, so he was arrested, but he didn't stay in jail for long before he was bailed out. I'd started my shift after he'd been booked, and they mentioned his name and address. That's when I realized that he was probably related to Franklin. You know, they don't look anything alike."

"That's because he's not our brother," Grace said.

Officer Collins looked puzzled, as he opened up his black binder.

"He's not?" He asked.

"No. Franklin and I recently found out that our mother adopted him when he was two."

"Oh, that explains why they don't favor," he said, writing in his black binder.

"I hadn't seen Franklin in years, up until I passed by him last November. I'd made an arrest on your street."

Grace remembered after they picked up Auntie Mabeline from the airport, they all noticed Big Tuna sitting in the backseat of the police cruiser, when it passed by.

" Big Tuna ?" She asked.

"Well, that's his name on the street, but his real name is Jefferson Corbin" he said.

"Oh!" Grace said. "I didn't know that."

"Well, enough about that. I'm glad you came in to talk to me. I'd spoken briefly with Franklin and informed him that I was working on the case of the woman who was murdered across the street from you. I'm guessing that's why you're here, because Franklin said that he would talk to you, to see if you knew something about that. Do you have any information?"

Grace took a deep breath as Macie held her hand tight.

"You can do it," Macie whispered.

Grace began telling Officer Collins everything from Momma's fall, to overhearing Big Tuna talking to a woman whom she couldn't identify, to her vicious sexual assault that blurred her vision, to the lady across the street who saved her and bought her back home. She provided details on how the woman smelled, and the bright orange crocs that she wore that made so much noise as she exited the apartment. She continued on, telling the officer how she found David drunk on the couch the next morning, with an empty bottle of Hennessy in his room and another bottle by the couch, up to discovering that the same woman who saved her, the previous night, was found dead. She shared how she witnessed the woman's body being rolled out on a stretcher.

"Just breathe, Grace," Macie, said, coaching Grace.

Officer Collins mentioned that one of the officers took a statement from an older gentleman.

Grace confirmed that it was her neighbor, Old Man Joe, who happened to be Big Tuna 's father. Officer Collins scoured through his notes, attempting to connect the dots. Grace went on to tell him how she remembered watching him, as he pointed his cane in the direction to where they lived.

She spoke about the fear that paralyzed her, making her too afraid to go out, thinking that the killer would come for her.

"I don't want to revictimize you, but can you share any details about the assault? Just tell me when you need to stop."

Grace shook her head yes.

"Do you remember anything about him?" Officer Collins asked.

"He was bigger than me and he wore Timberland boots. There were no lights on in the house, only the streak of light from the hallway, so I couldn't see his face. Everything happened so fast! Once he punched me on the side of my face, I blacked out."

Macie sat still, listening to the details that Grace had left out when she'd shared the assault with her.

Officer Collins continued writing. "Did you wake up?"

"Yes. Once he started dragging me down the stairs. I remember the pain I felt in my body as my back hit every step."

Macie winced.

"Once we were outside, I could hear a car turn the corner, and I remember a bright glow ... I assumed that it was car headlights. He dropped me right in front of the car, on the ground. I could hear him running away from me, although I couldn't see him or what he had on. Just a shadow. I tried to get up, but I stumbled back to the ground. That's when the person driving the car slammed on the breaks, and I heard a car door opening. Next thing you know, I vaguely saw a shadow standing over me. I knew it was a female, once she started talking to me. She helped me up, off the ground. She told me that she almost ran me over," Grace said.

"Did she provide details of what the assailant looked like?" He asked.

"No. She witnessed him running off toward the bushes," she said. "She yelled something at him. I don't quite remember."

"Who do you think could have done this to you?" He asked.

"It could only be one of two people," she said.

Officer Collins began writing, as he looked up.

"Who?" He asked.

" Big Tuna or David?" She said boldly.

"David? You mean, the guy who was raised like your brother, but he's not, based on what was found in the safe?" He asked, looking baffled, writing in his notebook. "I have to take a look at what's in that safe."

"Yes," she responded.

"Both he and Big Tuna are shaped the same way," she said. "They are actually half-brothers."

"What?" Officer Collins asked.

"Yes, you know the man who the cops were speaking to the day the woman was discovered, Old Man Joe . . . he's their father," she said.

"Wow! We didn't know that they were half-brothers," Officer Collins said.

"Well, they don't know it either," Grace said, referring

to David and Big Tuna . "I don't know if Old Man Joe knows that David is his son."

"This sounds like a soap opera," Macie said, chiming in. "Don't forget to tell him about the flowers and the letter," she added.

"Oh, yeah. While I was in the hospital …"

Officer Collins cut her off.

"Why were you hospitalized?Are you okay?"

"Yes," Grace responded. "I gave birth to my son."

Officer Collins looked intently, as he began to connect the dots.

"I don't want to assume but I'm trying to put the pieces together. So, the person who assaulted you, is the baby's father?" He inquired.

"Unfortunately, yes!" Grace said. "I want him to be brought to justice! He needs to pay for what he did to me!" she exclaimed.

"Yes, I agree. Trust me, Grace, I will do everything in my power to see that it happens," he said.

Grace continued.

" Big Tuna sent me flowers to the hospital, and he wrote me a letter. I received the letter when I got home from the hospital."

"Do you have the letter with you?" He asked.

"Yes, "Grace said.

Grace reached into her pocketbook and pulled out the letter that Big Tuna wrote handing it to Officer Collins.

The officer carefully read the letter before looking up.

" Big Tuna , well, Jefferson Corbin, is the person that you overheard talking when you were on the porch, right?" He asked.

"Yes," Grace said. "He said that he's gonna get some tonight."

"Here we go! I knew this was sounding all too familiar," Officer Collins said, pouring over his handwritten notes. "Well, let me tell you what I know about Mr. Corbin. His father is Joseph Corbin. The elder Corbin was a well-known businessman in his younger years, with a thing for the ladies. He's also the one who was interviewed the day the woman was found murdered," Officer Collins said. "Most people call him Old Man Joe. Other than the several disgruntled women he impregnated, he's a well-liked man. He was a generous philanthropist back in the day. Prior to getting caught up in the court system with child support hearings, he was always donating to mom and pop venues. He always helped the underdog."

Grace listened intently. She never knew Old Man Joe's or Big Tuna 's government name. Although she knew that Old Man Joe was a lady's man, it was news to hear how popular he was in the city and how giving he was. She remembered Momma telling them how he helped her get the job in the cafeteria where she met daddy. Grace started feeling bad about how she had treated Old Man Joe.

Officer Collins began turning the pages of this notebook, looking at more notes that he previously wrote.

"Jefferson got the name " Big Tuna ," while in prison. He worked in the kitchen, and he was known to make the best jailhouse tuna fish sandwiches. We actually had him questioned about the woman across the street. He's was very cooperative with us," he looked up at Grace. "He actually mentioned David."

"What did he say?" Grace asked.

"He informed the detective that he and David run in the same crowd, but they are definitely not fond of each other. I cannot say too much, because it's still an active investigation" he said.

Grace tuned Officer Collins out, as she reminisced back to the day she and David returned from the mall. She remembered how mad David had gotten, after his and Big Tuna's heated exchange. Big Tuna even mentioned it in the letter he wrote her.

Officer Collins continued to pour over his notes.

"The detectives had gone to your apartment and knocked on your door, but no one responded. Jefferson had mentioned to the detectives that you all were home, because he'd heard you walking above his head but you didn't answer the door."

Grace started to realize just how much of a snitch Big Tuna was.

"Yeah, Momma didn't like us opening the door if she wasn't home," Grace said.

Officer Collins interrupted Grace.

"But we can rule him out," he said.

"BIG TUNA? WHY?" Macie exclaimed, looking at Grace, then at the officer.

"He was in custody. We got a call from the woman you heard, but didn't see," he said.

"Who was she?" Grace asked.

"A girl that he was dating," he said.

"Oh," she said. "What did he do?" She asked.

"I can only tell you because the case is closed, and it was in the newspaper. He'd asked her to take him to get ecstasy pills, and she bought them from an undercover cop. He's not your guy!"

"But what about him locking a woman in his trunk? I heard that," Grace asked, not mentioning where she heard it from.

"We can't go off hearsay, but I can tell you, that's still

an active investigation. I cannot speak on that," he said.

Grace and Macie gasped.

"I'll see if we can get David to submit to a DNA test," he said, closing up his notebook.

CHAPTER 76

Four days had passed since Grace found out that Big Tuna was not the person who sexually assaulted her. She kept it to herself and waited patiently for Officer Collins to contact her about David's DNA results, but her hopes were soon dashed.

She thought she'd covered her tracks by secretly going down to the police station with Macie, but since she didn't leave a number for Officer Collins to contact her, he immediately reached out to Franklin looking for her. Franklin hit the roof when he found out that she'd talked Macie into taking her to the police station the morning he watched Justice. Franklin lit into her, giving her the third degree for betraying him before giving her the silent treatment. Auntie Mabeline simply jumped on the bandwagon, refusing to speak to her simply because she didn't get the opportunity to forewarn David!

Apparently, Officer Collins had more questions. Grace overhead Franklin asking Officer Collins if he could stop by the house on Thursday. Grace was on pins and needles. She wondered if he'd gotten David's DNA results back that soon. She wanted nothing more but to gloat once Officer Collins read the results, confirming that David was indeed Justice's father, since neither Franklin nor Auntie Mabeline believed her. She also kept quiet about knowing that Big Tuna was definitely not her attacker.

Officer Collins calmed her fears with the truth. She came to the conclusion that Big Tuna was truly harmless and genuine.

Today also marked something special. It was the day that Anna Mae was coming home from the hospital, so everyone was putting on a united front when they were anything but!

Franklin made an executive decision to leave Grace home with Justice, and that he and Auntie Mabeline would pick Anna Mae up from the hospital. He and Auntie Mabeline decided that they would inform Anna Mae about her incarcerated husband. The nurses had informed Franklin that she'd been constantly asking for Rufus. Auntie Mabeline thought that she'd come up with a brilliant idea to wait until they got Anna Mae into the car to tell her that Grace had a baby. She was afraid that Anna Mae would go ballistic in the hospital, thinking that Grace took her baby, and they'd all end up right where Rufus and David were, in jail!

"Grace, we're getting ready to head out," Franklin said. "I'll pick up dinner on my way home."

"You talking to me?" Grace asked.

"Who else would I be talking to? Justice?"

"Well, considering that you and Auntie Mabeline haven't spoken to me in four days, maybe."

Franklin put his hands on his hips. "Are you going to

be here when we get back?"

"Where am I supposed to go?" She asked.

Franklin just walked away. "I hope you have a better attitude when we get back!" He yelled.

The nerve of him, Grace thought.

She overheard Franklin telling Auntie Mabeline that it's time for them to go. Grace heard them as they walked out the door.

"Bye to you, too!" she said, hurrying into the living room to lock the door.

Grace looked at her discharge papers. She stared at the number a few times. She decided that it was time. She picked up the phone, dialing the number. The phone rang five times before a woman answered.

"Lakewood Community Hospital Trauma unit," the upbeat woman said.

"Hello, I'm wondering if Trevor is available?"

"Who?" the woman asked.

"I'm sorry, Mr. Cooper," she said, quickly correcting herself.

"He's with a patient right now. Can I take a message?" She asked

"Yes. This is Grace Johnson. I wanted to confirm my

appointment with Mr. Cooper for tomorrow?"

"Hold please," the woman said, placing Grace on hold, as the smooth jazz filled her ears.

"Hello, Grace."

"Hi!" Grace said, sounding upbeat. "Trevor?"

"Yes. I just walked through the door and my secretary said that you were on hold," he said.

"Ah ... yeah. I wanted to confirm our appointment for tomorrow," she said.

"Yes. I will be there at 46 Rosehill Way at 2 p.m.," he said.

"Great! I'm looking forward to it! Anna Mae comes home today, so you'll get to meet the rest of the family," she said.

"Oh, do you think we should postpone it? It's probably too premature for her to have visitors," he asked.

"NO! I need you to come tomorrow!" Grace exclaimed.

"Oh ... okay," he said. "Is everything okay?" He asked.

"Oh, yeah. I'm just anxious to start my meetings," she said.

"Oh, okay. How's your son doing? Are you both adjusting well, now that you're home?" He asked.

"Yes. We are. He's doing well, thanks for asking.

Well, I know how busy you are, so I'll let you go. See you tomorrow!" she said, abruptly ending the call.

Grace was hopeful that Trevor would be able to break whatever curse was on her family, although she could hear Momma's favorite song ringing in her ears, "Let Jesus Fix it For You."

The phone rang just as she was walking out of the kitchen.

She immediately ran back over, hoping that it wasn't Trevor calling back to cancel.

She picked up the phone on the third ring.

"Hello!" she said.

"You have a collect call from the Nirvana Heights State Penitentiary."

Grace froze. Why is Big Tuna calling again, she wondered? Since Franklin wasn't there to put the kibosh on the call, she decided to accept the call. She needed to know the real reason behind the flowers, letter, and calls! Officer Collins calmed her fears by telling her that he didn't assault her and likened him to the jolly green giant.

"Yes, I accept," she said.

"Hello!" The caller said, sounding anxious to have gotten through.

"Hello," she said, sounding surprised. "Rufus?"

"Yeah, Grace, it's me," he said.

"Why are you calling from the penitentiary?" She asked.

"The prosecutor is trying to screw me over. They're trying to pin something on me that happened in St. Louis, Missouri, a few years back. I didn't do it!"

"Do what?" She asked.

"It's a long story, and I don't have time to go into it. I'm trying to reach my wife. I called the hospital, and the nurse said that she was unable to talk. I called back today, and they told me that she had been discharged!"

"Well, maybe she doesn't want to talk to you!" Grace said, knowing Anna Mae had been asking the nurses for Rufus, according to Franklin. "The doctor told Franklin that she's been talking up a storm! When did you call her?"

"It was one day last week, before I went into the hole."

"You fell in a hole?" Grace asked.

"Grace, I don't have time to explain it right now. Google it! I need to talk to Anna Mae before they get to her."

"Who's they?"

"The prosecuting attorneys. They are gonna make her testify against me."

"Why would she do that?" She asked.

"Lies … they are making up a bunch of lies about me," he said.

"I heard that they let Franklin go," he said.

"Yup!" she said. "As far as we know, David is still in jail."

"Oh," Rufus said, sounding stunned. "Anna Mae knows I would never hurt her."

Grace could hear Auntie Mabeline's voice ringing in her ear, saying that she talks too much.

"Well, I got to go. Franklin and Auntie Mabeline will be back soon. They went to pick Anna Mae up from the hospital, and you are everyone's least favorite person right now, so I don't want them catching me talking to you! Auntie Mabeline said that you should have taken that bullet for your wife!" Grace said, feeling powerful.

"Your aunt is nuts!" He said. "Just tell Anna Mae I'll call her back tomorrow, and that I love her, and to not talk to anyone until after I speak to her. You got it?"

"O-kay," Grace said, hesitantly.

"They should be back soon if you want to call back."

"I can't. I have to make one more call." He said.

"Well, bye!" she said.

"Oh, Grace, before you hang up . . . your neighbor's here," he said.

"What neighbor?" She asked, already knowing the answer.

"That big dude," he said.

"I don't know what big dude you're talking about," she said, dishonestly.

"Yes, you do. The dude from the first floor. Big...... Big....Tuna!" He said.

"Oh. Well, at least you got one friend," she said, jokingly.

"Yeah, he mentioned to me that you had a baby," he said.

"Since when did I become breaking news! Please stop talking about me to those jail birds! Please keep my name out of your mouth!" she said.

Rufus continued.

"I figured after talking to Big Tuna that's why Franklin called Anna Mae up to the hospital that day. We had no idea why he was acting all secretive. So, what did you have?" He asked.

"Why is it any concern of yours?" She asked.

"Stop being so difficult," he said.

"I had a boy," she said.

"Cool. What's his name?" He asked.

"Justice," she said.

"O-kay. Must be a reason behind that," he said. "So how are ya'll doing?"

"Us, as in all of us?" She asked.

"Grace, I know you don't like me much, but I'm not as coldblooded as you think. You and the baby?"

"Good. Didn't you say you had to go?" She asked.

"Yeah. Just don't forget to give Anna Mae my message," he said before pausing. "Grace, I have to go. There's a line now, and these dudes are starting to get riled up."

Grace hung up. She picked Justice up out of his bouncer and headed into the living room, preparing for Anna Mae's arrival. She plopped down on the couch. It didn't take long for her and Justice to doze off to sleep.

About 45 minutes later, Grace awoke to the slamming of car doors. She laid Justice on the couch, securing him with pillows and she walked over to the window, looking out. She could see Auntie Mabeline getting out the front seat carrying three bags. She saw Franklin opening the rear car door. Franklin carefully assisted Anna Mae with getting out of the backseat. She almost couldn't believe what she saw. Anna Mae no longer looked fancy. She looked like a plain Jane. Grace watched as she made slow movements, like a mummy.

Grace's calmness turned into nervousness. What

would Anna Mae say to her? Would she blame her for getting shot? She didn't know, but she was sure about to find out.

Chapter 77

It seemed like an eternity for Franklin, Auntie Mabeline, and Anna Mae to make it up the stairs. She could hear Auntie Mabeline giving Franklin direction.

"Go slow, Franklin. Don't bang her body into the banister!" she exclaimed.

"Auntie, I'm good," Anna Mae said, sounding very weak.

It was the first time Grace had heard Anna Mae's voice in months, since Momma's funeral. It was a far cry from the annoying voice that she was used to.

Grace rushed over to the couch and picked up her baby boy and held him tight, and then walk back over to the door and opened it.

She could see Franklin in front of Anna Mae, as he walked up the stairs backwards, holding Anna Mae's hand. Auntie Mabeline walked closely behind her, supporting Anna Mae's back with one hand, as they all took a step at a time.

Grace stood back, so that she would be out of Anna Mae's view.

Franklin reached the top step.

"Okay, one more, and then you can rest."

"Okay," she said, faintly. She took a deep breath.

Grace backed up into the apartment. Anna Mae looked as if she was in excruciating pain as Grace watched her lift her leg up, planting it on the top landing.

"You did it!" Franklin said.

Grace hid partially behind the door, allowing Franklin to guide Anna Mae into the house. He held her arm as he walked her over to the couch. He quickly grabbed some pillows, stacking three on top of each other.

"Okay, go down slow," he said, guiding Anna Mae into a sitting position.

"Child, we're gonna need some help," Auntie Mabeline blurted out. "I don't know if I have the patience for all this!"

Franklin ignored her.

"I hate to be a burden," Anna Mae said.

"You're no burden," Franklin responded, giving Auntie Mabeline the side-eye.

Anna Mae let out a deep sigh.

"Don't worry about Rufus. He's a grown man and can take care of himself. You'll stay here with us until he comes to get you," Franklin said, with doubt.

"Okay. Where's Grace?" She asked.

Franklin's tall frame blocked both Grace and Justice.

"I'm right here," she said, moving from behind Franklin.

Anna Mae held her arms open wide.

"Grace, come over here and give me a hug," she said.

Grace didn't know what to do. "Is this a set up?" She wondered.

"Go on over there and hug your sister," Auntie Mabeline squealed. "You haven't seen her since your Momma's funeral!"

Grace reluctantly walked over to Anna Mae. She bent over and gave her a warm embrace with one hand, as she held Justice snug in her right arm.

"Oh, that's your baby?" She said, hugging both Grace and Justice. Justice stared at her.

"He's such a cutie, Grace," she said.

Grace had a loss for words. Anna Mae never paid her a complement unless it was backhanded.

"Thank you," she said.

"How are you feeling?" Grace asked.

"Well, I'm in pain, but I'm grateful to be alive. Never in a million years would I have thought something like this would happen to me. I'm still in shock," she said, looking sad. "When I woke up and saw all the bandages, I thought I had the c-section, but then the nurse told me that I had been shot, and how lucky I was to be alive. I remember bits and pieces about the shooting, but I don't know who would want me dead . . . besides Diamond."

"WHO? DALIA'S SISTER?" Grace asked.

"COME AGAIN!" Auntie Mabeline exclaimed.

"Franklin, you didn't tell them?" She inquired.

Franklin stood cold stoned.

Anna Mae continued.

"Franklin gave me an ear full, once I got to the hospital. He told me that Diamond was bad mouthing me. This was before Rufus and David came in," she said, looking at Auntie Mabeline and Grace.

"Franklin, what is this child talking about?" Auntie Mabeline asked.

Franklin looked closely at Anna Mae, remembering what he'd shared with her.

"While I was waiting for Anna Mae at the hospital, Diamond and I were talking. She was telling me all of the things that Anna Mae had done to her, when we used to help Momma in the soup kitchen. Yeah, she still seemed a bit mad about it, but if you're thinking she shot you, I think you should erase that from your mind. Besides, you just got home. I don't think we should talk about this now," Franklin said, looking back at Anna Mae. "What's important is that you are alive."

"That's easy for you to say! Gracie got that cousin of hers coming up here to the house. They're probably in cahoots together!" Auntie Mabeline said.

"Trevor is not in cahoots with nobody. I agree with Franklin. Although I don't know Diamond as well as Dalia, I don't think they are vindictive. Diamond don't look like she could pick up a weapon. She's very petite!"

"That don't mean nothing! Down in the country I got me a little revolver that I keep under my pillow, just in case someone wants to come in and disturb my sleep. They'll get a bullet right between the eyes!" Auntie Mabeline said. "Don't you go running your mouth about that, Gracie! I know you like to talk, and my piece is unregistered!"

"The last thing you need is a gun," Grace said.

"I agree with that!" Franklin said.

"You need to share this with that cop! Not about me but about that child, Diamond. I don't trust no one!" Auntie Mabeline said. "I've come across many a people in my time who appear nice on the outside, but they are hell on wheels on the inside!"

"I don't think it's a bad idea to let the cops know," Anna Mae said. "It would make me feel more at ease."

"Okay," Franklin said. "I'll think about it."

"Think about it nothing," Auntie Mabeline said. "You better be about it! Protecting your sisters should be your number one priority. Never mind some fast-tale girl!" Justice began to whimper.

"Grace, can I hold him?" Anna Mae asked.

"He's heavy," Grace said.

Grace looked at Franklin, who gave her a nod.

"The doctor said that she can hold up to 15 pounds for right now," he said.

"Okay," Grace said. Grace grabbed a pillow and propped it on Anna Mae's lap, so she didn't bear all 10 pounds of Justice's weight.

"Hi, little man," Anna Mae said, doting on Justice.

Grace watched closely as Anna Mae spoke to Justice in baby talk before looking up at her siblings and aunt.

"Rufus and I will just have to try again. But until then we can all spoil . . . what's his name?" She looked up, asking Grace.

"Justice," she responded.

"Has Big Tuna seen him yet?" She asked.

Grace almost flipped her lid.

"WHAT?? WHO SAID IT WAS BIG TUNA'S BABY?" Grace said looking at Franklin and Auntie Mabeline, who clearly let Anna Mae in on what happened to her.

"Child, stop. He's here now. You can't hide nothing no more!" Auntie Mabeline said.

Anna Mae looked confused. "Did I say something wrong?" She asked.

"Nope!" Auntie Mabeline blurted out.

Grace looked at Franklin, wondering if he's in agreement. Franklin stood in silence, with his arms folded.

Grace decided to not tell them what Officer Collins confirmed about Big Tuna . She wanted them to hear it directly from Officer Collins.

"FRANKLIN, WE NEED TO SHOW THEM WHAT'S IN THE SAFE!" Grace yelled.

"You don't need to convince me!" a disgruntled Auntie Mabeline said.

"Grace, just calm down and say less!" He said. "Anna Mae just got home. She's still groggy from the meds. I don't want to overwhelm her. I'll show them! Just stop!" He said. "I need to go get us some food. I wanted to get Anna Mae home first," he said, taking his keys out of his pocket.

"Let me have my baby," she said, taking Justice out of Anna Mae's lap.

"I'm sorry, what did I say? I swear it's not me but the

medicine," she said, looking heartfelt.

"It's not you, Anna Mae," Grace said, as she stormed out of the living room and into her bedroom, slamming the door. Grace called the only person besides Momma who understood her.

"Hi! It's me," she said.

"Hey, Grace," Macie said. "What's up? You just caught me on the tail end of my break." Grace spent the next 15 minutes venting to Macie.

"Well, I'm glad that Anna Mae is finally home, but you should just tell them that Big Tuna is not the baby's father," she said. "What's the point of waiting?"

"Since they don't believe me, I want Officer Collins to tell him. I want to see all of their mouths drop to the floor. I know who did this to me. It was David. For some odd reason, Auntie Mabeline is sticking up for him and acting as if he's innocent. Franklin's been acting like a jerk!" she said.

"Well, you have to remember, he's probably feeling really bad and damn near depressed, because he was the one who called Anna Mae up to the hospital. She in turn called her husband and David. So, I'm sure he wishes that he could turn back the hands of time, but he can't. Put yourself in his shoes," Macie said, sounding levelheaded.

"Well check this out … Anna Mae thinks that Diamond shot her!" Grace said.

"What? Little Diamond, the secretary?" Macie laughed. "Okay, they're reaching now. That timid girl is scared of her own shadow. If you say boo to her, she'll run off!"

"Yeah. Apparently, she was bad mouthing Anna Mae to Franklin before Anna Mae got to the hospital. She used to help Momma in the soup kitchen, along with Franklin and Anna Mae, when they were teenagers."

"I'm not convinced on that one! Diamond is definitely not that type of person, and I don't even like her like that! She's bougie! Always bragging about her rich husband. She's definitely not willing to trade in her cha-ching-ching for the clank-clank," Macie said laughing.

"I know right! Her sister Dalia thinks she's all that too," Grace laughed. "But Franklin just seems so different from the day we found all of the stuff in the safe, until now. It's like he's doubting me."

"Well, just talk to him," Macie said.

"You think so?" Grace questioned.

"I would," Macie responded.

"I will … tomorrow, when Trevor comes," Grace said. "Franklin just told me to "say less.' Yeah, I'll say more tomorrow."

"Oh, Mr. Cooper?" Macie asked.

"Yes," Grace replied.

"Wow! Look at you with the connections! Do you have any idea how long the waiting list is for patients to see him?" Macie asked.

"No," Grace said.

'Girl, like a year out!" Macie said.

"Well, they should have gone to school with him and fed him free ice cream," Grace said. They both laughed.

"Okay, Miss Grace, my break is up. Just stay calm. Stop getting yourself all worked up. You know the truth, and that's all that matters. Let them think what they want about who Justice's father is. Just remember, Justice feeds off your energy! You definitely don't want to raise a worrisome little boy!" Macie said. Grace looked down at her son, almost forgetting that she has to be a role model for him, even if he doesn't quite understand what is going on.

"Yeah, you're right," she said. "Okay. I'll talk to you later."

"Bye, Grace," Macie said, hanging up.

Chapter 78

Grace heard chatter coming from the kitchen. She opened her door and followed the smell of Chinese food.

Auntie Mabeline, Franklin and Anna Mae we're sitting at the table. Auntie Mabeline and Franklin were grubbing away, as Anna Mae sipped on one of those nasty liquid drinks, Franklin picked up from the store.

"Grace, the food is inside the oven," Franklin said.

"Okay," she said, seeming unphased.

"Grace, where's the baby?" Anna Mae asked.

"He's taking a nap," she responded.

"Oh. I think he looks like you," Anna Mae said.

"Yeah, I do, too," Grace said, not knowing where Anna Mae going with her comment.

"Oh, Anna Mae, you received a call earlier."

"From who?" Anna Mae asked, looking surprised.

"From your husband," Grace said.

"WHAT? Franklin chimed in. "You're just now mentioning it?"

"Well, had you not pissed me off earlier, I would have remembered to tell her," Grace said. "He called from the penitentiary."

"The what?" Anna Mae asked.

"The penitentiary," Grace said, with assurance.

"That's where he needs to stay!" Auntie Mabeline exclaimed.

"I think you need to focus on getting better Anna Mae," Franklin said.

"Listen to your brother. A good man would have jumped in front of you and would have taken that bullet in your place," Auntie Mabeline said.

"I don't know about all that," Franklin said.

"Well, I know that Rufus loves me, and he would never do anything to hurt me. I wish I was here to tell him that we lost the baby. We both were so excited," Anna Mae said solemnly.

"Anna Mae, I wish none of this happened. I feel responsible for you losing your baby," Franklin said.

"I'm sorry, too," Grace said.

"We'll just try again," she said. Auntie Mabeline showed no sympathy toward Anna Mae.

"Why?" Auntie Mabeline said. "He can't do nothing for you behind bars. He can't comfort you, hold your hand. Child, please," she said, sucking her teeth.

"Why did you accept the call anyways?" Franklin asked, looking at Grace.

Grace couldn't bring herself to tell him that she thought it was Big Tuna .

"I don't know. I just did," she said.

"What did he say?" Anna Mae inquired.

"He said that the prosecutor may contact you to talk you into testifying against him," she said.

"What? For the shooting?" Franklin asked.

"No, apparently something went down in some other state, and he said they found out, and the prosecutor is trying to pin it on him," Grace said. "I guess that's why they're still holding him."

"Anna Mae, what in the world did this man do?" Auntie Mabeline asked.

"Yeah, why would he say that?" Franklin asked. Anna Mae looked at both of them in shame.

"I don't want ya'll to judge him," she said.

"What did he do?" Franklin asked, looking perplexed.

"Well, before he moved here, he was living in St. Louis, Missouri," she said.

"I don't think none of us knew how you met him," Auntie Mabeline said, making sure Anna Mae didn't spare not one detail.

"I met him online," she said.

"Say what?" Franklin exclaimed.

"I knew it! I told your Momma that!" Auntie Mabeline interjected.

"That's why I never told you all, because you are so judgmental," Anna Mae said.

"Just let her finish," Grace commented.

Anna Mae continued.

"Well, he told me that he had a twin brother who robbed stores and banks," she said.

"OH, MY GOSH!" Grace exclaimed.

"Girl, what kind of family did you marry into?" Auntie Mabeline asked. Franklin put his hands on his head. "Unbelievable!"

"Rufus never finished the story. He would get so upset just thinking about how the cops took his older brother away from the family that every time I bring it up, he would break down and cry," Anna Mae said. "I think my brother-in-law is still in jail. I've never met him."

"Have you spoken to him on the phone? I'm sure if they are as close as you're saying, he must've called the house," Franklin asked.

"No," she said. "He would call Rufus's cell phone. He told me that he didn't want him to run up our land line phone bill."

"You are so gullible!" Auntie Mabeline said shaking her head.

"Did he say anything else?" Anna Mae asked Grace, ignoring Auntie Mabeline.

"Yeah, he also said that he called the hospital, and the nurse said that you couldn't talk."

"When was that?" Anna Mae asked.

"I think he said one day last week. He called earlier today, too! He said the nurse told him that you had been discharged, but he just wanted me to tell you to not talk to the prosecutors before you have a chance to talk to him."

"See that! He doesn't care nothing about you! He didn't even ask how you were doing or where you're staying? Child, he doesn't care if you are dead or alive!" Auntie Mabeline said.

"Sounds that way to me, too," Franklin said.

"My husband cares about me! I know that he would never do anything to hurt me. He loves me!" Anna Mae exclaimed.

"What's love got to do with it? Not a darn thing!" Auntie Mabeline said.

"Oh, he said that on the phone. He said that he would never hurt you," Grace said, in agreement.

"He also mentioned that he was in the hole. I asked him what did that mean? Did he fall into a hole? He told me to google it!" Grace exclaimed, shrugging her shoulders.

"Woah! That's serious! That means they are no longer holding him in jail, he's actually in prison. In the military, we call it the SHU. It stands for "Security Housing Unit." It's used for prisoners who get in trouble. I wonder what he did? It's not like he's been there for a long time," Franklin said, looking puzzled.

"I don't know. I asked but he wouldn't tell me," Grace said.

"I bet it's whatever his brother did," Anna Mae said. "He looks a lot like Rufus. Rufus told me that when they were growing up, people would mistake him for his brother. He's always being accused of things his brother did."

"And you believe him?" Auntie Mabeline said, shaking her head.

"Yes. He's never lied to me," Anna Mae said.

"How do you know that? Oh, because he told you," Auntie Mabeline said, grunting.

Anna Mae had a blank expression on her face as she looked at Auntie Mabeline.

"He heard that Franklin was out of jail," Grace said.

"Heard from who?" Franklin asked. "I don't know anyone that's in there with him!"

"He didn't say," Grace said, refusing to share that Rufus was in the same company as Big Tuna .

"I told him what you said, Auntie," Grace said.

"What? Don't speak for me," Auntie Mabeline said.

"I told him that you said he should have taken the bullet for Anna Mae."

"Well, that's the truth. Yeah, I'm glad you told him that. Yes, indeed!" she exclaimed.

"Anna Mae, I just feel so bad that I called you up to the hospital," Franklin said. "I know that if Momma was alive, she would have wanted us to be there for Grace. I thought if I told you over the phone, you wouldn't come. I wish this never happened."

"I told you, it's not your fault," Anna Mae said, as she looked over at Franklin, before looking at Grace.

"It's not yours either, Grace," she said, surprising everyone.

"I didn't tell you all this, but after David left here last November, he was blowing up my phone begging for a place to stay. I asked him why didn't he want to stay at home? He said that he kept having flashbacks of Momma's fall," Anna Mae said.

"He should feel guilty!" Franklin said.

"That's not what I got from it. I think he blamed himself," Anna Mae said. "He was a hot mess, but he'd met this girl at the hospital who seemed to take his mind off of what happened."

Franklin, Auntie Mabeline, and Grace listened intently to Anna Mae talk about Sharmaine.

"We met her," Franklin said.

"You all did?" Anna Mae said, looking around.

"Yeah, she was about to be your nurse, up until Franklin went out with her and discovered that she was dating David," Auntie Mabeline blurted out.

Franklin smirked, as he looked at Auntie Mabeline. "Well, I had no idea that she was dating David."

"What? I've never met her. David only showed me a picture of her," Anna Mae said.

"Well, she knew a lot about you. She told me that you and Rufus had taken David in," Franklin said. "You didn't mention that when you came to the hospital."

"We helped him out, but you know David. He's a rolling stone," Anna Mae said.

Grace just listened to them talk. She couldn't believe how insensitive they were, casually talking about David.

Anna Mae continued.

"At first, I told Rufus that we couldn't house him, even though we have a two bedroom. You know, with the baby coming in all. I know how David could be, and I didn't want him to get too comfortable and not leave!" She paused. "Well, that was before I lost the baby."

"If I was in a position to help my sibling, no matter what it was, I would do it! Don't talk about it … be about it!" Auntie Mabeline said.

"That's not what you said when Grace mentioned that David can move to Georgia with you," Franklin said.

"My place is too small," Auntie Mabeline commented.

Franklin and Grace gave Auntie Mabeline the side eye. Grace held her tongue. She had the comfort in knowing that Officer Collins would set her aunt straight, with facts, all pointing to David.

"I guess you were gonna play a Gracie," Auntie Mabeline said.

"WHAT'S THAT SUPPOSED TO MEAN!" Grace said sharply.

"Hold that baby as a secret until you gave birth," Auntie Mabeline said.

Grace was hot as fire. She had enough! Father time couldn't hold her tongue any longer! She lost it!

"YOU ARE ACTING AS IF I GOT PREGNANT ON PURPOSE!" Grace continued, unleashing all of her frustrations on Auntie Mabeline.

"Grace, calm down! You know she didn't mean any harm," Franklin said.

"I meant what I said!" Auntie Mabeline said, not backing down.

"Auntie, I don't think we should jump to conclusions," Anna Mae said.

"I'm shocked that's coming from you!" Auntie Mabeline said, looking perplexed.

Anna Mae seemed heart felt.

"The shooting changed my life. I remember laying on the ground, hearing voices but unable to respond. It was like my life flashed before my eyes. I really thought I was going to die," Anna Mae said. "I couldn't imagine not seeing any of you again." Anna Mae looked at Grace. "I'm sorry for the way I treated you through the years."

Grace, Franklin, and Auntie Mabeline listened intently.

"I hope you accept my apology, Grace," she said.

"I don't know what to say," Grace said. "I mean .... I always wondered why you treated me a certain way, when I've never done anything to you. It just seemed as if you had a vendetta to pay, and you wrote my name all over it."

"Part of it was that I was unhappy with my own life, and you just always seemed so happy-go-lucky," Anna Mae said.

"Child, just say you were jealous and move on!" Auntie Mabeline blurted out.

"Since, we are all making our wrongs rights, I'm sorry that I couldn't protect the both of you!" Franklin said, directing his attention to Auntie Mabeline and Grace. "I know you are probably wondering what's been going on with me lately. I know I've been in a funk. I've just been depressed."

Grace was relieved that Franklin revealed why he'd been acting so distance lately.

"I'm just glad you told me," Grace said. She looked over at Anna Mae. "Your apology means a lot to me. So, thanks."

"I ain't apologizing for nothing that I've said! I know all of you kids like the back of my hand," Auntie Mabeline said.

"David should be living on the street after what he did to me! He raped me!" Grace blurted it.

"WHAT?" Anna Mae exclaimed.

"Here we go!" Auntie Mabeline said.

"We don't know if he did or not, but I'm starting to believe Grace based on what we found in Momma's closet," Franklin said, looking over at Grace.

Franklin couldn't hold his tongue any longer.

"There's no sense of keeping things hidden from each other. Grace and I discovered that David is not our brother!" He exclaimed.

"I know!" Anna Mae said.

The entire room fell silent.

Chapter 79

Franklin and Grace stood with their mouths wide open.

"How'd you know?" Auntie Mabeline questioned.

"Momma told me a while back. She gave me $200 and swore me to secrecy. I told Momma that I would never tell, but if ya'll ask me, I would tell the truth."

"Momma bribed you?" Grace asked.

"Yes, you can say that," Anna Mae said, "with good intentions though."

"You knew all this time?" Franklin asked in disbelief.

"Yes, I did," Anna Mae said.

"So, why didn't you tell us?" Grace asked.

"Didn't you just hear what I just said? I promised Momma that I wouldn't tell," she said.

"So, when did all this take place?" Franklin asked, trying to hold in his anger.

"Well, right before David turned 18, I was on my way over, when Momma called and asked me to grab the mail on my way upstairs. This was right before I changed my mailing address, so my mail was still coming here to the house. So, as I was going through the mail, I noticed something from an adoption agency. When I asked

Momma about it, at first, she was being evasive. I know she wasn't feeling well, so I left it alone. As I walked out of the room, Momma called after me and asked me to come back and close the door. She asked me to sit down on the side of the bed, and she proceeded to tell me about David," Anna Mae said.

"What did she say?" Auntie Mabeline asked.

"Well, she started talking about her friend Ms. Purlie, and how they were thick as thieves growing up," Anna Mae said.

"Auntie, do you remember her?" Franklin asked.

"Yeah, I remember that woman," Auntie Mabeline said.

Anna Mae continued.

"Momma began to tell me that when they were younger, she and Ms. Purlie were joined at the hip. She helped Momma down at the dance hall sell chicken dinners. But she said, one day, Ms. Purlie just vanished. She'd told Momma that she messed with the wrong man and got burnt. Momma assumed that she was pregnant. Momma tried to get in contact with her, but nothing. A few years ago had gone by since she'd seen or heard from her. Then one day, before we left out to church Momma heard a faint knock on the door. She went to the door and opened it up to see this little boy sitting on the step with a note attached to his lapel. She said, it was crazy because he was dressed for church, too."

"Auntie, you don't remember Momma telling you that?" Grace asked.

"Gracie, I was probably down in Savannah by then," Auntie Mabeline said.

"Any mother who would do that, don't deserve to have kids," Grace said. "I could never see myself leaving Justice on anyone's doorstep."

"Auntie, I thought Momma shared everything with you," Franklin commented.

Auntie Mabeline shrugged her shoulders.

"I'll never forget the day that Ms. Purlie called out of the blue. Whatever she said to Momma, got Momma fired up," Grace said.

Anna Mae interjected, as she continued.

"Momma was telling me, something in her spirit wasn't sitting right. She just could not get it out of her mind that Ms. Purlie would do such a thing. Not to mention, Ms. Purlie had told Momma that her tubes were tied."

"From what I can remember, that woman always lied like a rug," Auntie Mabeline said.

"Did Momma tell you that David was a twin?" Franklin asked, looking at Anna Mae.

Auntie Mabeline and Grace hung on every word.

"Momma alluded to it. One day Misty was over

doing Momma's hair, and she was telling us that she was adopted. Momma said to me in private, that she had a hunch that Misty was related to David. If you notice, they both do that thing with their eyes," Anna Mae said.

"Squint. Yeah, I noticed that too," Franklin said.

"I was with that child all day at court. I don't remember her doing such a thing," Auntie Mabeline said.

"You must not have looked at her closely, because they do it all the time, especially when she's reading something," Grace said. "You're not going to believe anything we say anyways."

"Now, I've told you about that sassy mouth of yours. Just because you've had a baby don't give you no license to pop off at the mouth," Auntie Mabeline said sternly to Grace.

They were interrupted by Justice's high-pitched cry. Grace rushed out of the kitchen.

"Auntie, what do you know about Ms. Purlie," Anna Mae asked.

"She would always be at our house eating us out of house and home. She was the size of a toothpick. I always wondered where the food went! But in my opinion, she was a fast-tail hoochie Momma, who couldn't keep her legs closed, always chasing other people's men. She annoyed the living daylights out of me!" Auntie Mabeline said.

"Wow! Tell us how you really feel," Franklin said, as Grace walked back into the kitchen with Justice.

"Well, I had enough of this talk," Auntie Mabeline said standing up.

"Don't forget that Trevor will be here tomorrow at 2 p.m. for the counseling session," Grace said, casually sliding it into the conversation.

"He's coming to meet with you! No need of reminding us!" Auntie Mabeline exclaimed. "You can use an attitude adjustment!"

"Well, we all do! He is willing to talk to us as a family, so he can help us through our issues," Grace said.

"Speak for yourself!" Auntie Mabeline said as she walked off. "I will be down at Joe's!"

"The nurse had told me about him," Anna Mae said. "She said he's one of the best councilors, and he's very professional. I don't mind talking to him, Grace."

"I want to stick around to see if I remember this dude," Franklin said.

"Do I know him?" Anna Mae asked.

"Maybe. He's Diamond and Dalia's cousin," she said.

"Oh, I didn't know that. On second thought, I really don't want to discuss my business with him," Anna Mae said.

"I think you should give Trevor a chance. He has to keep things confidential," Grace said, attempting to reassure Anna Mae.

"Well, right now, I need to lay down. I'll see how I feel in the morning," Anna Mae said, slowly getting up from the chair, as Franklin rushed over to help her stand up on her feet.

"What day is the officer coming?" Grace asked catching Franklin off guard.

"I should be asking you!" He said, referring to Grace's secret trip to the police station. "He'll be here Thursday to talk about the death of the woman who was murdered across the street!"

"They still haven't found her killer?" Anna Mae questioned.

"No," Franklin said, "but it seems like they are closing in on whoever did it."

"Oh wow! They need to find the crazy person who killed her! Whoever it is needs to pay with their life!" Anna Mae said.

"I agree!" Grace said, as she cleaned the table.

"It's good to be home," Anna Mae said.

CHAPTER 80

The next morning Grace woke up bright and early. She walked into the kitchen to find Auntie Mabeline at the kitchen table writing out all of her bills. She was not going to allow anything or anyone break her positive vibes.

"Good morning," Grace said, sounding upbeat.

"Morning, Gracie," Auntie Mabeline said, not looking up.

"I thought I'd get up early and take care of my business before that counselor comes," she said.

"Oh, you changed your mind about participating?" Grace asked.

"Heck no!" Auntie Mabeline exclaimed. "I'm getting out of here! I'm going with Joe to his doctor's appointment at nine. We'll be gone most of the day. He needs to pick up some things from the market, too."

"Oh," Grace said. "Well, before you go, can you keep an eye on Justice, so I can go help Anna Mae?"

"Yeah, as long as you don't play one of your disappearing acts! Just put him over there in his bouncer. I'm not going to sit here and hold him," she said.

Grace placed Justice in his bouncer that sat on the table.

"I fed him already."

"I would hope so," Auntie Mabeline said.

Grace ignored her comment and walked to Franklin's room, where Anna Mae slept. She was surprised to see Anna Mae sitting up on the side of the bed. She helped Anna Mae into the shower and assisted her with changing her bandages. About an hour later, they joined Auntie Mabeline in the kitchen.

"Good morning Auntie," Anna Mae said, carefully sitting down on a pillow.

"How are you feeling?" Auntie Mabeline asked.

"Well, it's good to be able to stretch out, even though I miss my own bed."

"Yeah, I bet," Auntie Mabeline said, looking up.

"Hi, Justice," Anna Mae said, as she played with Justice's chubby hands.

Auntie Mabeline stacked her envelopes up in a pile.

"Gracie, can you go drop these in the mail for me? That mailman comes so early. I've missed him twice. I can't afford to miss him again," she said.

"Sure," Grace said.

"I'll look after Justice," Anna Mae said.

Auntie Mabeline handed Grace the pre-stamped envelopes.

"I'll be right back," Grace said.

Grace stopped in her bedroom putting on her flip flops, as she tossed the envelopes on her bed. She picked up the mail, perusing through it as she walked out of her bedroom. She nearly bumped into Franklin, as he wiped his crusty eyes.

"Oh, my God!" she exclaimed, stopping dead in her tracks.

"What?" Franklin asked.

Grace held up the envelope.

Franklin wiped his eyes again.

"What's that?" He said, reading the envelope.

Franklin looked down at Grace, pulling her into his room.

"Why is she writing David?" She asked.

"What? . . . Good . . . question! Did you tell her what was in the safe?" He whispered looking at the envelope.

"No! I thought you did!" she exclaimed.

"There's something she's not telling us," he said, recalling the other day when they found out that Auntie Mabeline was accepting calls from David.

"Don't you think we should confront her?" Grace asked.

Franklin stood, thinking.

"No! Not yet," he said. "Give me the letter," he said, extending his hand out to Grace.

"But . . . what . . . if she finds out that I didn't mail it?" Grace asked.

"Well, let her think that you mailed it. Don't let on that you saw it," Franklin said. "Do not say a word."

Grace reluctantly gave Franklin the letter intended for David.

"Are you going to open it?" She asked.

"Not now! Just go mail those," he said pointing to the mail in her hand. "I'll go into the kitchen and distract her," he said, placing the envelope in his top dresser drawer.

"Okay," Grace said.

Franklin peeked out of his bedroom door, looking toward the kitchen.

"Okay, she's standing with her back to the sink, go ahead!" He said, waving Grace toward the front door.

Grace hurried into the living room, slowly opening the door, as she heard Franklin with his loud "good morning" cue.

She flew down the stairs, dropping the mail into the mailbox, before rushing back upstairs before Auntie Mabeline had time to question the length of time she'd been gone.

She could hear Auntie Mabeline talk about her upcoming birthday. She mentioned how she told Macie that she wanted a celebration, similar to what she did for Grace. She filled Anna Mae in on what Macie did the day Grace left the hospital, not sparing any detail.

"Wow! I wish I was there," Anna Mae said, looking excited.

Grace walked in the kitchen, overhearing the latter part of the conversation.

"It was very special," Grace said, panting, pulling out the kitchen chair and sitting down at the kitchen table.

. "You'll meet Macie soon. She's a sweetheart."

Franklin was sitting across from Auntie Mabeline. His eyes focused on his aunt.

"So, Auntie, it's hard to keep anything from you, so what do you want for your birthday?" He asked.

"Well, I wish all the family could be together like old times," she said.

"Well, that's a wish we can't grant!" Franklin said, bluntly.

"Then why did you ask me? Ya'll kids just think of something," Auntie Mabeline said, sounding annoyed.

Grace looked at him, wondering if he was going to let

her know that they saw the letter addressed to David.

"Surprise me!" she said.

"How about Old Man Joe jumping out of a cake," Grace said.

"I'll take Joe over Leroy," she said.

"Leroy?" Anna Mae asked. "Not that ..." she said, before Franklin cut her off.

"Yeah! The security guard that you had words with. Come to find out, he knows Momma and Auntie. He's actually a cool dude," he said.

"Hmmm," Anna Mae said.

"I like surprises, but don't do anything behind my back that's going to get me vexed with ya'll kids," Auntie Mabeline said.

"Yeah. No one likes to be set up. If we do something behind your back, it's something that you'll like," he said, looking over at Grace, who's eyes bugged out.

"We'll think of something," Anna Mae chimed in. "I know I won't be able to cook like I used to. Maybe we can invite a few folks over and ask them to bring a dish," Anna Mae said.

"I don't know about that. I don't eat everyone's food. Just don't forget Joe," Auntie Mabeline said.

Grace changed the subject, her mind clearly on the

counseling session.

"Trevor will be here at two o'clock, so I'm going to start getting ready," she said, standing up from the table. Franklin, Auntie Mabeline, and Anna Mae looked at the wall clock.

"It's only 10 o'clock," Anna Mae said.

"I know," Grace said. "It's not just me anymore. I have to get Justice ready too!"

Grace picked up Justice and walked out.

"She likes that boy," Auntie Mabeline whispered in earshot of Franklin and Anna Mae. Anna Mae giggled.

"I heard you, Auntie," Grace yelled.

Chapter 81

The morning had flown by. Auntie Mabeline had left out about noon. She high stepped down the street with Old Man Joe in toe.

Grace had helped Anna Mae into the living room, laying Justice next to her, while she did a quick wardrobe change before her counseling session.

Surprisingly, Franklin was home. He was in Momma's bathroom, trying to unclog the toilet that Auntie Mabeline had clogged up. He came out of the bathroom sweating profusely, just as Grace was coming out of her room, fixing her shirt.

"Excuse me!" He exclaimed.

"What?" Grace asked.

"Umm . . . where do you think you are going?" He asked.

"I'm getting ready for the counseling session," she said.

"Grace, really? Dressed like that?" He asked.

Grace had cut a pair of her jeans and made them into booty shorts. Her breasts looked like two plump melons, clearly filled with breast milk, in her fitted hot pink cotton t-shirt.

"You know if Momma was living, you wouldn't dare

be dressed like that," he said. "I know you are 19, but you really need to go change. Trevor won't be thinking about healing the family. He'll be ready to lay hands on you, and then I'll have to lay him out!"

Grace looked at Franklin. She knew he was just being an overprotective older brother. The last thing she wanted was for Trevor to get hurt. Just like a two-year-old having a tantrum, she turned around and stormed back into her room. Fifteen minutes later, she came out with a royal blue maxi dress, that nearly hit the floor and a short denim, sleeveless jacket.

Franklin was in his room, laying on the bed, as Grace passed by his bedroom door.

"That's better!" He yelled, holding his head up.

"Whatever!" she said.

"Grace, I heard a car door close. I think that may be your counselor," Anna Mae said.

Grace hurried over to the window. She spotted Trevor getting out of a dark green Mercedes Benz. She watched him open the back door, grabbing his briefcase, after buttoning up his fitted dark blue suit.

"He's here!" she said with excitement.

"How'd do I look?" She said, turning around to Anna Mae.

"Like someone who is ready for the convent," she said,

poking fun at Grace.

"Well, Franklin was tripping and acting like my daddy, so I changed," she said.

"Should I open the door or wait until he knocks?" She asked.

"Grace, stop being so silly. Open the door, go downstairs to meet him and bring him upstairs," Anna Mae said.

"Yeah, I'll do that," she said, opening the door, hastening down the steps.

She nearly bumped into Trevor as he was coming up the steps.

"Hi Trevor! We are upstairs," she said.

"Hey, Grace. How are you?" He asked.

"I'm doing great," she said, being careful to not trip on her long blue dress.

Grace sashayed up the steps in front of Trevor. She reached the top step, walking into the apartment. Trevor was one step behind her.

"Did you live here while we were in high school?" He asked.

"Yes. Ever since I was a baby," she said, as they walked into the apartment.

"This is my sister Anna Mae," she said pointing to

Anna Mae sitting on the couch. "That's my son, Justice," she said.

Trevor walked over to Anna Mae.

"Don't get up. It's okay," he said, extending a handshake.

"Hi, Trevor," Anna Mae said. "It's nice to meet you. I heard some things about you."

"I hope they were all good," he said, looking at Grace, smiling.

"Yeah," Anna Mae said.

He reached down, pulling on Justice's chubby arm.

"Hey, little man. It's so nice to meet you," he said.

Grace interjected.

"Can I get you something to drink?" She asked.

"I'll take a bottled water, if you have one," he said.

"Yes. I'll be right back," she said. "You can have a seat over there," she said, pointing to the recliner.

Grace rushed into the kitchen. She could hear Anna Mae talking to Trevor about the incident at the hospital and how she thinks Diamond shot her.

Trevor quickly dispelled that notion and began to talk about how his cousin Diamond was raised with high morals and values. He talked about how his aunt was a huge advocate against gun violence, and how she often had Diamond and Dalia on the front lines with her, marching for safer streets, in support of gun reform.

Graced opened the refrigerator, grabbing the bottle of water and hurrying back into the living room, afraid that Anna Mae would say something that would scare Trevor off.

She handed Trevor the cold bottle of water.

"Here you go!" she said.

"Thanks, Grace," he said.

"You're welcome," she said, joining Anna Mae and Justice on the couch.

"Oh, my sister Anna Mae wants to join the session today," she said.

"Okay. That's great! Is anyone else going to join us?" He asked.

"My Auntie Mabeline left out earlier, and my brother is here, but I'm unsure if he's going to join us," she said.

"Your brother is welcome to join us if he wants," he said. Okay, well, we can get started."

Trevor opened his brief case and took out his black binder.

"Anna Mae, let me just start off by telling you what I do," he said, opening his binder.

"I am a grief and trauma counselor. That means I help people get through the pain of any type of trauma or grief that they've experienced. I give them ways on how to deal with and push past their pain. I specialize in all sorts of traumatic experiences, such as loss of a loved one, a sexual assault, or trauma that affects the sense of one's safety and happiness, like the shooting incident, that you shared with me, or experiencing the loss of a mother."

"Okay," Anna Mae said.

"Well, experiencing a significant loss of a loved one can be complicated and traumatic to deal with. I teach you ways on how to deal with grief and trauma as a result of losing a loved one. Any questions for me?" He asked.

"Well, ever since I've gotten shot, I feel as if someone is trying to kill me," she said.

"That's expected," he said. "Getting shot is a very traumatic experience. I know that it is difficult; however, you have to separate the experience from your desire to move forward toward your healing. You also have to realize that you are around people whose main goal is to keep you safe," he said, looking at Grace. "Face your fears head on!"

"That's true. I do feel better knowing that I am surrounded by my family," she said. "But I really miss my husband."

"I understand," Trevor said.

Trevor looked over at Grace.

"Is it okay if we discuss your assault?" He asked.

"I guess," she said.

"How are you doing with healing your emotional wounds?" He asked.

"Well, I've just been keeping myself busy by taking care of Justice, so I really don't dwell on it much unless someone accuses me of asking for what happened to me. That's been happening a lot!" she said. "Then I get really upset. I don't even want to mouth his name, but they force me to bring him up, you know … I am always feeling as if I am defending myself."

"Well, that's not good. You need people who are going to stand with you and help you get through this. They must understand that you have a reminder, every time you look at your beautiful son. Having family that does not support you can be extremely difficult. Grace, I want you to remain positive, and when they come at you with negativity . . . I want you to inhale and then exhale. Release that negative energy, and just remember that this was not your fault," Trevor said.

"Can I call you?" She asked.

"Of course, you can," he said, smiling. "Matter of fact, I will give you my cell number before I leave."

"Franklin and Auntie Mabeline need to hear this. They

are the only two who are accusing her of sleeping with the jail bird who lives downstairs," Anna Mae blurted out.

Grace looked sharply at Anna Mae.

"He is not Justice's father!" Grace exclaimed.

Trevor stood up, removing his suit jacket, as he demonstrated his breathing technique for Grace. He took in a long deep breath and let it out very slowly, raising his hands over his head. "I want you to have only positive vibes."

Grace mimicked Trevor's breathing technique, as she stood up beside him, raising her hands over her head and then placing them by her side.

"Wow! I feel better already," Grace said.

Trevor sat back down. Franklin could be heard walking toward them.

"Hey! How are you doing?" Franklin said, as he boldly approached Trevor, shaking his hand, placing the screwdriver on the side table, next to Anna Mae.

"How are you? I'm great! I'm Trevor Cooper. I'm a grief and trauma counselor for the hospital," he said extending a handshake to Franklin.

"Yes, Grace told us all about you. You're the one who used to come up to the ice cream truck. Diamond and Dalia's cousin."

Grace looked at Franklin sharply, not knowing what was about to come out of his mouth.

Trevor chuckled, as he patted his stomach.

"Yeah, that would be me. I remember that your route was in my cousin's neighborhood. No more ice cream for me. I became lactose intolerant," he said, patting his stomach.

"ME, TOO!" Grace chimed in, as if she was happy to have something in common with Trevor.

"I see! Looking good man! You look almost as good as me!" Franklin said, even getting a smile out of Grace.

"So, are you going to join us?" Trevor asked.

"Yeah, just for a few minutes. I'm trying to get this toilet fixed before our aunt gets back."

"Oh, I see," Trevor said.

Anna Mae began to whisper to Grace. "He's fine! You should see if he's single. I don't see a wedding band on his finger."

The two giggled, like two high school girls with a crush.

Their friendly banter was interrupted by a knock on the door.

"This is probably our Auntie now. I don't know why she just doesn't open the door. She knows it's unlocked.

Excuse me, while I get this."

Franklin hurried over to the door, opening it widely. His mouth dropping to the floor.

"WHAT THE HELL ARE YOU DOING HERE!" He yelled.

Trevor and Grace rushed over to the door, attempting to hold Franklin back as he lunged toward the unexpected visitor.

CHAPTER 82

Franklin, please don't be mad at me!" Sharmaine said, as she stood at the door, next to David.

Grace thought her eyes were deceiving her. She hadn't seen David in months!

"OH, NO! HE CANNOT COME IN HERE!" Grace yelled.

"WHY THE HELL WOULD YOU BRING HIM HERE, WHEN YOU KNOW THAT HE'S NOT WELCOMED!" Franklin yelled.

"HE IS NOT TAKING MY BABY!" Grace yelled.

Grace darted over to the couch. She picked up Justice and ran into her room.

"He didn't do it! He didn't assault Grace!" Sharmaine said, pleading on David's behalf as David stood tall behind her.

"HELL, NO, I DIDN'T! SHARMAINE TOLD ME EVERYTHING! YOU GOT THE WRONG ONE, SON! I AIN'T DID NOTHING TO NO ONE!" David said, yelling, his hands flaring in the air behind Sharmaine's Cola-Cola bottle frame.

Trevor looked as if he needed to intervene and diffuse the situation.

"Hi, my name is Trevor," he said, calmly, extending his hand, as he stood next to Franklin.

"Man, who are you?" David said, in a snide manner.

"I'm the grief and trauma counselor from the hospital," Trevor said, calmly.

"Oh! I've seen you around the hospital before," Sharmaine said, as if she was looking for her next male encounter.

Sharmaine turned her attention to Franklin.

"Franklin, you got to believe David. He called me and told me that they were releasing him today. That's when I told him that I met all of you, and I couldn't be around him, after what he did to Grace. That's when he told me that he would never do anything to hurt Grace," Sharmaine said, looking past Trevor at Franklin and back at David.

"Well, unless we have a DNA test, we are not buying anything that he's selling!" Franklin said.

"I think we should all sit down and talk this out," Trevor said, attempting to be diplomatic.

"Franklin, just let him come in and talk this out. I am taking Trevor's advice. I need to face my fears head on! I need to know why he shot me!" Anna Mae said, as she sat on the couch, reaching for the screwdriver.

Trevor looked back at Anna Mae. "Well, the part that I failed to address is that we don't want to be confrontational in facing our fears."

Anna Mae slowly put the screwdriver back on the side table.

"I DIDN'T SHOOT YOU!" David yelled, over Sharmaine's head. "YOU NEED TO CHECK YOUR HUSBAND! ASK YOURSELF, WHY IS HE STILL IN JAIL!"

Sharmaine began to plead with Franklin.

"Franklin, you got to trust me. I would not bring David over here if I felt in my heart that he assaulted Grace and shot Anna Mae. Please, just hear him out," she said.

Franklin began to rub his head. The bad decisions that Sharmaine mentioned the other night, in her choice in men, played in Franklin's mind like a bad karaoke singer. He was perplexed about letting David in, but he wanted to hear the truth.

"Now, I'm just an outsider, but I really don't think they would come over here looking for trouble," Trevor added, looking at Franklin. "I can help you all work through this situation, only if you allow me to."

"Franklin, I think we should just hear him out," Anna Mae said. "Just be ready to drop kick David if he tries any funny stuff."

"ANNA MAE, JUST STOP! I LIVED WITH YOU! DID YOU SEE ME TRY TO HURT YOU WHILE I WAS THERE?

NO!" He said, answering his own question. "I WAS TOO BUSY TRYING TO DEFEND YOU FROM THAT ABUSIVE HUSBAND OF YOURS!"

"WHAT?" Franklin yelled, looking back at Anna Mae. "What is he talking about?"

"Rufus slammed me up against the refrigerator once . . . well, maybe twice," she said.

"And you didn't think that was important enough to tell me this?" Franklin asked.

"Well, I know how you can fly off the handle. I know he didn't mean to put his hands on me. In spite of David's low-down dirty attempt to put my husband on blast, I know that Rufus really loves me. I shouldn't have made him so mad that day," Anna Mae said.

"THAT DAY AND EVERY OTHER DAY YOU CALLED ME, BEGGING ME TO COME TO YOUR RESCUE!" David yelled.

"You have got to be kidding me right now!" Franklin said, looking irate.

"Can we come in?" Sharmaine said, sounding cautious.

"You're practically in now … so you might as well!" Franklin said, keeping a close eye on David.

Sharmaine and David came in, both sitting on the love seat.

David looked across at Anna Mae, who was clearly perturbed.

"Anna Mae, I'm sorry for putting your business out there. I appreciate everything that you did to help me out, but you have to understand that he's no good for you! He's abusive! You also have to realize that I would never hurt you or Grace! Grant it, I know that we didn't always get along, but I love my family. I really do," David said, sounding emotional.

Grace slowly opened her door, listening to David talk.

David continued.

"When Sharmaine came to pick me up from jail, she started telling me everything. I must admit, I can understand why you all are mad. It was messed up, what I did after Momma died. I left Grace here by herself, and I didn't tell her that I was leaving. But ya'll have to understand that I was going through a lot. I really felt guilty for what happened to Momma. I blamed myself," he said.

"I told you that Franklin," Sharmaine said, sounding proud.

Trevor slowly sat down on the arm of the chair.

"David, this is good that you are letting it all out. This is part of your healing," Trevor said.

"What happened?" Franklin asked, bluntly.

"Where do you want me to start?" David asked.

"From the day of Momma's suspicious fall," Franklin said.

"Suspicious? Oh, here we go!" David said. "Well, Grace was in the kitchen cooking. I heard Momma ring her bell, but I was too tired to get out of bed. Next thing you know, Grace had come into my room, waving a spatula in my face, telling me to get up and go help Momma. When I got into the bathroom, Momma was holding onto the sink, trying to move about. I was wiping the crust out of my eyes, when all of a sudden, she lost her balance. By the time I tried to grab her, she'd hit her head on the tub and was laying on the floor. I must admit, I was in total shock, even after Grace came into the bathroom, asking what happened. I couldn't move. Seeing the blood coming from Momma's head paralyzed me. It was like a blur. I could see Grace running out of the bathroom into Momma's room, searching for the phone. It seemed like everything was in slow motion. She called 911. Grace really was a hero that morning. Well, she was mine. I hate the sight of blood."

Grace continued to listen from her bedroom, as she stood near the doorway rocking Justice, who'd fallen asleep. She was shocked to hear David refer to her as a hero.

Trevor looked over at Anna Mae and Franklin.

"Is there something else that you wanted to know, regarding your mother's fall?" He asked, sounding like a well-trained mediator.

"Yeah! Why didn't you tell us all this before?" Franklin asked.

"I was scared!" David said. "I honestly was scared!"

"So, how can you prove to us that you didn't assault Grace?" Franklin asked. "It just doesn't add up that Momma would fall, then the same day Grace gets assaulted, and she just so happens to find you on the couch, drunk the next morning."

Grace gently placed Justice in his crib and boldly walked toward the living room. She had to hear this for herself.

"First of all, I would never hurt Grace. EVER! When Sharmaine told me all of this, I was in total complete shock. Why would I do that to her! Ya'll are SICK! I knew that I was not going to be welcomed, but there was no way in hell, that I was going to allow you all to dog my name and make me out to be some sick, incestual rapist! Not on my watch!" David said.

"I don't believe you!" Grace said, shocking all of them by her presence.

David stood up and walked toward Grace.

"AH, NO! I think you should take a seat," Franklin said, as he and Trevor rose up to their feet, ready to restrain David.

David slowly sat back down.

"You were acting all crazy, blasting music when you know that Momma didn't like that!" Grace said. "Then you got piss-poor-drunk! You turned into someone that I no longer recognized!"

"Grace, I'm sorry! I blame myself for what happened to Momma. I don't know . . . but listening to the Sugar Hill Gang always made me feel hyped. Besides, Momma wasn't here."

"You see what I mean?" Grace said, looking at the others. "Everything to him is a joke!"

David looked up to the ceiling.

"This is hard for me to say, but I guess I have to admit, I have a drinking problem! I know this, and I'm trying to deal with it!" David yelled.

"Grace, just hear him out," Anna Mae said. "Stop jumping to conclusions."

"Well, let's just all lower our voices and talk to each other and not at each other," Trevor interjected.

"This doesn't make sense," Franklin said. "You were the only one here. So, it's hard for me to believe that you didn't do this to Grace."

"I don't get why all of you would think that I would look at my sister in a sick way! Bro . . . ya'll are the sick ones!" David said. "Ya'll seriously have some issues! I may have a drinking problem, but I think ya'll need more than this dude standing here looking like a choir boy," he said, referring to Trevor's bow tie and fitted navy blue suit. "Ya'll seriously need a real shrink! Yeah . . . I may not have made all the right choices. I may not be able to hold a job on a consistent basis, but what ya'll are not going to do is make me into some sick monster that goes around having sex with his siblings! Get out of here with that man!" David said, shooing them off with his hand.

"It's okay, baby. I believe you," Sharmaine interjected, as she reached out for David's hand.

Grace smirked. "So, ya'll are a couple again?" She said, not waiting for a response. "Just ridiculousness!" she said, shaking her head.

Franklin looked closely at David. He was starting to think that David had no clue about the contents of the safe, which meant that he had no clue that he wasn't their brother.

"Well, if it wasn't you, then who was it?" Anna Mae asked. "You were the only one here!"

"Ah ... no I wasn't!" David said.

"Duh! We know that Grace was here, but she obviously didn't do this to herself," Anna Mae said.

"I don't know ... why don't you ask your husband!" David said.

Anna Mae gasped!

"DON'T YOU GO ACCUSING MY HUSBAND! LEAVE HIS NAME OUT OF THIS!" she yelled.

"Anna Mae, you need to calm down. You don't want to exacerbate your injury. You are still healing from your wounds," Trevor said, sounding concerned.

Trevor looked over at David.

"David, why would you say such a thing? I know that when people feel that they are being accused, their first line of defense is to unleash on others and deflect the blame," Trevor said.

"Man. Get out of here! I'm not deflecting anything! It's simple . . . the night of Momma's fall, I was heading out to go back to the liquor store when I saw Rufus pull up," David said.

Everyone under the sound of David's voice hung onto every word that was coming out of his mouth.

"He'd asked me where I was heading to. I told him to the liquor store. He mentioned that Anna Mae asked him to swing by and drop off Momma's diamond earrings."

Grace looked at Anna Mae, remembering their conversation the following morning, when she called inquiring their whereabouts because Rufus had come by. Anna Mae never mentioned that Rufus had bumped into David outside. Perhaps, Rufus didn't tell her.

"I told him that Grace was upstairs but she was asleep. I was trying to get to the liquor store before they closed." David looked over at Grace. "Remember, we had words, so I wasn't trying to deal with you then."

David continued.

"Rufus was still sitting in his car, after I turned the corner. It was dark out, but I could see that his phone was lit up, so I assumed he was calling the house phone or Anna Mae. I have to admit; I may have left the door open by mistake because I couldn't find my house key, but my intentions were not bad. I knew that Grace was all in her feelings, so I definitely was not about to call her and ask her to let me back in."

Franklin stood up, with his arms folded. All of them were shocked at what they were hearing.

David looked at Anna Mae. "You called me and asked where I was at, and I told you, Anna Mae. So, don't go acting like you didn't know that I wasn't home! You knew that I was out! Remember, I told you that I was out, but Grace was at the house. That's when you said that Rufus was swinging by to drop off Momma's earrings. I don't know why you just didn't hold onto to them yourself!"

Grace held onto her heart. Her mind was spinning out of control. She reminisced back on the inappropriate comments that Rufus used to say to her. She remembered how Momma took notice and watched him like a hawk. She recalled the day of the cookout, shortly after he and

Anna Mae tied the knot, that he came up behind her, pressing his privates against her butt and said, "if you weren't my sister-in-law." She felt sick to her stomach!

"What I am NOT going to do, is sit here and allow you to accuse my husband!" Anna Mae blurted out, as she looked over at Franklin. "You and Auntie Mabeline told me that Grace was messing with Big Tuna behind everyone's back!"

"WHAT? I TOLD THAT DUDE TO STAY AWAY FROM GRACE! I CAUGHT HIM CHECKING HER OUT THE DAY WE CAME BACK FROM THE MALL!" David yelled.

"I know! I remember you telling me that baby," Sharmaine interjected, like a supportive girlfriend.

Grace knew that she could no longer wait for Officer Collins to drop the bomb. She knew that Big Tuna was innocent. She also knew that the truth would set her free and she had to face her fears.

"It was not Big Tuna !" she said.

Everyone turned their attention from David, to Grace.

"Oh, no, you are not going to use my husband as a scapegoat!" Anna Mae said, sounding lethargic and out of breath. "Franklin and Auntie Mabeline told me all about it! You must've been creeping downstairs or he was creeping up here, when David wasn't home!"

Trevor stood up and walked towards Grace.

"Grace, how do you know that it wasn't Big Tuna?" He asked, in a calming voice.

Grace began to speak.

"The other day when Macie took me to the police station, Officer Collins told me that there was no way that Big Tuna could have sexually assaulted me," she said.

"Based on what?" Franklin asked.

"Just let me finish," Grace said. "After I'd gotten home from seeing Momma the night of her fall, David was in the living room blasting his music. As he said, I had gotten mad at him for disrespecting Momma's house. So, I stepped out onto the porch. That's when I overheard Big Tuna talking to a woman. I could not see them or make out her voice. He'd just gotten out of jail and said that he was going to "get him some tonight." I told Officer Collins what I'd overheard and thought that maybe it could have been either Big Tuna or David who'd assaulted me. That's when he told me, early that evening, they'd arrested Big Tuna and his girlfriend for buying pills from an undercover officer. They were arrested after I heard them. He told me that they both spent the night in jail."

Franklin walked over to Grace and stood next to Trevor.

"Grace, why didn't you tell us that?" He asked.

"Well, all of you were accusing me of sexing Big Tuna

, and I'd planned to wait until Officer Collins came by tomorrow and have him tell all of you, since you didn't believe that I was telling the truth!" she said.

"I still don't believe it!" Anna Mae said.

Grace looked down at Anna Mae, who was adjusting herself on the couch.

"Well, believe it Anna Mae! He did not do it!" Grace said.

"So why did he send you flowers and the letter?" Franklin asked.

"He heard that I was in the hospital, either by his friend who works at the hospital or Old Man Joe, who came to the hospital to see me with Auntie Mabeline."

"Where is she at any ways?" David asked.

Franklin, Anna Mae, and Grace all looked at him, giving him the same look.

"With Old Man Joe," they said in unison.

Grace continued.

"That's how Big Tuna found out that I had a baby. Actually, Officer Collins told me that his real name is Jefferson Corbin."

"What? Okay," Anna Mae said, looking as if she ate something distasteful.

Grace continued.

"As for the letter, he wrote to ask if I could go down and look after his father. You read the letter for yourself," she said looking at Franklin. "His mother was supposed to look after him, but for some reason he couldn't get in touch with her."

"Well, your Auntie won't have none of that!" Sharmaine exclaimed, thinking back to her rocky encounter with Ms. Mabeline. "That's for sure!"

"Well, you can say what you want; Rufus is not the father of that boy! I know that he would submit to a DNA test in a heartbeat to prove it! I knew I shouldn't have come back to this house! It's nothing but drama!" Anna Mae exclaimed, flaring her arms in the air.

"You bought the drama when you married him!" David exclaimed.

"Anna Mae, it's starting to add up. I know it's not what you want to hear but think about it, he's not just in a city jail, he's in the state penitentiary. The fact that they released me and David, speaks volumes. Grace shared with us last night that he called saying that something went down in St. Louis, Missouri. You even said yourself, just last night, that he has this twin brother that you never met but he talks so much about. Doesn't that strike you as odd?" Franklin asked. Anna Mae looked upset. Trevor noticed her confused look.

"I understand that you all want to get to the bottom of this but keep in mind that your sister is still recovering, not to mention the meds that she's on probably have her memory a bit jumbled," Trevor said. "So be easy."

"THERE IS NOTHING WRONG WITH MY MIND! STOP SPEAKING FOR ME!" Anna Mae exclaimed.

"Woah, okay," Trevor said, backing up.

The tension was cut by Justice's loud wail. Grace ran into her bedroom, picked up her son and returned to the living room to join the others.

"Can I hold him?" Sharmaine asked.

Grace was hesitant, but she knew that everyone was on guard. She walked over and handed Justice to Sharmaine as she stood up. Sharmaine slowly sat down, admiring Justice. David looked over at his nephew for the first time.

"This kid doesn't look nothing like me! Are you serious? He has Rufus' egg head! He looks just like him!" He exclaimed.

Trevor, Franklin, and Grace came closer as they looked intently at Justice.

"Yeah ... I can see it now!" Franklin said.

"Well, I have never met Rufus, so I don't know," Trevor added.

"Me either, but Justice is still a cutie, no matter who

his daddy is," Sharmaine said, as she played with Justice's full cheeks.

"YA'LL ARE JUST GOING TO STAND HERE AND DISRESPECT ME!" Anna Mae yelled, mustering all of her strength.

"Ah, no, your husband disrespected you!" David said.

Franklin stood back, not letting David off the hook so quick.

"What about the pictures in your desk?" He asked.

"What are you talking about?" David asked.

"Yeah, Franklin and I saw naked pictures that you had of me in your desk drawer," Grace interjected.

"Okay, you two have really lost every bit of sense that I thought you had. I have naked pictures of my sister?" He said, looking at Sharmaine, who seemed to be the only person who believed in him. "Do you believe this? This is why I didn't want to do this!"

"Franklin didn't tell me that when I was out with him! Is that true?" Sharmaine said, said, looking strangely at David.

"HELL NO, IT'S NOT TRUE!" He yelled.

"I didn't hear about this!" Anna Mae exclaimed.

Franklin and Grace looked at each other.

"The day that I was discharged from the army was the same day that I found out that Grace was pregnant. She'd told me that she saw a safe in Momma's closet. Well, I don't want to get into what we found," he said, not wanting to divulge the family business in front of Trevor and Sharmaine.

"The funny thing is someone had busted the lock on the safe. So, somebody knew that it was in there. The question is, who besides Momma, would know that the safe was in there?" Franklin said, looking over at David. "Something told me to go check your room. So, Grace and I went into your room, and I busted open your desk drawer, and that's when I discovered all of these pictures that you took of Grace, and some of these pictures were taken a few years ago. So, what, someone planted those? It wasn't you? Right?" Franklin said, folding his arms.

David laughed.

"IT'S NOT FUNNY!" Grace yelled.

"Grace, calm down and talk about your feelings. Yelling will get us nowhere," Trevor said.

"I'm laughing because this is just a joke!" David said.

"You're the joke!" Anna Mae said.

"No! You're the joke, and your husband is the joker! He is playing you!" David exclaimed. "Okay ... I know, I may be an alcoholic but my memory is still sharp as the pointed tip of your eyebrows," he said, looking at Anna

Mae. David continued.

"I admit, on the day of Momma's funeral, I was highly intoxicated, but I was not that much out of it that I didn't know what was going on," he said.

"You told us that you got into a fight!" Franklin said.

"Yeah, I am man enough to admit that I lied about that!" David said, looking at Sharmaine. "I'd actually got into a car accident. I know I was banged up pretty bad, but I still wanted to attend Momma's funeral. That's when I came home and … well … you know the story. You made the executive decision and told me that I wasn't going to Momma's funeral," he said, looking up at Franklin. "I was drunk! After ya'll left, slamming doors and all, I woke up to what I thought was my head pounding. Then I realized it wasn't my head; it was someone actually banging on the door. I figured that ya'll were back, not even looking at the time. I was surprised to look out the peep hole to see Rufus."

"So, he came back here? I was wondering where he went," Anna Mae asked.

"Yeah, your husband was here," David said.

"I'd asked him where were ya'll at? He said that ya'll were at the funeral. So, I'd asked him, what was he doing here? That's when he said something about Old Man Joe had busted him in the head with his cane on the way to the church. I guess Old Man Joe thought his curls were dangling worms or some sh..." David caught himself.

"Or something like that. I remember telling him that my head was banging and I had to go lay back down. Well, I remember telling him that I was going back to bed.

He'd sat down in the living room and eventually came into my room. I can't even tell you what he was talking about, but I remember he sat at my desk.

Well, he was talking to himself because when I woke up, he was gone. You know I don't keep the neatest room, but it did look as if someone had gone through my stuff. I didn't think anything of it, until the day that I was looking for my watch that Sharmaine bought me. That's when I realized that it was missing. I knew where I had put it. It was on my dresser, near my clock.

About a month or so after Momma's funeral, I'd bumped into Rufus at the barbershop and noticed two things: he'd cut his jerry curl, and he was wearing a similar watch, like the one I was missing. When I questioned him about the watch, that's when he said that he borrowed it and didn't think I would mind. I was like, this dude is a kleptomaniac!" David said.

"Rufus has a lot of watches, and he doesn't steal," Anna Mae interjected.

"Are you sure about that?" David said, leaning forward, towards Anna Mae's direction. "Because he took the watch off his wrist and gave it back to me, and he admitted to taking it!"

David continued.

"I changed the subject and started telling him how I was looking for a job, and that I'd been helping Misty out in the shop, and she's been letting me crash there at night. That's when he told me that I was family, and that he and Anna Mae could help me out. When I asked, in what way, he said that I could crash at their house, until I got myself on my feet."

"See that! Ya'll are trying to make my husband out to be some villain, when he's not!" Anna Mae said, looking at David. "We helped you out, and you did nothing but make messes for me to clean up!"

"Seems to me that he was simply trying to take the attention off of him," Franklin said.

"Uh huh," Grace commented.

"I wonder if he knew that the safe was in Momma's closet?" Franklin asked.

"Now, I didn't know nothing about no safe!" David said, holding his hands up in the air.

"Someone knew about it, because they broke the lock on it," Grace added.

Anna Mae looked as if she'd seen a ghost.

"I may have mentioned to Rufus that Momma had this

big old safe in her closet, but that was a long time ago. He probably forgot all about me telling him that."

"BINGO!" David said, looking at Franklin and Grace. "Told you!"

Sharmaine listened closely.

"You're not telling us nothing!" Anna Mae exclaimed.

"Anna Mae, if he knew that the safe was in there, he may have rummaged through it, while we were at the funeral."

"Yup!" Grace interjected.

Anna Mae shrugged her shoulder. "Think what you want!"

Trevor walked over to Anna Mae.

"Anna Mae, you need to breathe. Inhale and exhale. It will help your diaphragm," he said.

"Get out of my face!" Anna Mae said. "You are starting to work my nerves!"

"Anna Mae, stop being rude to him. He's only trying to help!" Grace said.

"I don't need any help!" Anna Mae responded sharply.

"Anna Mae, I know this is all difficult for you to hear, but you do need help. This is why you are here," Franklin said.

All of a sudden, their attention shifted to the sound coming from the door.

Franklin walked over to the door.

"Maybe that's Auntie Mabeline," he said, opening the door.

"Hey ya'll!"

"What are you doing here?" Franklin asked.

Dalia and Diamond stood in the doorway, holding a fresh bouquet of yellow flowers.

"Hey Franklin!" Dalia said, batting her eyes, dressed in a fitted two-piece black skirt and top. She gazed into the apartment, past Franklin.

"Hi, Franklin," Diamond said, looking equally seductive. She was dressed casually, in a hot pink strapless maxi dress and black stilettos that matched her hot pink matted lipstick.

Both ladies, huffed and puffed, as they caught their breath.

"I DON'T WANT HER HERE!" Anna Mae yelled.

"JUST BREATHE!" Trevor exclaimed.

"THEY GOT TO GO!" Grace said.

"Oh snap! She can talk!" Dalia said.

"What is wrong with her?" Diamond asked Franklin.

"We wanted to stop by and drop off these flowers for Anna Mae. I looked on the computer and saw that she was discharged the other day."

"Isn't that against policy?" Sharmaine chimed in. "You're not supposed to look at the patients records and then show up to their house."

"Girl, we go way back. We know them!" Diamond said.

"But that's still a privacy violation," Sharmaine said, sounding as if she was of mind, body, and sound judgement.

"Girl, you taking things way too serious," Diamond said. "I don't know you like that, but I've seen you around with your men friends," attempting to put Sharmaine on blast.

Sharmaine slid back into the couch.

"There's my cousin!" Dalia said, running past Franklin and over to Trevor, giving him a hug.

Trevor didn't look at all surprised that his cousins had shown up to the house.

"Hey, what's going on?" He said. "You know I'm in the middle of a session."

"Boy, stop playing. You know you told us to stop by in case something jumps off," Dalia said.

Anna Mae looked over at Grace.

"I thought you said that he kept things confidential?" Anna Mae said. Grace looked stone-faced.

"Well, we are not going to stay. You look like you have things under control," Diamond said, looking around the room, locking eyes with David. "Oh, my word! When did you get out?"

"Hey. I got out this morning," he said.

"Oh! Well, I hope you stay on the right side of the law this time. That goes for the both of you," she said, looking keenly at Franklin and David. "STOP THE VIOLENCE!" she chanted, raising her fist in the air.

Dalia walked over to Anna Mae.

"Anna Mae, these are for you," she said, extending the colorful bouquet of flowers. Anna Mae gave her a blank stare.

"I'll take them," Grace said, grabbing the flowers from Dalia.

"Ooooh, girl, you need to make an appointment and come back into the shop! Your hair is looking like who done it and ran, and came back and tried to do it again and failed!" Dalia said, with attitude.

"Okay, I'm not even going to apologize for being rude. We need ya'll to exit stage left," Franklin said, opening the door wider.

"Whatever! Just remember, I saved your sister's life,

while you and your brother were playing cops and robbers in the emergency room!" Diamond exclaimed.

"Trev, text us when you leave, so we know that you are okay," Dalia said, as she sashayed past Franklin, out of the apartment with her sister Diamond.

"Oh, Franklin, this is for you," Diamond said, handing Franklin a piece of paper.

"What's this?" He asked.

"A bill for the glass table that you shattered in the emergency room, when you threw the chair at him!" she said, pointing to David.

"Bye ya'll!" they both said in unison, as they hurried down the stairs.

"I am so sorry!" Trevor said.

Grace stared at him blankly.

"Well, I think it's time for me to wrap up this session," Trevor said, looking at his watch. "Oh my! I didn't realize how late it was. The session was only supposed to be one hour. It's almost four o'clock," he said, looking up at Grace. "I'm going to have to charge you for the extra time that I spent here."

Grace walked over to the door and stood next to Franklin. She used the flowers to direct Trevor out the apartment. Once he got into the hallway, she whipped the flowers at him, hitting him in the back of the head.

"No wonder why ya'll have issues! The whole family is violent!" He said, hurrying down the steps.

CHAPTER 83

Everyone looked wiped out.

Grace sat down on the couch next to Anna Mae, just staring off into space.

Sharmaine rested her head on David's shoulder.

"David, we better go. You know they are not going to allow you to stay here tonight," she said. "Plus, I am getting tired."

"You got that right!" Grace said.

"Yeah, ya'll should get going!" Franklin echoed. "We just need some time to process everything that you mentioned. A lot has been said today, and we're all just trying to figure it all out."

"I understand," David said. "But you got to believe me. I would never hurt the people that I love."

Grace looked at David closely. Although she didn't want to put it in the atmosphere, she finally believed that David was telling the truth. She had a hard time comprehending that Rufus raped her but all hands pointed to him. She thought back to the telephone conversation earlier, of how he was interested in how she was doing, and how he inquired about Justice but not his own wife.

Anna Mae sucked her teeth.

"I knew I should have left you on the street, where Rufus and I found you!" she exclaimed.

"Anna Mae, think what you want," David said. "We all have hidden scars, and it's time that we pull the band aid off, expose our scars, and work on our healing."

"I like that analogy, babe," Sharmaine said.

Franklin looked to be deep in thought, as he looked at David.

"Anna Mae mentioned that before she got shot, you had reached into your waistband," Franklin said. "What was that all about?"

David looked mentally exhausted, as if he was on the witness stand for hours.

"Yeah," Anna Mae said, as if Franklin had jogged her memory.

"It's simple. I was walking up to the hospital in the pouring rain when Rufus pulled up next to me and asked if I needed a ride. I told him I was going to the hospital, he said hop in. I told him that Anna Mae had called me and left a message after I'd left their house. So, as I got into the car, I was about to sit in the passenger's seat when I noticed Anna Mae's phone stuck in the seat. So, I picked it up and mentioned to Rufus that Anna Mae dropped her phone. Rufus said that it must've fell out of her rain jacket as she got out the car, because she was on her phone the entire ride, trying to call us. He realized it when he heard the phone ringing. It was Auntie Mabeline returning Anna Mae's call. He noticed that I was soaking wet, and he said that Anna Mae had taken the only umbrella that was in the car, so he let me out at the emergency room door. That's when he asked me to give the phone to Anna Mae, because he was sure that she would be looking like a bat out of hell, because she didn't have her phone with her. I guess he was right!" David said.

"My husband wouldn't say that!" Anna Mae said, although she was surprised that Rufus did not mention his conversation with her aunt.

Franklin, Anna Mae, Sharmaine, and Grace hung on every word that David was saying.

He continued.

"I didn't want Anna Mae's phone to get wet, since I didn't have an umbrella, so I simply put her phone in my waistband, so that it would stay dry."

The room fell silent.

Anna Mae looked as if it was finally clicking for her.

"So, right before the gunshots rang out, I reached into my waistband to give Anna Mae her phone, and the next thing I knew, she was on the floor. The flash from the gun nearly blinded me. I didn't know where the gunshot came from," he said. "The next thing I knew, I saw Anna Mae on the floor, with blood streaming out of her. Similar to when Momma fell, I had a flashback and just froze!"

"Oh my gosh!" Grace said, gasping and covering her mouth. It was at that moment that she really believed David.

"Are you okay?" Franklin asked, looking at Grace with concern.

"It was Rufus! It was Rufus!"Grace exclaimed. Anna Mae became hysterical, as she started to hyperventilate.

Sharmaine jumped up, her nurse skills fully intact, as she ran over to Anna Mae, booting over, coaching her on breathing. She gently held onto Anna Mae's stomach.

"Anna Mae, just breathe! It's okay. Inhale and exhale. Take small breaths," Sharmaine said. "It's okay. You will be okay."

Anna Mae followed Sharmaine's instructions. She began to take tiny breaths, which helped her to calm down.

"I can't take any more of this!" she said, barely getting it out.

"I'm sorry!" David said. "I really didn't mean to upset you Anna Mae."

Grace began to cry. Her tears flowed, as if they had been built up for years. She finally got the answers that she needed.

Franklin ran over to console her.

"It's okay Grace. We now know the truth," he said.

"We'll make sure that Rufus pays for what he did to you!"

He hugged Grace so tight, refusing to let her go.

David sat back on the loveseat, looking somber but relieved.

"I'm sorry that I've been a total jerk, as a brother. I've always felt as if I was the black sheep and didn't belong. I don't know why I've felt that way for years, but I know that we have much love for each other, because that's how we were raised. I will do my best to do better and get myself together," he said, his voice cracking.

He took a deep breath and continued.

"Sharmaine said that she would go with me to Alcoholics Anonymous, so that I can get the help that I need. I know that all of you don't feel 100 percent comfortable with me staying here, so I'll be at Sharmaine's until I find a place."

Anna Mae began to wail, as if she was in pain.

"Rufus, why? How could you do this to us?" She said, sounding weak.

Grace, Franklin, and David went over to where she and Sharmaine were and they embraced her.

"Grace, I am so sorry that he hurt you!" Anna Mae continued to wail.

"I'm okay, Anna Mae," Grace said, still crying. "I'm okay. He can't hurt me anymore, and we won't allow him to hurt you! We will continue to rise up!" Grace said, relishing in their breakthrough.

David and Sharmaine felt with all the bad news that they all could use some good news. They shared with Franklin, Anna Mae, and Grace, that Justice will soon have a playmate. Sharmaine was three months pregnant. Franklin vowed to help David find a job, to help support his family. They were elated.

"I love you guys" David said.

"We love you, too, man!" Franklin said.

"I love all of ya'll" Sharmaine said.

There was not a dry eye in the apartment. They all let out a good cry, as they clung to each other, embracing their unity and healing.

They had broken the curse on their family.

After they all let out a good cry, Sharmaine and Grace helped Anna Mae shower and change her bandages.

David and Franklin sat in the kitchen, doting on Justice and talking about how they missed being together as a family; each one competing on what sport Justice would play when he grows up. Franklin insisted on him becoming a basketball player, and David boasted about how he's going to be the high school quarterback. Each one, wanting Justice to follow their dreams.

Franklin filled David in on the surprise birthday

party that they were planning for Auntie Mabeline. He also encouraged David to come back over the following day, for the meeting with Officer Collins to discuss the neighbor's death across the street.

David mentioned to Franklin that he heard that the cops had found evidence in the house, but had yet to name a suspect.

The two, disappeared to pick up pizza, and returned chopping it up like old times, into the wee hours of the early morning, until David and Sharmaine finally left.

Chapter 84

The next morning, Franklin was up in the kitchen cooking breakfast at seven.

It was as if Momma had poured her unified spirit on all of them last night.

Grace followed the sweet smell of maple bacon coming from the kitchen as she carried Justice, meeting Anna Mae in the hallway.

"Good morning, Anna Mae," Grace said. "I was going to come help you get out of bed. I was bringing Justice in the kitchen first, so Franklin could watch him."

"Good morning, Grace. Hey, Justice," Anna Mae said, leaning over, kissing Justice on his forehead. "I feel stronger today than I felt in a long time. I was able to get right out of bed! I feel as if a load has been lifted from my shoulders."

Anna Mae hugged Grace around the shoulders, as they both entered the kitchen.

"I am so sorry for what you been through, Grace. I just …" she said, before Grace cut her off.

"It's not your fault," Grace said.

Anna Mae stopped in her tracks.

"I need to say this. You should tell the cops everything

you know. I support you. If Rufus did this to you, he should pay," she said looking down. "He's put his hands on me one too many times, and he needs to pay for what he's done to me and to you."

"Thank you, Anna Mae. I appreciate your support, and I agree," Grace said, as they continued walking into the kitchen.

"Good morning, Franklin," they both said in unison.

"Hey, how did ya'll sleep?" He asked, as he picked up the bacon slices, turning them over on the griddle.

"Like a baby," Grace said, laughing.

"Me, too! I was telling Grace how strong I feel today," Anna Mae said.

"That's good to hear," Franklin said.

"I have a newfound appreciation for Sharmaine. I think she is good for David," Anna Mae added.

Franklin and Grace were in agreement.

"Yeah, after seeing her interact with David and with us, I was thinking the same thing. I like her. She'll make a good mother," he said, turning his back to them.

"I told you that she was a good person," Grace said, smiling and stealing a piece of bacon from the plate that sat on the counter.

Franklin observed his sisters. They looked as if a

load had been lifted from their shoulders, although he knew that they were both emotionally scarred. He had the consolation in knowing that they were at peace and everything was going to be okay.

"Trevor left me a message, and he apologized for asking Diamond and Dalia to come over to check on him," Grace said. "He also told me that he is going to waive the extra hour that he was here."

"Good!" Anna Mae exclaimed. "I don't think you should use his services anymore. He needs to be reported!"

"Yeah, that was pretty messed up," Franklin said, agreeing with Anna Mae. "Anna Mae, I was proud of the way you handled Diamond."

"Well, I know that everything happens for a reason," Anna Mae said.

"I was about to slap her and Trevor into tomorrow," Grace said.

"Well, that wouldn't have solved anything, but he did do some good. I was starting to like him," Franklin said. "So, I think you should give the man a pass and don't report him, but Anna Mae is right, don't use him anymore."

"Yeah, I suppose you're right," Grace said.

"Where is Auntie Mabeline at?" Anna Mae asked.

"I thought I heard her come up earlier this morning, when I was feeding Justice," Grace said.

"Yeah, I heard her too! That's what woke me up, but after I used the bathroom and came into the kitchen, she was gone," Franklin said. "I fixed the toilet, so I don't know why she needs to live down at Old Man Joe's."

"Me, either," Grace said. "She's been working my nerves, so she can stay down there, for all I care!"

"Funny hearing you say that," Anna Mae laughed.

"Well, she's rubbed me the wrong way, too, but it would be good for her to stay upstairs, so she knows what's going on. I asked David to come back over today. Officer Collins said that he will stop by at 11 this morning," Franklin said.

"Oh! I almost forgot!" Grace said. "Thanks for the reminder."

"Did you tell Anna Mae?" Grace asked.

"About?" Franklin responded.

"The letter," she said.

"Why are you both talking in code?" Anna Mae asked. "Tell me what?"

"Go ahead, since you bought it up," Franklin said.

"The other day, Auntie Mabeline asked me to mail her letters. In the pile was a letter addressed to David," Grace said.

"Okay?" Anna Mae said. "What's the issue with an aunt keeping in contact with her nephew. Big deal. After last night, I would let it go. I finally believe David."

"We do too, but it is a big deal," Franklin remarked. "Auntie Mabeline just seems to be doing things behind our backs. She's been acting secretive. I don't know, it's kind of suspect to me."

"I agree!" Grace chimed in.

"I don't know. I don't see anything wrong," Anna Mae said.

Grace grunted.

"That's because you haven't been around her long enough since you've come home from the hospital," Franklin said.

"Maybe," Anna Mae said.

He opened the microwave, taking the stack of French toast out and sitting it on the table, along with the scrambled eggs and crisp bacon.

"This looks so good! Thanks, Franklin," Anna Mae said.

"No problem! Eat up," Franklin said.

"I thought you said that Justice has an appointment coming up soon?" Anna Mae asked.

"OH MY GOSH! I THINK I MISSED IT!" Grace said.

Graced looked up at the wall calendar, realizing that

Justice's appointment is today!

"OH, NO! Justice's appointment is today at nine!" Grace said frantically, woofing down her breakfast.

"I'll drive you over there," Franklin said.

"But what about Officer Collins?" She asked.

"Well, it's not going to take two hours, is it?" Franklin asked.

"I don't think so," Grace said.

Franklin sat down and joined his sisters for a quick breakfast, before heading out with his sister and nephew to Justice's pediatric appointment.

Chapter 85

It was 10:45 am when Franklin, Grace, and Justice arrived back at the house. Anna Mae was sitting in the living room watching Steve Harvey.

"How did it go?" She asked.

"It went well," Grace said walking into the room. "Justice weighs 12 pounds, and he did very well getting his immunizations."

"Yeah, he was a trooper," Franklin added.

"Oh good," Anna Mae said. "David called earlier, and he said that he'd be over before 11, so he should be here shortly."

"Okay, good," Franklin said.

A voice could be heard from outside. Franklin walked over to the window, looking out, noticing Officer Collins talking over the walkie talkie.

"Well, Officer Collins is here," he said.

"Wow! He's prompt," Anna Mae said.

Franklin hurried downstairs to meet the officer. He could be heard, through the open window, greeting the officer and informing him that they live upstairs.

"Alrighty," Officer Collins said, as he ended his

conversation with the dispatcher.

"Come on in," Franklin said, as they reached the top landing.

Officer Collins walked in, looking around, as if he was casing the apartment.

"Hey, how are you?" He said, noticing Anna Mae, sitting on the couch. "You must be Anna Mae Payne."

"Did you perform a background check on me?" She said, smiling.

"Should I have?" He said. "No," he laughed. "I'm Officer Collins."

"Hi," she said.

"Where's Grace?" He asked.

"She should be out soon," Franklin said. "David will also be joining us. He should be coming in any minute now."

"Yeah, we had to let him go. His prints were not found on the weapon," Officer Collins said.

"Yeah. He was over on yesterday, and he told us," Franklin said. "We were all shocked but relieved!"

Grace walked into the living room, holding Justice.

"Hi Grace. It's nice to see you again," Office Collins said, with a warm smile.

"Hello! Same here," she said, still a little miffed that he'd contacted Franklin behind her back and informed him that she'd come to the precinct to talk to him.

"So, that's your son?" He asked.

"Yeah, this is Justice," she said.

"He's beautiful," he said.

"Thanks," she said, coldly.

"Please have a seat," Franklin said, directing Officer Collins to the recliner.

"I shared with Grace that I remember you from high school," the officer said. "Did she tell you?"

"No. Really? I don't remember you," Franklin said.

Officer Collins laughed.

"Yeah, I had a feeling that you would say that. You were on the basketball team, and I was part of the cheerleading squad."

"OH, WAIT!" Franklin said, connecting the dots. "You were the one with the red hair."

"You are too kind. Yeah, the chubby one with red hair," the officer chuckled. "After high school, I followed in my father's footsteps and joined the police academy. I dropped the weight in no time."

"Well, you look good!" Anna Mae said, sounding as if

she was flirting with Officer Collins.

"Oh, thanks," Officer Collins said, looking embarrassed but accepting the compliment, before quickly changing the subject.

"I'm sure you know by now that Grace came into the police station to talk to me," the officer said.

Anna Mae and Franklin shook their head, yes.

Grace looked even more annoyed but remained silent.

"She'd told me all the events that led up to your mother's fall that resulted into her untimely death and of her sexual assault," he said, speaking as if Grace was not present.

"I'm sitting right here," she said.

"I'm sorry, Grace. I don't mean to talk as if you were not present," he said.

Franklin chimed in.

"I was waiting for David to get here, but I wanted to let you know that when he came by last night, he told us what we were all waiting to hear. He didn't cause our mother's fall, and he was not the one who sexually assaulted Grace," Franklin said.

"I know," Officer Collins said.

"How'd you know?" Grace asked, inquisitively.

"An anonymous call came into the station after your mom's fall. So, we did a thorough investigation on David. He's been under surveillance for a few months. We found nothing on him," he said, looking over at Anna Mae.

"WHAT?" Franklin asked. "Who called in?"

"Oh, my gosh!" Grace added.

Anna Mae gasped. "Don't look at me! It wasn't me!" she said.

"We cannot divulge that because all callers' identity is protected when they call into the crime stoppers line. I can tell you that the doctors were equally suspicious and called law enforcement. David's prints were not found on your mother's body or any of her clothes. The medical examiner determined that her injuries were consistent of a fall and not of someone hitting her in the head."

"Why didn't you tell me that when I came in?" Grace asked.

"The investigation was still active at that time. I cannot speak on active investigations. It's simple as that!" He said.

Grace looked peeved.

"Oh, okay," Franklin said. "Well, David's checked more boxes off for us. I feel much better now."

"You can believe him. He didn't do it," Officer Collins said, as he looked over at Grace. "We left no stone unturned."

"We received a call from a woman, looking for David. Apparently, she had mailed a letter to the jail and accused us of not giving it to him. We assured her that he received every piece of mail that came through. She also inquired about his bail money. She was informed by the officer that he'd been bailed out already," Officer Collins said.

Franklin, Anna Mae, and Grace looked at each other.

"Did the officer tell you her name?" Franklin asked.

"No. He just said the woman said that she was a relative, and that she knew he didn't do it," Officer Collins said.

"That sounds a lot like our aunt. She's been acting very strange lately," Franklin said.

"How so?" Officer Collins asked.

"Well, just what you said. We discovered that she was writing David while he was in jail. Even after Grace had initially thought that he'd assaulted her. She's been acting strange and distant."

"Where is she now?" the officer asked.

"She should be downstairs with the neighbor, but no telling where she's at," Grace added.

"I will probably want to talk to her," the office said.

"Good luck! You'll need tracking device to find her," Grace said.

"Anna Mae, I know this is going to be hard to hear, but my fellow officers worked with the hospital security team pouring over hours of footage the day of the shooting. We had to find the tape that got the angle, right before the shooting. The video clearly shows David reaching into his waistband, removing a cell phone. At the time of his hand movement, Rufus, your husband, moved in closer to David and took a gun out of his inside pocket, aiming it low and shooting you in the abdomen. Two of the bullets pieced the magazine rack that was behind you," Office Collins said.

Anna Mae let out a huge cry.

Grace rushed over, consoling an inconsolable Anna Mae.

"Do you want to take a break from all of this?" Officer Collins asked.

"No. I need to hear this. I need to know all of what Rufus did," Anna Mae said.

"We came to the same conclusion last night. All signs pointed to Rufus. We assumed he was the one who also assaulted Grace," Franklin said.

"Your assumption is right! As for Grace's sexual assault, we got a confession out of Rufus Payne," he said, turning his attention to Anna Mae. "I'm so sorry!"

"OH MY GOSH!" Grace gasped, covering her mouth.

"Yes. We grilled him for almost four hours," Officer Collins said.

"Thank you for believing in me," Grace said.

"What you did was one of the bravest acts I've ever witnessed," he said, looking intently at Grace.

"What did he say?" Franklin asked, inquisitively. "How'd you get him to talk?"

"It wasn't hard. I think he knew that his game was up. Plus, we also had him under investigation for crimes that he committed in St. Louis, Missouri. We were working with their police department. He was pretending as if he had a twin brother and tried but failed to pin his crimes on his imaginary brother," Officer Collins said.

"What type of crimes?" Franklin asked.

"Well, he robbed stores and banks and shot a security guard in the groin," Officer Collins said. "The gun used in the hospital shooting matched the gun used in the shooting in St. Louis."

Franklin looked over at Anna Mae, not saying a word.

"We also linked him to the neighbor's death, across the street," Officer Collins said.

"WHAT?" they all exclaimed in unison.

"Yes," Officer Collins said. "As part of the evidence, we found a small bottle of activator with traces of blood on it in her house. We sent it down to forensics and the prints matched his 100 percent, and it was her blood!"

"OH, MY GOSH!" Anna Mae exclaimed.

Officer Collins was interrupted by a knock on the door.

"This must be David," Franklin said, getting up and answering the door.

"Sorry I'm late!" David said, rushing in.

"David, this is Officer Collins," Franklin said. "He was just bringing us up to speed on what you shared and the developments about the woman who was murdered across the street."

"It was Rufus, huh?" David said.

"How'd you know?" Franklin asked.

Office Collins listened intently.

"Last night after I left, I couldn't sleep. Things weren't adding up. The streets were starting to talk, but no one was mentioning his name. I remember the guys at the barbershop were saying how the day he came in to cut his jerry curl out, they were booked up, and he threatened to grab their clippers and cut his own hair. He also mentioned the woman across the street, and said that he heard the woman was a snitch. But the guys at the barbershop were skeptical. Everyone knows everyone, but they hadn't seen Rufus before. They thought it was suspect, when Rufus blurted that out. Not only did Rufus blurt it out, but he tried to say that I had something going on with the lady," David said.

"Why didn't you tell us this yesterday?" Anna Mae questioned.

"Right!" Franklin added.

"It was a very emotional night, and I didn't think Anna Mae could take any more bad news," David said.

"But the guys at the shop knew that Rufus is my brother-in-law, so they told me, but when I confronted Rufus, he said that he would never speak ill against me."

"Yeah. He's a smooth talker," the officer said.

"Rufus had us all fooled. I defended him against Auntie Mabeline," Anna Mae said somberly. "I decided that I will talk to the prosecutor! I want Rufus to rot in hell for what he did to me, Grace, and that poor woman across the street! Anna Mae said, as tears rolled down her high cheekbones.

Grace handed Anna Mae a tissue.

"So, who was the woman?" Grace asked.

"I was just about to ask the same thing," David said. "As long as I've been living here, I've only noticed the SUV when it was out there during the day, but I never saw anyone get in or out of it, and I'm always outside," David said.

"Her name was Purlie Louise Prichard," Officer Collins said.

"WHAT? NO IT CAN'T BE!" Grace exclaimed.

"Come again?" Franklin said. "Our mother's best friend's name was Ms. Purlie."

"Well, it cannot be a coincidence. Ms. Prichard was a professor at the university. She taught trigonometry at night. She was born here, but had relocated to Burnt Corn, Alabama, according to her aunt, whom we contacted after her death. She'd come back here to help care for an old friend," Officer Collins said.

"I wonder if that was our mother's friend," Grace asked.

"That, we are not sure of," Officer Collins said. "She did have a brush with the law, and the Alabama sheriff's office had a warrant out for her arrest, but she turned herself in."

"What did she do?" Anna Mae asked.

"She was dating a guy who ran a brothel. The Alabama sheriff's office thought she had something to do with it, but she was cleared," he said. "Apparently, she was dating the guy, and she had no idea that he was running an illegal business out of the basement of the house they shared."

"I wonder if that's what she was telling Momma that day I overheard Momma tell her that she was tired of getting her out of her sinful situations," Grace said.

"That's possible," Officer Collins said.

"We'll never know" Franklin added.

"Wow. Seems like she had some skeletons deep in her closet," David added.

"She was known to live a flamboyant life. The guy ended up in jail," the officer said.

'Do you know if she had any children?" Franklin asked.

"Her Aunt that I mentioned said she couldn't have kids."

They all looked at each other.

"I told ya'll!" Anna Mae said. "Momma said that!"

"This keeps getting weirder and weirder," Grace said.

"This doesn't make any sense though," Franklin asked.

"Tell me about it," David commented.

"Believe it!" the officer said. "Her aunt was sharp as a tack. She provided us with such detail. She knew every mark that was on her nieces' body. She recalled that her niece got caught up in a scandal when she lived here in her early 20s. A young lady had twins and said they were kidnapped and tried to pin it on Ms. Purlie."

"That sounds crazy!" Franklin said.

"Oh, Momma told me that!" Anna Mae said. "Ms. Purlie almost had to serve jail time because of what happened to her! But she cleared her name! Momma said it took a few years, and that's why she relocated to a different state because people around her didn't trust her!"

"What?" Franklin said, as they all looked at Anna Mae keenly. "You're just now sharing this."

"Yeah, I forgot!" Anna Mae said. "You know I'm on all this medicine".

"Now you are. What was your excuse before?" Franklin asked.

"I researched it, and it's true! Ms. Purlie was a prime suspect in the disappearance of the twins, but we later found out that someone had stolen her identity and was pretending to be her. She went through hell trying to prove it. The kids were ultimately placed up for adoption," Officer Collins said."

"That's crazy!" David said. "Who would do that! Those poor kids!"

Franklin and Grace looked at each other.

"WAIT! I think I ran into her at the liquor store. This was right around the time of Momma's falls. She was standing behind me and commented on my cap. I told her that I love hats and had my own mini collection at home. She'd offered to pay for my E&J. I told her that I had money on me, but she insisted. She said that she'd seen me around the neighborhood and liked the way I dressed. I didn't think anything of it. I always get compliments on my clothes. Then she started asking me about the neighborhood and asked if I lived here for a long time. That's when I told her that I've lived in the neighborhood since I was two, and that Momma bought the apartment building on this street after we lost our father. She told me that she had moved back here recently but had lost contact with some of her old friends. She said I wouldn't know them because she could tell I was young. I told her, yeah, 21. I would've asked for her number, but Sharmaine was waiting out in the car. I just remember she was older but she was fine!" He said reminiscing.

"Momma told me that before her identity was stolen, she was Old Man Joe's main woman when he had all those side chicks that had him in and out of court. But once they drained his pockets, Ms. Purlie dropped him like a hot potato! Momma said that the other ladies would do things to her, out of spite, to get back at Old Man Joe! One lady put sugar in her tank and ruined a car that Old Man Joe had bought her, but he just bought her another one. Well, before he went broke!" Anna Mae said.

"One of ya'll need to go get Auntie Mabeline from downstairs," David said.

"I told Grace, Mr. Joe Corbin was a philanthropist. It didn't surprise me that he had a lot of nice-looking woman on his arm back in the day, who he spoiled rotten. He was well off. He had a weakness for women in general. He had a lot of kids. We don't know exactly how many. The courts lost track. If I had to guess, I would say he about 35 kids. Well, they would be young adults now because he is in his 70s," the officer said.

"Was my husband having an affair with her?" Anna Mae blurted out, referring to Ms. Purlie.

"It doesn't appear that they had been acquainted before, based on what the homicide investigators discovered after recreating the scene. I provided them with the information that Grace gave me the other day. Ms. Pritchard just happened to be at the right place, at the wrong time. It appears that Rufus saw her and killed her thinking that she could identify him as Grace's attacker," Officer Collins said, looking over at Anna Mae and Grace.

"Don't worry, Rufus will never see the light of day."

Anna Mae and Grace looked relieved.

"I think we need to show you what Grace and I discovered in the safe," Franklin said. He knew that the safe was a bombshell in itself. David would finally find out that he is no kin to them, and that Old Man Joe was his father.

"Yeah, ya'll keep talking about this safe that everyone seems to know about but me," David said. Grace looked at Franklin. Her expression was that of trepidation.

"I'm about tired of hearing about the safe, too!" Anna Mae said, thinking back to the day before when they accused Rufus of rummaging through it.

"Well, Grace and I had planned to show it to Auntie Mabeline, but she's been playing disappearing acts lately, and I just had a lot on my mind," Franklin said. "Someone definitely knew that the safe was in the closet. It had been pried open," he said, looking at Anna Mae.

"Well, I told you that it wasn't me! Bump that!" David said, rising to his feet. "Where's it at?" He said, looking at Franklin and Grace.

"It's in Momma's closet," Grace said, hesitantly.

"I would definitely like to see its contents," the officer said, as he took out his small writing pad, taking notes.

"I'm going to get it," David said.

"I'll go, too! The safe is heavy, so I know you won't be able to carry it by yourself," Franklin said, flexing his muscles.

"Man, please," David said, smirking.

Franklin followed David into Momma's closet. He knew it was time that David learned the truth.

"Can I get you something to drink?" Anna Mae asked Officer Collins.

"Do you have bottled water?" He asked.

"Yes. Grace, go get the officer bottled water," Anna Mae said, looking at Grace.

As Grace passed by Momma's room, she could hear Franklin and David bickering back and forth. She got the water and passed by Momma's room again, listening to the two. She walked into the living room and handed the bottle of water to Officer Collins.

"That must be one heavy safe," he said, cracking open his bottled water and taking a swig.

Franklin and David came back into the living room.

"Oh, you need my help?" Officer Collins said, smirking.

The two stared blankly.

"No. The safe is missing," Franklin said.

CHAPTER 86

David raised his hands in the air. "I didn't have anything to do with it!" He said. "I told you, I didn't even know that it was there!"

"Don't look at me," Anna Mae said.

"When was the last time that you saw it?" Officer Collins asked.

Franklin stood, looking bewildered, as he rubbed his temple.

"The day I went into labor," Grace said. "That was a few weeks ago!"

"Yeah." Franklin agreed. "Something isn't right here. The safe was too heavy for one person alone to pick up. I don't know," he said.

"Tell me about it! You struggled that day just trying to move it from Momma's bed into the kitchen," Grace commented.

"Do you want to fill out a police report?" Officer Collins asked.

"It's just odd," Grace said. "You had to be Hercules to move that thing!"

"Well, before we do that, I would like to speak to our aunt. She was staying in our mothers' room. So maybe, she knows what happened to it. Besides that's not the only thing missing," Franklin said.

"What else is missing?" Anna Mae and Grace said in unison.

"All of Momma's clothes that you bagged up," Franklin said, looking at Grace.

"That rules my husband out because he's no cross dresser!" Anna Mae exclaimed.

"WHAT?" Grace exclaimed, as she ran into Momma's room to look for herself before rejoining the others.

"Yup! They're all gone! We need to report this!" she said.

"Yeah," David said, placing his hands on his hips.

"Let's not jump to conclusion. We need to rule out Auntie Mabeline first," a levelheaded Franklin said.

He looked over at Officer Collins.

"Our mother wanted her clothes donated after her death, so before Grace had Justice, she had gone through our mother's closet and bagged the clothes up. Our auntie is about the same size as our mother, so she could have very well did something with them," Franklin said.

"Okay," Officer Collins said. "It just seems that if it was too heavy for two grown men, I don't see how a woman would be able to carry it."

"Well, easy. If all of the contents in the safe were removed, which it had to be, then the safe would probably be about 30 pounds. Nothing was left behind," Franklin said.

"You sure you don't want to join the force?" Officer Collins said, looking closely at Franklin. "We could use a few good men!"

"No. I'm good!" Franklin said, before continuing. "The money Momma left is gone too!"

"MONEY?" David questioned. "Momma had money up in there?" He asked.

"Yes. She was saving some money," Franklin said, as Anna Mae shook her head in agreement.

"You knew that, too!" Franklin said, looking at her.

"Yeah. That's why when Momma was asking me for help with paying her bills, I told her that she needed to go into the safe and use that money that she was saving," Anna Mae said.

"What was she saving the money for?" David asked.

Franklin, Anna Mae, and Grace all shrugged their shoulders. It was obvious that Momma had informed Anna Mae, who the money was for … David.

"Well, it's gone now, so it doesn't matter what she was saving it for," Franklin said.

"Gone my eye! If ya'll don't need it. I can use it!" David blurted out.

"Auntie Mabeline probably is downstairs spending it on Old Man Joe!" Anna Mae said.

"Let's not jump to conclusions," Officer Collins said, closing his black note pad. "Franklin, let me know what you find out from your aunt. As for the case, I think I have everything I need to make sure that Rufus stays locked up," he said, looking around. "Grace, you are very brave to have gone through what you did and to still be alive to talk about it. It says a lot about your strength."

"Thanks! I'm just taking one day at a time," she said, looking down at Justice.

"Me, too! She wasn't the only person that he hurt!" Anna Mae uttered. Officer Collins continued.

"Ms. Payne, he'll never be able to hurt anyone else. The prosecutor will be in touch with both you and Grace. You will be asked if you want to testify but, in all honesty, with the evidence found at the crime scene and the fact that he admitted to sexually assaulting Grace, resulting in your pregnancy, you really don't have to. There's no stronger proof than that little man right there," he said, referring to Justice.

"We can also get the DNA test done on him, while he's locked up."

"I'm just at the point where I want to put all of this

behind me. I've been traumatized enough," Grace said. "I do not want to testify."

"Well, he tried to jack up my reputation!" David blurted out. "You didn't mention the pictures. Did he admit to planting those naked pictures of Grace in my desk drawer?"

"Actually, he didn't have to. When we confiscated his phone, the pictures were on his phone," Officer Collins said.

"I told you he was a dog! Oh my God, you saw them?" Grace gasped, looking at Officer Collins, embarrassed.

"Well, yeah … it was evidence," he said.

"I don't want to hear anymore!" Anna Mae blurted out.

Office Collins turned his attention to Anna Mae.

"Mrs. Payne, I am really sorry about all of the pain that you are going through. No pun intended. I know that it must be very difficult to find out that you are married to a conman, but be thankful that you are alive. Rufus also went through a mental health evaluation. He has sociopathic tendencies. People like him are antisocial and have no regard for the rights of others. They exude charm that can easily attract others to them before they're victimized. People with his type of behavior do not care who they hurt, and usually it's those closest to them. You definitely have an angel looking out for you."

Anna Mae shook her head, yes.

"In some ways, I can relate. I know all about having someone in your life who you have unconditional love for and idolize. You look at them as your bright and shining armor, just to find out that they are anything but," Officer Collins said.

"Are you okay?" Grace asked.

"I know man. You're like a day late for the shrink who was here on yesterday," David said, smirking.

"Oh, that fake shrink Trevor? Please, he's the last person you want to talk to!" Anna Mae exclaimed.

"He's not a shrink! He's a grief and trauma counselor," Grace said, correcting them.

Officer Collins took a deep breath.

"There is one other thing that I want to share with all of you," he said.

"Don't tell us that you're not really a cop?" Anna Mae said.

"He is a cop!" Grace said. "He's legit! I saw him at work!"

Officer Collins placed his notepad under his arm and started to wipe the sweat beads that had formed on his forehead.

"I've been very interested in getting you justice for

what you've been through for a number of reasons," he said, as he shook his head.

"Why?" Grace asked.

Franklin sat on the arm of the couch. They all looked intently at Officer Collins. His whole demeanor had changed.

"I mentioned earlier that I followed in my father's footsteps. Well, that's partially right. He became a cop well before I was born, but he was a dirty cop. I remember right before he got sick, he sat me and my siblings down, there's seven of us," he said.

"What was wrong with your father?" Anna Mae asked.

"He had Parkinson's, "Officer Collins replied.

"Dang, sorry to hear that!" Franklin exclaimed.

"Man, what are you trying to say?" David asked.

"Just let him finish," Grace said.

Officer Collins continued.

"Well, as long as I could remember … I'll say, right before I hit my junior year of high school, my father seemed to struggle with depression too. Before he got really sick, he'd always seemed to fly off the handle, putting my mother and all of us kids on edge. We walked on egg shells any time we were around him.

Well, a few years before he died, he'd confessed to us

that when he first got on the force, he was the type of officer who would shoot first and ask questions later. He said that he was just an angry man, who knew that as soon as he put on his uniform and loaded his gun, he had power over the powerless. Well, he told us about a robbery that took place many years ago, not far from here," Officer Collins paused before continuing.

"My father told us about a young black man who was coming out of a gas station, holding a pack of cigarettes in one hand and his change in the other, who he mistook as a robbery suspect. He said the young man wasn't doing anything wrong but walking out of the gas station, minding his own business. But before he knew it, he'd gunned the young man down in cold blood, shooting him three times in the chest, killing him instantly. He said, he'll never forget the look on the young man's face as he dropped the box of cigarettes, looking right at my father, as he fell to the ground."

Franklin, David, Anna Mae, and Grace gasped as they looked on horrified, as Officer Collins shared the details from that dark day that Momma told them about their father's murder.

Tears began to roll down Officer Collins face.

"My father admitted to us, right before his death, and after I had joined the police academy, that he didn't want me to be anything like him. He wanted me to really represent all of the people and to really meet them where their needs are. I am truly sorry for the loss of your father, but I want you to know that it haunted my dad for many years."

"Oh my gosh!" Grace exclaimed, as tears rolled down her cheeks.

The sound of sniffles filled the room.

Franklin walked toward his former high school classmate and placed his hand on his shoulder.

"As a black man, we know that the cops are not our friends. We," he said looking at David, "know that every time we walk the streets, there is a chance that we may not come back to our families. We live this nightmare every day but it also looks as if the sins of your father have carried over to you. We want you to know that it wasn't your fault."

The two men embraced, as Officer Collins wept.

After Officer Collins left, Franklin didn't waste any time. He went downstairs banging on old Man Joe's door looking for Auntie Mabeline. He questioned Auntie Mabeline about the missing safe. Auntie Mabeline admitted that she'd called the thrift store and asked them to come and pick up all of the stuff in Momma's closet, including the clothes that Grace had bagged up because she knew that she couldn't fit them. She'd gotten up early one morning, before Franklin and Grace were awake and had the employees from the thrift store, go into Mommas closet and remove everything that was on the floor.

Franklin didn't believe her, until he called the thrift store and spoke to the manager. The manager agreed that his crew came to the house at six in the morning and were advised by Auntie Mabeline, to take it all, including the safe. He'd told Franklin that once he looked through it, he knew that it was something taken in error by the contents but he couldn't get in contact with Auntie Mabeline, since she'd called from Old Man Joe's house. They'd called Old Man Joe but thought it was someone trying to get a hold of his social security check, so he kept hanging up on them. The manager told Franklin that they would drop the safe back off to him. When Franklin asked about the contents of the safe, namely the money, the owner assured him that all of the money is there, and he'd put it up for safe keeping.

Franklin was relieved that Auntie Mabeline told the truth … this time!

Three weeks later, Officer Collins paid an unexpected visit to the Johnson household. He came over and informed them of some shocking news. A correction officer had found Rufus dead in his cell. At first, they thought that Rufus had taken his own life, but they further discovered he died from food poisoning!

They all had mixed emotions, which surprised Officer Collins. Although Rufus had lied on David, David felt bad for him. Anna Mae, on the other hand felt that his premature death, was appropriate for his crimes. All Grace could think of was that she knew Big Tuna worked in the kitchen. She couldn't help but think that he had something to do with Rufus's untimely death, but she decided to bury her thoughts along with the imaginary hatchet that had Rufus's name written all over it. As for Franklin, he didn't want to see his sisters have to relive all the pain and be put on the witness stand, to face this monster because he didn't know what he would do to Rufus! He didn't vocalize it, but he was relieved that someone else did the dirty work, and they could finally put the pieces of their lives back together. He knew that although they would never see Rufus again, a part of him remained … JUSTICE, but he found consolation in knowing that Rufus could never hurt his family again.

CHAPTER 87

Although hearing the details of daddy's senseless murder at the hands of Officer Collins's father, along with Rufus's surprising murder, shocked them, they knew that they had so much to be grateful for. Momma and Daddy had instilled in them the importance of forgiveness, even though not all of them were at the forgiving stage yet. It was also very important for them to carry on their parent's legacy with pride and honor, and the morals and values that were instilled in them.

Grace had contacted the church secretary, the night that Officer Collins had left, to see if Pastor Fallback could squeeze in Justice's dedication after Sunday service. He agreed. She invited Macie and Sharmaine, and surprisingly she extended the invite to Officer Collins. David and Sharmaine had agreed to meet them at church.

To their amazement Anna Mae felt well enough to attend service. Although Auntie Mabeline spent a good part of her visit downstairs with Old Man Joe, Grace made sure that she didn't forget about her, although she had been MIA most days. In classic Auntie Mabeline style, she showed up to the church with Old Man Joe in toe. He looked more like her pimp daddy. All Grace cared about at that moment was that her family was all together.

During the church service, Grace looked around and spotted Diamond and Dalia. Diamond sported a bright yellow top with a fitted pencil flowered skirt, with sunflowers at the bottom. Dalia had her hair in fat braids, with a hint of red and wore a red fitted dress, with puffy shoulders. Both Diamond and Dalia came over to all of them before the ceremony, apologizing for their ratchet behavior, and asked Grace if it's okay if they stayed for Justice's dedication. Grace knew that it was time to show a sign of maturity and gave them both a nod. She came to the conclusion that as a mother, she would have to pick and choose her battles, not only for her growing son, but for those she encountered. She vowed to never allow people to get the best of her or take her to a place that was beneath her. She would conduct herself, just like her name, with Grace.

One other thing that she had no regrets about was selecting Misty and Franklin as Justice's godparents. Both Misty and Franklin stood tall and poised, as they surrounded Grace and Justice, listening intently to every word that Pastor Fallback said. They both looked elegant. Misty wore a fitted hunter green dress. Her hair was in a cleopatra style and dyed platinum blonde. She looked amazing, as usual. Franklin wore a dark blue suit with a paisley blue, yellow and hot pink tie. He looked finer than the teeth on a hair comb. Since he'd been home, he hadn't cut his hair but he and David took a trip to the barbershop, where one of the guys used a texturizing crème kit that made the top of Franklin's hair, curly, just like Justice's.

In a short amount of time, Anna Mae had made drastic improvements that she didn't even need physical therapy.

Although she was walking better, she opted to use a cane, to take some of the pressure of her abdomen. She sat on the front row, dressed much simpler than she'd ever dressed before. She wore a deep purple muumuu, mainly for comfort. In classic Anna Mae style, she'd taken the matching head wrap to her dress and wrapped it around her cane, proving that she was still the fashionista!

Sharmaine was finally starting to show signs of her pregnancy. She looked adorable in her canary yellow drop waisted dress. David appeared to be moving into his fatherhood role. He had on grey pants, a white short sleeve shirt and wine-colored suspenders, that matched his bowtie. He and Sharmaine openly displayed their affection for one another. They sat in the front row holding hands, as if they were on a date at the movies.

Macie was all business. She wore a grey suit with a white tank top underneath and black pumps.

Auntie Mabeline and Old Man Joe's outfits were a symbol of their relationship....out of order! If you looked at them too long, you were bound to get dizzy. Auntie Mabeline had on a dark blue dress with fire engine red polka dots, and Old Man Joe had on a plaid suit that had every color of the rainbow, with a burnt orange ruffled shirt and a wool grey top hat that blocked the vision of those sitting behind him.

Grace kept it simple. She wore a beige lace maxi dress that got Franklin's approval and a short beige sweater with pearls that lined the neck.

Justice was growing like a weed. If Grace had put the dedication off for another two weeks, she would've had to wrap Justice in a white sheet. His suit that Misty bought him fit him like a glove. He was chubby like a chunk bar. He cooed the entire time, as if he was talking back to Pastor Fallback.

Pastor Fallback had gotten down to skin and bones. A true testament that First Lady had stopped feeding him those nasty cheese sandwiches. He'd shared with us that all that cheese blocked him up and raised his cholesterol through the roof! So, he had to cut those sandwiches, out of his diet all together. He began to reminisce about all the good food he missed that Momma used to make.

The ceremony was short and sweet. Those who stayed behind came up and greeted Grace and Justice, as Misty and Franklin stood next to them. Grace looked up to surprisingly see Officer Collins dressed in his uniform. He thanked Grace for inviting him, but said he had to head into work. Grace gave him a warm embrace, thanking him for coming. Franklin vowed to keep in touch with him.

After Justice's dedication, they all decided to go to the buffet restaurant for dinner. Diamond and Dalia declined, which was fine with the rest of them.

Auntie Mabeline sat at the end of the table near David, catching up with him, since she hadn't seen him since Momma's funeral.

Franklin sat at the other end of the table with Anna

Mae, Grace, Justice, Macie, and Misty, watching Auntie Mabeline and David's interaction. David was telling her all about his experience in jail, as Sharmaine cozied up next to him.

Something still was not sitting right with Franklin about his aunt, but he knew that this was not the place to bring it up. Instead, he whispered to Misty and Macie that they were planning to have a surprise birthday party for Auntie Mabeline and invited them to come.

Everyone seemed to be enjoying each other's company. That's all he could ask for, at this moment.

CHAPTER 88

The month of August had finally arrived. It was the day of Auntie Mabeline's surprise birthday.

Franklin, Anna Mae, David, and Grace decided that they would each prepare something special for an undeserving Auntie Mabeline and present it to her at her birthday party.

Sharmaine had dropped David by before she went to work, so that he could help with the preparations. Grace passed by David's bedroom, pressing her ear to the door, as she held Justice. She could hear him warming up his vocal cords. It was safe to say, that he was preparing a song for Auntie Mabeline. She heard David walking toward the bedroom door. She snickered, as she hurried into the kitchen.

David came out of his room and walked into the kitchen.

"Well, I'm ready for my surprise for Auntie Mabeline's birthday party tonight," he said.

Grace pretended to act dumb founded.

"What are you doing?" She asked.

"I ain't telling you," he said. They both laughed.

"I'm going to hate to see Auntie Mabeline leave. I can't believe she's rolling out tomorrow," he said.

"Well, it's not like she's spent a lot of time with us, so I'm fine with her leaving," Grace said.

"So, what are you doing for her?" He asked, "Since you want to be all up in my Kool-Aid."

"I'm not telling you, but Justice and I will be ready. I just hope she likes it," she said.

"Where is she at anyway?" David asked.

"I don't know. When I got up, I didn't see her. My guess … downstairs with Old Man Joe," Grace said, rolling her eyes.

"I don't know about that. I was standing outside talking to Big Tuna on the porch, and I heard their door slam. She may have left out," he said.

"WHAT? HE'S OUT?" Grace asked.

"Yeah. He told me that they dropped the charges and let him out with time served," David said.

"Oh my gosh! I didn't know that."

"He asked about you. I told him that you and little dude were cool. We even squashed that beef we had from last year."

Grace fell silent.

"I don't know what was going on downstairs. I guess he walked in on Auntie Mabeline and Old Man Joe having a lover's quarrel or something last night. He told me; he was bouncing for the weekend. He said Auntie Mabeline was going off. I guess they were looking through Old Man Joe's pictures albums because he saw them stacked up on the kitchen table, and she saw something that made her hit the roof," he said. "But he noticed that she had cut all of Old Man Joe's his ex-girlfriends out of every picture he had in his picture album."

"That's just wrong! I wonder what got her so mad?" Grace asked.

"I don't know. He didn't ask. Whatever it was, that was what? Like thirty years ago. Old Man Joe probably cannot even get it up!" David said, laughing.

"I'm not trying to get into his business, but I'd bumped into him at the pharmacy before and he was picking up his Viagra prescription. As I told Franklin, you can't speak for Old Man Joe," she said, smirking.

"Well, maybe so, but she don't need to be tripping over that old man. She needs to get over it, or this will be her last birthday. She won't need those blood pressure pills no more!" David said. "I don't see what she sees in him anyways. The dude got what, 35 kids?"

"Well, I know she definitely didn't go with Anna Mae and Franklin to the supermarket. They purposely left early, so she wouldn't be up to tag along," Grace said.

"Well, I'm going to get in the shower. Franklin said he will call when he gets here, so we can help him bring the stuff up the back steps," Grace said.

"So how are we going to get Auntie Mabeline out of the house, that's if she comes back! You know she's nosy," David grinned.

"She may be back downstairs making up with Old Man Joe," Grace smirked. "We have a plan. While we were at the buffet, we spoke to Misty about it. We were saying how we didn't want Auntie Mabeline walking in on us, as we were decorating. So, Misty volunteered to do her hair. We had her talk to Auntie Mabeline before we left the restaurant. She told her how lucky we were to have such an awesome Auntie who filled in the gap, after losing Momma and how jealous she was of us and that she wanted to do something wonderful for her before she left. Yada, yada, yada," Grace said, laughing. "Auntie agreed, once Misty told her she was doing her hair for free!"

"Misty is a good egg. I hope she really finds out who her family is. She mentioned it to me when she let me stay at the shop. She's really obsessed with finding out," David said. "I know she's done a lot for me. If I wasn't involved with Sharmaine, I would try to holla at her but she's more like a sister to me."

Grace wanted so bad to tell David about his twin sister but she didn't want to do anything else behind Franklin's back, since their relationship was mended.

"Auntie Mabeline had suggested a friend of hers, who's a genealogist but Misty said she fell through. I guess her number was disconnected, so she hired a private investigator to find her birth parents. He sent her a letter the other day," Grace said.

"Oh really? Good for her," David said. "I can only imagine how difficult it is to be an only child and not feel like you belong."

Grace fell silent, before responding.

"Yes, but she still hadn't opened the letter yet because she's a little nervous." Grace said. "He told her that he had to do some deep digging but he's sure she will be satisfied with the results because he found a match."

"STOP PLAYING!" David said, with excitement.

"Anna Mae had told her that since we will all be together at Auntie Mabeline's birthday party, that she should bring the letter over, since she'll have all of us to support her," Grace said.

"Yeah, that makes sense. I know she's done a lot to help me out, even when others weren't willing to give me a chance. She gave me a job and a place to stay." David said, sounding appreciative.

David and Grace were interrupted by ringing on the house phone.

"I'll get it," she said. "It's probably Franklin."

Grace rushed over to the phone.

"Hello . . . he's here," she paused. "Okay, I'll tell him." She hung up.

"That was Franklin. He and Anna Mae are downstairs. He needs your help carrying up the bags upstairs," Grace said.

"Oh, Franklin also said that they passed by Auntie Mabeline. She looks like she was walking to Misty's shop. She didn't see them."

"Oh good!" David said, before darting down the back steps.

Two hours had gone by, as they continued to prep for Auntie Mabeline's surprise birthday party.

"Okay, we have to get the table set," Anna Mae said, as she sat down giving orders.

"David, you have to pull the tablecloth over some more," she said.

David gave her the side eye.

"I understand that you are recovering from your injury but your hands still work! You can set the table while you're just sitting there. A pack of paper plates don't require heavy lifting!" David said.

"Alright! Stop the bickering," Franklin said, attempting to gain some order. "Misty said that Auntie Mabeline is under the dryer. She's gonna stall and keep her as long as we need her to. I told her, wait until about 5:30 p.m. and then tell Auntie Mabeline that I can't come back and pick her up, but she'll drop her off."

"She's gonna be mad as fire," Grace said, laughing.

"I know," Anna Mae said. "We saw her walking that way at 11. Her appointment was at 11:30," they both laughed. "She's gonna be fit to be tied once she come up in here. Franklin that was smart of you to give her money to feed Auntie Mabeline. At least she won't be hungry!"

"I know, right! She's gonna say "that's why I do my own hair. I got less hair than an ear of corn, why in the world would it take six hours," Grace said, mocking her aunt, as she placed Justice in his bouncer.

"Well, hopefully she'll be so shocked, in a good way that she forgets all about that," Franklin said.

They all stopped doing what they were doing and stared at Franklin.

"OH, NO, SHE WON'T!" The trio said laughing, even getting a giggle out of Justice.

"You even got the baby laughing at you," Anna Mae said.

"I appreciate you all working together," Franklin said. "We haven't done this since Momma was alive … If she could see us now," Franklin said.

"Yeah, she would be proud," Grace added.

Anna Mae started counting the chocolate frosted cupcakes that she baked.

"Okay, I made 15 cupcakes. One is missing," she said.

They all looked at David.

"Why is everyone looking at me?" He asked.

"BECAUSE YOU ARE GREEDY!" They said in unison.

"You still have enough," he said.

"GUILTY AS CHARGED!" Grace said, laughing.

Anna Mae began to rattle off who they invited.

"The four of us."

"FIVE! Don't leave my baby out. He wants his own cupcake," Grace said.

Anna Mae continued counting.

"Pastor Fallback, First Lady, Misty, Old Man Joe."

"Franklin, is Leroy coming?" Anna Mae asked.

"He said he'll try to swing by if he can get a break at work. But he was doubtful."

"You may want to leave Old Man Joe downstairs," David said. "Big Tuna told me earlier that Auntie Mabeline was yelling at him about something before she stormed out of his apartment."

"I told you that was him Franklin!" Anna Mae said.

"We saw him getting into a Lyft."

"When did he get out?" Franklin inquired.

"I guess the other day. He told me they let him out for time served. Oh, I forgot to tell you too, Grace, he was at the same place as Rufus."

"Let's not even ruin our day. I just hope that Big Tuna does the right thing now that he's out. It's kind of bittersweet, because someone will need to help his father out since Auntie Mabeline leaves tomorrow."

"That's true. I sure ain't going down there to babysit him," Anna Mae said.

"Grace, you're quiet. You okay?" Franklin asked.

"Yeah, I'm fine. Big Tuna didn't do anything to me. I'm not afraid of him," she said.

"Good. Let us know if you ever feel uncomfortable around him."

"Is Macie coming to the party?" Anna Mae asked.

"No. She picked up a double shift. She can't make it."

"Same with my baby. I told her to don't overdo it now that she's pregnant," David added.

"Well, you need to get your butt a job, so she doesn't have to!" Anna Mae said.

"Funny that you would bring that up. I was going to

surprise ya'll later at the party but Sharmaine hooked me up with a job at the hospital. I started last Monday."

"Congratulations!" they all said in unison.

"That's great David. I had been looking for a job for you," Franklin said.

"Doing what?" Anna Mae asked.

"I'll be a supervisor for housekeeping," David said.

"Cool!" Grace said.

"I'm real proud of you man," Franklin said. "We were also saying how Sharmaine is good for you. We all really like her. Momma ..." Franklin caught himself, "We know you'll make great parents."

"Thanks man. I appreciate that. Yeah, she's a keeper. I have to give credit to Momma," he said, kissing his two fingers and raising them to the ceiling. "I met her at the hospital, the day Momma was admitted."

"Yeah, we heard," Anna Mae said. "Just don't mess it up!"

"Oh, and she told me that you all went out," he said looking at Franklin. Franklin looked as if he'd been caught with his hands in the cookie jar.

"Trust me! I'm good. I am not interested," Franklin said.

Franklin welcomed Anna Mae's timely interruption.

"David, you are lucky. We'll have seven extra cupcakes, well, six if Old Man Joe don't come," Anna Mae said.

"Hide your kids, hide your cupcakes! David's back!" Franklin said, bursting out in laughter.

They all laughed uncontrollably.

CHAPTER 89

Okay, they're walking up the steps," Franklin said, looking out the peep hole.

"Does she look mad as fire," Grace asked.

"Yup, like a steamed locomotive," he said.

"Oh yeah, I can hear her fussing at Misty," Anna Mae said.

"What did she leave the house wearing?" Grace asked.

"A tight yellow jogging suit...and green beads," Anna Mae whispered.

"Oh, Miss fashionista, she's gonna be mad with you for letting her go out the house looking like big bird," Grace said, giggling and pointing at Anna Mae.

"I think we need to pray!" Pastor Fallback said, as First Lady clung to him with her mink shawl daintily hanging off her bare shoulders, dispelling Deaconess Franzine's rumor of trouble in their marriage.

"Too late, Pastor," David said.

"On the count of three," Franklin said. "One, two, three!" He said, opening the door wide.

"SURPRISE!"

Auntie Mabeline stopped talking in mid-sentence.

"What in the dickens is going on!" she said, looking shocked.

"We got you!" Misty said, hugging Auntie Mabeline, as they walked in the house.

Pastor Fallback hijacked the birthday song, and he and First Lady began to sing the churches' version, as the others looked on, displaying their annoyance.

He sang off key, patting his feet, as First Lady Fallback clapped her hands, off beat.

"Okay, that was cute," David said. "Now to the version we know."

They all began to sing Stevie Wonders version of "Happy Birthday to Ya, Happy Birthday to Ya ... Happy Birthday . . . Happy Birthday to Ya ...."

Auntie Mabeline beamed with pride, as they circled around her, singing joyfully and ending the song strong.

"Ya'll need to come on down and join the choir. We could use some more faithful choir members," Pastor Fallback said. "We even got a men's choir," he added, looking at David and Franklin.

"Oh, I'm good," David said.

"All this for me?" Auntie Mabeline asked.

"Yes, Auntie. We wanted to surprise you and celebrate your birthday before you leave tomorrow. We're gonna miss you," Franklin said, being the spokesperson for his siblings, and made sure to say the right thing, although her visit was anything but pleasant.

"How'd you all know that it was my birthday?" She asked.

"Me and Anna Mae were cleaning up, and we came across Momma's bible. Momma had written it in there, August 11th," Grace said, smiling.

"And remember you told me it was coming up," Misty added.

"Oh," Auntie Mabeline said.

"Now we ain't gonna ask you how old you are Sister Mabeline. My wife taught me well," Pastor Fallback said, looking over at First Lady.

"Sister Mabeline, I made you some toasted cheese and cold cut sandwiches. I cut them up small, so we'll have room for dessert," First Lady said, handing the tray to Auntie Mabeline.

"Thank you," she said, unable to hide her expression of distaste.

"I'll put them in the kitchen for you," Grace said.

"I got it, Gracie. I have to go change my clothes. I didn't know we were expecting company," she said, looking keenly at Anna Mae.

"You look fine Auntie! Your hair looks great! I'm loving those finger waves!" She added.

"It should! Misty had me down at that shop for hours. I almost lost my mind," she said. "She added a little paint to me face too!" she said, showing off the cherry blush on her cheeks.

"Nice!" Grace said.

"I'm sorry, Ms. Mabeline, but it was all part of the surprise," Misty said.

"You can blame me," Franklin said.

"Does this mean I have to pay you?" Auntie Mabeline asked.

Misty laughed.

"Oh no! This was my gift to you! I wanted to show you how much I appreciate you! I could never repay you for being there for me. I appreciate all of our conversations and your words of encouragement."

Do you mind if I use the restroom?," Misty asked.

"Don't be silly. You don't have to ask," Franklin said.

"Thanks, Franklin," Misty said.

"Ok, I'll be right back," Auntie Mabeline said, carrying the platter into the kitchen.

Misty and Auntie Mabeline walked down the hall

toward the kitchen together, arm-in- arm. Misty placed her pocketbook on the back of the kitchen chair before entering the bathroom, while Auntie Mabeline looked to see where she could hide the platter of soggy sandwiches.

"Let's get this party started," David said to those in the living room.

"David, I got an eight-track tape in my truck with some fast songs. I can go down and get it," Pastor Fallback said.

"No, thanks," David said. "I got something even better for you. I know how my auntie gets down."

David turned the volume up to a reasonable level. James Brown's "Funky Good Time" filtrated through the house.

"Oh boy! That's my jam, too!" Pastor Fallback started tapping his feet to the music as he rose to his feet, moving to the beat of the music. "Ooooh, First Lady come and dance with me," he said, as he began singing to the music, pulling her up from the couch.

"Ooooh, sooky, sooky now," she said, bashfully standing up dancing with him, as they two-stepped across the living room floor.

"We're gonna get funky tonight," he sang in his baritone voice.

"Go Pastor!" Anna Mae said.

"I'll go help Auntie Mabeline," Grace said, walking

down the hall, nearly bumping into Misty as she exited the bathroom.

"I'll take my godson," Misty said, reaching out for Justice. "We're going back into the living room to help Uncle David get the party started."

Grace walked into the kitchen just as Auntie Mabeline dumped the platter of food into the trash.

"Auntie!" She said looking back down the hall to make sure no one saw them. "Why did you do that?"

"Ain't nobody going to eat that mess! She might as well had gone down to the food pantry and bought me a block of that government cheese on a platter. Besides who's eating cold cuts this time of night! Them sandwiches smelled like the mayonnaise was bad!" Auntie Mabeline said, washing the platter.

"What are you going to say when they ask about them?" Grace asked.

"I'm gonna tell her they fell on the floor," she responded.

"But that's lying," Grace said.

"Well, a little lie ain't gonna hurt nobody. It's those big ones that cut deep, like broken glass!" Auntie Mabeline said.

Grace looked perplexed.

Auntie Mabeline looked at the lime green and yellow

streamers hanging from the ceiling.

"The decorations are pretty," she said.

"We all pitched in and helped," Grace said.

Auntie Mabeline walked over to the table looking at all the food.

"I hoped ya'll helped Anna Mae. She's not supposed to pick up anything heavy," she said, looking at Grace. "Including Justice."

"I know. We did the heavy lifting for her."

"Okay," she said. "Everything looks good. It looks like your Momma has been here."

"She's here . . . in spirit," Grace said smiling. "Anna Mae put us to work. I think if Justice was old enough, she would have given him some things to do, too!" They both laughed.

"What we got here . . . macaroni and cheese, barbecue chicken, string beans, corn bread, potato salad, candied yams," she said, looking over at Grace. "And you concerned about some cheese & cold sandwiches."

"Anna Mae baked a cake and some gourmet cupcakes. She got the recipe online," Grace said, as they turned their attention to the dessert table. "Franklin had to bring the cake in the kitchen, so we could keep an eye on it. David attacked the cupcakes."

"Ya'll leave that boy alone. He told me the other day, that he nearly starved while he was in the jail," Auntie Mabeline said. "Everything looks so good!"

"Well, we have a few more surprises for you before we eat. We should get back in there," Grace said.

Auntie Mabeline and Grace went back into the living room to find Pastor Fallback and First Lady grooving. Franklin and Misty were attempting to keep up with them. David was in the corner dancing with Justice near the stereo as Anna Mae sat dancing on the couch.

"The birthday girl is back!" David said, turning down the music. "I know ya'll go to bed early, so we better get this party moving along." He said looking at the Fallbacks and Auntie Mabeline.

"It's time to open your gifts," Anna Mae said.

"Auntie, this chair is for you," Franklin said, as he held Auntie Mabeline's hand, guiding her to the straw chair.

"Grace, why don't you go first," Franklin said.

"Okay," Grace said, as she handed Auntie Mabeline a yellow envelope.

"Auntie, this is from me and Justice. We hope you like it," she said.

"Well, let's see," Auntie Mabeline said, wasting no time prying the envelope open.

Auntie Mabeline beamed with joy! "I LOVE IT!" she exclaimed.

"What is it?" Misty asked.

"It's a certificate for two-month supply of frozen baby back ribs that Auntie likes, from Roxie's," she said smiling.

"Gracie knows I love them! Every time I come up, she brings me over there, and I ship a few slabs back home," she said.

"Well, for the next two months they will ship you two slabs a week," Grace said.

Auntie Mabeline placed her hand over her heart.

"Don't eat too much of those ribs, Ms. Mabeline. All that pork isn't good for anyone," Misty said.

"Girl, hush up," Auntie Mabeline said.

"No, she didn't," Misty said, laughing to herself.

"You and Justice come here. You'll soon be sucking on one of them delicious rib bones," she said, squeezing Justice's full cheeks and giving them both a hug. "Thank you, Gracie."

"Sister Mabeline, you need to ship me some of them ribs after you smoke them on that grill with some of that hickory smoked barbecue sauce," Pastor Fallback said, as if he was dreaming of holding a rib between his hands. He woke up from his dream after First Lady forcefully elbowed him in his rib cage.

"Well, I know it's hard to come between a woman and her ribs, but I hope you like my gift, just as much as you enjoy them delicious ribs," Franklin said handing Auntie Mabeline a small dark blue box with a baby blue bow on top.

"Oh, what could this be?" She asked looking at the box, then shaking it.

"Open it," Anna Mae said.

Auntie Mabeline ripped the wrapping paper off. "Oh, you shouldn't have," she said, looking up at Franklin and then back at the jewelry box.

"Open it up," he said.

"I hope it's a one-way ticket to the Bahamas! I can use a vacation. Joe wore me out!" she said.

"I bet he did!" David said.

"I want to go to Jamaica!" Grace exclaimed.

"Don't we all!" Franklin said. She opened the box, pulling out the medallion.

"What am I going to do with this thing?" She asked, holding up the bronze star.

"Oh, nice!" Pastor Fallback exclaimed, seeming to be the only person other than Franklin who understood the significance.

"Auntie, while I was in the service, I risked my own life to save one of my comrades who was injured. I was awarded the bronze star for my heroism. I can't think of anyone else, besides Momma, who I would want to hold onto it . . . but you!" He said.

"Oh, okay," she said, looking puzzled. "I have to find somewhere to put it."

"Franklin, that's awesome! You never told us that!" Grace said.

"Your mother would be so proud of you!" Misty said.

"Yeah man . . . you are truly a hero," David added.

It was Anna Mae's turn to surprise Auntie Mabeline.

"Franklin, can you get my gift?" She asked.

"Yeah," Franklin said, standing up to reach behind the couch, dragging the huge box in front of where Auntie Mabeline sat.

"Oh my, what is this?" She said.

"You'll have to open it and see," Anna Mae said.

Auntie Mabeline tried to shake the box.

"Oh, this is heavy. It feels like a bunch of dead weight. I hope this ain't your husband's body, wrapped up in a box," Auntie Mabeline said. "If it is, I don't want it!"

Franklin, Anna Mae, David, and Grace suspiciously

looked at Auntie Mabeline.

Everyone laughed, except for the siblings.

"I'm a widow!" Anna Mae exclaimed, curtly correcting her.

"You're better off," Auntie Mabeline said, coldly.

Pastor Fallback cut Auntie Mabeline off.

"Anna Mae … First Lady and I want to extend our deepest condolences. We are so sorry," Pastor Fallback said, feeling obligated to say something, although he knew the story. "I guess, I won't be meeting him now!"

"I'm so sorry, too!" Misty said.

"There's nothing to be sorry about," Anna Mae said, before responding to Auntie Mabeline. "Auntie, it's something that you're going to love!"

"I wish Justice was big enough to help me break into this thing," she said, looking at the big box, noticing all of the tape that Anna Mae had on it.

"I can help you, Auntie," Grace said.

Grace sat on the floor Indian style, picking at the corner of a piece of tape.

"Dang Anna Mae, are you sure you want her to have this?" Grace asked. "We cannot even open it."

"Here, use my pocketknife," Franklin said, as he

popped the tape off of the sides.

Auntie Mabeline popped the cover off, removing the paper from the top. She reached down into the box, pulling out the gift.

Auntie Mabeline yelped!

"WHAT THE HECK IS THIS?"

"It's one of Momma's fur coats that she had hanging in the coat closet," Anna Mae said.

"CHILD, YOU KNOW THAT I DON'T WEAR NO ANIMALS!" she exclaimed.

"I'm part of PETA!" she said.

"Who's Peter? Don't tell me that you're cheating on Old Man Joe," David said, being facetious.

"Get out of here, David! It's an animal's rights organization. I don't wear anything that looks like it walked in the forest," she said. "Looking over at First Lady and her mink shawl.

"I didn't know that," Anna Mae said.

"That is dope! Ms. Leola always dressed to kill. No pun intended," Misty said, laughing at her own joke. "I'll take it!"

"Get this thing away from me!" she said kicking away the box.

"That's what you get for shopping in Momma's closet," Franklin said.

"Well, it's my turn," David said. "We saved the best, for last."

David walked over to the stereo.

"I hope you ain't playing no rap music," she said, looking at David keenly.

"No, this is safe, even for Pastor Fallback," he said, nodding his head to the pastor and his wife.

"Auntie, I just want you to know that you're my hero," David said.

The instrumental began to play in the background, as David cleared his throat.

"Oh, I know this song by heart! I got the CD in my collection at home," Auntie Mabeline said. "I love listening to them Levert men singing this," she said smiling and fanning herself. David began to sing in his baritone voice.

"It must have been cold there in my shadow

To never have sunlight on your face

You were content to let me shine

That's your way

You always walked a step behind

See, I was the one with all the glory

While you we're the one with all the strength.

Yes, you were

Only a face without a name

I never once heard you complain, no

Did you ever know that you're my hero?

You're everything I would like to be

I could fly higher than an eagle

Cause you are the wind beneath my wings

It might have appeared to go unnoticed

But da ..."

"Okay . . . okay enough of that. You about to make me ruin my makeup," Auntie Mabeline abruptly interrupted David.

"I wanted to hear the rest!" Anna Mae exclaimed.

"Me too!" Misty said.

"Now, he can sing!" Pastor Fallback said, looking up at David.

"Auntie, I wanted to prepare something special for you. Well, I hope you enjoyed it, although you interrupted my flow," David said.

"I most certainly did .... and I got something for you, too," Auntie Mabeline said.

"You do?" David said, smiling, looking excited. He shared with Auntie Mabeline, over dinner, after Justice's dedication, that he got a job. Now he needed a car to take some stress off of Sharmaine. Auntie Mabeline had told him how responsible he was and mentioned that even when his siblings didn't believe in him, she did. He thought maybe she was waiting until now, to surprise him. Although he left out the part that his license had been suspended.

"What it is?" He said, as everyone looked on with excitement.

"You've been working so hard, and I am so proud of you, but today is my birthday," she said, "so you gonna have to wait until tomorrow." Everyone in the room busted out laughing. "I'm going to give it to you before I leave."

"You sure about that Auntie?" Franklin asked. "We'll need to be at the airport by five a.m."

"I'll be up," David said, putting the jazz CD in the CD player.

"Says the log, that sleeps in the forest," Grace said, laughing.

"It's time to eat," Anna Mae said. "I think we should bring the party in the kitchen where the food is."

They all went into the kitchen strutting to the beat of the jazz music.

"This is nice!" Pastor Fallback said. "You know, me and First Lady can't let our hair down around everyone."

"Yeah, I bet it's hard to find folk who you can be yourself around, without judging you," Franklin said.

"Oh, yes," Pastor Fallback said, as First Lady shook her head, in agreement.

"Oh, now this is a spread!" Pastor Fallback said. "It reminds me of Ms. Leola's home cooking."

"Wait . . . where's my platter?" First Lady said.

"I was carrying it into the kitchen and Gracie bumped into me, and every one of them sandwiches fell on the floor," Auntie Mabeline said, unapologetically including Grace in her lie.

Grace looked sharply at Auntie Mabeline.

"Momma taught us the five second rule. If it hadn't been down there for more than five seconds, she would tell us to pick it up and eat it," David said.

"That's true," Franklin said, laughing.

"Well, David, you can go over there and dig them out the trash," Auntie Mabeline said.

"Yuck!" Misty said, turning her nose up. "It's been longer than five minutes!"

First Lady folded her arms, clearly angry, as she cut her eyes at Auntie Mabeline and Grace.

"Let me pack a plate to go," Pastor Fallback said, sensing that Auntie Mabeline was being untruthful about the platter incident. "Tomorrow is first Sunday. Come on down to the church after you drop your Auntie off at the airport. Don't wait for another baby dedication to come back! You too, Misty! It was nice seeing you. You have a lot of clients that attend my church. You ain't using none of that cheap hair, either. I can tell when they get their hair done . . . the tithes are extremely low on the first and third Sunday's. You need to lower them prices. You can't beat God's giving, no matter how you try!"

Misty was speechless.

"Besides, we got a lot of wholesome brothers down there at the church, looking for a good woman!" He said.

"I'm all set," Misty said, smiling. "I have way too many exes up in your church! I bumped into one after Justice's dedication. He said, he didn't remember me looking this good when I was with him. I told him, that's because he didn't bring out the best in me!"

"Oh snap! Drop the mic on that one!" David said, laughing.

"I know, right!" Grace agreed.

"Well, looks like we've worn out the welcome mat," Pastor Fallback said. "First lady and I appreciate your hospitality. Thank you for including us on this festive occasion." He directed his attention at Auntie Mabeline.

"Ms. Mabel, you will be blessed for bringing this family back together. Now, give me a hug, so me and First Lady can get out of here and go get our beauty sleep."

Pastor Fallback walked toward Auntie Mabeline as she reluctantly stood up from the kitchen chair, giving her a bear hug.

First Lady was still upset that Auntie Mabeline tossed out her food. She stood in the kitchen doorway, as she waited for her husband. "Bye everyone," she said, turning her nose up at Auntie Mabeline.

Franklin walked the Pastor and First Lady out, while the others continued eating in the kitchen.

Franklin re-entered the kitchen to roaring laughter, as they sat around the table enjoying each other's company.

Misty had fixed Franklin a plate.

"That plate is for you Franklin," she said, pointing to the plate that sat on the counter.

"Thanks, Misty."

"I'm full as a tick!" Auntie Mabeline said, rubbing her stomach. "Thank God for elastic waisted jogging suits."

They all laughed, as David and Misty cleared the table.

Auntie Mabeline took notice.

"Ya'll are going to make a great help mate one day," she said looking at Misty and David.

They both looked at each other, as they grinned.

"You don't mean us, like together?" Misty asked.

"Oh, no," Auntie Mabeline said.

"Oh ok, I was going to say, David's like a brother to me. Plus, he has a beautiful girlfriend and a baby on the way," Misty said.

"A BABY!" Auntie Mabeline exclaimed.

"I forgot you didn't know that me and Sharmaine are expecting a baby Auntie," David said as he walked to his room.

Franklin, Anna Mae, and Grace, wondered if they should use this time to tell Misty that David is her brother."

David returned quickly, holding a bottle of Hennessey.

"It's turn up time!" David yelled, swaying to the music as he unscrewed the cap on the Hennessey bottle.

"Eh! Eh! Eh! Misty said smiling as she pumped her small fist in the air, joining in on the celebration. Let's do a toast to Auntie Mabeline," he said, as Franklin and Grace reluctantly raised up their empty glasses.

"David, what's that man?" Franklin asked. "Alcohol wasn't on the list. Didn't you tell us that you have a drinking problem?"

"Yeah. I start my classes soon," he said.

"Ya'll need to stop being so anal, and let the boy live a little. Besides it's my birthday. A little drink is not going to hurt anybody," Auntie Mabeline said, looking at David. "Don't you make me no drunk now."

Franklin, Anna Mae and Grace observed how lenient Auntie Mabeline was being on David.

"I'll pass," Anna Mae said.

"None for me either. I'm still breastfeeding. Apple juice for us," Grace said. They all laughed.

"I'm down," Misty said, raising her glass up. David began to pour the alcohol, as it freely flowed into Misty's glass.

"Now the birthday girl," David said, as he poured an ounce of Hennessy into Auntie Mabeline's glass.

"Stop! That is enough," she said. "You know I got to get up in the morning and catch my flight." Franklin, Anna Mae and Grace looked stunned. they'd never seen Auntie Mabeline consume alcohol, unless it was in the ribs that Momma used to make.

"You're gonna make it, Auntie," Franklin yelled out. "You may be a little saucy, but you will be on time."

They all laughed.

"I am sure gonna miss everything about all of you all," Auntie Mabeline said.

"Auntie, stop talking like you'll never see us again," David said.

"I appreciate you coming to check on me," Grace added.

"I'm sure gonna miss you, Ms. Mabeline," Misty said. "I have to come down to see you."

"Oh, child, you are welcome anytime. All of you are welcome. I have a one bedroom, but ya'll can make a pallet on the floor. I am really glad that I got to spend a little time with you." She said, getting choked up.

"When I came up here a few months ago, I didn't know what I was getting myself into. Ya'll had so much going on and part of me wanted to jump back on that plane and runaway, but I know that with your Momma gone, I needed to face the music and deal with what lay ahead. I've always been a runner, just like I ran to Georgia, but ya'll have taught me to not run away from things but to run to them," she said looking around the room.

"Gracie, I watched you ... seems like overnight, you changed from a little girl into this strong young woman and mother, who found her voice. You've taught me that losers never win and winners never lose! We all make mistakes. I'm not saying that this baby is a mistake, so get that out your head. I'm saying that, I definitely ain't perfect. I may have disappointed you during my stay. I'm sorry for that. Just know, that in order to move forward, you must forgive but never forget. Continue to be the strong young woman and mother that you have been to that little handsome boy!"

She looked at Anna Mae.

"Anna Mae, you taught me about resilience. Just a few months ago, you were sitting up in a hospital, shot in the stomach. You had tubes going every which way. Lord knows, I was shocked to hear from Big Tuna that your own husband was the one who pulled the trigger, but through your own adversity, I've seen you bounce back so quick. I know when you have your quiet time, you're probably mourning his loss in private, but you have no reason to hang your head. Hold your head up high! You are up and about, cooking, cleaning, and cutting up, but more importantly, you've turned this tragedy into triumph. The bond between sisters is like no other. I am so proud of your progress."

They all realized, at that moment, Big Tuna had informed Auntie Mabeline of Rufus murder in jail.

She turned her attention to Franklin.

"Franklin, I knew when you were a little boy that you were destined for greatness. You are so much like your daddy. You're strong, you're a protector, and a provider. You can be headstrong, too! I know we clashed while I was here, but I know, you only want the best for your family. One day, you are going to meet the woman of your dreams. She may not come in the form that you're used to and may even be a little rough around the edges, but she will be designed especially for you! Continue to be the leader that you've been to your siblings. I know your parents are so proud of you. I am equally as proud."

Auntie Mabeline looked at David.

"David come over here," she said. Auntie Mabeline reached for David's hand. "I am so proud of the man that you've become. You are a living testament to never judge a book by its cover. I hope that one day, you will find it in your heart to forgive everyone who did not have faith in you or who have failed you along the way. Your healing will begin when you can finally let go of the hurt, pain, and disappointment. Only then will you start to live your blessed life. I want to be here for the birth of your baby and for the wedding, which I hope comes before the baby."

"The pressure is on," he said, as they all laughed. "Let me take one day at a time."

"This is so emotional," Misty said, sounding as if she had too much to drink, as she wept openly.

"I know. I feel like we're at a funeral and not a party," Anna Mae said.

Sniffles could be heard around the room.

Anna Mae had picked up the tissue box, passing it around, as they pulled a Kleenex for themselves before handing it to the next person. There wasn't a dry eye in the place.

"Misty," Auntie Mabeline said.

"Me," Misty said.

"Is there another Misty that I don't know about," she asked, with a smile.

"Misty, Leola always talked about you. Just as much as she did these kids here. I want you to know that I can see why you held a special place in her heart. She used to tell me that you were like a daughter to her. You are everything in a daughter that any mother would want. I must say, within these past few months, I have really gotten to know you. Just know that in life, we all are faced with decisions that we must make. We don't know how the outcome is gonna be, but just know that everything will work out for the best. Things may not happen in our time, but they always happen right on time." She reached over, grabbing Misty's hand. "You have been a blessing to those around you, but what you will become is a blessing to the world."

Misty jumped up and hugged Auntie Mabeline.

"Ms. Mabeline, I love you so much! I want to stay in contact with you!"

They all stood up and made a circle as they hugged each other.

"I ain't perfect. I'm a work in progress, but you all have taught me about 'me,'" she said.

"Okay, if I'm going to make this plane, I need to go to bed," she said, looking at her watch. "It's 11 o'clock!"

"I better get going. I don't want to hold you all up," Misty said, grabbing her pocketbook from the back of the chair, as she went around the room hugging everyone. "No matter what, you all will always be my family."

"Oh! You were supposed to read the results to us," Anna Mae said.

"Oh yeah! I bought the letter from the private investigator who found my birth parents," Misty said, as she reached for her pocketbook, opening it up. "Ms. Mabeline, I didn't get a chance to tell you earlier at the shop, after your friend fell through, I reached out to a private investigator, and he said he found my birth parents! I told Anna Mae and Grace that I was so nervous to open it up by myself."

"The genealogist that I gave you didn't work out?" Auntie Mabeline asked, sounding surprised.

"No. Her number was disconnected," Misty said. "I know you need to get in the bed, but this shouldn't take long, plus you said that if you were here, you would support me." Misty said, looking at Auntie Mabeline.

"Okay. Just hurry up. I'm tired!" Auntie Mabeline said, as they all looked on as Misty rummaged through her pocketbook, looking for the letter. She sat down, sitting her pocketbook on the kitchen table, looking for the letter.

"Where did it go? I know it was in here. It was in my side pocket. Hmmmm ... I must've dropped it in the car."

"If you can't find it, we'll all be home tomorrow, after we drop Auntie Mabeline off at the airport. You are more than welcome to come back, and we will eat some more cake and hold your hand as you read the results," Franklin said, smiling.

"Yeah, that's your best bet! It's going on midnight," Auntie Mabeline said.

"It is getting late, and we want to make sure that you get home safe," David said.

"We can still include Auntie Mabeline tomorrow because I showed her when I was in the hospital how to use the video chat on her cell phone. That way, she is still included, and we can all see your results," Grace said.

"Hmmm . . . okay," Misty said, looking disappointed. "Well, Ms. Mabeline, I hope I can find it."

"You will. Just remember, I live in the country, so I hope when ya'll call, I have service. You know those towers are fickle. Sometimes I can get a connection, sometimes I can't."

"We'll work it out," David said. "I'm staying here tonight, since I had a few drinks."

"That's wise," Franklin said, as he turned his attention to Misty, handing her a to-go plate. "Are you going to be okay to drive?"

"You know I live around the corner. I could have walked here," Misty said. "Besides, I cannot keep up with David. I know my drink limit."

"Call us when you get in," Anna Mae said.

"Let me walk you out," Franklin said.

They all followed Franklin and Misty back into the living room.

"Okay, see you tomorrow," Misty said.

"Bye Misty," they said in unison, as she and Franklin exited the apartment. Franklin returned a few minutes later, rejoining them in the living room.

"I really enjoyed the party. Ya'll really outdid yourselves," Auntie Mabeline said. "Let me catch my breath before I go to bed. My bags are already packed."

"Okay, we're rolling out at 0300 hours in the morning," Franklin said.

Grace and David began to tidy up the living room, as they brought the drinking glasses back into the kitchen. Justice lay asleep, across Anna Mae's lap.

"Ping!" Anna Mae looked down at her phone.

"Misty's home."

"Good!" Franklin exclaimed, as he, Auntie Mabeline,

and Anna Mae sat quietly, looking exhausted.

"Did you hear that?" Anna Mae said.

"Hear what?" Franklin said, as he stretched out on the love seat.

"I didn't hear anything," Auntie Mabeline said.

"I thought I heard tapping," Anna Mae said.

"That's David and Grace in the kitchen," Franklin said.

"No, it ain't. I just heard it too," Auntie Mabeline said.

The noise appeared louder.

"TAP, TAP, TAP, TAP."

Franklin jumped up, looking out the window. "I don't see anyone out there."

"TAP, TAP, TAP, TAP," the noise was louder than before.

"Is someone at the door?" Auntie Mabeline asked.

Franklin walked over to the door.

"WHO IS IT?" Franklin asked, in a deeper tone than usual, as he looked through the peep hole.

"SURPRISE!" the voice said.

Franklin looked at his watch. "It's old Man Joe," he said, with a smirk.

"LET ME IN! I'M READY TO PARTY!" Old Man Joe yelled.

"DON'T LET THAT MAN IN HERE. THE PARTY IS OVER!" Auntie Mabeline said, seeming to still be agitated from earlier.

"GO HOME, OLD MAN JOE!" The trio said in unison.

CHAPTER 90

The next morning David woke up to the house dead quiet. He looked at the fluorescent blue clock on his dresser.

"OH, SHOOT!" He said, whipping the blanket off. It was 12:30 p.m.! He'd missed Auntie Mabeline.

He grabbed his short pants that were laying on his room floor and put them on. He walked into the kitchen, noticing the separate Tupperware bowls of pancakes, sausages, and eggs.

He opened the refrigerator and took out the carton of milk, taking the cap off and placing it towards his mouth.

"Oh no, you are not!" Anna Mae said, surprising him, as she held Justice.

"Dang! You scared me!" he said.

"I can't believe I missed Auntie Mabeline."

"Well, we tried to wake you up, and you seemed like you were having a fight with the blanket, so we left you alone. She told us to tell you that she loves you," Anna Mae said.

"That's it?" He asked.

"Yup!" Anna Mae said, as she rocked Justice in her arms.

"She said she had something for me," he said, looking disappointed.

"She didn't mention anything this morning before she left," Anna Mae said.

David took a plate from the cabinet and began to fix himself breakfast.

"Sharmaine was blowing up your cell phone. I answered it and told her that you were dead to the world. She said, she'll pick you up after she gets out of work."

"Okay," he said.

Grace and Franklin could be heard entering the living room, chatting it up, as they walked into the kitchen.

"Hey, what's going on?" Franklin asked, dropping the stack of envelopes on the kitchen table.

"David is in his feelings again. He thought that Auntie Mabeline had something for him," Anna Mae blurted it out.

"Oh, she did," Grace said, reaching for the envelope in the pile that that Franklin had just dropped on the table. "It's mixed in with the mail."

"She had something for all of us," Franklin added.

"Yeah, she gave me $200," Grace said. "Franklin got a hundred more than me. I guess it's because he's older. Anna Mae, you probably got the same amount. I don't know how much she gave you David."

"Here it is," Grace said, handing Anna Mae and David their envelope.

"I'll take Justice," she said, taking Justice from Anna Mae.

"Who's the other envelope for on the table, Justice?" David asked.

"No! Auntie Mabeline was generous. She said that she didn't want to leave Misty out. I think she felt bad that her genealogy friend, who she referred Misty too was a bust! She has something for her, too!" Grace said. "Oh … Misty pulled up just as we did. She's sitting in her car on the phone. She seemed upset. But she told us that she'll be up after her phone call."

"David, are you happy now? You're such a big baby." Anna Mae said, poking fun at him.

David laughed, as he stuffed the pancakes in his mouth, trying to hurry up, so he could open the envelope.

"I'd mentioned to Auntie Mabeline that the car that I wanted was $2000. She said that if she could, she would help me get it," he said, beaming with joy. "Once I get my license back, I'll be straight!"

"I think I hear Misty at the door," Anna Mae said.

"I'll get it," Franklin said.

Franklin could be heard consoling Misty, as they walked into the kitchen.

"What's wrong?" Grace asked.

"Hey guys. I searched my apartment when I got home, and I couldn't find the envelope. I paid all of that money to the private investigator, just to turn around and lose the documents. I could've sworn that I had it with me yesterday. I retraced my steps, tore up my car up, and I still cannot find it," she said.

"Can't he print you another one?" Anna Mae asked.

"I just spoke to him. Yeah, he said for $300! I just paid him $1,500 to get it done," Misty said, wiping her tears away.

"Oh wow, I'm sorry to hear that Misty," David said.

"Yes, that's not good," Grace added.

"Well, I know what will make you feel better," Anna Mae said, handing Misty a generous slice of leftover red velvet cake, as she sat across from David at the kitchen table. "Cake always makes me feel better," she said smiling, hugging Misty around the shoulders.

"Okay, we got to cheer you up. You cannot come over here sulking," David said.

"I know what will cheer her up" Grace said, handing Misty the envelope from Auntie Mabeline.

"What's this?" She asked.

"Just open it, girl," Anna Mae said.

"How about if we see who can open their envelope the fastest," David said.

"Auntie Mabeline was generous, and she gave us all money," Grace blurted out.

"Money? What? Why would she give me money?" Misty asked.

"You're talking too much," David said, playfully. "Let's go."

David and Misty began to open up their envelopes from Auntie Mabeline.

They both ripped the envelope open at the same time. Hundreds of dollars fell out of each of their envelopes."

"What tha ..." Franklin said.

"That's not fair! Ya'll got more than we did!" Grace yelled, as Franklin and Anna Mae looked on dumbfounded.

"Oh my gosh! That's generous of her," Misty said, looking shocked, yet elated.

"Oh shoot, we were supposed to video call her," Grace said.

"I'll call her! Now I'm mad," Franklin said, as he dialed Auntie Mabeline. "I want to know why they got more money!" The phone rang.

"Oh my God!" David said, as he and Misty began to count the hundred dollar bills.

"2200, 2300," he counted the five ten dollar bills that were at the end. "$2,350! YES! Now I can buy my car!"

Misty trailed behind him, as she slowly tallied up her money.

"She's not answering," Franklin said.

"Isn't there something else in the envelope," Anna Mae said, being observant.

David picked up his envelope, just as Misty picked up hers. They both checked. A smaller envelope fell out onto the table.

"Wait, this is the envelope that I was looking for!" Misty exclaimed.

David ripped open the envelope to find a letter.

"We didn't get a letter," Franklin said, hanging up the phone.

David looked at all of them, as he unfolded his letter.

"This is the report from the private investigator!" Misty exclaimed, with excitement.

"Why would Auntie Mabeline have it?" Anna Mae asked.

David had started reading his letter. He looked up in complete and utter shock, as if he'd been dealt a sharp blow.

"What does it say?" Anna Mae asked.

"Don't tell me she bought you a car. What is it, a Benz?" Franklin said.

Misty looked up.

"I don't have anything else in my envelope," she said.

"Read it out loud?" Grace said.

David read the letter out loud.

Michael (David),

I write this letter with a heavy heart and a guilty conscience. By the time you get this letter, I will be back in Georgia. But you deserve to know the truth.

Growing up, I was born to an alcoholic mother. As a result, I had a host of issues. She ended up putting me in foster care, where I bounced from foster home to foster home, until I was adopted at the age of 5 by the Johnsons. They had one spoiled daughter, Leola. I was nothing like her, but did everything to emulate her. I was a handful as a toddler and a menace as a teenager, I got into everything and anything that I could and wreaked havoc wherever I went.

In my late teens, early 20s, I lived a promiscuous life

and wound up getting pregnant by my sugar daddy, who was much older than me. I was in no way ready to be a mother. After my adopted parents found out, they put me out on the streets, with nowhere to go. Everyone turned their back on me, including the man I was in love with. That's when I decided to pack up and move to Georgia, for a fresh start. I started hearing through the grapevine that I was not the only one he'd gotten pregnant. I ended up coming back here to confront him. I went right to his house and knocked on his door. That's when this woman opened the door and proceeded to tell me off. That woman was Leola's best friend, Purlie. Even more hurtful was that Leola was there, and she defended her best friend. I was shocked to say the least. Purlie told me that the man, who we were both involved with, didn't want anything to do with me and suggested that I go find another sugar daddy. That's when I lost it! I did the unthinkable! I stole Purlie's identity and did everything that I could to make her life a living hell. Some things I'm still asking God to forgive me for, like when she moved away and I told the FBI that she and her new beau was running a brothel. Well, they raided the place, and her face was plastered all over the news.

I didn't tell anybody, not even Leola, that I was pregnant, or that I was contemplating giving my kids up. After Leola lost her parents, she blamed me for sending them to an early grave.

I eventually gave birth to twins, a boy and a girl. I named my son Michael and my daughter Malaysia. I found myself, a young mother, with no support from your father. I did the best that I could do at the time, but I was struggling. For years, I held so much resentment toward Leola, for introducing Purlie to your father, when they used to sell those dinners at the dance hall.

After putting my baby girl up for adoption, I did the unthinkable and it still haunts me. I typed up a note, pinned it to your lapel, and left you on Leola's doorstep and signed Ms. Purlie's name. Purlie swore up and down she had her tubes tied. I knew if Leola knew it was my child, she would have hunted me down and dropped you back in my lap. I wanted to get back at Purlie for stealing my man and my sister, causing me a life of heartache and pain! I know now that I was dead wrong. But I knew that Leola would be able to raise you better than me. For years, Leola and Purlie's relationship became strained! After Purlie disappeared, Leola and I started to get close. I will never forgive myself for not telling her the truth. I'll take that to my grave.

For years, I felt guilty as a teacher, spending time and investing in other people's kids, when I threw my own away. I will never forgive myself.

As for the safe, I knew what was in it. I purposely had the thrift store pick it up along with all those clothes that Gracie had packed up in Leola's closet. After the manager spoke to Franklin, he called me to give me a heads up. So, Joe and I took the bus over there to pick it up. I wanted to make sure that you and your sister got the money that Leola was saving from the rent she got from your father.

After meeting my Malaysia, I didn't feel right leaving her out. So, I split the $4,700 between the both of you.

I'm sorry that I didn't have the courage to face you and your sister and tell you the truth, but I am your mother, whether you want to believe it or not! Old Man Joe is your daddy and yeah, Jefferson is your half-brother. His Momma showed up when I was there, while he was in jail and, well, we had some words. I encourage you and Misty to not shut Joe out. He really needs you.

P.S. - I know that Misty is with you right now. I am so proud of the young lady she's become. She reminds me of myself. She's just smoother around the edges. I hope she won't be upset with me for what I'm about to say about the genealogist. The number I gave her was my old number that I had when I moved from Macon to Savannah. It was disconnected four years ago! I hope she can forgive me, too! I'm sure she knows now, she didn't misplace her results from the private investigator, I took it when she left her pocketbook hanging on chair in the kitchen! She got to be more careful and keep her pocketbook strapped to her body! I know that Franklin, Anna Mae, and Grace will be mad with me, too, because I lied and deceived not only them, but their Momma, after she opened her home up to me year after year. I've grown to love them, and I could not have picked better siblings for you to be raised with. I know they will be your biggest supporters!

Michael - you and Malaysia may never forgive me, but I have no regrets. You had a good life, and I am grateful that I was able to be a part of it.

I will always love you both!

Your mother, Mabeline

The entire room fell silent. David dropped the letter and placed his head in his hands.

David and Misty were in complete and utter shock as they looked at each other.

Tears streamed down Misty's face.

Anna Mae hugged Misty, just as Franklin and Grace embraced David.

"Man, I am so sorry," he said, as he looked over at Misty. "Misty, I just don't know what to say. We feel bad for the both of you."

"I'm so sorry guys," Grace said, tearing up.

"She is a no-good trip! She had the audacity to wreak havoc in my life! Looks like the only one chasing a no-good fool was her!" Anna Mae said.

"Anna Mae, they don't need to hear that right now. We're all in a state of shock," Franklin said.

"I can't believe this! I went to court with her. I had her at my shop, and she couldn't look me in my face to tell me that she was my birth mother, after I poured my heart out to her, and told her how much I wanted to find my birth parents? I feel like a fool," Misty said.

"Misty, this is not your fault. She was a coward," Franklin said.

David was so angry, he looked as if he was about to blow a gasket.

"Did you guys know?" David asked, looking around the room at them.

Misty looked at the three of them, with bated breath, waiting on their response.

"No ... I mean, yeah ... Well, we didn't know that she was your mother, but one of the things that we found in the safe were documents saying that you were not our biological brother and that you had a twin sister," Franklin said.

"And none of you thought to tell me?" David said.

"We wanted you to see it for yourself but then the safe came up missing. We had no idea that Auntie Mabe ..." Grace caught herself, "that she was your mother. We thought it was Ms. Purlie".

"She's right," Anna Mae said. "Momma told me a few years back that Ms. Purlie was your mother and left you on the step for Momma to raise but we know now that wasn't the truth. Momma obviously didn't even know the truth."

Misty began to wail. Grace ran over to her and comforted her, along with Anna Mae.

"YOU WHAT? YOU ALL KNEW?" He said.

"Don't be mad at us. We just wanted to protect you both," Anna Mae said.

"PROTECT US? YOU HID THIS FROM US."

"Well, actually your Momma hid it from you," Franklin said, attempting to be diplomatic. "We don't think Old Man Joe knows that you are his kids."

"So that means you have a boatload of sisters and brothers out there that look just like you," Anna Mae said.

"Anna Mae. Just stop! You're not making this any better!" Franklin exclaimed.

"I know right!" Grace added.

"I can't believe this. You're my brother," Misty said, looking at David from across the table.

David remained silent and just stared at Misty.

"Misty, what does the report say?" Grace asked.

Misty slowly opened the envelope with her genealogy report in it.

"What does it say?" Anna Mae asked, as they all looked frozen in time.

Misty unfolded the document reading it aloud.

"The undersigned conducted an investigation at your request to locate your birth parents," Misty skipped down to the results.

"We have located your birth parents," she scanned the document with her eyes. "Yup. It's right here. Ms. Mabeline Dixon and Mr. Joseph Corbin."

"It confirms everything that David just read. She is our mother," Misty said, looking up at David.

David covered his face with his hands, in disbelief.

"I'm glad I didn't give her Momma's fur coat!" Anna Mae exclaimed.

"I WANT MY MEDALLION BACK!" Franklin exclaimed.

Chapter 91

Two months had passed since Misty and David found out that they were siblings.

They were more different than alike. Unlike David, Misty longed for a relationship with her father. David didn't want to have anything to do with Old Man Joe. As for their mother, David seemed to be more forgiving than Misty. It could be the money she gave him for the car he wanted but couldn't drive yet, since his license was still suspended. Misty, on the other hand, didn't want anything to do with her birth mother. She couldn't understand how a mother could be so selfish, deceiving the very people that put their trust in her. They both still had questions that haunted them.

If something was spot on, it was that they had Franklin, Anna Mae and Grace to lean on.

Auntie Mabeline had called the house a few times to apologize, but the only one that was hearing her out was the answering machine. Franklin, Anna Mae, and Grace had cut all ties with Auntie Mabeline, in solidarity with David and Misty.

If there was one thing that David and Misty embraced, it was their relationship with their half-brother Big Tuna . The trio started hanging out on occasion, dragging Grace, Justice, and Sharmaine along.

The stories that Big Tuna shared about their father pulled on Misty's heart strings. Those conversations with her brother unveiled the real reason why their mother spent so much time downstairs with Old Man Joe. It wasn't because they were getting their groove on. It was because his memory was failing. She was caring for him and had turned into his personal caretaker.

Big Tuna told them after he told their father about them, their dad kept vigil near the window, waiting for the day when they would come visit him. He did everything that he could to be a part of their lives. He called them every day. David would not only ignore his calls, but when he came to visit the Johnson kids, he passed by his father's apartment, just like he did so many times before. David was still unforgiving, despite what he was taught, growing up. There was no turning the other cheek! He wanted to inflict the same pain on him that he felt. He resented his father. He was angry.

On occasion, when Misty wasn't busy at the shop, she would call her father and check on him, promising to stop by one day. For weeks, she gave excuse after excuse. She would say not today; I have a client or tell him how tired she was. He would continue to call, and she would consistently give him more excuses. She couldn't be mad at him for not reaching out, since he never knew she nor David existed. Besides, she had the consolation in knowing that she had a fabulous life and never went without.

Those rare days, when she felt resentment against

her father, were the times that she would avoid his calls, like the bubonic plague, until the day that Anna Mae and Grace paid her a surprise visit.

Anna Mae and Grace had surprised her by making homemade blueberry muffins and bought them to the hair salon. It had been months since the Johnson sisters had been in the shop. All the ladies doted on Justice, who was six-months-old. Anna Mae and Grace talked about how much they missed their mom, and wished that she was there to see how close they'd grown as sisters and could see her first grandchild. More importantly, they wanted Misty to see that life is too short to harbor ill feelings, and that she had to learn to forgive what her mother withheld from her. It was beyond her control.

Whatever Anna Mae and Grace said had a major impact on Misty. The following day she decided to call her father. The phone rang off the hook, until he answered, sounding exasperated.

"Hello," he said, coughing.

"Hi, Daddy. It's me," she said.

"Hi, you," Old Man Joe said, sounding hoarse. "I've been calling you."

"Yeah, I know, but I told you how busy I get at the shop," Misty said.

"Yeah, I know," Old Man Joe said.

"I just called to tell you that I'm going to try and stop by today after my last client, but I won't make any promises," she said abruptly.

"Oh, ok, then, I won't hold my breath. I've held it so long waiting on you that I'm surprised I haven't passed out," he said.

Misty had mixed emotions. She couldn't hold back her feelings any longer; she knew today was the day that she had to tell her daddy how all this has made her feel. He had to know how his absence affected her and the nonexistent relationships with men.

"Okay, Daddy, you don't have to hold your breath any longer; I will definitely stop by later."

"Oh, okay. I haven't been feeling like myself. I've been a little short winded, and my head has been hurting like a bad toothache. So I'm gonna unlock the door so you can let yourself in when you get here. I don't know where your brother went to. I think he had an appointment," Old Man Joe said, as he coughed. "I can't wait to see you, baby girl."

"Well, I got to go Daddy. I'll be over around 6:30 this evening," Misty said.

"Okay, baby. I look forward to seeing you. I love you," Old Man Joe said.

"Yeah, me too. Bye," Misty said, still uncomfortable with telling her father that she loved him.

Misty finished up her client's hair, but was still reluctant to stop by her father's, although she told him that it would be today.

"Let me just get this over with," she muttered.

Misty pulled up in front of her father's place at 7:15 p.m. She knew she was 45 minutes later than what she'd told him, but she didn't care. Why? He didn't care about the events that he missed, during her formative years. She sat in the car in front of the very apartment that Mrs. Leola owned. She thought of the many times that she'd entered this same apartment building to visit Ms. Leola, Anna Mae, and Grace, unknowing that her own daddy lived feet away. A part of her wondered if Ms. Leola knew who her real birth mother was or maybe Ann Mae was right... she was bamboozled like the rest of them. She recounted the times that she wished she had brothers to defend her, from the trifling men that she'd dated. She thought about the selfish people who robbed her of the chance of having a relationship with her brothers. Her bitterness took control.

She looked at the first-floor window where Old Man Joe lived. She could see the television through the 12-inch slit on the dingy shade. "Wow! He's just ridiculous," she mumbled.

Her ringing phone broke her concentration. She reached into her pocketbook and saw that it was her daddy. She pressed ignore, which sent his call straight to voicemail. Although she was just feet away from seeing him, he needed to understand that she was doing this on her time, and he was not going to rush her.

Misty clicked on Facebook to see what her friends were up to. She scrolled through her newsfeed as she sat in the car laughing. Grace had posted the group picture they all took at the shop yesterday, when she and Anna Mae popped in for a visit. She loved Grace's post and posted a comment of her own, "My nephew is getting big. Thanks for bringing him in to see us! God-mommy loves you little man." Grace immediately loved her comment and quickly responded, "How are you Misty? It was nice to see all of you!" Misty was hesitant about telling Grace her whereabouts. She responded with, "I'll see you all soon." Grace immediately loved her comment.

"Ding!"

Old Man Joe had left her a voice message. "Oh gosh! I'm not even listening to that!" she said, tossing her phone into her pocketbook.

"Let me get this over with," she grumbled.

She looked at the clock that read 7:31 p.m. She was now an hour late from when she told her father that she would be there. She wished her brothers were here with her. When she asked David to come with her, he hung up the phone. Big Tuna had a prior obligation. It was his day to check in with his probation officer. She remembered what her adopted mother would always say to her anytime she faced a problem: It's in the most difficult of situations that we find out what we are really made of.

She stepped out of her white jeep, clicking on her key fob, making sure her doors were locked. It seemed like an eternity as she walked up the steps that led to her father's apartment. She opened the door, leading into the hallway. The strong stench of cat urine smacked her right in the face.

She held her breath as she picked up her pace, quickly walking toward her father's door, attempting to avoid inhaling the stench.

She knocked on the door.

There was no answer.

She knocked harder.

Still no answer.

She looked down at the doorknob that was soiled with what looked like dirt and dried peanut butter.

"I am not touching that," she uttered, looking into her pocketbook for her pack of tissues.

She could hear music playing through the door.

"HELLO, I'M HERE!" she yelled, as she knocked on the door a third time, attempting to get Old Man Joe's attention.

She remembered her father saying that he would leave the door open for her.

She couldn't inhale the stench any longer. She lightly

placed her fingers on the edge of the doorknob, using minimal contact as she turned it slowly.

She walked into the dark apartment. To her surprise, it was neater than she had imagined. She assumed that her mother tidied up before she went back to Georgia, two months ago. She looked across the dark and dingy room to where the music played. She could hear Donny Hathaway singing "A Song for You." A deep sadness fell over her. She wondered why Daddy would be playing such a depressing song like this. She thought, maybe this was his way of telling her how he felt, since he couldn't verbalize it. This meant more than the pathetic written apology that her birth mother gave them. A tear rolled down her cheeks. She didn't realize this would be such an emotional step for her.

A strong aroma of chitterlings smacked her in the face, breaking her concentration. "Oh, my gosh," she said, as she gagged, covering her mouth with her shirt.

"Daddy, you know that I don't eat chitterlings," she said.

She could hear what sounded like running water. She'd visited Ms. Leola's several times, so she was familiar with the layout of the apartment.

She walked down the hall, looking at all of the school pictures of her half brothers and sisters as they'd matriculated through school. The walls looked more like a shrine. She couldn't tell if they were old or recent pictures and wondered if she was older than the kids in the pictures.

She proceeded toward the kitchen. The sound of the running water become louder.

"Daddy, I'm here. Sorry I'm late."

"Daddy . . . daddy . . . you need to get a hearing aid," she said, laughing.

As she entered the kitchen, she immediately noticed that the sink had overflowed, as water gushed onto the floor.

"Oh, my God!" she exclaimed.

She rushed over, turning the water off.

"Daddy, what are you doing?" She said, looking around to see where Old Man Joe was.

She grabbed the mop that stood in the corner and began soaking up the water. As she moved the mop from left to right, she hit a hard object. She peaked on the other side of the table to find her daddy, sprawled out on the floor, with his cell phone clutched in his hand.

"OH MY GOD!" Misty said, dropping the mop, as she crouched down near her father.

"DADDY, DADDY, WAKE UP!"

www.ingramcontent.com/pod-product-compliance
Lightning Source LLC
Chambersburg PA
CBHW032255020726
47495CB00001B/119